W9-AQD-613

Red, Red Rose

Marjorie Farrell

A TOPAZ BOOK

TOPAZ
Published by the Penguin Group
Penguin Putnam Inc., 375 Hudson Street,
New York, New York 10014, U.S.A.
Penguin Books Ltd, 27 Wrights Lane,
London W8 5TZ, England
Penguin Books Australia Ltd, Ringwood,
Victoria, Australia
Penguin Books Canada Ltd, 10 Alcorn Avenue,
Toronto, Ontario, Canada M4V 3B2
Penguin Books (N.Z.) Ltd, 182–190 Wairau Road,
Auckland 10, New Zealand

Penguin Books Ltd, Registered Offices:
Harmondsworth, Middlesex, England

First published by Topaz, an imprint of Dutton NAL,
a member of Penguin Putnam Inc.

First Printing, February, 1999
10 9 8 7 6 5 4 3 2 1

 REGISTERED TRADEMARK—MARCA REGISTRADA

Printed in the United States of America

This one is for my father,
Major (ret.) John Aloysius Farrell,
Pearl Harbor survivor and a man
who has faced all of his life
with great courage.

It is also dedicated to the memory
of Leslie Baker, my "instant sister,"
who gave me what Charlie gave to Val:
unconditional love.

Author's Note

I am greatly indebted to four books which gave me the background for my story: *Wellington: The Years of the Sword,* by Elizabeth Longford; *A History of the Peninsular War* by Charles Oman; *Britain and the Defeat of Napoleon: 1807–1815* by Rory Muir; and *The First Respectable Spy, the Life and Times of Colquhoun Grant,* by C. Haswell.

The historical situation is accurate: The British troops did sit behind the Lines of Torres Vedras for months, waiting for Massena to make a move. At the same time, the question of a Regency was being debated back in England. It seemed plausible for my story to suggest that Massena might be receiving inside information, although there is no basis for this in fact.

I have taken the greatest liberties with Colquhoun Grant, since his scenes seem to suggest he spent more time behind a desk than he did on a horse! In fact, he was one of Wellington's most indefatigable exploring officers.

I was also inspired by the Richard Sharpe stories, written by Bernard Cornwell and brought to the video screen by the BBC. I bought all of them and immersed myself in another fictional representation of the Peninsular War while I was writing.

Music is always an inspiration for me. To anyone who wishes to hear "A Red, Red Rose," I recommend *The Songs of Robert Burns* sung by Andy Stewart, a Green Linnet CD. "Bonny Light Horseman," sung by Eliza Carthy, is found on *Troubadours of British Folk, Vol. 3* on Rhino Records.

Prologue

"Val . . . Val, it is time to go."

The boy was brought out of his reverie by the familiar voice. He was in his mother's garden, standing in front of her favorite rosebush with his eyes closed. If he didn't open them, if he just wished hard enough, then she would be there, with her garden shears, cutting the dark red blossoms and dropping them into her basket. She would turn to him and smile, he would take her hand, and he would know that the last month had been only a nightmare.

But when he opened his eyes, she was still gone. Oh, he had wished and prayed hard. And cried even harder in his bed at night. But nothing would bring her back. The roses swayed in the breeze, waiting for her, as he did.

"Val! We will miss the stage."

The boy reached out and snapped off a half-blown rose. He pulled out his pocket handkerchief and carefully wrapped the flower and put it in his jacket pocket. When he got to his aunt and uncle's, he would press it in one of his books. It was the only thing of his mother's that he had.

Nancy would have disagreed. Nancy, who had been their maid of all work, could have told him that he had more of his mother than he knew: her gray-blue eyes, her dark brown hair, her strength, and her warm heart. In fact, as he walked around the corner of the cottage to where Nancy was waiting, she nearly started crying again at the thought of losing all that was left of her beloved mistress. But she had to be strong for the boy.

They were just arriving at the King's Head when they heard the coachman striking his yard of tin. It all happened quickly—the coach arriving, the bustle of passengers getting on and off, the coachman grabbing Val's small bag—that

neither Nancy nor the boy had time to do more than franti-
cally hug each other before he was in the coach and looking
down at her with tear-brightened eyes.

"You will soon be happy in your new home. Your aunt
Martha will be like your mama. And you will learn a
trade."

"I'll miss you, Nancy." The boy's lower lip was trembling.

"And I'll miss you, my brave boy. Don't forget your
Nancy."

The coach had started to move. "I won't forget you,
Nancy," he called back to her. "I'll never forget."

It only took a day to reach Westbourne. The boy was
out and handed his luggage, and the coach was off before
he knew what was happening.

He waited a full hour, a forlorn little figure in the new
black suit bought for his mother's funeral. He had what he
guessed was a good sum of money in the old purse tucked
in his bag, but it was to go to his aunt and her husband,
for taking him in. The local solicitor had told him that and
so he was afraid to pull it out and buy himself supper.
Finally he was getting chilled and made himself go across
the street and into the inn.

The innkeeper looked down over the counter at him and
said with rough humor, "We don't serve no midgets here."

"I am looking for the Burtons' house, please, sir. George
Burton is a blacksmith. They were going to meet me."

"George Burton, eh? And who might you be?"

"I am Valentine Aston, Mrs. Burton's nephew, sir."

The man lifted his eyebrows. "Valentine, is it?" he said
sarcastically. "Well, Master Valentine, I wouldn't be expecting George Burton to be a-meeting anyone. You had
best get yourself there. Come, I'll point the way," said the
innkeeper, somewhat sorry he had teased the boy. There
was an air of sadness about him, as well there should be,
if he was going to the Burtons'.

"There, just past the livery stable, is the Burtons' shop.
And their house is right after."

The boy whispered a thank-you and, picking up his bag
again, trudged down the road. It wasn't a long way and he
found the house easily enough.

It wasn't a large house, not as nice as his mother's cottage. But it was to be his home. And, he guessed, smithing would be his life. He squared his small shoulders and knocked on the door, first tentatively and then harder.

The woman who opened it was older than his mother and the boy could see a resemblance. It was as though his mother had been a fresh, vivid watercolor and this woman was the same painting, only years later and very faded.

"I am looking for Martha Burton. I am her nephew."

The woman's face lit up and she invited him in. "You *did* find us yourself. George said you was old enough to. I wanted to meet you," she confided, "but George said if you was old enough to travel alone, you could make your own way. And George was too busy himself to go after you."

The boy got the impression that some of what his aunt was saying were her own words, and some of them her husband's. But her welcome seemed genuine enough; he was just relieved to have arrived and comforted by her resemblance to his mother.

"Valentine! Valentine Aston! Wot kind of a name is that, boy?" George Burton wasn't a tall man, but with his red face and huge hands and loud voice, he was frightening enough.

"I don't know, sir. My name, sir," said the boy.

"It were his father's name. Well, one of his father's names, George," said his wife placatingly.

"His father! The boy's a bastard, Martha. He has no father."

The boy blanched. He had heard the word "bastard," of course. He knew what it meant. It meant shame and ridicule for Samuel, a local farmer's brother. He had asked his mother about it after hearing the farmer call his brother the squire's bastard in a fit of temper. She had sat him down and carefully explained to him that some people had two parents who were married before they had children, but that some parents didn't marry at all. "But whatever the parents had done, whatever mistakes they made, it had nothing to do with their children."

"His father is the Earl of Faringdon, George," Aunt Martha said. "Charles Richard Valentine Faringdon. He seduced my sister when she were visiting our mother's brother. How do you think she lived all these years? Maintained a home? The earl sent her an allowance. Why would he do that if he weren't the boy's father?"

They had forgotten he was there. He had a father? He had thought his mother was the widow of a soldier and that his father was a very brave man who had died in the service of his country. His father had never married his mother? He was one of those shameful things people talked about, joked about?

"I don't give a tinker's damn who his father is, Martha," growled the smith. "And you had better put on no airs, either, you little bastard," he added, turning to Val. "You are lucky I am willing to take you in for your aunt's sake. And you'll be lucky to learn a trade from me. Now off with you. You'll need to be up early at the smithy with me in the morning."

Val had been imagining his new home, his new room; longing for a place where he would be alone at last and could put out his clothes and his three books and his tin soldiers that he received for Christmas last year. One of the soldiers he had imagined to be his father. He had fought up and down with that soldier, risking his life in many a battle.

When he reached the small attic room, he did take out his books and place them on a rickety table next to his bed. He pulled out his handkerchief and unwrapped the faded rose and placed it between the pages of the small leather-covered Bible his mother had given him. Then he took out the soldier. He grasped its head and twisted and twisted until the neck snapped. He took off his clothes, folded them carefully on the chair as Nancy had taught him, and climbed into bed, the headless soldier clutched in his hand. He lay there dry-eyed for hours until he fell asleep. And when he went to the smithy for the first time with George Burton, he dropped the two pieces of his soldier into the fire.

Going from his mother's cottage to being George's apprentice was like going from heaven to hell. The first two weeks, Val cried himself to sleep. The only good thing he could say about the man was that he was a genius at his trade. But he was a hard master and pushed the boy to the point of exhaustion.

Once his aunt spoke up in his defense, timidly asking her husband if he didn't think he was working the boy a bit hard. "After all, George, he is only eight." Burton's response was to slap her and tell her not to be an interfering bitch. "I am not going to coddle the little bastard, Martha, just because he's an earl's by-blow."

By the end of the first week, everyone in Westbourne knew that George Burton had been kind enough to take in his sister-in-law's bastard. And by the second week, all the children delighted in taunting Val by calling him "Bastard Aston."

The first six months he thought he was going to die of heartbreak. His mother was dead. Her sister, who had some affection for him, was bullied and beaten by her husband into not showing it. The children in the village hated him, merely because of his birth and "fancy" name. And he was so tired all the time that his whole life was a blur of waking up, working in the forge, and falling into an instant sleep.

He was young and healthy, however, and began to adjust. He also began to enjoy part of the work, particularly watching George shape something intricate like a church screen. He hated George, but hating him didn't mean he couldn't admire the man's talent and strength.

He tried not to think of his mother and earlier life. After a while, he began to get angry at her. Probably his father was this earl. How else could she have afforded their cottage? He had always believed his father's pension supported them, but how much would a foot soldier leave anyway? If she had never been married and yet had had him, then she was a . . . He couldn't bring himself to say the word. But the children said it all the time. And his name? Why had she named him Valentine? Had she wanted people to know? Didn't she care that it made his life miserable?

Underneath his anger, he loved and missed her. But he couldn't afford to think of her too much. So he concentrated on surviving: getting enough rest, enough to eat, and avoiding George's casual whacks and drunken punches.

By the time he had been there seven years, he was swing-

ing the hammer himself and George allowed him to work
on simple things. He had reached his adult height early
and, had he not been smithing, perhaps he would have
looked weedy. But the work developed his arm and chest
muscles, so he was as well-built as he was tall. And the day
he turned fifteen was the last day George Burton laid a
hand on him. Val leveled him with one blow. "If you ever
touch me again, drunk or sober, I will kill you," he said,
balancing the hammer in front of him with both hands.
And both of them knew he could and he would.

One day in late summer when Val was fifteen and a half,
a well-sprung coach bearing a coat of arms on the door
pulled up in front of the smithy. George had gone to the
next town to buy nails and Val was in charge for the day.
He watched curiously as the groom opened the coach door
for a boy who looked about ten or eleven and a distin-
guished-looking older gentleman.

Val wiped his hands on his leather apron and stepped
forward. "Can I help you, sir?" he asked the older man as
he at the same time assessed the condition of the coach
and team.

"I am . . . we are looking for George Burton."

"Well, you have found his smithy but not him," replied
Val with a smile. "He is away and won't be back until late
this evening. I am his apprentice. What can I do for you?"

"We were looking for Mr. Burton or his wife to make
inquiries about their nephew, as a matter of fact."

"Their nephew?"

"Yes. I believe his name is Aston. Valentine Aston."

Val hesitated. "I am Aston. What do you want with
me?"

As soon as Val identified himself, the boy's face lit up with
a delighted smile. "I knew we would find him, Robinson!"

The older man placed his hand on the boy's shoulders
as if to calm him. He looked with barely disguised distate
at the young man before him, who stood, arms crossed,
with no hint of obsequiousness. His face and hands were
dirty, his sleeves rolled up, exposing his muscular arms, and
his shirt soaked with sweat.

"What is your first name, Aston?"

"Valentine."

"And your mother's name?"

A subtle change came over Val's face. "Who are you, and what has my mother to do with anything?"

"Please answer him," broke in the boy.

Val looked down at the open, pleading face. He liked the boy. He didn't know why, but he did.

"All right. I don't see how it could hurt anything. My mother's name was Sarah Aston. She died when I was eight and I came to live here. And what is it to you?" he added angrily.

The boy tugged at Robinson's sleeve. "May I tell him?"

"Yes, my lord."

"I am Charles Thomas Faringdon, Viscount Holme. Son of the Earl of Faringdon. We are brothers," he added with a shy smile.

"*Half*-brothers," intoned Robinson.

Val was too accustomed to hiding his feelings by now to allow any of his surprise and distaste to show. He just stood there looking expressionlessly at his two visitors and there was a long uncomfortable silence, until the boy said hesitantly, "Perhaps you didn't know who your father was?" His face was flushed with embarrassment and he was looking down at the toe of his leather pump, which had a fine dusting of dirt on it.

"I've been told I am the earl's bastard often enough," Val replied harshly.

The boy's face grew white as though he had been slapped and then flushed even redder. "I didn't know I had a brother until just a few months ago," he said softly. "I only found out after my mother died. . . ." His voice trembled and when he finally lifted his eyes to Val's face, Val could see the tears brimming. For one moment, Val was eight again and wanting his mother. It was as though in the boy in front of him he saw himself.

"It is hard to lose your mother," Val said gently.

The boy only nodded.

"Well, now, my lord, you have met your brother," said Robinson, his distaste at Val's appearance obvious, "and now we may leave."

"Oh, no, Robinson. Papa agreed that I could invite him home."

"My lord," protested Robinson.

Val waited a beat and then repeated the words. "My lord."

"My name is Charles. We *are* brothers, whether you choose to acknowledge that or not," he added with the dignity of one born heir to an earldom.

"I would say that you are the one doing the acknowledging, my lo—I mean, Charles," replied Val with an ironic smile.

"I only hoped we could get to know one another . . . perhaps become like real brothers. I begged Papa to let me come."

For all of a moment, when Val had first heard the boy's name, he had experienced a wild hope that the earl had finally decided to acknowledge him, even had revealed some feeling for his eldest son. He despised his father, of course, for not marrying his mother, but perhaps they might have gotten beyond that. Now it was clear that the contact had only been made because of the young viscount's whim. Yet there was something about Charles that pulled at him. He knew he was being foolish, but all he could think of was, *He's lost his mother.*

"I could not leave the smithy even if I wanted to," Val replied.

The boy's face lit up. "Oh, Robinson is prepared to compensate Mr. Burton for your time."

Perhaps it was his sympathy for the boy. More likely it was the desire to see the look on George Burton's face when the earl's man bought him out of a few weeks' work that made him agree. Val nodded and said slowly, "All right. If George agrees, I'll come."

Two days later, as the coach drew closer to Faringdon, Val wondered if it had been worth the look of consternation on George's face when approached by Robinson and the young viscount. George hated Val for the combination of noble blood with ignoble birth, and would have refused if the money hadn't been so tempting. Greed won out, but George's parting words had been, "Ye'll be coming back full of yourself, I'm sure, but I'll work it out of you."

Val looked over to where Charlie—it had only taken a few hours in his brother's company before he was calling him that—leaned against the squabs sound asleep. Robinson had kept his eyes resolutely on the landscape as it rolled by, clearly not eager to engage in any conversation with the earl's bastard. Well, the earl's bastard wasn't particularly interested in speaking with such a stiff-rumped old bugger anyway, thought Val.

He hadn't been able to avoid conversation with Charlie, though. He smiled to himself. The boy babbled like a brook, about his new mare and how Val would love Faringdon and he couldn't wait to take him fishing in the river. He had a warm heart, this half-brother of his, Val had to admit. No one had shown him any interest or affection for so long that, like a fool, he'd let himself be moved by it. Well, it would be a short visit, for Val had mainly come for the opportunity to tell the earl just what he thought about a man who seduced and abandoned a woman like Sarah Aston.

They arrived in the late afternoon and Charlie was out of the coach and up the front steps of the house before either Robinson or Val had stepped down. He was back almost immediately. "Father is out inspecting the south field," he announced, a disappointed look on his face. "But that gives us a chance to clean up for dinner. He left word that he would be in the library at six."

Val was standing there trying not to look the dumbfounded yokel as he took in the magnificence of his surroundings. The main part of the hall clearly went back to Tudor times, but the east and west wings were of more recent origin. Several footmen had come out to get the luggage. A dignified older man in black—whom, Val was embarrassed to confess to himself, he'd first thought was the earl when he had followed Charlie out—greeted them politely.

"This is Baynes," said Charlie. "He's been here ever so long, since before I was born."

Val nodded stiffly and followed Charlie into the hall, very aware that the eyes of all the servants were on him. He could only imagine what they must be thinking: that their sweet young viscount had foolishly brought home his bastard brother, a dirty blacksmith's apprentice.

Oh, God, and he looked the blacksmith's apprentice. Val

groaned despairingly as he looked at himself in the pier glass. His best suit of clothes had been made for him over a year ago and he had only worn it to church on Sundays for a few hours, so it was stiff and uncomfortable . . . and too small. He had filled out considerably over the last year and it seemed the weight of the blacksmith's hammer had stretched his arms more than a few inches, he thought with grim humor as he looked at what seemed like yards of white shirt which were exposed. He had to leave the top button of his jacket unbuttoned or else he was afraid he'd rip the seams. But he straightened his shoulders, reminding himself that he might be a blacksmith's apprentice, but he was a damned good one, and the muscles produced by hard work were nothing to be ashamed of.

He was so eager to get his ordeal over with that he was the first in the library.

"His Lordship and the viscount are not down yet," Baynes had informed him. "But there is a fire going and I will pour you some sherry, sir."

Baynes was suiting action to words when Val stopped him. "No, thank you, Baynes, I'll wait until the others come down."

Actually, looking at the fragile glasses, Val decided he'd wait till hell froze over. He was used to solid tumblers of ale, not flimsy crystal that looked like it would break if he tightened his fingers around it.

"I'll leave you, then, sir."

"Er, thank you, Baynes."

The library was a more inviting room than he had expected. The fire was burning cheerily, throwing strong light upon a deep red Turkish carpet. There was a large desk tucked into the bay window and rows and rows of books on the walls.

Val had read and reread his *Robinson Crusoe* and third volume of Shakespeare over the years. He had been hungry for new books, but the only time he had brought one home from the lending library, George had mocked him unmercifully about his pretensions—although George was happy enough to use his reading and calculating skills in the business. Now George didn't have to ask his wife to read orders or keep the accounts for him: He had Val to do it.

There were shelves of books in many languages, Val discovered before he came upon a name he recognized: *The Tragedies of William Shakespeare,* in a leather-bound volume. He lifted it down carefully and opened it slowly; there it was, the same table of contents: *The Tragedy of Hamlet, Prince of Denmark; Othello;* and *King Lear.* Val turned to *Lear* immediately, searching for one of his favorite passages, Edmund's speech at the beginning of Act One. Val had read it to himself many times over the years, so that he had it by heart:

> ". . . Why bastard? Wherefore base?
> When my dimensions are as well-compact
> My mind as generous and my shape as true,
> As honest madam's issue? Why brand they us
> with base? With baseness? bastardy? base, base; . . .
> Now, gods, stand up for bastards!"

Once or twice on a walk through the local woods, Val had declared the whole speech, shouting out the last line as though someone might hear him and come to his rescue. Edmund might have been a villain, but Val couldn't help but feel sympathetic.

He had been so caught up in the play that he didn't hear the library door open and he jumped and nearly dropped the Shakespeare when a man's voice greeted him.

"You enjoy Shakespeare, do you, Mr. Aston?"

Val was tempted to tug his forelock and say, "Oh, ay, my lord, I do be fond of auld Will, what I can make out of him, that is." The earl's comment sounded innocent, but Val was sure he was surprised his bastard son could read at all. But he resisted the temptation and merely placed the volume down on a side table before facing his father.

It was immediately clear that Charlie closely resembled the earl, for despite the fact that the man's hair was lightly streaked with gray, it was the same as his son's: a dark gold. His blue eyes were a shade lighter than Charlie's, but at first glance, Val only thought, with a pang of loneliness that surprised him, how much it must please the man to have a son so like him. Then he began to notice details. The earl's gaze was cool and shuttered, where Charlie's heart was in his eyes. His face was long and narrow, and

his nose . . . Val unconsciously reached up and traced his
own. He had thought he was very like his mother: curly
dark hair, gray eyes, and a complexion that browned in the
sun. But his nose was as aquiline as the man's before him.

"Ah, yes, the Faringdon nose," said the earl. "If I'd had
any doubts, that would have done away with them," he
continued with dry humor. "Charlie has my coloring, but
his mother's face and nose. While you . . ." The earl hesitated. "You have Sarah's coloring and my beak."

He said Val's mother's name so *easily.* There was no
shame in his voice, just a statement of fact, uttered in the
blandest of tones. Val had imagined this scene many times.
He would confront his father. When the man spoke dispar-
agingly of his mother or denied her, he would challenge
him and beat him within an inch of his life. He would rail
at the Earl of Faringdon as Edmund had railed. He would
demand satisfaction.

But in his fantasies, the earl had been a gross man, a
corrupted member of the nobility, not this elegant person
before him who gazed at him with quizzical interest.

"You do not deny me, then, my lord," Val finally said.

"Why should I?"

"Yet you never sought me out?" Val worked very hard
to keep his tone as even and unemotional as his father's.

"Your mother and I agreed that it was best I stay away
from you both," the earl answered noncommittally.

Val wanted to ask, "Best for whom?" but he remained
silent and after a moment his father—*no,* he would not call
him that—the earl continued.

"Charlie was very affected by his mother's death. When
he accidentally found out about your existence, he kept
after me. He has a very loving heart, Charlie," said the earl
with a quick, almost apologetic smile, "I thought it might
be good for him to find you, once he learned of your
existence."

"But you never would have told him of me yourself."

"No," the earl admitted softly. "But here you are, and
we might as well make the best of it, shall we?"

Val never knew what he might have answered, if anything. He was ready to stride out the door and walk the
long way back to Westbourne when Charlie came into
the library.

"I am sorry I am late, Father. Val." He was trying to act the sophisticated young viscount, but his eyes were as curious and eager as a puppy's.

"We were just getting acquainted, Charles," said his father. "I was asking Valentine if he enjoyed Shakespeare."

"Do you, Val? I find him a great bore, myself," Charlie confessed with an exasperated grimace that made Val smile.

"I am afraid I do. At least the plays I have had the opportunity to read."

"You *see,* Father," said Charlie.

"Charles, we agreed not to discuss this now."

The interchange was so quick that Val almost didn't notice it. He didn't understand it, at any rate, and put it out of his mind.

"Would you like some sherry, Valentine?"

Since the earl was already pouring it, Val realized that it was a rhetorical question and extended his hand, praying that the glass would be safe.

"Charles?"

"May I, Father?"

"I think that the occasion calls for it. After all, it is not every day one discovers a brother," the earl said dryly.

Once the glasses were filled, Charlie lifted his and, looking over at Val shyly, gave a whispered toast: "To your homecoming, Val."

The earl's eyes widened, but he lifted his glass at his son's words, and Val drank his sherry wondering how such a sweet, heavy liquor could leave such a bitter aftertaste.

Charles Faringdon thought the evening would never end. Thank God for Charlie, he told himself later as he stood in his bedroom, looking out the window. At least the lad had kept the conversation going, asking his brother questions about hammers and horseshoes.

Val had smiled more than once at Charlie's questions, and Charles had thought his heart might break, for it was Sarah's smile that lit up the boy's gray eyes, which were Sarah's eyes.

Sarah had been right to keep him away. He knew that with his mind. He had been betrothed to Helen when he'd met her. It was a match arranged years ago by their fathers,

but he was also very fond of Helen. But the only woman
he had ever loved passionately and completely had been
Sarah Aston.

He would have married her if she had let him, thrown it
all to the winds: the estate, the earldom, his reputation, her
reputation. But she had refused him.

"It would not work, Charles," she'd told him. "I am only
a farmer's daughter."

"Your father has been very successful, Sarah," he had
protested. "He sent you to school. You are a real lady, far
more one than some of the members of the ton, I can
assure you."

"He did send me to school, and I stayed until I could
bear the loneliness no longer, Charles. I never fit in there
and I would never fit in here or in London. I am afraid, in
time, you would grow ashamed of me and regret your
decision."

"Never."

"And I could not be the cause of a breach with your
family, Charles. Nor the reason for a young woman's humiliation and heartbreak."

"But you *love* me, Sarah."

"And I will forever, my dear. But I cannot marry you."

"Then I will find you a home, Sarah. Here and in London. If you won't marry me, then we can still be lovers."

"No, Charles, I will not be your mistress," she answered
angrily. "That is no way to start off a marriage."

"It is the way most marriages are, my dear."

"In your world, perhaps, but not in mine." She was silent
for a moment and then said, with a quaver in her voice,
"But I do need you to find me a place, Charles, where I
can raise our child."

"My God, Sarah, you *have* to marry me," he'd exclaimed, bruising her arms as he'd grabbed her and given
her a shake as though that would get through to her.

"I don't *have* to do anything, Charles," she'd replied, her
eyes flashing.

And that was part of why he'd loved her. She had no
respect for his rank or fortune. She, a farmer's daughter,
was less in awe of him than some of the young women he'd
met during the Season. She loved him for himself. But she

also respected herself. There was no false humility in Sarah Aston, only a hard-earned realism.

It took two more painful scenes before she convinced him. And so he sent his secretary out to find a suitable dwelling far enough from Faringdon and her home that she would be unrecognized, where she settled in as the newly widowed Mrs. Aston.

Despite his promises, he had been driven by desire and heartbreak to try one last time to change her mind and he visited her dressed in a shabby suit so no one would guess at his rank. She had been a month away from giving birth and he thought she had never looked so beautiful as when she struggled up from her knees when he found her in the garden.

"Charles! Oh, my dear, I have so wanted you to come," she cried, unable to hide her joy at the sight of him.

He walked with her in the garden, holding her arm and casting shy glances at her swollen belly.

"Do you wish to feel your child kick, Charles?" she asked and placed his hand on her side. She laughed at the look of amazement on his face. "He . . . or she . . . is very active."

"Oh, Sarah, please come home with me," he begged, knowing it was useless, but unable to stop himself.

"It is best this way, my dear. You know it is."

"How could it be best to marry a woman I will never love?"

"You know you are very fond of Helen. You will grow to love her, but only if we are apart, Charles."

"You are a strong-willed woman, Sarah."

"I have to be, Charles, for both of us."

They walked back to the rosebushes and Sarah leaned down and took a flower out of her basket.

"Here, Charles. Roses have always been the flower of love. When you look at this, know that I will always love you. That it is only love that enables me to give you up."

"This is what I think of your love, Sarah," he said with sudden, fierce anger and he ripped the petals from the rose and threw it at her feet. She flinched as though he'd slapped her, but only said a calm good-bye and walked slowly into the house. He watched her go, knowing he would never see her again, and, reaching out, plucked a half-blown rose, glad of the pain as a thorn stabbed the soft pad of his thumb. He thrust it into his jacket and rode away from her and all that had given his life meaning.

Sarah had been right: He did come to love Helen, although he didn't realize it until Charlie was born. But his love for her was very different from what he had felt for Sarah, who had been the love of his life, his "red, red rose," while Helen was his everyday companion, someone who over the years became an integral part of his life. When she died, he was desolate, only able to take comfort from their son, who was so like her.

He hadn't wanted Charlie to find Val. He had hoped the boy would be rough and crude and that Charlie would recognize he had made a mistake and not invite him. Or that Val wouldn't come.

Now here he was, looking just like his mother. He was a bit rough around the edges, but Faringdon was sure Sarah would have been proud of their son and happy to know that father and son had met at last. And he knew she would have wanted him to get Val away from Burton. Robinson had made inquiries and it was clear from village gossip that the blacksmith was a brutal man.

Valentine had evidently survived his harsh adolescence, but whoever he had been before Sarah died—and Faringdon could not imagine Sarah raising anything but a warm-hearted boy—was hidden deep inside. His conversation with his father had been respectful, but the earl was sure that the boy despised him. And why not? As far as he knew, the earl had deserted mother and son years ago, except for his financial support. Perhaps someday he would be open to hearing the story, but now the earl was sure any attempt to establish a relationship would end in Valentine telling him to go to hell. Faringdon smiled. One other thing he had inherited from Sarah: her damned pride!

It took the whole first week, but at last Val began to relax and even enjoy his visit. Charlie was irresistible: full of enthusiasm and eager to show Val all his favorite haunts.

Val enjoyed their rides and rambles and fishing expeditions. He had been working since he was eight and it was glorious to wake up in the morning and realize he was not at George Burton's beck and call. That he could do whatever he wanted that day and the next. It would be hard to go back, but for now he'd decided not to think about it.

He really could do what he wanted, he realized. Charlie was so pleased to have found a brother, so eager to make Val feel at home that he started out every day with, "What should we do this morning, Val?" At first Val would reply politely, "Whatever you wish, Charlie," but after a few outings, Val began to express his own preferences. One visit to the village was enough for him; he was so conscious of people staring and gossiping. Everyone knew he was the earl's bastard and he'd be damned if he'd be insulted here as well as at home. He loved fishing the river and an outing to Fern Pool was his most frequent request.

One afternoon of his second week, he and Charlie were returning to the hall, their baskets holding three and two trout, respectively. As the earl and Robinson watched from the window of the library, Charlie punched his brother's arm and said, "Tomorrow I'll come home with four, I promise you, Val."

Val reached out his hand and tousled his brother's hair. "I'll wager you a ride on Shadow that you don't. My lord," he added humorously.

"Oh, no, you don't 'my lord' me," said Charlie with a laugh. "Nor get a ride on my favorite mount, Val."

"Your son seems to have become very fond of his brother, my lord," said Robinson.

"To which son are you referring, Robinson?"

Robinson cleared his throat in embarrassment.

The earl smiled. "I know. Charlie is happier than I have seen him since his mother died. And Valentine seems to enjoy his company. Perhaps it is time to broach Charlie's plan. Will you send the boys in to me after they have cleaned up, Robinson?"

Val felt more than mere enjoyment in Charlie's company. His half-brother was very likable, he'd told himself the first few days. But by now, as his visit was coming to an end, he knew his feelings for Charlie went beyond mere liking. Charlie's warmth and ease with physical affection had opened a place in Val that had been long closed. He would miss his younger brother terribly, he realized. He would miss

Faringdon and this part of Devon. Somehow the fields and
trees and moors had begun to feel like home to him. The
only person he wouldn't miss would be the earl. The man
had never shown him the least sign of affection. Not that
Val wanted him to. Nor had he even attempted an explanation of his behavior with Val's mother. Not that Val expected him to. And nothing he could say could excuse it
anyway. So when he entered the library, he had his face
fixed in his usual expression: a superficial look of respect
that almost but not quite disguised his disdain.

Charlie was already there and Val gave him a quick
smile.

"Come in, Valentine, and sit down," said the earl. "We
have something of importance to discuss with you, don't
we, Charles?"

Charlie's face lit up. "You are going to ask him, then?"

"Why don't you," said the earl with an encouraging
smile.

"I have had a private tutor for years, Val."

"Yes, you told me about Mr. Cordell. He is on vacation."

"A well-earned vacation, I might add," said the earl.

"Father thinks it time for me to go away to school, Val."

Val nodded, wondering what this had to do with him.

"But I told him I didn't want to leave Faringdon. Not
alone, anyway. I want . . ." Charlie glanced over at his
father for confirmation and the earl nodded. "We want you
to come with me."

Val was too surprised to keep his face expressionless.
"Are you mad, Charlie? I'm a blacksmith's apprentice. And
I couldn't get out of my articles even if I wanted to."

"Father will buy you out."

Val looked over at his father, astonishment on his face.
"Whyever would you want to do that, my lord?"

"Charles needs to be away with other boys his age, Valentine. His mother wanted to wait, and when she died, I
hesitated to send him. But with you accompanying him, he
would feel less alone."

"George Burton would never let me go," Val said flatly.

"Oh, I daresay he could be persuaded," the earl replied
with an ironic smile.

"Please say yes, Val," Charlie pleaded.

Val ignored him and stared at the earl. "Might we converse alone, my lord?" he asked formally.

"Of course. Charles, please wait in the drawing room."

"Father . . ."

"*Charles.*"

"Yes, sir." Charlie left with a pleading backward glance at his brother.

"Well, Valentine?"

"Why would you do this now, my lord? After all these years?"

"Because Charles has grown fond of you. And because I think your mother would have liked you to have the opportunities your birth fits you for."

"My birth! That's a fine joke, my lord. I am nothing but your bastard. By-blow of an earl and a farmer's daughter. And I'll thank you not to imagine what my mother would want. How would you know, once you deserted her?" All the anger Val had been holding in flared up and the words were out before he realized it.

"You may be a bastard, Valentine," the earl responded calmly, "but you are, as you put it, an earl's bastard. And your mother held schooling to be very important."

"That hasn't seemed to concern you all these years."

"It was your mother's wish that I stay away from her and you. She had given guardianship to her sister long ago. I had no way of knowing until recently that your aunt was so different from Sarah. Your allowance went through my solicitor. It wasn't until Charlie found out about you that I discovered the truth about George Burton."

"I don't believe you," Val replied hotly.

"Be that as it may, I am now offering you an education and freedom from a laborer's life."

"And what would I do with such an education? Become the best-read blacksmith in Devon?"

"If you wished. But I would suggest considering the law or perhaps estate management as an alternative," the earl replied with dry humor.

Val was quiet for a long time and his father waited patiently while the boy considered his offer.

To go to school? To be out from under George Burton? To have some choice in his life? Not to lose Charlie? How could he say no? Yet how could he accept this from a man who was only acknowledging him fifteen years after his birth?

"It is a hard decision to make," Val finally choked out.

"I understand." And Faringdon did. The boy was proud and did not want to be beholden to the man he saw as the victimizer of his mother. "But it would be so helpful to Charles. . . ."

If the earl had mentioned his mother or his position, Val would have said no immediately. But Charlie? How could he not give something back to the first person who had offered him affection since his mother died?

"I will try it, for Charlie's sake," said Val, standing up. "But I will not thank you for it, my lord."

"No, I suppose I did not expect gratitude," Faringdon replied. "Well, then, I will send Robinson to Burton to buy you out."

"I wish to go with him, my lord. To say a farewell to my aunt and thank her. It has been hard for her all these years, trying to protect me and at the same time remain loyal to her husband."

"Very well. You should be ready to leave tomorrow."

The look on George Burton's face when Robinson informed him of the earl's intentions was reward enough for all the years the man had brutalized him, thought Val. The man was outraged, greedy, and obsequious all at the same time. He accepted Robinson's third offer, not realizing that he could have held out for more.

"This will more than provide you for another apprentice, Mr. Burton," said Robinson as he handed over the earl's draft.

"Aye, one I'll have to train from the very beginning," he grumbled.

"Do you have anything to collect, Valentine?" Robinson asked in a kinder tone than Val had ever heard from him before.

"Yes."

"Well, then, get your things and meet me at the inn. I would like to be off within the half-hour."

Val turned his back on George Burton and the shop and headed toward the house. He collected his books and two shirts, leaving behind a patched pair of corduroys and an old pair of brogues. There wasn't much, even after seven years, he thought sadly.

His aunt was in the kitchen, setting out the bread to rise, and his appearance at the door startled her. "Why, Val, I thought you'd be staying a few more days. Did you not enjoy your visit?"

"I am only here to collect my things," Val told her gently.

His aunt looked over at him, a puzzled frown on her face.

"The earl wishes to send me to school."

"But George?"

"The earl has paid him well for the last year of my articles," Val reassured her.

His aunt put a hand over her heart, as though to calm it. "Oh, Valentine, this is what your mother would have wished. I have often felt so terrible that I couldn't do better for you."

"You did what you could, Martha," Val told her. "And it has not been so bad, once I grew strong enough."

They both knew he didn't mean strong enough for the hammer, but strong enough to keep George from beating him.

"I always tried to stop him," she said with helpless regret.

"I know, but he needed to hear it in his own language, Martha," Val said with a reassuring grin. "Now, come and give me a good-bye hug and wish me luck. God knows I'll need it."

Martha clung to him for a long time. When she finally pulled away she had to wipe her eyes on her apron. "You remember you are Sarah Aston's son, Val. She was a good, strong woman, so don't let anyone make you feel ashamed."

There was color in Martha's cheeks and for a moment Val saw his aunt's resemblance to her sister that became apparent from time to time. He caught her in his arms for another long hug and this time it was his eyes that were filled with tears. "I will keep in touch, Martha," he promised.

"I know you will, Val. God be with you."

With all the times he had wished for his freedom and dreamed of his escape, Val had never imagined it would be hard to leave the smithy behind. And yet, as he walked down to the inn, he realized he was leaving the only home he had known since his mother died, and his closest connection to her.

He had learned a lot from George Burton, he had to admit. First, how to survive cruelty, which was no small thing. Second, how to stop a bully. And third, a trade that had made him physically strong and with which he could support himself if he ever needed to. In a strange way, he was even grateful to the man, he realized with a grin as he stepped forward to greet Robinson and begin his new life.

Queen's Hall was a smaller version of Eton and Harrow, educating, as they did, the sons of the nobility so they could take their places helping run the nation.

Or ruin the nation, Val thought cynically after his first month there. He wasn't sure what he'd expected of the legitimate issue of earls and marquesses, but certainly something different than the young ruffians of Queen's Hall. With the exception of a few boys in every form, the majority were as mean-spirited and intolerant as the worst of Westbourne. They pounced on any weakness and exploited it. The upper-school boys tormented the lower-school boys just because they were younger and smaller.

He only saw Charlie at meals and then it was from three tables over. There were occasional stolen moments in the hallway when Charlie would give him a smile that lifted his spirits for a few days. And there were a few free hours on Sundays after chapel.

That seemed to be enough for Charlie, who recovered quickly from his first few weeks of homesickness and threw himself into his schoolwork and games. It became obvious to Val that his brother was immensely popular and had the makings of a natural leader.

Val was not faring as well. While Charlie was entering school only a few years after boys his own age, Val's classmates had been at the Hall for seven years. They knew the routines, the schoolwork, and, most of all, each other.

Val's natural intelligence and hunger for knowledge helped him to catch up in most of his classes. But Latin was Greek to him. He was sent to the lower school to sit in a small chair with the seven-year-olds, his baritone voice overshadowing their piping tenors as they repeated their *"amo, amas amats."* Finally the humiliation became too much and he visited the school's head to convince him Latin was a subject not required for someone who would most likely end up an estate manager. The head needed no convincing, for he regarded Val's presence mainly as an interesting social experiment and an additional source of income. It wasn't that the Hall hadn't educated the occasional by-blow before, but never one quite so muscular, he thought after Val left.

Things might eventually have turned out well had it not been for Lord Lucas Stanton. He was an arrogant upper classman who from the first had whispered slurs just loud enough for Val and one or two of Stanton's lackeys to overhear, but never anyone in authority. It wasn't easy for Val to ignore him, but he did, knowing any response would only feed Stanton's desire to humiliate.

Then Val caught him in the washroom one day twisting the arm of one of the skinnier eight-year-olds while commanding the boy to lick his boots clean. On the one hand, Val knew the lad was lucky it was only Stanton's boots he was being asked to lick. On the other, he couldn't ignore the pain and fear in the boy's eyes, so he ordered Stanton to let him go.

"And who are you to give me orders, Mr. Aston?" sneered Stanton, all the while twisting his victim's arm even harder. Val quickly grabbed Stanton's free arm and twisted it behind the bully's back. Stanton yelped in pain and Val motioned the younger boy to the door. The lad, tears pouring down his face, gave Val an admiring and grateful look, and fled.

Stanton struggled but was no match for Val. "How does it feel, Stanton?" asked Val, twisting his arm even harder. He let go suddenly and Stanton staggered and almost fell. "You are a pathetic excuse for a gentleman," said Val with disgust. "If I ever catch you torturing a small boy again, I'll make you lick your own boots clean."

Stanton had never been a friend, but it was now clear that Val had made an enemy. The insults became more frequent and instead of sotto voce, were often uttered aloud and in public. Val continued to swallow them, know-

ing there was no alternative unless he was willing to fight.
But fighting was against the rules, he thought angrily, while
tormenting little boys was not.

On one rainy Friday at the end of a long, rainy week,
things came to a head. All of the boys were feeling pent
up, having been confined indoors for so long. They gathered around the tea tables, ravenously eating biscuits and
muffins, jostling one another, and rattling their teacups. Just
as Val entered the room, Stanton said from across the floor,
loud enough for all to hear, "Here he is, Faringdon's bastard. Do you know, I've found out who his mother was: a
tuppenny whore who died of the pox."

Of all the insults he had endured and ignored—and Val
had ignored many—this was the first time Stanton had commented on his mother. He pushed his way through the
openmouthed boys.

"What did you say?" he demanded in a low voice.

"I said, Aston, that your mother was a tuppenny whore."

"That's what I thought." Val's arm swept the teacup out
of Stanton's hand and the sound of the shattering china
quieted the room immediately.

"Come outside, Stanton."

Stanton glanced out the window. "I think not, Aston."

Val's hand was at Stanton's throat in an instant, grabbing
his cravat and twisting it. "You *will* come outside, Stanton.
Or are you afraid to?"

"I'm not afraid of a rude fellow like you, Aston," Stanton managed to choke out.

"I'll meet you behind the kitchen, then," said Val and,
turning on his heel, he walked out of the room, ignoring
Charlie's hand on his arm and his desperate plea to "Ignore, him, Val. You'll be thrown out for fighting."

The tearoom emptied in a minute, and half the school
gathered outside with the other half crowding the hall
windows.

Val had stripped his shirt off and was standing in the
rain, the hard little needles hitting his chest and arms, but
his anger so energized him he didn't feel cold or wet. When
Stanton came out he stripped quickly and rushed Val, pushing him down into the mud. As Val stood up, Stanton
caught him a blow on the chin and a muffled gasp went up

from all the boys. This wasn't going to be an imitation of a bout of fisticuffs at Jackson's.

Val pulled himself back up and rubbed his chin. "No gentleman's rules, Stanton?"

"You're a bastard, not a gentleman, Aston," Stanton sneered.

Val moved so fast that Stanton never saw him coming. He swept the viscount's leg with his and Stanton went down to his knees. With his two hands together as though he were holding a blacksmith's hammer, Val smashed him on the side of the face and Stanton went over into the mud. Val looked down at him. "Where I come from, you don't kick a man when he's down, Stanton, so get yourself up."

Stanton stood up, and landed a blow to Val's right eye.

As Val went down, he was blinded by the blood from his split eyebrow and didn't see Stanton's boot coming until it was too late to avoid it. He knew his nose was broken as soon as it was hit. He was down on all fours like an animal when Stanton grabbed his hair and, lifting his head, said, "Would you agree, Aston, that your mother was a pox-ridden whore?" He was just raising a hand to hit Val's face when Val grabbed him between the thighs and squeezed. Stanton doubled over and then they heard a new voice.

"What the hell is going on here, Stanton?"

"Why, er, nothing, Wimborne," Stanton grunted, trying to straighten up. "Just a little sport, that is all."

James Lambert, Marquess of Wimborne, looked around at the silent spectators and then down at Val. "I don't call it sporting to insult a man's mother, Stanton," said the marquess, looking at Stanton with disgust. "And your fighting techniques belong in Seven Dials. Now all of you, get yourselves out of here before the head finds out. Henry, help me with Aston."

The marquess and his friend lifted Val up and when he tried to pull away and stand on his own, James said with sympathetic humor, "Relax, Aston. I'm only taking you to my rooms to get you cleaned up a bit before supper." So Val let himself be led.

The Marquess of Wimborne was in his last year at Queen's Hall. He was one of the best-loved pupils in the school, both by the boys and the masters. To be his fag was like being adopted, not enslaved, for while he used the younger boys for errands, he also jollied them out of their homesickness, encouraged the shy ones, and controlled the bullies. Val, who was two forms below him, knew of him and had even received a smile in the hall, but had never expected to speak with him, much less be rescued by him.

"I've been watching you, Aston," said the marquess as he cleaned the blood off Val's face with a wet towel. "Stanton has been after you for weeks, but you've managed to ignore him. Which is always the best course with bullies like that," he added with a warm smile. "What set you off?"

"I am used to being offered insults to myself, my lord," Val answered, "but he insulted my mother's memory."

"Yes, I thought it might have been that," murmured the marquess as he gently ran his fingers down Val's nose. "I fear 'tis broken, Mr. Aston, and you will have an even more raptorlike look in the future," he joked as Val winced. "Not that it won't make you more interesting to the ladies," he added.

"I doubt that any *lady* will be interested in me, my lord," Val replied with a strained smile.

"Nonsense, you are just the rugged sort they love. Now then, Henry, can you get me a clean shirt from the clothespress?"

Val started to protest, but the marquess just put up his hand. "Do you wish to be sent down, Mr. Aston?"

"No."

"I thought not. I have heard that you are quite good in all your classes . . . except, perhaps, Latin?"

Val looked up, expecting an insult and finding only a sympathetic twinkle in Wimborne's eyes. He grinned. "I must confess I felt like a bullfrog amongst the peepers, my lord."

"An apt metaphor, my friend," said the marquess with an appreciative laugh. "I saw you with your knees up around your ears."

They both laughed and Val felt all the muscles in his back relax. He realized that it was the first time in weeks that he wasn't holding himself guarded and tense.

"Look, old fellow, I *know* Stanton is a brute," said the marquess seriously. "I try to keep the youngest boys safe from him, if you know what I mean."

Val nodded. He knew what went on. Some of the boys relieved their tension by stroking themselves, and others were drawn to one another out of loneliness. A few, Val knew, had genuine affection and desire for their own sex. He'd heard of two men like that, in the next town over from Westbourne. He didn't really understand it, and didn't know quite what he felt about it, but what he did mind was the way some of the older boys were rumored to force those of the lower school. To him, that was buggery, pure and simple, and he had had a hard time accepting that it was the way things were done. Val was happy to know that his new friend deplored the practice as he did.

"I know a little of your story," continued the marquess. "I am sure you wish to stay, both for Charlie's sake and your own."

Val nodded.

"Then ignore the bastard."

Val flinched at the word. He couldn't help himself.

The marquess decided to ignore it. "Now let me look at you. What do you think, Henry?"

"He could have walked into a door."

"It is too bad we can't come up with anything better than that old saw," said the marquess with an ironic smile, "but I suppose it will have to do. Now, what do you think the head will say about Stanton walking bent over his balls?" asked the marquess, an eyebrow lifted inquiringly.

Henry and the marquess laughed aloud and, after a moment's hesitation, Val joined them. For the first time since arriving at the Hall, he felt a sense of camaraderie.

Val was sure the teachers knew what had happened, but since no one, especially the two combatants, was willing to tell, nothing happened except for a few weeks of being under very close scrutiny. The next Sunday Charlie told Val that the younger boys had taken great satisfaction, especially when Val had attacked Stanton's privates.

"Stanton has never, er, bothered you, has he, Charlie?" asked Val, suddenly worried about his brother. "You know what I mean?" he added, not wanting to have to put it into words.

"He wouldn't dare. I'd kick him right where you squeezed him!"

*   *   *

For the Christmas break both boys returned to Faringdon and the pattern that had been set during the summer continued. Val was polite to his father, spoke when spoken to, but kept his distance, and the earl wondered if he would ever be able to form a relationship with his oldest son. It seemed the only thing they had in common was their love for Charlie.

Val had managed to slip off from time to time into the village and had convinced the local blacksmith to let him use the forge. He had fashioned Charlie two small wrought-iron bookends for Christmas and was embarrassed at the pleasure and surprise in Charlie's eyes when he opened the heavy parcel.

"They are splendid, Val!"

"Indeed they are," agreed the earl, admiring the workmanship and thinking how very odd it was a son of his had been a smith.

"George was a good teacher, if a hard one," Val said gruffly.

One of Charlie's presents to him was an illustrated copy of Ovid's *Metamorphoses*. "I thought you might like something more enjoyable than a grammar."

"I doubt that I have enough Latin to make it out," said Val as he paged through the book. "I never did get much beyond conjugations, but thank you, Charlie."

Returning to the spartan atmosphere of Queen's Hall was difficult after three weeks at Faringdon. The school was big and ill-heated and half the boys at any one time were suffering from coughs and sniffles. One Sunday, when Charlie was one of those in bed with a cold, Val decided to go for a walk across the neighboring fields. He had a good long tramp and was within a mile of the school when he met the Marquess of Wimborne.

"You look like you had a healthy walk, Aston," said the older boy with a smile.

"And you too, my lord."

"Please call me James."

"Then you must call me Val."

"How was your holiday, Val? You spent it at Faringdon?"

"Very enjoyable, my lord. I mean, James. In fact, I was surprised at how difficult it was to return."

"This was your first holiday there, wasn't it? Do you and your father get along?"

"The earl can be very pleasant," Val answered stiffly.

It did not escape James's notice that Val had referred to his father by his title, but he decided to ignore it. "Fathers can be most difficult. Mine is determined to marry me off to recoup the family fortunes. Oh, not immediately," said James, responding to Val's look of surprise. "But he would love to celebrate a betrothal in the next few years. There is a suitable girl, old friend of the family's, excellent dowry . . . that sort of thing."

"You don't care for her, then?"

"I don't dislike her. But I haven't met any woman I would wish to marry." There was an undertone of sadness in James's voice that took Val by surprise. He wondered what such a privileged young man had to be sad about.

"I saw you in the library with your grammar out, swotting away. I thought you had given up on Latin," teased the marquess.

"Charlie gave me a copy of Ovid for Christmas, but I find it hard going."

"I'd be happy to help you with it. Come up to my room tonight for some chocolate and we'll see what we can do."

Val had received so little affection in his life and had never had a close friend, that it took him a while to open up to James's overtures, but gradually they fell into a routine of tramping the moors together every week, no matter what the weather, and warming themselves up later with tea or chocolate and whatever they could cadge from the tea table. Val did not become one of the marquess's intimates, of course. He was two forms below him, after all. But their friendship was genuine nevertheless, although Val could never understand why someone of James's rank would be drawn to an outsider like himself. He developed an affection for the older boy that was close to rivaling his feelings for Charlie, although he would have had a hard time expressing either.

In March, the boys were thrilled to discover that a recruiting regiment had arrived in the village and on their visits to town, the younger boys especially were enthralled by the recruiting sergeant's speeches outside the local pub.

"Poor bastards," said James one day as they watched some of the local men sign up. "They are nothing but 'food for powder.' "

Val had seen recruiting regiments in Westbourne. "But at least they'll have food in their own bellies before they feed the guns. Most men who sign up are poor laborers or vagrants, you know."

"Or men who would otherwise be transported. Have you ever considered the army, Val? I'm sure the earl would purchase you a commission if you desired it."

"He seems to have either the law or estate management in mind for me, James. And with my Latin, I think it will be the latter!"

Between Val's humiliation of him and James's protective friendship, Lucas Stanton had stopped his harassment except for an occasional whispered insult in the halls that Val could easily ignore. Although he still did not feel like a Queen's man, he was surprised at how he was beginning to enjoy his spring term and was even looking forward to his second year.

Then he caught Lucas Stanton with Marcus Towle, a cherubic nine-year-old. He and Charlie had been passing by the barn one Sunday afternoon when they heard crying.

"Go on, Charlie," said Val, "and I'll find out what it is."

"I'll go with you," Charlie protested.

"No, you just get yourself to evensong on time."

Lucas Stanton was just coming out of one of the back stalls, buttoning up his trousers. He looked surprised to see Val, but only gave him a leer and a smile as he passed by, saying, "If you want some, Aston, he's all yours."

Marcus was huddled in the corner of the stall, weeping heartbrokenly, his face buried in his hands. Val knelt next to him and put his hand gently on the boy's shoulder. "Are you all right, Marcus?" The younger boy shrank against the wall. "I'm not going to hurt you," Val reassured him. "What did he do to you?"

"He made me . . ." The boy wiped his mouth with the back of his hand. "He made me . . . take it in my mouth—"

Marcus turned and retched into the straw while Val patted his back awkwardly.

"I didn't want to," the boy sobbed after he'd stopped heaving. "Truly I didn't. I know some boys who might, but I didn't."

"It's all right, Marcus, I understand."

"He's been after me all spring, but I managed to keep out of his way until today."

"Can you stand up? He didn't do, er, anything else to you?"

The boy pulled himself up, looking blankly at Val, obviously still unaware that anything else might have befallen him, so Val just patted him again on the shoulder. "All right, then. Why don't you tell your prefect that you don't feel well, and sleep in the infirmary tonight."

The boy shivered. "I don't feel well. I think I shall do that."

Val caught up with Stanton outside the chapel.

"Stanton," he called.

Stanton only looked over his shoulder and, whispering something to his comrades that made them laugh, walked on.

"Are you afraid of me, Stanton?" Val called.

Stanton had to stop then. "Afraid of you? Hardly. What is it, Aston? Little Marcus not give you as much pleasure as you thought?"

Val thought his head might explode at the strength of the fury that flowed through him. He ran at Stanton with all the force of a battering ram and, just as Stanton turned, brought him down. This time, there was no contest. Val was on top of Stanton, trying to drive his face into the ground, when two of the teachers managed to pull him off.

"Aston, get yourself to your room and stay there till you are sent for. Is Stanton all right?"

"He's been beaten unconscious, sir," said one of Lucas's friends.

Val was still trembling when he was finally summoned to the headmaster's office.

"Lucas Stanton is missing two teeth and has a possible concussion. What have you got to say for yourself, Aston?"

"He . . . he . . ." Val couldn't think of the right words.

"He made Marcus . . . give him pleasure, sir," he finally choked out.

"Well?"

Was that all the head could say? *Well?*

"Well, what, sir?"

"Was there any other excuse?"

"Marcus is a nine-year-old boy, sir. Lucas Stanton violated him." Finally he had found the right word.

The headmaster looked down at his desk. "Yes, that does happen from time to time. Boys living together. Young men being what they are. It is no excuse for near murder."

"Young men being what they are?" Val's fury, which had died down, flamed up again. "Where I come from, young men don't do that. If they tried it, they'd be run out of town on a rail. Sir."

"I am sure that laboring men have the same urges, Aston," the head said disdainfully.

"Having urges is one thing. Forcing yourself on young boys or girls is another."

"It may not be right, Aston, but it happens."

"And you just pretend it doesn't? Just pretend Marcus wasn't sitting on the barn floor, puking his insides out?"

"He'll get over it in time. Boys do." They were both silent and then the head sighed again. "I shall have to dismiss you for this, Aston. I am sorry, for despite your, uh, unfortunate background, you seemed to be adjusting, but I can't overlook this."

Val gave him a disgusted look. "Don't worry, sir. I'll be out by morning. I don't want to adjust to such goings-on as this."

James was at the end of the hall, waiting for him.

"I am sent down. But I'd have had to leave anyway," Val told him.

"What happened?" James asked him quietly.

"I found Marcus in the barn. He was throwing up what Stanton had made him swallow," Val said harshly.

"Oh, God," said James.

"Yes. Well, I understand that this does happen here from time to time, this violation of innocence," said Val with savage irony.

"Most of the boys learn how to stay out of Stanton's way."

"I am not sure what I think about the boys who are clearly made this way," said Val, "but I can't accept this kind of perversion."

"Lucas Stanton isn't made that way, you know," the marquess commented quietly.

Val looked over at him with surprise.

"He'd bugger a sheep if he couldn't find anything else," James added with a wry smile. "He just enjoys hurting those weaker than himself. I pity the woman he marries."

"Then that is the real perversion, James."

"It may be, Val, but it will never be seen as such. Not amongst gentlemen, at any rate," he added sarcastically.

"Then I am glad I am not one of you."

"Ah, but in some ways you are, Val. What will you tell your father?"

"The truth," Val replied shortly. "Or nothing. I haven't decided yet what I am going to do."

"Why, what can you do but go home to Faringdon?"

"Go home to Faringdon" was the last thing he could do, thought Val as he packed his books. Charlie would still be at school and the earl would surely not want him at the hall. Home. He wished he knew where home was. It seemed to him he hadn't had a real home, one where love and affection reigned, since his mother died. The earl and Charlie loved each other. But the bastard son was only there because he made Charlie happy.

He certainly could not, would not, count George Burton's house as home, no matter how his aunt wanted him to think so. So the question before him was how he was going to make his living. Perhaps if he showed up, George might take him on as a partner. And pigs would fly! He supposed he could tramp around Devon looking for a smithy, but most men would already have apprentices. He had no money to set up on his own, although he knew he could eventually make a good living at it. If he asked the earl . . . ? He laughed out loud then. He could not ask the earl for anything, not the man who had rejected him for so long.

He sat on the edge of his bed, wondering where he would go, his bag packed, his head in his hands. After a while he became conscious that a plaintive tune was running through his head, a tune he knew from his mother's singing to him in childhood. Now, why had that song come back to haunt him? And then he remembered. In the town a week ago, one of the men accompanying the recruiting sergeant had been singing it. Well, singing the same tune, but the words were different:

> "There's forty shillings on the drum
> for those who volunteer to come. . . ."

He'd forgotten the verse, but remembered the chorus:

> "O'er the hills and o'er the main
> In Flanders, Portugal, and Spain
> King George commands and we obey
> Over the hills and far away."

The man had sung it in that deep baritone that country folk used and although the man had only sung three verses, they led you on, the last notes not bringing the verse to an end, but going up instead of down, as though promising something: another verse, another sea to cross, another battle to fight before the song was over.

Suddenly he knew what he was meant to do. He would go for a soldier. He would follow that imaginary "father" of his into the army, just the way he had dreamed he would when he was a boy. And the Earl of Faringdon be damned.

Chapter 1

Elspeth Gordon looked herself over in the pier glass and then gave her shoulders a little shrug as if to say, "I have done the best I can." She knew her dress, two years out of date, would not help. The wives and daughters of the Portuguese officers and diplomats would easily outshine her, with their satins and silks and black lace. And the few Englishwomen at this supper were new arrivals and, no doubt, had trunks full of the latest fashions.

And all of them, no matter how they were dressed, would be smaller than she was, thought Elspeth with a smile as she bent her knees to get a better look at her hair in the glass. She smoothed back a few strands that had escaped the knot she had twisted and secured with a silver pin.

She shrugged again at her reflection and said, "Ah, ma wee lass, ye're a sight for sore eyes," which was how her father always greeted her. And she added, with a twinkle in her hazel eyes, "Handsome is as handsome does, Elspeth," which was one of her mother's favorite sayings. "Now, Elspeth," she reminded herself, "everyone is here for Maria's birthday and not to see you. Your gown may be two years out of date, but it *was* fashionable at the time and it brings out the green in your eyes.

Fortified by that thought, she threw a shawl of soft white wool lace over her shoulders and went downstairs to join her hosts.

Elspeth Gordon, daughter of Major Ian Gordon and his wife Margaret, was in no danger of being ignored at a supper dance. She had come over to Portugal a year ago after finishing what she considered a tedious two years at Mrs. Page's School for Young Ladies. Her parents had offered her a Season, but she had refused. "After all those years in India, Mama, I just don't fit in. Truly, all I want is to join the two of you."

Had Elspeth been small and conventionally beautiful, perhaps her parents might have insisted upon a Season for two good reasons. One, had Elspeth combined beauty with her wit and spirit, a Season would no doubt have seen her married, if not blissfully, at least happily. The second reason was that bringing a Pocket Venus to live amongst the officers of Wellington's army would have been like setting a cat among pigeons. Or perhaps a pigeon among cats, as her mother had said.

As it was, Elspeth was very popular amongst the officers precisely because she was not an Incomparable. With the exception of her years at school, she had lived all her life in the army, for her mother had declared at the beginning of her marriage to the then-Lieutenant Gordon that she refused to sit home weeping and waiting either for his infrequent returns or a letter that announced he would never return at all.

Margaret Gordon's family had protested her decision as they had protested her marriage to a man who was the son of a Scottish vicar, while she was the granddaughter of an earl. But Margaret ignored their protests, determined to follow her husband wherever the army might send him, and she had never regretted her decision.

Elspeth wished her mother had come with her to Lisbon as she usually did, but Major Gordon had just recovered from a bout of Guadiana fever and Mrs. Gordon was convinced only her continuing presence would keep the major from suffering a relapse. So Elspeth descended the stairs alone, looking around for a familiar face.

The Count de Sousa sent his son over to escort her in to supper and Elspeth smiled gratefully as he took her arm. To her relief and pleasure, she was seated next to Lieutenant Morrison and chatted away with him, all the while wondering whether the empty seat to her right would eventually be filled or whether the count's guest had had to cancel at the last minute.

Just as they were beginning to serve the first course, Elspeth heard a stir at the door and the count's butler entered the dining room and whispered in his master's ear. "Tell him to come in," said the count.

"I beg your pardon, my lord, Lady de Sousa. I was unavoidably detained. I tried just to leave my apologies with your butler. I didn't want to disturb dinner."

"Nonsense. José, show Captain, my Lord Wimborne to his place next to Miss Gordon," said the contessa.

James's face lit up when he heard the name and Elspeth had a warm smile for him when he sat down.

"Jamie! What a delightful surprise. I am so happy to see you. Did you just arrive from England? And how is Lady Maddie?"

"She is still in alt, planning her coming Season, Elspeth."

"Her last letter was very enthusiastic," said Elspeth with a grin. "And Maddie is such a dear and attractive young woman that I am sure her Season will be everything she is hoping for. She also told me of the heavy responsibilities you had to take on after your father's death, James," Elspeth added more seriously. "She is very grateful to you for making sure she had a Season."

"And I am grateful to her for understanding it had to be put off last spring. Her only disappointment is that you will not be making your come-out with her, Elspeth."

"I prefer the army to Society, as you know, James. But I am hoping, depending upon the situation here, to attend Maddie's come-out ball. Now, what brings you here, James? I thought you were stationed at Whitehall."

"I have been asked to join Wellington's staff, Elspeth."

"Why, that is splendid."

"I was pleased. Especially since it meant getting out from under Townsend."

"I can understand why. Papa does not hold the colonel in very high regard, James," said Elspeth with a straight face but a twinkle in her eye.

They both grinned at the thought of the unrepeatable comments Major Gordon had made on his last leave about his superior officer. He had at one time or another cursed his ancestors, his stupidity, and his vanity, not to mention threatening his life and his manhood.

"May I claim a dance after supper?" James asked before he turned to do his duty to the lady on his other side.

"Of course."

* * *

Elspeth was a great favorite with both the British and allied officers and she only sat out one dance, and that with Lieutenant Morrison, who was recovering from a leg wound. All the men enjoyed her down-to-earth manner and her dry sense of humor. Dancing with Elspeth Gordon was like dancing with your sister or your best friend from childhood: a breath of fresh air after being mesmerized by the exotic flowers of the Portuguese nobility.

Elspeth enjoyed herself as she usually did after her initial self-consciousness wore off, but she looked forward the whole evening to her dance with James Lambert. The brother of her good friend from Mrs. Page's, he was someone she felt an intimacy with that went beyond the friendship she had with the other officers.

It was a comfortable intimacy, she mused, as they made their way to the dance floor. She had danced with James before, but only country dances, and she wondered whether a waltz, that daring Continental dance, would add another element to their friendship. But as well as they danced together, the warmth she felt from his hand lightly guiding her was the warmth of affection. There was no additional heat sparked between them by the closeness of the dance.

Elspeth had to confess she felt a twinge of disappointment. James had become a friend over the two years she had known Maddie and she had wondered from time to time whether the easy camaraderie they had with each other might transform into something more. But for all he was one of the most handsome men she knew, she had to confess that her flickers of curiosity were only that. Perhaps if he had acted differently, she would have felt something more for him. Or perhaps if she had been moved to flirt with him, he might have responded.

But it seemed clear to her at least that their pleasure in one another's company was uncomplicated by any more sensual feeling. It was too bad one of the men she most liked in the world was only a good friend. " 'Only,' Elspeth," she scolded herself later. A good friend of either sex was a precious thing, she reminded herself, but occasionally she couldn't help longing for something more, something she was likely not destined to have.

* * *

Not for the first or the last time, Val cursed the stony, narrow tracks of the Portuguese mountains slowly and fluently in English and Spanish and Portuguese as his horse stumbled and almost fell going downhill. He had to dismount yet again if he wanted to keep the animal's legs sound. "I know it isn't your fault," he said as he led the horse along, the reins looped over his right arm, his rifle in his left.

Below him was a wider road that he thought wise to avoid, considering the dispatches he was carrying, and when he heard an approaching vehicle, he dropped down behind an outcropping of boulders to see who would be traveling so late in the afternoon.

He was not expecting a private traveling coach. Nor the small group of bandits who swarmed down upon it from the other side of the hill, taking the driver and the guard completely by surprise.

It was hard to tell from where he was if the driver was English or Portuguese. Not that it mattered, he thought with a grimace. There was little one man could do against five. He was turning away when he heard the woman screaming.

The guard was dead, that was obvious. The driver might be, though Val thought he saw him twitch a few times. The woman was alive—for now, at least. After they got through with her, she would be happy enough to be dead.

Except, of course, he couldn't stand by and do nothing while that happened. So in a few minutes, they would both be dead, he thought with an ironic smile: he from a bandit bullet and she from one of his own to save her from worse. He pulled his pistol from his belt and, giving a yell that echoed across the pass, brought down one of the bandits. As he reloaded, he saw the woman, who had slumped against her captor, bite his hand before pulling away from him. As the man's mouth opened to yelp his surprise and pain, his head exploded. The woman had been as quick as a cat, thought Val, with a somewhat horrified grin. She'd taken her captor's pistol and blown his head off, by God! But now she was standing there with an empty weapon. He hit one of the remaining three in the arm and then scrambled down the side of the trail, trying to keep his footing and dodge the bullets at the same time.

They didn't expect one man to rush them and surprise was on his side when he swung his rifle butt at one villain who was trying to reload. The other two were occupied: one trying to drag the woman backward to throw her in the coach, the other heading for the driver's seat. But Val had been right: The driver was still alive and thrust at his attacker with a knife. They died together, the bandit from the knife across his throat and the driver by the shot fired as the bandit's finger convulsively closed over the trigger. Val silently blessed the driver for his sacrifice as he rushed the fifth and last man.

His weapons were empty and he only had his hands. He butted the man in the kidney, which made him let go of his prisoner. As the man turned, Val kneed him in the groin and, as the man fell, broke his neck with one swift downward movement of his boot.

He stood there, dazed and winded, amazed to be alive. Then he heard the woman retching. My God, if it hadn't been for her quick reflexes, they'd both be dead.

He let her empty her stomach before he approached her. She was about to wipe her mouth on her skirt when he thrust a handkerchief at her.

"Here. It's not very clean, but it's better than your dress."

She looked up at him blankly as if she had no idea who he was and then sank back against the coach with a little moan as she saw the twisted neck of the bandit on the ground in front of her. She looked up and said with a combination of thankfulness and horror, "You broke his neck." Her eyes flickered over to where her own victim lay. "And I killed a man," she whispered.

Val took his handkerchief back. "Have you any water?"

The woman looked at him blankly.

"A canteen?"

She nodded slowly, but it was clear she was too much in shock even to gesture, so Val rummaged around until he found it. He held the canteen to her lips and said, "Here, drink some." She took a few weak swallows and then Val took the canteen and drank thirstily. He poured some water on his handkerchief and, asking "May I?", gently began to wipe her face. It wasn't until the square of linen turned pink that she realized why and looked down at herself.

When she saw how her cloak and her dress were spattered with blood, she gagged.

"Take a deep breath, ma'am, and try to keep that water down," Val told her gently. Her face was so white he was afraid she was going to faint, so he crouched down beside her and pushed her head between her knees and gingerly rubbed his hand in light circles on her back. When her breathing became less ragged, he pulled back and she lifted her head and looked at him thankfully. Her eyes were hazel and Val had the fleeting thought that they were the most open and honest eyes he had ever seen.

"You are a British officer?" she asked.

"Lieutenant Valentine Aston. Late of the Eleventh Foot, and recently reassigned to Captain Grant's service. I am one of his exploring officers."

"Then that explains what you are doing out here alone."

"May I have the pleasure of your acquaintance, madam?" Val asked with dry humor, as though they were in a drawing room.

She blushed. "I am Elspeth Gordon, Lieutenant. My father is Major Ian Gordon."

"I have not yet had the pleasure of being introduced to him, Miss Gordon, but I know he is a well-respected officer."

"One of Wellington's best," she said proudly.

"Are you on your way to visit your father?"

"Oh, no, I am on my way home from Lisbon. My mother and I have followed the drum since I was little," she added with a smile.

The coach moved forward a little as the horses grew restless and Val suddenly remembered where they were: far from Lisbon and not close enough to Wellington's quarters to be safe from any other bandits who may come upon them.

"We've got to get out of here, Miss Gordon," said Val, standing up and offering her his hand. She took it and he helped her to her feet. "How well do you ride?"

"Very well," she answered stoutly.

"You can take my horse and I'll cut one of the coach horses free," said Val, moving as he spoke. "If there is anything you desperately need from the coach, please take it, but we can't bring all your luggage, I'm afraid."

Elspeth looked down at her dress again. "I . . . I would so much like to change my dress, Lieutenant. I can do it quickly," she added as she saw him begin to open his mouth in protest. "That is, if you can help me?" She was already untying her cloak and Val just stood there as she approached him. "If you could just unpin me?" she asked shyly.

He stepped forward and tried to pretend she was one of the women he had helped undress over the years. He had had a few respectable women, so he was not ignorant of how to unfasten a fashionable gown. He didn't think he'd ever undressed such a *tall* woman before, though, he thought with a quick smile as he realized her head came up to his chin.

"Thank you, Lieutenant." Miss Gordon held up the bodice of her gown with great dignity and climbed into the coach to pull her other traveling dress out of her bag.

She had been quick about it, Val admitted as he helped her fasten the light wool burgundy gown she had changed into. He placed her cloak around her shoulders and she gave him a smile. "I am grateful for your understanding, Lieutenant. I don't think I could have faced another minute in that dress," she added with an involuntary shudder.

It wasn't until Elspeth was in the saddle and they were on their way down the narrow track that paralleled the road that she became fully conscious of her situation and her surroundings. It had all happened so fast: the rifle fire, the men surrounding the coach, pulling her out. She could feel the bandit's fingers tightening cruelly over her arm and smell the garlic on his breath as he leaned forward to smack his wet lips against her cheek, promising her more where that came from. She had gone limp with shock and fear and hopelessness. But then she'd heard another rifle shot and, seeing one of the men go down and without even thinking about it, she'd bitten her captor's hand and twisted away from him while grabbing the pistol tucked in his sash. She started to shiver again as the sounds and smells came back, but made herself take deep breaths as she concentrated on how her horse picked his way slowly over the rocks that studded the narrow trail.

Almost as if he knew what she was thinking, Lieutenant

Aston turned in his saddle and asked, "Have you ever fired a pistol before, Miss Gordon?"

"My father made sure I knew how to fire a rifle and a pistol by the time I was thirteen, Lieutenant. I've never had to use one on a human being before," she added, her voice trembling.

"The first man you kill and know that you kill is always the hardest," Val said automatically.

"I sincerely hope that my first man was my last, Lieutenant," she said simply, her voice steady again. "I appreciate your attempt at comfort, however," she added with a grin. "It sounds like something you've said before?"

Val blushed. "Yes, I guess it is. I didn't realize how automatic the words sounded."

"*Does* it get easier, Lieutenant Aston?"

"I have never enjoyed it, if that is what you mean. But you do get used to it. And I have been lucky. I have not been in combat that often."

"I don't think I could ever get used to it," Elspeth replied with a shudder.

"Then you are lucky you are not a soldier, Miss Gordon. But we are both lucky you killed a man today. We'd both be dead if it wasn't for you and your driver."

"Whyever did you fire, then, if you thought it was hopeless?"

"I couldn't stand by and watch them . . . er . . . molest you, Miss Gordon. I would have shot you before I let that happen."

Elspeth blanched. "*You* would have killed me?"

"Or let you have my pistol to do it yourself," Val replied matter-of-factly. "Believe me, death would be preferable to being in the hands of such men. And they would have killed you afterward anyway," he added bluntly. "So we both have reason to be grateful to your unconventional upbringing!"

The sun was almost down and when Elspeth's horse stumbled over some loose rocks, she looked longingly at the road beneath them.

"Can't we travel on the road, Lieutenant, now that it is getting dark?"

Val pulled his horse up and turned to face her again. "I'd like nothing better myself. But I am carrying a stolen dispatch back to headquarters and cannot risk being caught with it. I am sure that those bandits were not the only ones around. When they are found, I want to be well hidden."

Elspeth sighed. "Will we ride all night, then, Lieutenant?"

"I'd like to get as far away from here as possible while we still have some light. Can you hold out?"

"I can," Elspeth replied stoutly.

"That's my girl," Val said without thinking, and then stammered an apology.

Elspeth smothered a grin and told him not to be foolish. "We have gone through enough together to release us from some of the formalities."

As they rode on, Elspeth began to pay more attention to the man in front of her. He was a little above average height, she thought, with satisfyingly broad shoulders and muscular thighs. He was a natural rider, moving comfortably with his horse as it made its way up and down the rises along the track. Once in a while he would put his hand on the horse's haunches to shift himself, and she realized that if she was getting stiff and tired, he must be even more so, for at least she had a saddle.

Still, her legs were being chafed raw, she realized, shifting a little herself. She was used to riding astride, with breeches under a split skirt.

Her cloak kept her covered over her hiked-up dress, but it couldn't protect her against the hard leather of the saddle, and her cotton stockings did nothing to keep her legs from rubbing against the stirrup leathers. Perhaps the lieutenant was the more comfortable one after all, she thought as she shifted again.

It was growing dark and the moon was not yet beginning to rise when they heard it: the faint sound of horses' hooves and jingling bridles. The lieutenant was off his horse and lifting her down before she had a chance to think.

"Perhaps they are English, or Ordenanza," she whispered.

"They may be, but I want the horses out of sight just in case. Stay here," said Val, pushing her down behind a boulder.

Elspeth huddled there as the rider came closer. Val was back in a moment and crouched down next to her. The riders were getting closer and finally they could tell they were Portuguese. Elspeth let out her breath in a half-gasp, half-sigh. "They could be allies," she whispered hopefully.

"I doubt it and we can't risk waiting. They will have seen the coach and know that someone is out here. They are going slowly because they are looking for us. We must find a place to hide before the moon comes up."

Half-crouching, half-crawling, they made their way off the track and up the rocky hill. Every few minutes a stone would dislodge and go rolling down behind them. Whenever it happened, Elspeth would freeze until Val pulled her along behind him.

A minute or so later, Elspeth heard him breathe a soft sigh of relief and then for one terrifying moment, he disappeared. She froze against the hillside. Had he fallen off some ledge she couldn't see? What would she do without him? Suddenly he was there in front of her again, holding out his hand. "Hurry!" She scrambled as fast as she could and found herself in front of a small cave—although it may have been generous to call it that, for it was so small it was more of a hollow in the rocks. But there were actually a few scraggly bushes in front of it, an almost miracle in this barren landscape.

"It is a bit cramped, but I think it will hide us well enough," Val whispered as he guided her in. "Be careful of your head."

There was no room to stand. Indeed, there was hardly room to sit down and be able to stretch out their legs.

"Not the most luxurious of accommodations, I admit, Miss Gordon," Val said ironically.

At least he had a sense of humor, this Lieutenant Aston, Elspeth thought as she sat down. Their shoulders brushed and she immediately tried to slide to her right, but the side of their "cave" was too low and forced her head down.

"I am afraid where we are is the most comfortable," said Val as he felt her shift away and then back again.

Elspeth nodded her head and then felt ridiculous, for of course he could not see her in the dark.

She heard a horse whinny, but could not tell if it was one of theirs or belonged to the bandits. She heard voices getting closer and when she realized they were climbing up the track, she stopped breathing.

"You can breathe, Miss Gordon. They can't hear you,"

said a soft whisper in her ear. She let out a ragged breath
and tried to ignore the way her heart was beating. It was
thumping around in her chest like a parade drum and when
she next heard the bandits, she could tell they were just
below them, on the path. How could they not hear her
heart if she could hear every shuffle of their boots? She
gave an involuntary little moan of fear and then felt a
strong, steady hand close over hers as the lieutenant shifted
and brought their shoulders closer together.

Her fear didn't go away, but as she let herself take in
the strength and warmth of his hand and the solidity of his
shoulders, it receded a little. As the moon rose, she could
see the shadows of rocks and bushes take shape. "Dear
God, please don't let them find us here. Please let me see
home again," she prayed over and over as they huddled
there for what seemed hours.

It was probably less than half an hour, Elspeth realized
later. The ruffians' voices grew fainter and she began to
hope that they had ridden on. Between her great relief
and the chill of the rocks behind her, she began to shiver
uncontrollably.

"Are you all right, Miss Gordon?" whispered Val.

"J-j-just c-c-cold," she replied, her teeth literally hitting
against one another. "I c-c-c-can't stop."

"Here, lean back against me," Val said, pulling her in
front of him and opening his legs so that she could rest
herself against his chest instead of the rock walls. She was
beyond modesty, she realized, as she felt his arms come
around her, pulling her back against him. He closed his legs
around her, surrounding her with his body heat.

"It is shock as well as cold," he murmured reassuringly.

"Are they gone?"

"I think so. But I want to wait just to be sure. Close
your eyes and get some sleep, Miss Gordon."

At first Elspeth couldn't relax. She had never in all her
life been so close to a man's body and she was aware of
the lieutenant's every breath and slightest movement. Her
backside was tucked right between his legs and she was
aware that she was resting right against his . . . private
parts. But as the warmth penetrated her body, her shivers
stopped and her eyes grew heavy. Without volition, she
relaxed against him and finally slept.

Chapter 2

Val was grateful for the cold sharp rocks that bit into his back, for they distracted him from the sensations caused by his enforced intimacy with Miss Gordon. *She* had relaxed enough to sleep, but he doubted he'd close his eyes that night. Miss Elspeth Gordon might be tall and slender, but she was not all bones and angles; she was soft warm curves as well, and Val felt he was in contact with every one of them. His vigil was a combination of pain and pleasure, for his body was stiffening with the cold even as he enjoyed the sensation of a woman in his arms. It wasn't until the sun rose and light began to penetrate their small hideaway that he realized the implications of their night together. Had she spent the night with any other officer, the man would have been a gentleman and able to remedy the fact that she'd been compromised. He would do the right thing and offer to marry her, but he doubted Major Gordon would want him as a son-in-law. Miss Gordon would certainly not want him as a husband. He felt the old shame rise up in him and as Miss Gordon stirred awake, his voice was brusque as he gave her a good-morning.

"Why, it is growing light!" she exclaimed. "I can't believe I slept through the night." Then, as she remembered just where she had slept, she struggled to stand up. "Be careful, Miss Gordon," Val whispered at the same time as she hit her head and gave a little yelp. She dropped to her knees and said, "I am sorry. Dear God, what if they heard me?"

"They are long gone, Miss Gordon," Val reassured her. "I've been awake all night and haven't heard a thing."

Elspeth looked at him with grateful sympathy as he hobbled around, trying to work the stiffness out of his back and legs. "I had a much more comfortable night than you did, Lieutenant. Thank you for keeping watch."

Val only nodded and, after a few more stretches, said, "I am going to see if they found our horses, Miss Gordon. You can take care of any of your, er, private needs while I am gone."

Elspeth desperately needed to relieve herself and, as soon as Val was out of sight, crawled behind one of the bushes. Val had left the canteen in front of the cave, and when she was finished, she picked it up and shook it. It was only about a quarter full, so she only took two sips, one to rinse out her mouth and the other to ease her thirst. She was walking around in small circles to work the stiffness out of her legs when Val returned.

"They got the coach horse, but my gelding got away," said Val. "I've found a small path that is an easier way down to the track."

"Thank God," said Elspeth with a relieved smile. "I was afraid I'd have to stay here forever, because I could not imagine going back down the way we came up."

When they reached the track, Val gave a low whistle and Elspeth heard his horse trotting toward them.

"You and your mount seem to have a friendship which is strange for an infantryman," she teased.

"Yes, and the men in my old regiment are always telling me I won't be able to keep up with them anymore. But a good horse is a necessity for an exploring officer. This isn't the first time Caesar has saved my ar—er . . . my life."

Val rummaged around in his saddlebags and pulled out a lumpy parcel. "This bread and cheese isn't very fresh, but it will keep us going, Miss Gordon," he said apologetically as he opened the wrapper and offered her some. The cheese was almost as dry as the bread, but they washed it down with a few sips of the water and then Val held out his hand. "Come, let's get you up on Caesar."

"But surely you are going to ride too," she protested.

"He can't carry two of us on this track, Miss Gordon. Once we are through the pass and it seems safe on the cart road, I'll ride."

He was different this morning, thought Elspeth as she watched him walking in front of her. Yesterday she had felt like they were . . . not friends, but at least comrades.

What they had gone through had brought them close and although she knew nothing at all about him, at the same time she felt she knew Lieutenant Aston better than some men she had known for years. Facing death certainly broke down conventional formality, she thought, as did a night spent huddled together on a mountainside. Perhaps it was just embarrassment, she thought, and decided that she would have to break through the lieutenant's reserve.

"How do you come to be working for Captain Grant, Lieutenant?"

"I was with him in the Eleventh Foot for many years, Miss Gordon. As his sergeant," he added stiffly.

"Oh, but you are a lieutenant?" Elspeth asked without thinking. "You must have done something to distinguish yourself, then, to obtain a field promotion," she added quickly.

"My father purchased my commission, so I arrived here a lieutenant. Then, after Captain Grant began serving as Wellington's intelligence officer, he asked for me to join him."

"I see," Elspeth said brightly. She didn't see at all. To purchase a lieutenant's commission took money, so Lieutenant Aston's father must be at least of the merchant class, if not gentry. But then why wouldn't he have done so to begin with? she wondered. Unless there had been some bad feeling between father and son? Given the lieutenant's tone and the brevity of his reply, she didn't think he would tell her more, no matter how friendly her questions, so she turned the conversation in a different direction.

"I have met Captain Grant, Lieutenant, and it is not hard to understand why Lord Wellington chose him. Not only is he a most competent officer and fluent in Spanish and Portuguese, he is an utterly charming companion."

"He is also one of the most courageous men I have ever encountered. I was very pleased when he sent for me."

From the lieutenant's tone, it was clear to Elspeth that she was not going to be successful in her attempts at friendly conversation. They made their way down the track in silence for a good long while until they began their descent to the road. There was a small stream that had formed a pool in the rocks as the track ended. Val stopped and helped Elspeth down.

"We can take a short rest here, Miss Gordon. Caesar is thirsty and I know I am."

Elspeth cupped her hands and drank. Although its surface had been warmed by the sun, the pool was deep enough that the water underneath was cool and refreshing. She splashed her face and neck and stepped back so Val and his mount could take their turns.

"How are you feeling, Miss Gordon?"

"I desperately needed that drink, Lieutenant. And I am dusty and dirty enough to wish I could immerse myself in that pool. But other than a little chafing, I am fine. This is not my usual riding outfit, you know," she added with a wry smile.

"I would guess that we are only a few hours from camp."

"Well, then, I shall survive the rest of the ride by dreaming of a long hot soak in my father's copper tub," Elspeth said lightly.

"Yes, well, perhaps we'd best get on our way," Val said quickly and Elspeth blushed from having mentioned something so personal.

"You *are* going to ride now that we are on better ground?"

"Actually, I had thought if you rode pillion behind me, you would be a bit more comfortable also," Val told her.

"I won't feel very secure, though," Elspeth said with a slight frown. "I must confess I don't ride sidesaddle very often. I think I will sit astride behind you, if that is all right."

Val mounted and, leaning down, grasped Elspeth's hand as she put her foot in the stirrup, and drew her up.

"You can put your arms around my waist when you need to, Miss Gordon," he said stiffly.

"Thank you, Lieutenant."

At first Elspeth kept her balance with her knees. But sitting astride a horse's rump, though kinder on her legs than the saddle leather, was not the easiest way to ride, and when Val kicked Caesar into a trot, Elspeth was forced to throw her arms around his waist whether she wanted to or not. For the first two hours, they alternated trotting and walking, but when Caesar showed signs of tiring, Val kept him at a walk and Elspeth was able to relax, which was a mistake, because almost before she knew it, she was dozing off, her head against Val's back.

Val knew immediately that she had fallen asleep when he felt her slump against him and her arms loosen. He let go of the reins with one hand and covered her right arm with his to support her. They rode that way into the camp and when Val identified himself to the sentry, he felt Miss Gordon begin to stir.

"Which way to Major Gordon's tent?"

"He is in a house in the village, sir. All the way down and to your right."

"Are you all right, Miss Gordon?" he asked as they moved through the encampment.

"I am, Lieutenant. I am just ashamed I fell asleep."

"Don't be. You've been through a lot these last twenty-four hours."

"As have you, and you have not closed your eyes at all. You must be exhausted!"

When they reached the small stone house that was the Gordons' quarters, Val dismounted and held out his arms for Elspeth. Just as she was sliding down, a tall, gray-haired woman hurried out.

"Elspeth!"

"She is fine, ma'am."

"I am all right, Mama."

They both spoke at the same time and then Mrs. Gordon took her daughter into her arms.

"My dear, we have been so worried about you. You were to have been here by noon at the latest. Your father is beside himself. I kept telling him it could have been a broken axle, but you know what he is like where you are concerned."

Elspeth pulled herself out of her mother's arms and laughed shakily. "Yes, Mama, I do. This is Lieutenant Aston, Mama, and he is the reason I am here safe with you."

"How can I thank you, Lieutenant?" said Mrs. Gordon, reaching her hand out to Val's. "You look utterly done in, but might I ask you one more favor?"

"Of course, Mrs. Gordon."

"Could you find my husband? He is off trying to get a party

together to search for Elspeth. Then you must come and tell us everything. Come, my dear, let me get you inside."

Val met the major just as he was coming out of Wellington's tent.

"Major Gordon?"

Elspeth's father hardly glanced at him. "Later, Lieutenant," he said brusquely.

"Your daughter, sir . . ."

That stopped him. "My daughter? What do you know of her? You are one of the Colquhoun's new officers, aren't you?"

"Miss Gordon is safely home, sir. I just left her there."

"Thank God!" The major was already half-running toward his quarters and Val stood there openmouthed, when the older man turned and said impatiently, "Come on, Lieutenant, and tell me what happened on the way. Was there an accident? How did you come upon her?" He fired his questions at Val without giving him a chance to answer.

They were almost back to the cottage when Val reached out and pulled at the major's arm.

"Sir, may I speak to you privately for a moment?"

The major finally turned and really looked at Val. "Who are you, Lieutenant?" he asked quietly.

"Lieutenant Valentine Aston, sir," said Val, standing at attention. "Recently reassigned to Captain Grant's service."

"Was it a coach accident? A broken axle?"

"No, sir. Miss Gordon's coach was attacked by bandits."

"How did you become involved?"

"I was on my way back from a reconnaissance mission for Captain Grant. I saw the attack from the rocks above."

"They did not . . . harm Elspeth, did they, Lieutenant?" the major asked, his voice tight with fear.

"No, sir. They had only pulled her out of the coach when I began to fire on them."

"So she owes you her life?"

"Actually, Major Gordon, I may well be in her debt. And her driver's," Val added. "There were five of them and I didn't really have much hope when I took them on. I was only trying to get to your daughter before they . . . you know what I mean."

The major nodded his understanding.

"But Miss Gordon got hold of a pistol and shot one of them and the driver managed to wound another, which evened the odds. I would say that we saved each other," Val said with a smile.

"Had you not chosen to risk your life, my daughter would be dead, Lieutenant Aston," replied the major. "I will be forever in your debt. And Captain Grant will hear about this, I assure you."

The major held his hands out in front of him. "See how shaken I am." And indeed, the tremors were obvious, although as they both watched his hands finally grew still. "I am never like this, not even before a battle, but ma wee lass is very dear to me."

Val was so exhausted that despite his sympathy he almost collapsed in nervous laughter to hear the major call his daughter his "wee lass." But he managed to keep his face straight and all desire to laugh left him when the major invited him in to have a drink of whiskey. "For you look like you need it, lad."

Val looked down at his blood-stained trousers and dusty boots. "I am not fit for polite company tonight, Major Gordon. And I must speak to you of something serious."

"If you won't have a drink, then it can wait till tomorrow, for I can see you are dead on your feet," the major replied. He grasped Val by the hand and shook it. "You have my undying gratitude, lad, and don't you forget it."

Val was almost faint from fatigue, but first he had to report to Captain Grant and deliver the information he had gathered.

"I had hoped to be back sooner, sir, but I ended up with something else on my hands."

"I heard you came riding in with Miss Gordon, Lieutenant."

Val started to tell him the story, but Grant looked up at him with a quizzical smile on his face. "You haven't had any sleep for almost thirty-six hours, Lieutenant. I suggest you get some. And count yourself off-duty tomorrow. I can hear your story later."

"Thank you, sir."

* * *

Val stripped off his filthy uniform and, crawling under his thin army-issue blanket, was asleep instantly. He awoke briefly when he heard the camp stirring the next morning at reveille, and then, turning over, slept till noon. He awoke to the sound of an orderly carrying in a bucket of hot water and a shaving of soap.

"Captain Grant thought you might be needing this, sir."

Val rubbed his hand over his eyes.

"I brought you your saddlebags, sir, and laid out a clean uniform."

Val grinned. "This is luxury indeed, Corporal. Do you do this for all the exploring officers?"

"No, sir," said the man with an answering smile. "But this one time Captain Grant thought it would be appropriate."

"God bless Colquhoun Grant," whispered Val as he washed himself. "Although he is doing himself a favor, given how I look and smell!" He was just scraping the last of the dark stubble off his jaw when someone called from outside the tent.

"Are you awake, Lieutenant Aston?" When Val recognized Major Gordon's voice, his hand slipped and he gave himself a small nick with the razor. "Blast it," he muttered, "I'll be bleeding all over my clean tunic." He hastily wiped his face and stuck a small piece of plaster on his chin.

"Give me one moment, sir," he called out. As he hurriedly pulled on his jacket, he watched the major's shadow nervously. Major Gordon looked restless, for he was pacing back and forth.

When he was finally dressed, he opened the tent flap. "I am glad to see you, Major Gordon. I was intending to call on you the first thing this morning . . . this afternoon," Val amended after a glance at the sun. "Do you wish to come in?"

"No, no, lad, let's walk for a bit. I want to hear all that happened, for Elspeth was unwilling to say much about it."

"I can imagine that the memory is disturbing to her." Val told the major the bare bones of the story and then patiently answered every question put to him.

"Once again, I thank you for my daughter's life, Lieutenant," said the major. "I have already commended you to Captain Grant."

They had walked a little way outside of the camp and Val pointed to an old oak tree that would offer them some shade. "Shall we take shelter from the sun, Major?"

The closer they got to the tree, the more nervous Val got, so by the time the major took a seat on a large boulder, he just said bluntly, "You realize, sir, that your daughter and I spent the night together in rather, uh, intimate circumstances."

"She told me you were lucky enough to find a cave."

"I am sure you came to see if I would act the gentleman, Major Gordon. Your daughter spent the night asleep in my arms and is therefore compromised. Were I another man . . . were my circumstances different . . . I would not hesitate to ask for her hand."

Major Gordon looked up at Val with a puzzled look on his face.

"You see, sir, though I may wish to act the gentleman, indeed be considered one by virtue of my rank, in truth, I am none."

"I see. You have acted in some way dishonorably in the past?"

"No, sir."

"Then I do not understand, Lieutenant. My daughter says you were very much the gentleman with her."

"I am a bastard, Major Gordon," Val announced harshly. "My father is the Earl of Faringdon, my mother a farmer's daughter."

"I see," said the major, standing up.

"So we are in a pretty mess, sir," Val continued more softly.

"Well, we might be, if that was what I expected of you. Or Elspeth, for that matter," the major added with dry humor.

"I don't understand, Major. Surely you must expect me to make an offer under the circumstances?"

"The circumstances? You saved her life, you young idiot! And you kept her from freezing up there on that mountainside. And you brought her safely home to us and for that I bless you."

"But for a well-bred young woman, sir—"

"This is not Berkeley Square, Aston, in case you hadn't noticed," said the major, waving his arm around him. "We are in the middle of a war and those were extreme circumstances. Even if they weren't," said the major with a laugh, "my lass has been following the drum since she was three. She would never have expected such a sacrifice."

"It wouldn't have been a sacrifice, sir," Val protested.

"Perhaps not for you, sir. I was talking of her. We have tried to get her to live with her mother's family in London and take her place in Society. But she refuses to. So why should she sacrifice her freedom to satisfy the standards of polite society when she doesn't live amongst them?" The major looked over at Val and said shrewdly, "I suppose you have been agonizing over this since yesterday, eh, lad? Well, I admire you for your sense of honor and your honesty. As for the circumstances of your birth, well, you did not choose them. Any man chosen by Captain Grant is a man who has made something of himself." The major clapped Val on the shoulder and said, "Come on, lad, Mrs. Gordon is waiting to see you and so is ma wee lass."

Val's relief was so great that this time he couldn't help smiling at the phrase and the major laughed. "Oh, aye, she is above average tall, Lieutenant Aston. But she'll always be 'ma wee lassie' to me."

When they reached the Gordons' quarters, they were ushered in by his orderly to find Mrs. Grant and Elspeth presiding over tea.

"Lieutenant Aston!" cried Mrs. Grant with a smile of pleasure. "I thought that Ian had failed in his mission to bring you here for a cup of tea."

"Lieutenant Aston and I have been having a private conversation, my dear. Concerning you, lass," he added. "The lieutenant made you an offer of marriage, as a gentleman should, but I refused him for ye. I hope I was right in doing so," he added with a twinkle in his eye.

"Ian! You are incorrigible!" his wife exclaimed.

"Oh, aye, but it occurred to me on the way that I had not given Elspeth a chance to have her say."

Val, who was standing tongue-tied and red-faced, was thankful to see Miss Gordon was not fazed by the frankness of her parent. She merely inclined her head to Val and said calmly, "I am very grateful to you, Lieutenant, for your thoughtfulness. But I think neither of us need worry, given the extremity of our circumstances. I am sure my father told you I don't hold much to convention. At least, not empty ones. Now do sit down and relax."

Val gave her a smile that expressed his relief, admiration, and gratitude. Miss Gordon had put them all at ease by her commonsense reaction and Val could only be grateful that she had gracefully turned the conversation away from his gesture.

Unfortunately, the conversation could not be so easily turned from his heroism. Mrs. Gordon picked up her cup and then set it down and said, "Lieutenant Aston, I cannot eat or drink until I thank you from the bottom of my heart for your brave action."

"I only did what any soldier would have done, ma'am."

"From what I understand, you were quite prepared to sacrifice yourself in order to save Elspeth from an unspeakable fate, Lieutenant."

It was clear to Val that Elspeth's calm strength came from her mother. "I would have made sure she didn't suffer, Mrs. Gordon, if it had come to that," he answered seriously. "But the fact that it didn't was largely due to your daughter's quick thinking, ma'am," he added with a nod of appreciation at Elspeth.

"The major made sure a long time ago that both of us knew how to load and fire both rifle and pistol," said Mrs. Gordon.

"Well, I for one am grateful for his foresight!"

"I understand that you are newly arrived to serve in Captain Grant's service, Lieutenant?"

"Yes, ma'am. Captain Grant was my commanding officer in the Caribbean and he requested me when he'd heard I received a commission."

"You will have a hard time living up to Captain Grant's exploits, I think, Lieutenant."

Val smiled. "I have heard many of the stories, Mrs. Gordon, and I agree. I'll be lucky to do my job half as well."

"Aye, it is not everyone who can go behind enemy lines and bring back cattle to feed the army," said Major Gordon.

After almost an hour of conversation ranging from Wellington's plans to Val's experience in the Caribbean, he excused himself.

"I have quite overstayed my welcome, Mrs. Gordon," he apologized.

"Not at all. We enjoyed your company, Lieutenant. I am hoping you will come again. We often entertain the officers for dinner and I will include you when you are available."

"Thank you, ma'am."

"That is a fine young man, Elspeth," said her father after Val left. "It is too bad you couldn't accept his offer," he added with a teasing smile.

"I can't believe you embarrassed him like that, Ian," scolded his wife. "You did a good job of putting him at his ease, Elspeth."

"The lieutenant was rather distant in his manner yesterday. I am relieved to know it was his contemplation of his proposal rather than anything I did," Elspeth replied lightly. "He relaxed a little over his tea, I was glad to see."

"Did I understand him correctly, Ian? Did he come up through the ranks?" Mrs. Gordon asked her husband.

"Yes, my dear. He was serving as a sergeant under Colquhoun in the Eleventh Foot."

"He told me that, Papa. I thought it very unusual that his father hadn't purchased him a commission straightaway. Unless of course, they were estranged. . . ."

"The lieutenant told me very little about his relationship with his father except for the fact that the Earl of Faringdon never married his mother. Which was the real reason he was so distant, Elspeth. He believed he had put you in a unresolvable situation: If you didn't marry him, you would be compromised. If you did, you'd be wed to a bastard."

Elspeth sat there, her mouth open in a wide *O*.

"The Earl of Faringdon is his father, Ian? Why, then, Lord Holme must be his half-brother."

"I hear that Charlie's regiment will be arriving within the month, Papa," said Elspeth thoughtfully. "I wonder if they have ever met. And if they have, if they like each other."

"Who could not like the viscount?" asked Mrs. Gordon.

Elspeth smiled. "I can't imagine." Except perhaps his illegitimate older brother, she added to herself thoughtfully.

Chapter 3

Val took a long walk around the perimeter of the encampment and, when a wave of fatigue washed over him again, decided to skip supper with the other officers and go to bed so he would be fresh for his meeting with Captain Grant in the morning.

He awoke before dawn and lay in his cot for a few minutes, his eyes closed, thinking about the events of the past few days. As a seasoned soldier, he was used to violence, and the scenes with the bandits faded into the background. It was the sensation of holding Elspeth Gordon throughout the night that kept coming back, and the feel of her arms around his waist and the way she had finally relaxed against him. There was something about the way she gave herself over to her trust in him that moved him. He felt himself becoming aroused and he groaned softly. He couldn't afford to be daydreaming about a woman who was so clearly not for him. As he got up, he told himself that it was only natural for him to feel this fleeting attraction; they had been forced into an intimacy they would never have experienced under different circumstances.

It surprised him, this desire, for although he certainly admired Miss Gordon for her courage and humor, she wasn't the type of woman he was usually attracted to. He preferred a smaller woman, one toward whom he could feel protective. Miss Gordon was too tall and slender for his taste. And yet, he remembered how soft and yielding she was when she fell asleep in his arms. Not a convenient thing to remember, he thought humorously, when you were a soldier and the only women available to you the camp followers! For once he was grateful to the cold mornings, as he splashed his face with icy water.

*   *   *

Val had thought he would be meeting privately with Captain Grant, but he was directed from Grant's tent to Wellington's, where he found himself in the company of several other officers.

"Gentlemen," said Grant, "I don't think you have had the pleasure of meeting Lieutenant Aston yet, for he only arrived recently and I have made sure to keep him on the road these past few weeks! Lieutenant Aston, Lieutenant Lucas Stanton, Lieutenant George Trowbridge, and the Marquess of Wimborne."

Val just stood there, frozen in place, as did the others.

"Is something wrong, gentlemen?"

The marquess stepped forward, his hand outstretched. "Not at all, Captain. We are all in shock because of coincidence, is all. Lieutenant Aston is one of our former schoolmates. I am right—it is Val?" James asked with a smile.

"Yes, my lord, it is."

"Well, then, a belated welcome to Portugal."

"Lieutenant Stanton?" Grant was puzzled by the viscount's lack of response.

"Uh, yes, James is right. We were schoolfellows for a short while. Quite a surprise, that is all," he added blandly and waved vaguely at Val.

"Well, now that the reunion is over, let us get down to business. Lord Wellington will be here shortly, but I wanted you to know that Lieutenant Aston will be working directly under me, helping me with the reconnaissance between here and Santarém. Massena seems to have settled in there, and for a time will be better provisioned than he was on the other side of the Lines. But Lord Wellington believes that the French will have to make a decision soon—make an all-out attack on the Lines, or a full retreat into Spain—so every piece of information is crucial."

When the duke had finished briefing them on the current situation, he dismissed all of them except for Captain Grant. As Val left the tent he saw Stanton had walked on ahead with two other officers. They looked back at him curiously and Val knew that Lucas Stanton had effectively scotched his chances of feeling at home among the members of Wellington's "family." Having come up from the ranks was enough to set him apart—he had found that out the first three months after he'd received his commission—but Stanton would, no doubt, spread the word of his birth.

"It has been a long time, Val," said James as he stepped outside the tent.

"Twelve years, my lord, to be exact."

"Please call me James," said the marquess with a friendly smile. "We did agree on that once, you know."

Val hesitated and then gave him a quick smile back.

"It was a delightful surprise to see you this morning, Val."

"I was surprised that you remembered me."

"Ah, but you were a most memorable schoolmate, Val. I have never forgotten how you thrashed Stanton so soundly."

"I fear he hasn't either," said Val.

"Don't mind him. His temper hasn't improved over the years, but I don't think he'll cause you any trouble. And if you are working for Colquhoun, you'll be out of camp a lot anyway. Will you come and have a cup of tea with me in my tent? I want to hear all about what you've been doing all these years."

It was the first time since he'd received his lieutenancy that Val had received a friendly gesture from one of his fellow officers and the marquess's invitation touched him deeply, although he kept his face expressionless and merely said, "Thank you, James, I will."

The marquees's tent was less spartan than Val's, but by no means luxurious. Of course, having your valet with you was a sort of luxury, he thought, as he watched James's man bustling around.

"To old times, Val," said James, making a mock toast with his tin mug.

"I'd rather toast old schoolmates, James." Val took a sip of tea and sighed appreciatively. "This is a real treat and the second time in two days I've been offered some. I had tea with the Gordons yesterday," he added.

"The story of your rescue is all over camp and I want all the details," said James, "but first you must tell me where you went when you left the Hall. Charlie was heartsick, as I am sure you must know."

"I couldn't stay, James, even for Charlie."

"No, I can understand that. It is difficult always to feel an outsider, I know."

Val looked over at him quizzically and James said apologetically, "No, of course I don't know quite how it was."

"It wasn't only that. I'd gotten used to it by then. It was how they dealt with, or rather didn't deal with, Lucas Stanton." Val hesitated and then smiled. "Do you remember the recruiting regiment that was in town? I signed up the night I left."

"So you have been in the army all this time?"

"Yes, in the Devonshire Eleventh Foot. I made it to sergeant before I received my commission. Of course, I've been as much of an outsider in the army as I was at Queen's Hall. Too common for the officers but too educated to make me one of the men—although my years with George Burton stood me in good stead. I never thought I'd be thankful to him in my life, but I was those first few years. None of the sergeants could intimidate me after George!"

"Did you father . . . uh, the earl . . . know where you were?"

"I wrote to him and told him I had left school and joined the army, but I had the letter mailed from the north so he couldn't trace my whereabouts. Not that he would have wanted to, but Charlie might have gotten after him."

"And what about Charlie?" the marquess asked gently.

"We've kept in touch over the years as best we could. We saw one another once in London, before we were to ship out to the Caribbean. I wanted to say good-bye to him, just in case."

Val was quiet for a few minutes, remembering his last meeting with his brother. He had known Charlie was in London for the Season, having finished his second term at Oxford. He had been there too, with a thirty-six-hour leave while the regiment waited to embark for the West Indies.

He had put on his best uniform and made his way to the Faringdon town house on St. James Street. He had been planning to go to the kitchen door, but then thought, I'm his half-brother, damn it, and a soldier in the King's army, so he walked up to the front and rapped sharply.

Baynes hadn't recognized him, of course, and he had to

take off his shako and give his name twice before the butler's blank look was replaced by a quick smile.

"Lord Holme is having breakfast, but I am sure he will want to see you, Private Aston. Please come in."

"No, no, I don't want to disturb him." Damn, he'd forgotten how late breakfast was in polite society after all his years in the army.

"Just wait right here, sir."

Val had turned his back and was watching a young lady and her maid cross the street when he heard footsteps behind him.

"Just tell him good-bye for me, Baynes," he started to say when he turned around, and there was Charlie in his dressing gown.

"You had better tell me yourself. But goddamn it, Val, why are you here to say good-bye when you haven't come to say a hello in all these years?"

It had taken Val a minute to take it in: His half-brother stood at least three inches taller than he and was addressing him in a voice as deep as the earl's or Val's own. The last time he had seen Charlie, his brother had been a schoolboy, his voice just breaking. Today, with his gold curls in a fashionable Brutus and his silk dressing gown, he was very different from the Charlie of years ago. Without thinking, Val stepped back.

"Oh, no, you don't. You're not leaving. You must come in, Val, please," Charlie pleaded.

"Is your father . . . ?"

"Is *our* father in? No, he hasn't come up from Faringdon yet, so you are safe," Charlie added with dry humor.

"I can't stay long," Val told him as he took a seat.

Charlie made sure Val was served and then, looking at his own full plate, laughed and pushed it away.

"I can't eat, Val. I am too excited. God, you look splendid in your uniform. But why were you so foolish as to enlist? Father would have bought you a commission, I am sure."

"Yes, if you asked him, Charlie."

"No, if *you'd* asked him, Val."

"I couldn't. I explained all that in my letters."

"I have always looked forward to receiving them, Val, but letters are a cold comfort when you miss someone."

He hadn't changed, despite his air of sophisticated young man-about-town. He was the same Charlie, all his affection there to see in the warmth of his expression, the concern in his blue eyes.

"I missed you too, Charlie," Val said stiffly. Saying what he felt did not come easily to him.

"So what is this good-bye about, then?"

"The Eleventh is being sent to the Caribbean. We sail the day after tomorrow."

"I see."

"I thought . . . I was in London . . . just in case anything should happen to me . . ."

"Are you on leave?"

"Until the night before we sail."

"Then we will spend today and tomorrow together."

They rode in the park early the next morning.

"Lord, I am stiff," groaned Val when they returned to the house. "This is what comes of enlisting in the infantry! I haven't been on a horse in years."

"We'll stroll around the park instead of driving, then, this afternoon. That will loosen you up."

They arrived in the park just as the curricles and cabriolets were filling up the lanes. Val could tell that Charlie was as well-liked in Society as he had been in school from the number of drivers and riders who stopped to chat with him every few minutes. He introduced Val as his older brother and Val was amused to see the puzzled looks on people's faces as they tried to work out just how Charlie could have an older brother and still be viscount.

Charlie had suggested the theater that evening, since Kean was playing in *Richard the Third*. "I've seen the man and he is a wonder, Val. I am sure you would love it."

"I must be at the docks early in the morning, Charlie. I can't lie around like a slugabed like certain fashionable gentlemen do," Val replied with a teasing smile.

"Then we will have a quiet supper at home."

It *was* a very quiet supper, thought Val, for after chatting about this and that, Charlie became silent. Finally he looked over at his brother and said seriously, "I wish you weren't sailing tomorrow. You will miss seeing Father by only a day."

"I am sure he won't mind."

"That is not true, Val. I wish you would believe that. He is always asking me if I've heard from you. And he would purchase you a commission if you wanted me to ask."

"But I don't, Charlie."

Of course, as it turned out, Charlie eventually had asked and Val had almost refused the commission. But a letter from Charlie, setting out the logic of it, as well as his newly awakened ambition, had convinced him. He had served under an excellent officer in Colquhoun Grant, but once Grant was called into Wellington's service, his replacement was an incompetent son of a baronet who had no military experience at all. By that time, Val had been a sergeant for three years and was beginning to discover his talent for leading men and for making the sort of judgments that made them eager and willing to follow him. As a lieutenant he would have some decision-making power. He might even look forward to gaining a field commission, if the war lasted long enough.

So he had accepted it. And almost wished he hadn't the first time he walked into the officers' mess and every time after. As an exploring officer he may never make captain, but thank God to Colquhoun Grant for removing him from the constant humiliating reminders that he was not one of them.

"So what do you think of Miss Gordon?" James asked, breaking into Val's reverie.

"Miss Gordon?"

"*Yes,* Miss Elspeth Gordon, whom you rescued, Val."

"To tell you the truth, James, I am not sure who rescued whom. There were five of them and I went down there sure only that I'd be able to save her from violation, not death. I thank God that her father taught her to use a pistol. And that her driver lasted long enough to kill one of the villains before he died. I wish I could have thanked him," Val added with regret.

"I hear Major Gordon was beside himself with worry when her coach did not arrive by noon. You have made a friend for life and Ian Gordon is a good man to have on your side."

"Do you think that Miss Gordon's reputation will suffer?"

"Her reputation?"

"We were alone for the night in very close quarters." Val hesitated. "Actually, I offered to marry her, but of course I had to tell her father the circumstances of my birth."

"Of course," James replied dryly. "Being the officer and gentleman that you are."

"They would have found out soon enough with Stanton here," Val said stiffly.

"You are still carrying that chip around on your shoulder, aren't you?"

Val opened his mouth to protest, but James continued more gently, "I understand, Val, truly I do, though you obviously think otherwise. I admire you for your courage around this, but at some time you'll have to give over thinking it is the most important thing about you."

"I'll give over thinking it when those around me allow me to do so, James."

"I don't think your being the bastard son of an earl would mean as much to Ian Gordon or his wife and daughter as long as you're a man of honor and a good officer. His wife may be the granddaughter of an earl, but they've been in the army so long they value a soldier's skills above all else. Elspeth doesn't give a fig for what Society thinks. I wish my sister Maddie were more like her."

"You have a sister, James?"

The marquess smiled. "Yes, Madeline Jane, although we call her Maddie. She and Elspeth were at school together. She is a dear girl and relatively sensible, but at the moment she thinks and writes of nothing but her come-out this spring." James sighed.

"And you disapprove?"

"Not at all. How else will she find someone to marry? But my father was not known for his economical good sense, Val," James added with heavy sarcasm. "Or competent stewardship of our estate. The financial affairs of the family have taken up much of my time."

"I am sorry to hear that, James."

"Thank God I managed to find enough for Maddie's Season." James sighed and then continued. "But put your mind to rest about Elspeth, Val. Things are different in wartime, and I tell you, there are times when I feel luckier to be here than in London dealing with the expectations of Society!"

Chapter 4

As she started out on her morning ride, Elspeth's feelings were quite similar to the Marquess of Wimborne. Her divided skirt covered the leather breeches and allowed her to avoid a sidesaddle without scandalizing anyone. She felt far safer and freer riding astride here on the rough terrain of Portugal where a loose rock could send you "arse over teakettle," as Mags Casey would say.

Elspeth smiled at the thought of Mrs. Casey, one of the camp laundresses, of whom she was very fond for many reasons, not the least of which was the fact that she towered over Elspeth. Well, perhaps "towered" was an exaggeration, she told herself, but it was wonderful to feel smaller than another female. Mrs. Casey could only be described as strapping, a sobriquet Elspeth dreaded overhearing about herself. Mags was a large woman, which she needed to be, since she took in officers' laundry and got it as clean as anyone with modern facilities might, despite the fact that it took lugging water from the stream and chopping wood for the fire that heated it, and wringing it out by hand, since her small wringer was constantly breaking down.

Elspeth smiled as she thought about Mrs. Casey and her . . . well, she supposed Sergeant Tallman could be called her beau—certainly her intended, whether he knew it or not, for Mrs. Casey most definitely intended to marry him. Will Tallman was a good six inches shorter than Mags. Finer-boned too. The thought of the two of them together made Elspeth wonder if Sergeant Tallman ever felt lost in Mrs. Casey's arms.

Thinking of a man and woman embracing reminded her what it had been like to fall asleep against Lieutenant Aston. Despite the cold, there had been a warmth she had felt that came as much from her response to him as from the warmth of his body.

She had been attracted to a few men over the years. Indeed, she had imagined herself in love with one of them, an incredibly handsome lieutenant in her father's regiment. She had been fifteen and was convinced her heart was forever broken when the lieutenant announced his engagement to a young lady in England. She had even had to admire his financée's miniature, which he had passed around their dinner table one night. She had excused herself shortly after and cried herself to sleep.

At school, she and Maddie had spent hours discussing the ideal beau, and in their letters to one another, they occasionally alluded to Lord This or Lieutenant That who set their hearts beating a little faster. But their physical experiences with the opposite sex had been limited to dancing and, in Elspeth's case, what she had described to Maddie as a "slobbering kiss" by an intoxicated young officer.

As Elspeth remembered the relief of being pulled against Lieutenant Aston's body, she was flooded by sensations that were both very pleasurable and slightly terrifying. What if they had been in England? She would have been hopelessly compromised and forced to marry the Lieutenant. Yet she had to admit that the thought of him embracing her as his wife made her blush.

She blushed even hotter when she realized that the horseman who had been riding ahead of her and was now turned back and coming toward her was no other than Lieutenant Aston. She was tempted to turn her horse, for conversing with the lieutenant seemed impossible after entertaining such thoughts about him. But she was not her mother and father's daughter for nothing, and she stood her ground.

"Good morning, Lieutenant. I see you and Caesar have recovered," she said brightly when he pulled up in front of her.

"We have, Miss Gordon," he said rather stiffly.

"Are you on your way back to camp, Lieutenant? Will you ride with me?"

They rode in uncomfortable silence for a few minutes and Elspeth stole a few glances at her companion. He sat his horse as well as she remembered and he looked very different in his clean uniform. She realized that her strongest impression of him had been his strength and the warmth of his body and she had never really looked at him closely. As she examined his profile, she saw that his face was brown and lined by the sun. He had spent years in the Caribbean, she reminded herself. His dark and curly brown hair was longer than was fashionable, but it lent him a gypsyish air. His nose . . . well, if she hadn't known who he was, she might have branded him a gypsy. His nose wasn't quite as distinctive as Wellington's, of course. She would guess it had been broken at one time from the slight bump in the middle.

As if he felt her gaze, the lieutenant turned and Elspeth thought to herself, My goodness, if it weren't for his gray eyes, he would look a ruffian. But his eyes softened his appearance a little. "You don't look at all like Charlie, Lieutenant Aston. It is amazing to think that you are brothers."

Elspeth only realized she had spoken her thoughts aloud when she saw his cheeks flush. Her own grew warm with embarrassment, but there was no going back now. "Oh, dear, I am most definitely my father's daughter, Lieutenant, and am in the habit of speaking frankly. I apologize if I have offended you, but Papa did tell us that you had revealed your relationship to Lord Holme."

"Did he tell you why, Miss Gordon?"

Elspeth thought she must have imagined that night in the cave, for the lieutenant's tone was so cool she couldn't imagine him capable of any warmth.

"Yes, he did. He was impressed by your concern for me and your honesty. And so am I. Please forgive me for raising a topic that is so obviously painful to you," she added.

Val pulled up his horse and turned to face her. Although his face was still closed, his tone was not so icy. "I have recently been told that I am overly conscious of the circumstances of my birth, Miss Gordon. It is likely true. And you are right," he added with a quick smile. "Charlie and I are nothing alike, neither in appearance or temperament."

"Lord Holme is a delightfully open and warm person,"

said Elspeth and then grimaced. "Oh, dear, I did not mean—"

"Of course you did, Miss Gordon. Charlie makes friends wherever he is. He is both loving and lovable," Val replied in a matter-of-fact tone. "I am very grateful to have him as a brother and indebted to his generous nature for many things, not the least of which is my commission," he added.

Underneath his even tones, Elspeth detected a current of sadness. Did the lieutenant feel himself incapable of inspiring affection? Or giving it? And if so, was this merely the result of his birth? In for a penny, in for a pound, Elspeth told herself.

"My father raised me to believe that the circumstances of a man's birth should have little to do with the regard in which he is held. You have the high opinion of Captain Grant, which is no small thing, Lieutenant. You have my parents' respect. And mine," she added softly. "I have not had the chance to tell you that I was grateful for your proposal. My father told you the truth, you know. I would have refused if he had not, for I cannot think that a marriage dictated by convention would have much chance of succeeding. I hope the embarrassment of a proposal refused will not keep you from our dinner table," she said with a smile to lighten the tension between them. "I rather thought we had become friends after our adventure," she added wistfully.

It was the hint of vulnerability that broke through Val's constraint. Elspeth Gordon might be an intrepid young woman who had faced danger with the equanimity of her mother, but that didn't mean she didn't have feelings that might be hurt, he realized. They *had* become comrades in a short period of time and to ignore that would be unfair.

As ever, it was difficult for Val to put what was in his heart into words. He knew he still sounded stiff and uncomfortable as he said, "I am honored to count you as a friend, Miss Gordon. And I will look forward to dining with you and your family occasionally; that is, when I am in camp." Thank God they were almost back to camp, thought Val, for he couldn't think of another thing to say to her. He gave her a quick wave and rode off.

Elspeth watched him go and then, dismounting, led her mare in the opposite direction. They were certainly not at ease with one another, but she supposed that was to be expected. And she had *had* to speak about his proposal. It would have been ridiculous to have it sitting between them. She didn't have to speak of his birth, of course, she chided herself. But damn it, that would have been between them too, if she hadn't. She hoped he would come to dinner, for she wanted to know Valentine Aston better. This man who had served in the ranks, who admitted to his fondness for his half-brother but never mentioned his father, intrigued her. And, she had to admit, attracted her.

Chapter 5

Sergeant Will Tallman of the Eleventh Foot was sitting glumly in front of his small tent, cursing softly but fluently as he attempted to sew a button back on his jacket. "God's bleedin' bum," he exclaimed as he stabbed his thumb with the needle for a third time. He could reload and fire his musket three times in a minute. Why the hell couldn't he sew a bloody button on without drawing blood? He was sitting there with his thumb in his mouth, ready to throw the needle into the fire, when Val found him.

"I thought Mrs. Casey was taking good care of you, Will," Val joked as he sat down next to his old comrade.

"Oh, she'd sew it on for me, all right. She'd likely button my jacket for me in the morning if I let her, sir. That's just why I am sewing it on myself. If I am not careful, that woman will be taking over my life!"

"From what I've heard, if you are not careful, she'll have you in the parson's mousetrap, Will!"

Will glared at Val and then laughed. "I've managed to escape before, sir. No woman has gotten the better of me yet."

"Ah, but Will, you never had such a strapping woman as Mags!"

Will blushed to the roots of his receding red hair. "I am large enough where it counts, sir," he announced with great dignity and then winked at Val, who let out a whoop of laughter.

"I brought you some tea, Will. Can you brew us a cup?"

"Thank you, sir. I'd be happy for something to do that won't be sending me to the surgeon's tent!"

"Here, give me your jacket and I'll have a go at it."

Val was just tying off the thread when Lucas Stanton and George Trowbridge walked by. "I see you can't keep away from common soldiers, Aston. Have you turned seamstress now?"

"I am handy with many things, Stanton," Val replied calmly. "Needle and thread, blacksmith's hammer . . . sword, pistol."

It looked almost as if Stanton was going to stop and answer Val's implied challenge, but Trowbridge pulled him on.

"Who was that bleeding idiot, sir?"

"Lord Stanton. I met him years ago at school and would have counted myself very lucky never to have met up with him again."

"Here's your tea, sir. With a little sugar, as you like it."

"Where did you get the sugar, Will?"

"Mags has been hoarding her supplies."

"So, she is good for a little sweetness, eh?"

" 'Tis not that I don't like a little sugar in my life, sir. 'Tis just I don't like the feeling of being hemmed in, if you know what I mean. And what's the point of a soldier getting married anyways? Why any woman would want to be widowed four times, I'd like to know!"

"Four times! You mean there really *was* a Mr. Casey?"

"A private in the Connaught Rangers. The second died at Corunna. And before that a recruiting sergeant that died of the ague in Sussex."

"So Mrs. Casey has been following the drum for quite a few years, eh, Will?"

"Aye, she'd likely make a better general than Erskine by now," said Will with a smile.

"Anyone would make a better general than that drunken ass, damn his soul." They both nodded in comfortable agreement and sipped their tea, having dismissed one of

Wellington's officers to a place where their commander-in-chief would have been equally happy to send him.

"I hear that you are the hero of the Gordon family, sir."

" 'Twas as much luck and her quick thinking, Will."

"She's a good lass, Miss Gordon, from what I know. Neither she nor her mother think themselves too good to talk to the enlisted men or their wives. And they are here to stay, not just visiting, like some officers' wives." Will took another sip of tea and then said quietly, "The men miss you, sir. And so do I," he added with a quick smile.

"Thank you, Will. I miss them too. Sometimes I wonder if I should ever have accepted the damned commission."

"Of course you should have. I knew you were officer material the first time I laid eyes on you, sir."

"The first time you laid eyes on me, Will, I was a raw recruit who knew two things: how to read and how to swing a hammer, neither of which was much good to me in the ranks!"

"Ah, but strength and book-learning aren't a bad combination after all."

"I suppose not," Val admitted with a grin. "I never could have survived Sergeant Hawkins's drilling if I hadn't worked for a similar brute for years. And I'd not be an exploring officer if I couldn't read!"

"And you picked up French and Spanish marvelous fast, sir. Almost as good as Captain Grant."

"I'll never speak French well, Will. Not like Captain Grant. But I only need to read it. My Spanish and Portuguese are far better, thank God. But enough of me, Will. How do you like being in charge, now that you are a sergeant?"

"I like it fine most days. I waited long enough."

"So, if nothing else good came of my commission, at least it allowed you to move up."

"God bless the Earl of Faringdon," joked Will, lifting his cup in a mock toast.

"Rather God bless Viscount Holme, Will."

"Whatever you say, sir." Will was silent for a moment. "Some days I don't like being a sergeant. I had to have a man flogged yesterday."

"What had he done, Will?" Val asked, his tone sympathetic.

"Nicked a chicken from a local farm."

"He was damned lucky not to be hanged, then. You know how Old Hooky feels about that."

"I told him. Said I wouldn't report him higher this time, and that two hundred lashes should keep him from stealing again. I've always hated watching floggings, but when it's because of your own orders . . ." Will sighed.

"I know, Will. I remember the first time I had someone flogged. I could almost feel the lash myself. But you and I survived two hundred, Will, and this lad will live, at least until the next battle."

"Aye, sir, I guess you are right."

"There," said Val, who had finished his tea and taken up the needle and thread again. "There's your buttons on all right and tight. You owe me, Will," he added with a teasing grin, "for I've saved you from Mags Casey for a few days anyway."

"And I thank you for it! Come back again soon, sir."

"I shall, Will, if only to see if you are still single!"

As Val walked down the row of tents, he thought he could feel the scars on his back itching, although of course that was impossible. He felt sorry for that young soldier, though as he'd told Will, the man was lucky only to get a flogging.

He had only been in the army six months when he'd been flogged. The Eleventh Foot had been stationed in Kent. It was summer, one of the hottest summers the county had experienced in years. And all they did was drill, line to square, square to line, under the meanest sergeant Val had ever known, before or since. Sergeant Hawkins made George Burton look like a Quaker. He'd give a man fifty lashes just for a loose stock or a missing button.

"And why does he have us in these damned dog collars anyway, Will?" Val had complained after watching the third flogging that week. They were lying in their cots, unable to sleep because of the heat and Val's chafed neck was itching unbearably.

"Aye, he's a mean bastard."

"He enjoys it. He bloody enjoys seeing us ready to faint from the heat, marching us around like we were toy soldiers, damn it."

"Ah, but the marching does have a purpose, Val. The quicker the men can change formation, the most likely they are to survive."

"We're never going to get out of Kent anyway," grumbled Val. "I joined the army to go places. 'Over the hill and far away.' Not bloody likely!"

"I been wondering why a lad like you joined up," Will commented.

Val was silent for a moment. He had never told anyone his story, though it was clear from his bearing and speech that he was a cut above the usual recruit. Indeed, most of the men kept away from him, not so much in deliberate unfriendliness but out of their sense that he was different. Will Tallman was the only one who had not been put off by Val's obvious breeding. But then, Will Tallman was one of the friendliest men Val had ever met. He smiled and joked with everyone, even some of the officers. He was ten years older than Val and had taken him under his wing. Val supposed he owed Will the truth. And the fact was, he guessed he wanted to tell someone his story.

"I spent six years of my life as a blacksmith's apprentice, Will, so I am not really much different from any of you. Except for my father," he added bitterly.

"And what is your dad, then, Val? A marquess or a dook?" teased Will.

"Charles Valentine Faringdon, Earl of Faringdon," Val announced flatly.

Will whistled. "I were only joking, lad. Is that the truth?"

"I'm only his bastard, Will. He never married my mother. My half-brother discovered me and brought me to school with him last year. I learned a lot, not the least of which was that a public school can be as hard as the army. So I ran away."

"Wouldn't blacksmithing have been better than here?"

"I most likely would have had to reapprentice myself, Will. And the recruiting sergeant made it sound like such an adventure. . . ."

"You'll have your adventures, lad."

Indeed he did, and sooner than he'd thought. The next day, when Private Gillingham, a consumptive-looking new recruit, fainted while standing at attention in the noon sun after hours of drilling, Val was about to break ranks and go to him when Will held him back.

"Steady, lad, steady. There's nothing we can do."

But when Sergeant Hawkins started kicking the man and screaming at him to "get up, you lazy bastard," Val couldn't contain himself. He ran forward and, kneeling beside Gillingham, started loosening his stock.

"What the bleedin' hell do you think *you're* doing, Aston?" screamed the sergeant.

"He can't breathe."

"He can't breathe, *sir*."

"Yes, sir," Val muttered.

"Get up, Aston."

"I've almost got his stock opened. Sir."

"Get the hell up. Corporal Baker, take Private Aston and give him two hundred lashes."

Val could barely hold himself back from strangling the sergeant when he heard Will's cheery voice. "Might I go with the lad, sir? For company-like." Usually Will's open face and cheerful voice got him what he wanted.

"Of course, Private Tallman. And for speaking out without being spoke to, you can take two hundred lashes yourself. For company-like," he added, mocking Will's Devonshire speech.

After it was over (although it felt like it would never be over or that he would die before it was over), Val and Will stumbled back to the barracks, where they were met by Corporal Gillen.

"Come out back, lads," said the Irishman. "I've got a little something to help you get through the night."

He sloshed a few buckets of water over their backs and then a half-pint of rum. Val had to bite down on his own hand to keep from screaming as the alcohol hit the open wounds.

"That should keep you from infection, lads. And here's the other half to put ye to sleep."

"God bless you, Gillen," Will whispered. "You're a good man even if you are a Paddy."

He'd only been flogged that once, thank God. He couldn't imagine how anyone survived the lash twice. He'd learned to ignore the sergeant's brutality and when Private Gillingham died a month later, he'd felt relief more than sorrow, for the man clearly would never have made it to the winter.

He'd been in Kent less than a year when the regiment was sent to Belgium and then to the Caribbean and he'd happily left England behind. It was in the Caribbean he'd met the young Colquhoun Grant and learned that not all officers were sadistic brutes like Hawkins. Some of them took their responsibilities seriously and cared deeply about the men's safety. That sort of officer could lead you into hell and you'd follow gladly, for you could trust him to lead you in if you knew you could trust him to get you out.

As he looked back on his last twelve years, Val marveled. It was as though some fate had determined that he join the Eleventh Foot, that he would serve in Martinique, where he would learn French, that he would spend eighteen months in Madeira, where he would pick up Portuguese and Spanish. And that he would catch the eye of Colquhoun Grant, who, learning of his linguistic abilities, took every opportunity to speak with him. Of course, his own were nothing compared to Grant's, who was more than fluent and had several dialects down perfectly.

When Val finally accepted his commission, it was not long before he was offered his present assignment, which meant in a month's time he would see Charlie again. Val was not a religious man, but perhaps there was a kind Deity who had brought his brother into his life again.

On the other hand, he wasn't quite sure but that it was a cruel fate that had introduced him to Elspeth Gordon. She had embarrassed him earlier today and made him speak of what he usually kept hidden. At the same time, she'd done it out of a combination of forthrightness and kindness. She had been right to do so, he had to admit, for the awkwardness between them would only have gotten worse had they left things unspoken.

But maybe it was better to have had that barrier, Val considered, as he felt that phantom itching on his back again. For how could someone like himself, a man who had risen from the ranks and bore the indelible mark of illegitimacy, form a friendship with the granddaughter of

an earl and the daughter of an officer on Wellington's staff?
He would accept the occasional invitation to dinner, just to
be polite, but luckily he would be out on reconnaissance
enough to keep out of her way.

Chapter 6

Val was out of camp for most of the following week, for
Colquhoun Grant as well as his men were constantly ob-
serving the French camp at Santarém. Massena and his men
had been settled in for a month now and it did not seem
likely that the French had any plans for attack. Like a fox,
Wellington had gone to earth behind the lines of Tôrres
Vedras, an earth he'd had his engineers create and reshape
out of the harsh Portuguese landscape. The general was
determined to hold Portugal despite the Whig opinion that
it would be impossible. So there the two armies sat, the
British behind the lines and Massena's army thirty miles
away.

The question, thought Val as he lay on his stomach on
a rock outcropping overlooking the French camp, was how
long the French could hold out, given their numbers and
the lack of food. The Portuguese were old hands at destroying everything behind them when they had fled the Spanish
down the centuries, and Wellington's orders to lay waste
the terrain had been followed out around Tôrres Vedras.
Here at Santarém, the land offered a little more to the
French, but they would not long be able to live off the
countryside. Yet Massena showed no signs of moving.

His reports to Colquhoun had been repetitive and mun-
dane these past weeks and he felt he was doing very little.
On his last report he had apologized. "I am sorry, sir, but
things are the same."

"I am not sure why you are sorry, Lieutenant," Grant

had replied, with one of his quick, warm smiles. "I do not expect you to drive the French out, only observe them."

"Of course not, sir."

"Sit down, Lieutenant."

"Thank you, sir."

Grant sighed as he read Val's succinct but careful report. "I am afraid Massena's dug himself in. I suppose that is better than an all-out attack. But I fear he knows more about the state of things in England than we would like him to know. Or than he *should* know."

"What do you mean, sir?"

"The government has been supporting Lord Wellington in his determination to hold Portugal. But the king's illness . . . if Percival has to go for a Regency, the Whigs would be in power. They'd recall Wellington and Massena would march us right to the sea." Grant, who had been sitting back in his chair, suddenly leaned forward. "I am convinced that someone in the War Office has been leaking information of the political situation back home to someone here, who in turn is leaking it to the French."

"You mean a traitor, sir?"

"They do exist, Lieutenant," Grant said with dry humor. "I want you to keep your eyes and ears open for anything suspicious. And although I know that one of the reasons you joined me was to get away from the officers' mess, I need you to socialize with your brother officers. I hear the Gordons have invited you to dine."

"Er, yes, sir."

"Consider it to be a part of your duty, Aston. It shouldn't be onerous, since it gives you the opportunity to further your acquaintance with Miss Gordon," Grant added, his eyes twinkling.

"Yes, sir."

"But before you can enjoy Mrs. Gordon's good cooking, I am going to have to send you out again," Grant told him apologetically.

"Back to Santarém?"

"No, I want you to make the acquaintance of Julian Sanchez, Lieutenant. Not only do I believe that we can hold Portugal, but I am convinced we will be in Spain within a year. I need you to help maintain contact with the guerrilleros. You'll leave tomorrow. But when you return, dinner with the Gordons. That's an order."

"Yes, sir. Thank you, sir."

It took Val two days of hard riding before he reached the guerrilleros' stronghold. Sanchez, who had started with only a handful of men, now commanded over three hundred. They were as disciplined as any British regiment, Val had been told, although he had to admit their appearance was rather irregular, with their mix of tunics from one regiment and trousers from another, and bright sashes and wide-brimmed peasant hats.

He had been led into the camp by two sentries and once he had identified himself to their satisfaction, he was taken to Sanchez's tent.

"Buenos días, Lieutenant."

"Buenos días, Señor Sanchez."

"Sientase, Lieutenant."

"Gracias."

Val sat there while Sanchez rifled through the papers on his field table. Then, at the same time that he heard someone enter the tent behind him, he saw a smile light up the old guerrillero's face.

"Ah, Juan, you are back. Have you anything new for me?"

"Sí, Julian. *Pero, quien es este?"* The man was now standing next to Val's chair, looking down at him suspiciously.

"May I present Lieutenant Aston, Jack? Colquhoun's new exploring officer," Sanchez replied.

The newcomer's face lightened and he held out his hand to Val. "Delighted to meet you, then, Lieutenant."

Val's eyebrows lifted in surprise. The man, who was tall, slim, and dark-skinned and was dressed in the motley dress of a guerrillero, spoke perfect English.

"Lieutenant Aston, this is Captain Jack Belden," announced Sanchez.

Val rose quickly, almost knocking his chair over to stand at attention.

"Oh, put yourself at ease, man," said Belden, a twinkle in his brown eyes. "I am glad you've come, for I have a few dispatches to send back to Captain Grant," he announced, pulling papers out of his jacket and tossing them on the table. Sanchez opened all three and read them quickly.

"Are they of any use, Julian?"

"Two have information we already know, but the third gives a full description of one of Massena's spies," said Sanchez with a wolfish grin.

"Then he won't get very far in his information gathering, will he?" said the captain with a smile. "I'll make a copy and you can take the original back to Captain Grant, Lieutenant. I am parched. Can I offer you a drink, Aston?"

"Thank you, sir."

Belden's tent was only two down from Sanchez's, and when they entered, Belden gestured Val to sit down.

"I have some local wine, Lieutenant. Not quite as nice as a glass of ale, but it will help quench your thirst, especially since it has been mixed with a little fruit juice."

Val took a small sip and then a grateful swallow. He wasn't a heavy drinker, but the sweet wine with its hint of orange and lemon was delicious.

"I'd better be careful, sir," he said with a grin as the captain offered to top off his glass.

" 'Tis delightful after a long day in the saddle, isn't it?"

Val could feel his spine soften as the wine began to have its effect on him and as he relaxed, he asked the question that was uppermost in his mind.

"Just how did an Englishman end up with a band of guerrilleros? You speak Spanish like a native. Sir," he added as an afterthought.

"You must be fluent also, or Colquhoun wouldn't have sent you."

"Ah, I may speak the language fluently, sir, but I still have a slight accent. You have none."

"My grandfather married the daughter of a Spanish count, Lieutenant. She made sure her children and grandchildren spoke the language. That is one of the reasons Wellington sent me to Spain. The other is that I look as well as sound like a native. I must say, it was the first time my foreign appearance put me at any advantage. If you call joining the guerrilleros an advantage, that is," he added humorously.

"It is certainly an advantage for us, sir, if not for you."

"Oh, yes, I have been able to ease communications with our allies. Now tell me, what is Massena doing?"

"Nothing, sir. He seems to have dug in for the winter."

"Waiting for Percival's government to fall, I'll be bound. Does Captain Grant still suspect an informer?"

"He is convinced of it."

"It will be hard to smoke him out, if he is highly placed. These damn Whigs . . . and I am one, mind you . . ." the viscount said with a grin, "have no faith Wellington can hold Portugal, much less take Spain. If they get into power, Europe is doomed. But what is your opinion on the political situation, Lieutenant?"

"I have none, sir," Val answered stiffly. "I've spent the last twelve years as a common soldier and I have been much more interested in the competence of my officers than in that of the politicians."

"So you came up from the ranks, did you? I am surprised that you don't profess any republican sympathy."

"Oh, I am against tyranny in any form, sir, and that includes Bonaparte. It seems to me that anyone who has himself proclaimed emperor is no real friend of the working man, no matter what his origins."

"I agree with you, Lieutenant Aston, but I am afraid many of my peers wish for his defeat only out of fear that republicanism might spread to England. Thank God Wellington is a soldier and not a politician!"

"I have not served under him for very long, sir. Do you think he is capable of beating Bonaparte?"

"Old Hooky can if anyone can," Belden replied with a smile. "I wouldn't be here if I didn't believe that. I don't think any of us has yet seen what he can do, for so far he has been on the defensive. But the time will come when he will start to push back and then the world will see what he is made of. And what the Spanish people will do to take back Spain!" Belden took a deep breath. "I tend to wax long and eloquent at times, Lieutenant," he said, the passionate fire in his eyes dying down to a humorous warmth. "I believe those dispatches should be ready for you by now. Give my best to Captain Grant."

"I will, and thank you for the wine, sir."

"You are welcome, Lieutenant." He pulled a watch out of his pocket. "I have only a quarter hour to dress for my appointment with a most charming señora," he added, with a mischievous look in his eyes.

"I wish you a most enjoyable evening, then."

After he had placed the dispatches in the hidden pocket sewn into his saddle pad, Val mounted and set off. As he sat huddled under his cloak that night watching the glowing coals of his campfire die down, he thought back to his meeting with Captain Belden. He was obviously passionate about the fate of his grandmother's homeland. His dark and brooding countenance coupled with that mercurial temperament was sure to attract the ladies, Val thought with a grin. It was not surprising that he had a Spanish señora waiting for him!

Val reached the encampment midafternoon the next day and, after delivering the papers to Captain Grant, sought out his own tent. He had just fallen back on his cot when he heard a call at the tent flap.

"Lieutenant Aston?"

Val groaned and sat up. "Who is it?"

"Private Ryan, sor, with a message from Mrs. Gordon."

"Come in, then, Private."

"Sorry to be disturbing ye, sor," said the private, holding out a piece of vellum.

"Thank you, Private Ryan."

The man just stood there and Val looked up at him sharply.

"Beggin' yer pardon, sor, but I'm to stay for an answer."

It was a dinner invitation for that evening. "Bloody hell," Val whispered, running his hand over his stubbled chin.

"Does that mean ye won't be comin', sor?"

"It means I'd better start getting ready now, Private Ryan. Tell Mrs. Gordon I am delighted and will see her at six sharp."

"Yes, sor."

Val flopped back on his cot. Oh, God, he was beyond exhaustion after the past few days. All he wanted was his bed, but now he would have to clean himself up for polite company, not to mention summon the energy for making conversation. If it wasn't for Captain Grant's orders, he would have refused. Well, perhaps not, he admitted to himself, for not only would he be doing his duty, he'd also be seeing Miss Gordon again.

The Gordon family had been lucky to be billeted in a small whitewashed house in the nearby village. As Val walked down the road an hour later, washed, shaved, and in a clean uniform, he wondered who else would be present at the Gordons' table and how he would begin to ferret out information that might lead to discovering who was selling information to the French.

The door was opened by Private Ryan, an apron wrapped around his waist. He acted as an orderly to the major and helped out with household chores when necessary.

"Come in, sor. Ye're the first to arrive."

Damn. He was familiar enough with polite society to know that it was not done to appear too eager, but his aunt Martha had drilled the importance of punctuality into him when he was young and it was a lesson hard to unlearn. He sat down on a small bench near the fire and was so fascinated by the green and blue flames that he didn't hear anyone enter the room.

"Good evening, Lieutenant Aston."

He jumped up, knocking over the bench, and cursed himself for a damned fool. "Good evening, Miss Gordon." If she hadn't already known he wasn't born a gentleman, his early arrival and clumsiness would have alerted her!

Elspeth took a seat opposite him. "Do sit down, Lieutenant," she said and he realized he was just standing there, turning his shako in his hand.

"We used apple wood tonight, Lieutenant."

"Apple wood?"

"That is why the flames are green," she explained politely.

"Oh, yes. Quite."

"Mother will be right out and father is on his way."

"I am a little early. I apologize."

"Not at all, Lieutenant, you were right on time. Ah, Private Ryan."

"Beggin' yer pardon, miss, but ye're needed in the kitchen."

"Fetch the lieutenant a sherry, would you, Private? That is one good thing about being here, Lieutenant," she said with a smile. "There is no difficulty obtaining good sherry and port. Would you excuse me for a moment?"

"Of course, Miss Gordon."

*   *   *

The sherry *was* excellent. Val was just beginning to feel more comfortable when he heard voices at the door.

"Could you get the door, Lieutenant?" Elspeth asked, poking her head in from the kitchen. "We are having a small crisis here!"

He opened it and there stood Lucas Stanton and George Trowbridge.

"I was sure this was the Gordons', George," said Stanton.

"Clearly not, if the riffraff are opening the door."

Val, who was still holding his glass of sherry, was tempted to dash the liquor in Stanton's face. He was able to restrain himself only with the greatest effort.

"Miss Gordon asked me to greet whoever was at the door, gentlemen," he said coldly.

Both men gave him a look of distaste and, after scraping their boots, entered the room.

"Let me get you some sherry," Val offered quickly, eager to be out of the room, and praying that by the time he got back, someone from the Gordon family would have arrived.

"No, no, Lieutenant. Patrick will serve the drinks," said Elspeth when he appeared in the kitchen. "It was bad enough you had to act the doorman. I'll be out in a minute." So Val returned empty-handed to find the men standing in front of the fire.

"Private Ryan will be out with the sherry in a moment, gentlemen."

Stanton just looked at him with one eyebrow arrogantly raised. Thank God, just then Major Gordon came in, with James right behind.

"So, you've all had a chance to get acquainted, eh, lads?" the major said heartily, rubbing his hands together and stamping his feet. "It is getting damn cold out there. I don't blame you for seeking out the fire, Stanton. But where are Elspeth and Peggy?"

"Here, Ian," said Mrs. Gordon, who had just emerged from the back bedroom. She tucked her hand into her husband's arm and led him over to the fire. "I am sorry, gentlemen, but my errands this afternoon took longer than I thought. I only got home just before you arrived, Lieutenant Aston," she added with a warm smile at Val. "Now, where is Private Ryan with the sherry?"

"Here I am, marm."

"Thank you, Private. And please send Elspeth out to us."

"Yes, marm."

Elspeth was patting her hair into place as she came into the parlor. "Well, now, we are all here, then," said her father. "Let us have a toast. James, will you do the honors?"

"To Lord Wellington and the liberation of Portugal."

"Hear, hear."

There was only time for one glass of sherry before they were summoned into the adjoining room for dinner, a fact for which Val was grateful. At least at the table there was something to do with one's hands and Stanton's and Trowbridge's attitudes were not as noticeable.

There was little conversation during the first course, but as Private Ryan cleared the soup, he managed to spill some of the leftovers on Elspeth's gown.

"Damned Paddy! Here, let me, Miss Gordon," said George as he wet his napkin in his water glass and sponged awkwardly at her dress.

"Thank you, Lieutenant," Elspeth said coolly. "Never mind, Patrick," she reassured the private, who was standing there stammering out an apology. "It will not stain."

"I don't know how anyone expects us to win this war with almost half the troops damned bog-trotters," said Stanton.

"I wouldn't say that in front of Alex Wallace," said James in deceptively mild tones. "His Connaught Rangers have proved themselves more than once in battle."

"That may be, but most of them only know enough English to get by on the parade ground," complained Trowbridge.

"Lieutenant Aston, I hear you have just returned from a visit to the guerrilleros," said Major Gordon, neatly turning the subject. "What did you think of them?"

"I was very impressed by General Sanchez, Major."

"Indeed, and so is Lord Wellington. I've seen the two of them cheek by jowl many's the time at Freneida."

"Did you run into Jack Belden?" asked James.

Val was silent for a moment and then replied, "I met no one who appeared to be English, James."

"A good answer," murmured James.

"It is all right, Lieutenant Aston," the major reassured him. "All of us here know that Belden is with Sanchez."

Val smiled. "I *did* meet a gentleman called Juan, sir, who spoke both English and Spanish fluently."

"That's Jack, all right. Looks like a Spanish don, all melancholy-like, but could charm the birds out of the trees."

"They called him Jack of Hearts in London, didn't they, Major Gordon?" commented George.

"Indeed they did, for he was as lucky at cards as he was playing at love," replied the major with an appreciative chuckle.

"I don't imagine the young ladies whose hearts he collected were that amused, Father," chided Elspeth.

"And how did you hear of him, lassie?"

"Oh, his reputation reached us at school, Father," she replied, her eyes twinkling. "Polly Ewing's older sister was one of the young ladies he amused himself with. She was heartbroken when he turned his attentions elsewhere. Did you like him, Lieutenant?" Elspeth asked Val.

"I must confess I found him quite charming, Miss Gordon," Val admitted with a grin.

"I must compliment you on this dinner," James said to Mrs. Gordon, turning the subject.

"Why, thank you, James. Between Private and Mrs. Ryan helping us, we manage very well, don't we, Ian?"

"Yes, and since we are here in the heart of Portugal, I have managed to obtain some very good port. Shall we return to the parlor, gentlemen?"

"I warn you, Elspeth and I will join you momentarily," teased his wife.

The port was everything the major had promised and between a full stomach, the warmth of the fire, and the wine, the atmosphere in the parlor was considerably more relaxed than at the beginning of the evening. Val, who was finding it hard to stay awake, did more listening than speaking as the conversation ranged from the superiority of the Ordenanza over Spanish troops to the French army's ability to survive on practically nothing.

"It isn't quite nothing, of course," said James. "They pillage and steal whatever they can."

"Surely our men would be better off if they were able

to do the same," George Trowbridge complained. "Lord Wellington's orders sometimes seem unreasonable, especially when supplies from home are always delayed and, when they arrive, are always less than we need. What harm can stealing a chicken or two do?"

"We are here to liberate the people, not deprive them of what little they have," said Val, joining the conversation.

"Well, I am not here to liberate bloody Papists and garlic eaters, I can assure you, Lieutenant Aston. I'm here to keep the Jacobins out of England."

"Hear, hear, George," said Stanton. "Only in a civilized country does everyone know his place."

"Ah, but Wellington is nothing if not practical," interjected Major Gordon smoothly. "To keep Boney out of England, we must have the support of our allies. They are hardly likely to support us if we are raping their women and stealing food out of their children's mouths, don't you agree? Now, George, I hear you just received a letter from your sister. How *are* things on our civilized little island?"

"Percival is hanging on by his fingernails, Major Gordon, from what my sister tells me. Though that is merely a postscript, don't you know," he added with a laugh. "Her letters tend to be full of the latest gossip: who is bedding whom, that sort of thing. There was quite a scandal last month, she tells me."

"Someone run off with another of Old Hooky's sisters-in-law?" joked Stanton.

They were all silent for a moment, embarrassed for Lord Wellington, whose sister-in-law had caused such a scandal and kept him from summoning one of his best officers to the Peninsula.

"No, she says they finally raided some of those iniquitous clubs on Vere Street. It was the talk of the ton for a week. No one was caught in flagrante, unfortunately, but the damned mollies will not be flaunting themselves so openly."

"Too bad we can't press them all into the navy, eh, George? 'Tis a hanging offense on board ship."

"It is a hanging offense on land also," James offered quietly.

"So it is, so it is, but it is harder to detect a catamite who mixes in Society, isn't it, James?"

"Indeed, some are even married," he commented with a

tinge of sarcasm. "But here are the ladies, George. I think we should change our topic of conversation, don't you?"

Val, who had been fighting a losing battle to keep from yawning every other breath, excused himself early. He made his way back to his tent slowly, in a fog of fatigue and port. When he reached his quarters, he fell into his cot fully dressed except for his boots, which had taken him forever to get off. He tried to reconstruct the conversations of the evening, but the talk was not that different from most soldiers', whatever their rank: what were the French doing or planning to do, Wellington and his damned regulations, and what was the news from home. George and Lucas were fierce Tories, although that was no surprise, and would, of course, be a good cover to use. James acted as a sort of mediator, his even temper enabling him to stay cool no matter what the argument. Major Gordon hadn't said much. But it would be ridiculous to suspect him, wouldn't it? Val fell asleep thinking it would take a few more dinners before he gathered any useful information that would help in his investigation.

Chapter 7

Mrs. Margaret Casey was collecting dirty laundry from her officers' tents. It was her favorite part of the job, for dirty laundry gave one almost as much information about a person as good gossip. "Which is why we have the expression about airing dirty laundry, Mags," she told herself as she stripped Lieutenant Trowbridge's cot. There were telltale stains on the bottom sheet, she noticed with a grin. She knew the lieutenant's current favorite among the women had been with Corporal Biggins the last few nights, so it appeared the lieutenant had fallen into the habit of relieving his own desire. "Now, then, Mags," she clucked to herself, "so does many a man or woman alone." But she heartily disliked the lieutenant and it gave her a sense of satisfaction to know something that private about him.

His friend Stanton was equally distasteful to her. "He puts enough bloody grease on his hair," she muttered as she pulled off the pillow slips, "to silence a Portuguese oxcart!" She chuckled to herself over that one. All the grease in the world wouldn't silence the damned carts.

Captain James Lambert, Lord Wimborne, on the other hand, was one of her favorites. She loved rolling his title on her tongue. She never had to strip his cot or pick up his clothes off the dirt. No, there they were, his dirty linens and uniform tied neatly in a sheet. A monogrammed sheet. "Now, that's true quality, Mags."

She hadn't had a chance to approach Lieutenant Aston about doing his laundry. But as she came up to his tent she saw a shadow moving about and decided to stop and see if she could drum up a little more business for herself.

"Lieutenant Aston?" she called into the tent door.

"Who is it?"

" 'Tis Mags Casey, Sergeant Tallman's . . . friend." Now, that was a right genteel expression, Mags, she thought.

"Come in, Mrs. Casey, come in. What can I do for you?"

Mags Casey had to bend as much as the average soldier when she entered the tent, she was that tall. "I was wondering if you needed anything laundered," she said, looking pointedly at the wrinkled sheet on his cot.

"I suppose I do, Mrs. Casey," Val said with a wide smile.

My Lord, Mags, this one is dangerous, she warned herself. Not so tall, though taller than Will, but broad-shouldered and slim-hipped. Clear gray eyes that were such a contrast to his brown skin. He'd just been washing up, so his shirt was open and she could see that the hair on his chest was curly, like the hair on his head. She liked hair on a man's chest. Too bad Will had so little. But Will had other things to recommend him, she reminded herself. But she couldn't deny it: Lieutenant Aston made her pulse quicken!

"I charge tuppence for a shirt and four pence for each sheet. You get them back within the week, as good as new. I'll iron your shirts for only another penny," she added, "seeing as you're Will's officer and all."

"Not anymore, Mrs. Casey. I'm detached from the Eleventh Foot."

"You work for Captain Grant, don't you? Now, that's a gentleman whose laundry I'd love to be doing. But almost all my officers are lieutenants," she added with a rueful smile. "Maude Parrish gets the captains' and majors' business. Except for Major Gordon, who has Private Ryan's wife doing for him."

"Will tells me you've been with the army a long time."

"I have indeed, sir. My first husband was a recruiting officer. Died of a fever, he did, without ever leaving England. My second husband died in the retreat from Corunna."

"And Mr. Casey?"

"Private Casey was killed in a drunken quarrel," she said solemnly. "And I was married to each and every one of them, Lieutenant, no matter what you are thinking."

"Of course, Mrs. Casey."

"No 'of course' about it, Lieutenant. There's but a handful of us who's stood before the parson amongst all the soldiers' 'Mrs.' and we both know it. But I have managed to remain a respectable woman until now," she added sadly.

"Surely you are still a respectable woman, Mrs. Casey."

"I may be a real widow, Lieutenant, but Sergeant Will Tallman is very much alive," Mags said with a wink, "and we are still no closer to tying the knot than we were when we first met. Will says he's never been married and never intends to."

"I have heard him say that," admitted Val, keeping his face straight with difficulty as he thought of his conversation with Will. "Surely there are other men who might be more willing, for you're an attractive woman, Mrs. Casey."

"Ah, but I love Will Tallman, you see, Lieutenant."

"Well, a man can change his mind, Mrs. Casey."

"And this is true, Lieutenant. Now, if you have no objection, I'll collect your laundry once a week from your tent and I ask you to pick it up when it is ready. That way, anything that gets wrinkled or dirty on the way home, it won't be me as has done it. And all my officers pay me when they come to collect their things. I hope that won't be a problem, Lieutenant, for I make no exceptions, even for friends of my Will."

"Understood, Mrs. Casey."

"Then I'll just strip your bed, sir. If you have any shirts, just add them to the bundle."

"Thank you very much, Mrs. Casey," said Val as she was leaving. "I hope this is the beginning of a mutually rewarding acquaintance."

She was only just out of the tent when he followed and stopped her. "Mrs. Casey?"

"Yes, sir?"

"You say you pick up all your officers' laundry?"

"It works out easier, what with all you hither and yon with your soldiering. I have never been accused of stealing, Lieutenant," she added defensively.

"Of course not. I didn't mean that at all, Mrs. Casey. Who are your other officers?"

"Why, Lieutenants Trowbridge and Stanton, among others. And Captain Lord Wimborne," she added proudly.

"An impressive roster, Mrs. Casey," Val complimented her.

"And now I can add you, Lieutenant, and an exploring officer will impress all the other women."

"Thank you, Mrs. Casey, but I wouldn't be too happy, for you'll have a real challenge with me. Less laundry, but a whole lot dirtier!"

"Was there something you wanted to ask me, Lieutenant?"

"No, nothing, Mrs. Casey. Thank you and good luck with Will!"

"But he *did* want to ask you something, Mags," she declared as she trudged back with her bundle slung over her shoulder. "I wonder what it was."

Val smiled as he watched Mrs. Casey walk easily down the row of tents despite the heavy laundry she carried. She was a strong woman, and, it seemed, a sensible one. And she had ready access to a number of officers' tents, which was, at the moment, the fact he found most interesting. He didn't know her very well yet, but Will certainly did. He would have to spend some time with both of them. Perhaps Mags Casey would eventually be able to offer some assistance in his investigation.

* * *

When Val rode out the next morning, he was grateful for his heavy wool cloak, for as November drew to a close, it was getting colder. Caesar had become familiar with the track he took over the hills and for the first part of his journey to Santarém Val could relax and let the horse lead the way. The sky was pewter and there was a moisture in the air that felt like snow. He hoped that the winter would hold off, for he wasn't looking forward to these steep tracks when they turned icy.

He was riding directly into the wind and could feel his lips and face getting chapped. For a moment he was envious of his fellow soldiers back in camp: At least drilling kept you warm! He wasn't a drinking man, but he wouldn't mind being in front of the Gordons' fire and sipping some of the major's best port right now.

As he pictured himself there, he could hear George's derisory tones. So Lord Trowbridge was not fighting to free Spain and Portugal but to save England, not so much from the "Corsican Monster" but to keep her aristocrats safe from the dreaded Jacobins. Most Tories felt the same, Val supposed. No liberty, equality, or fraternity for them. Yet a number of Wellington's officers had Whiggish sympathies. Major Gordon probably did. And they fought to free Europe from tyranny. Val gave a short laugh and his gelding flicked back his ears. "It is an oddity, Caesar. Here is a man who began as a revolutionary and ends up declaring himself an emperor. Not king, mind you. France wasn't enough for his ambitions; only Europe would do. And he wants England too. And where do I stand in all this, Caesar? You may well ask."

It was a good question and he hadn't spent much time thinking about it over the last twelve years. Where did he stand? Why, right close to the man next to him. Right behind his sergeant and in front of his lieutenant. He stood on the hard-packed earth of the parade ground and he counted himself lucky to have still been standing on the bloody battleground of Talavera.

He hadn't become a soldier for patriotic reasons. He had enlisted because it seemed the only thing left for him to do. And it was damn sure that his comrades were there for the same reason. Oh, a few had been drawn by idealism and the glamour of the red coat. But there were few of them and they soon enough realized there wasn't much glamour in getting up at dawn, digging latrines, and drilling all day. Most of the army was made up of men like Val who'd had no choice. For them, it was wander as a beggar or enlist. Be transported or enlist.

He'd stayed a soldier because it offered him a home of sorts and a clear purpose. Despite the boredom of his years in Kent, it was a better life than most. And despite fevers and seasickness, he had traveled to places he'd never dreamed of.

He laughed out loud again. Of course he'd dreamed of them. He'd dreamed of little else as a young boy playing with the lead soldiers his mother had given him.

And here he was, following in his imaginary father's footsteps. Fighting to save the way of life of men like his real father and Lucas Stanton. Surely, if there was a God, He was having a good laugh at the likes of Val Aston, freezing his arse off in Portugal to defend a system of rank and privilege that had excluded him.

Ah, but there was more to it than that. He had come to know soldiering almost better than he'd known smithing and he'd never felt such satisfaction as on the day he'd received his sergeant's stripes. He'd served under many a blockhead, but his service under Colquhoun Grant had been a privilege, and he wagered he'd learned more in the last five years than men did at university. There was an art to being a good soldier, and he enjoyed practicing it. Accepting the commission had been a bittersweet experience, but he had to admit that for all the discomfort, he loved reconnaissance work. He had grown fond of the Portuguese and admired their struggle. So he guessed maybe he was fighting for them and their freedom. And against tyranny. And for Colquhoun Grant and Lord Wellington. "And those are not bad reasons, eh, Caesar?"

Massena's encampment looked the same. There was no sign of any troop movements, either in or out. It certainly appeared that the French had settled in for the winter. Wellington's lines had surprised them and stymied them. But Wellington's brilliance would mean nothing if the Whigs got in. Obviously, Massena was counting on that and was going to stay no matter how tight his men's bellies got, thought Val.

The stalemate was clear: Wellington safe behind his lines, but in danger from his own countrymen; and Massena, with no supplies, but the hope of a British withdrawal if the prince became regent. A tenuous balance, and one that Massena would only strive to maintain if he were receiving information from someone with an insider's knowledge of the political situation.

Chapter 8

Val had positioned himself to the east of Santarém. He spent a cold, uncomfortable night, for he didn't dare make a fire, no matter how small. He wrapped himself in his cloak and fell asleep long after midnight. He was awakened by the cold muzzle of a pistol pressed against his cheek.

"Sit up slowly, monsieur."

He opened his eyes and saw a French corporal standing above him. Damn, the sentries had been farther afield than he'd thought. But when he sat up and really looked at the man, he realized that he was not one of Massena's pickets, but a dispatch officer.

"Open your cloak, monsieur."

Val slowly pushed his cloak back.

"So, you are an officer. I am sure that the marshal will accept your parole. It is just too bad that bringing you in will delay my errand."

So he was on his way out of the camp, thought Val. Heading toward France. Val bowed his head as though in defeat and the Frenchman relaxed the pressure against his cheek.

"Come, come, monsieur, it happens to the best of us."

Val looked up again. The pistol was now at least six inches away and the Frenchman was getting up from his crouch. Val didn't think, he just acted, sweeping his arm against the man's heel and destroying his balance.

Val was up on his feet, diving for the pistol in an instant. He had his hand on the man's wrist, but the man was just as fast and as soon as Val grabbed him, he swung around behind. When he felt the Frenchman's arm around his throat, Val forced himself not to fight against the hold. He ducked his chin, which took some of the pressure off his windpipe, at the same time realizing if he wasn't choked to death, he was likely going to shoot himself, for the Frenchman was slowly forcing Val's arm back. His arm was shaking from the effort to resist, and Val knew he wouldn't be able to hold the man off for much longer, and so instinctively he collapsed his arm and, using the man's own strength against him, knelt down and brought the Frenchman over his shoulder. The pistol flew out of his hand, and Val dove for it.

"So, you are on an errand for the marshal, eh, monsieur?"

The Frenchman just looked up at Val with no expression.

"Get on your knees, man, and open your jacket."

Reluctantly the man opened his jacket, revealing a slight bulge in the lining.

"Take it off and toss it here."

Val kept his eye on his enemy as he picked up the jacket and heard the telltale crackling of paper.

"The marshal sent you off alone? You must be very good if he thinks you can make it past the guerrilleros."

"Sometimes a patrol draws unnecessary attention," the man answered calmly.

"Indeed." Val cocked the pistol.

"I am an officer like yourself, may I remind you, monsieur. I give you my parole."

"First you will give me the real dispatches, *mon capitaine,*" Val said with heavy irony in his voice.

"I assure you, those in my jacket are real enough."

"And too easily discovered. Get up and go over to your horse, Captain. I will be right behind you." Just as the Frenchman reached his mount, he lifted his arm, ready to hit the horse's rump and send him running. "Oh, no, you don't," Val told him, smashing the pistol into the side of his head. "That should take care of you for a while, Monsieur Frog."

There was nothing in the saddlebags but food, but that was only what Val had expected. He ran his hands carefully over the Frenchman's saddle searching for any odd lumps or seams. Finally, as he slipped his hand under the pommel, he found it, a secret compartment built right into the saddle. *"Voilà!"* said Val with a satisfied grin on his face as he pulled out a thin packet. "I will keep this safe for you, *monsieur le capitaine.*"

Taking a knife from his belt, Val pulled down the gray blanket tied behind the saddle and cut it into strips. The Frenchman did not regain consciousness until Val had bound his hands and feet.

"I am an officer and a gentleman, monsieur," the Frenchman protested "and I assure you if I give my parole, I will honor it."

"I mean no insult, Captain, but I can't let you go so close to the camp."

"Then I take it back," the man replied angrily. "If you do not accept my parole I will do everything in my power to escape. I will make the journey very tedious for you, Lieutenant."

Bloody hell, thought Val, he was right. He could make the ride home a misery or trust the Frog bastard.

"Do you give me your word, Captain?"

"I give you my word of honor, sir."

"All right. But you ride in front. One move to escape and you'll have a bullet through your head. Do you understand?"

"Mais oui, monsieur."

By the time they arrived back in camp it was almost suppertime. Val directed his prisoner toward Captain Grant's tent but found it empty.

"The captain dines with Wellington tonight, sir," Grant's orderly told him.

"Damn," muttered Val. He supposed he could wait, but Grant's orders to him when he had first arrived were to seek him out immediately when he had obtained important information. He didn't know yet how important the dispatches were, but he decided he'd better err on the side of caution.

"Venez avec moi, capitaine. You are going to meet Lord Wellington."

Val had met Wellington only once or twice, and that very briefly. Now here he was, going to interrupt the general's dinner.

"Your dispatches better be worth it, Captain," Val muttered as they made their way to the general's quarters, which were in a house quite similar to the Gordons'. The door was opened by the general's aide-de-camp.

"Lord Wellington is at dinner, Lieutenant," he announced.

"I offer my deepest apologies to His Lordship, but I must speak to Captain Grant, sir."

"Just a moment."

Thank God it was Colquhoun Grant who opened the door a minute later. "You have something for me, Lieutenant Aston?" he asked with a welcoming smile.

"I *am* sorry to disturb you sir, but—"

"But I ordered you to do so, Aston. No need to apologize. What have we here?"

"Je suis Capitaine Moreau," the Frenchman announced before Val could answer.

"He was on his way back to France, sir. I found two packets on him," said Val, as he pulled the papers out of his jacket.

"Two, eh?"

"One sewn in his uniform and the other in the pommel of his saddle."

"Ah, I have heard of these special saddles, Captain. I will have to see it for myself tomorrow. You have given your parole?"

"Oui."

"Corporal Painter," Grant called.

Wellington's orderly appeared at the door.

"Show Captain Moreau to the tent behind mine."

"Yes, sir."

"Now, Lieutenant Aston, come on in. The general has invited you to have supper with us."

"Oh, no, sir, I couldn't," Val protested. "I am filthy and not at all fit for a general's table."

"Lord Wellington will not be surprised by your appearance, I assure you, Lieutenant."

Val scraped his boots and slapped at his jacket and trousers before entering the house. He could feel his chapped face and hands begin to burn from the welcome but sudden warmth from the fire.

"Come in, Lieutenant, come in."

It was only a small gathering, and not all the members of Wellington's "family" were present. But Major Gordon was there and Val was relieved to see a friendly face.

"I apologize for interrupting your supper, my lord."

"Nonsense. Captain Grant's orders take precedence over my soup. Now what is it he's brought us, Colquhoun?"

"A few pieces of paper with nothing of particular importance in them. Nothing we didn't know already," said Grant, passing the first packet over to Wellington.

Val's heart sank. All that effort for nothing. It happened often in reconnaissance work, of course. He knew that by now. More than half of what was captured was known already. But to interrupt Nosey's supper for it!

"On the other hand, what was hidden in the saddle is very valuable," Grant continued with a warm smile directed at Val. "It would appear to confirm our suspicions that someone is in close communication with the French about the political situation at home, my lord. This is directed at Bonaparte. Massena assures him that after your retreat into Portugal, all he has to do is wait for the government to fall."

"Which will likely happen if a Regency is declared, my lord," said Major Gordon. "We all know how fond the Prince is of the Whigs."

"He also assures Napoleon that the French people are full of confidence in their general and chief."

"I should only be as secure in my government's confidence, Major Gordon," said Wellington with dry humor. "They continue believing a dead man's opinion over mine. Poor John Moore should only have had such respect when he was alive, eh, Captain Grant? I keep telling them I can hold Portugal. But I must confess," he added with a sigh,

"I had expected the French would have been starved back to Spain by now."

"Massena is holding on because of this information being fed him, my lord."

"Well, we are snug behind the lines," said Wellington calmly as he cut a piece of pork into small pieces and ate it slowly and deliberately. "And if we must eventually leave, then we will leave like gentlemen, out of the hall door, not the back door." He took a sip of wine and looked over at Colquhoun Grant. "You will determine who is sending this information, will you not, Captain?"

"Of course, my lord."

Val was extremely grateful that Captain Grant did not add, "I've got Lieutenant Aston working on it," given his lack of progress.

"Tell me about this French officer, Lieutenant. How did he plan to make it across Spain?"

"He was carrying clothing in his saddlebags, my lord. It appears he was going to disguise himself as a Spanish peasant. He was lucky that when I caught him he was in uniform."

"You sound a bit hoarse, Lieutenant. I hope you are not ill? The wine should help," added Wellington, gesturing at Val's glass, which stood untouched by his plate.

Without thinking, Val brought his hand up to his throat. "I am not ill, my lord . . . I, uh, suppose it is a result of the Frenchman's attempt to choke me, my lord."

"What is this, Lieutenant? You were the one taken by surprise!"

Val blushed. Wellington's tone was humorous, but Val suspected there was a certain amount of displeasure behind the question. "I had fallen asleep in the early hours of the morning, my lord. But I had nothing on me that would have benefited the French, had he succeeded in taking me."

"That is a relief. And I suppose you are to be complimented if you were able to turn the situation around."

"Thank you, my lord." Val almost added, "I think."

He excused himself from cigars and port, pleading exhaustion. After he left, Wellington turned to Major Gordon. "So that is the young man who rescued Elspeth. He is obviously a good hand-to-hand fighter, eh? And lucky that he is so, or he would be sitting in a Frog tent at San-tarém," he added with a smile.

"Lieutenant Aston is one of my best men, my lord," said Grant. "Actually, it is he who I have working to uncover the traitor."

"Are you sure a man of action is the one for such a delicate task, Colquhoun?" asked Major Gordon.

"Absolutely. Don't be misled by his rough appearance, my lord. He has brains as well as brawn."

"There is something very familiar about him," mused Wellington, absentmindedly fingering his nose. Colquhoun ducked his head to hide a smile. "His beak is almost as prominent as mine," the general added. "I know of only a few men in England who could say that," he added, his eyes twinkling. "One of them is Charles Faringdon."

"Lieutenant Aston's father, sir."

"Indeed! Does Charles recognize him?"

"The lieutenant isn't very forthcoming about his background, my lord, but I surmise, from the little I've heard, that it is Mr. Aston who rejects the connection. Or until recently. It was the earl who purchased his commission."

"How long has he been in the army?"

"Twelve years, my lord."

"You mean he has spent twelve years in the ranks!"

Colquhoun glanced over at Ian Gordon and raised an eyebrow. Wellington's attitude toward his army was a para-doxical combination of personal disdain for the rank and file and a high regard for their safety. As a man he had no affection for the common soldier; as a general he avoided throwing them into unwinnable battles, for as he had once said, "We only have this army and we must take care of it."

Because of this, the men put their trust in him and were willing to follow him anywhere, thought Colquhoun. Warmth and affection might endear you to your men, but it didn't always save their lives the way Wellington's cold but strong sense of responsibility did.

Chapter 9

The news of the captured French officer was all over the camp by morning. Elspeth heard about it from her father at the breakfast table. She was surprised at the pang of anxiety she felt as she listened to her father tell the story. Lieutenant Aston could so easily have been overcome and ended up as a prisoner himself, she realized. Any exploring officer ran that risk daily, she told herself. But Lieutenant Aston was a friend and it was natural she should have some concern about him.

But when she met the lieutenant later that afternoon on her way back from camp, she found herself trembling in relief at the sight of him, hale and whole, and then chided herself for her reaction. Lieutenant Valentine Aston was certainly a man who could take care of himself and where on earth was her excessive sensibility around him coming from?

"Good afternoon, Miss Gordon," he said politely.

"Good afternoon, Lieutenant. I hear from my father that you have had another adventure, sir, and come out the hero again." Elspeth tried to keep her tone light.

"Not exactly, Miss Gordon," Val told her dryly. "The Frenchman surprised me and I was damned . . . I beg your pardon . . . very lucky to have been able to turn the tables on him."

"My father tells me the dispatches you discovered were very important."

"They were," said Val, "but I would not like to think they would become common gossip, Miss Gordon," he added gravely.

"I assure you, my father has shared information with my mother and me over the years and none of it has become gossip, common or otherwise. Good day, Lieutenant."

"Please wait, Miss Gordon," said Val, reaching out and grasping her arm. "I didn't mean to imply—"

"But you did, whether you meant to or not, Lieutenant."

Val let her go and ran his hand through his hair. "I suppose I did," he admitted, "but more as a warning than an insult, I assure you. I don't see you as a foolish woman, Miss Gordon. But secrecy is of the greatest importance in my work. I *am* sorry."

Elspeth took a deep breath. She was not usually quick to take offense, but proximity to Lieutenant Aston seemed to keep her off balance. "I accept your apology, Lieutenant," she said calmly.

"Will you also accept my escort back to the village?"

"Yes, thank you," Elspeth told him with a smile.

They walked side by side for a few minutes and then Elspeth said, "The weather has become cold, Lieutenant Aston. I imagine in the mountains it must be quite bitter."

Val gave her a rueful smile. "It is hard on the hands and face, Miss Gordon. I suspect I'll be chilblained for the rest of the winter."

"Do you think we will be here that long?"

"It seems that Massena is dug in, Miss Gordon."

"I can imagine it must be nerve-wracking for the troops to be sitting in limbo, but I am glad that I don't have to worry about my father for a while," she added with a wistful smile.

"It must have been hard for you and your mother to be so close to danger all these years," Val replied, the sympathy in his voice very obvious.

"It would be very much harder to be waiting at home, Lieutenant. To only know of a battle days after it happened, to have to wait for the casualty lists. . . . No, my mother decided long ago that it was worth every discomfort to have as much time with my father as she could."

"Would you do the same, if you were to marry a soldier?"

"Of course. But given my advanced age, I am unlikely to marry anyone." It was said humorously, but Val could hear an undercurrent of sadness in Elspeth's voice.

"You sound so sure, Miss Gordon, but you are an attractive young woman and have surely refused many offers besides mine," Val responded, keeping his tone light in response to hers.

"You are kind, Lieutenant, but clearly you have not moved much in Society if you think above-average height in a woman is à la mode."

"You know I have not, Miss Gordon," Val responded stiffly.

Elspeth stopped and put her hand on his arm. "I *am* sorry, Lieutenant. I was so caught up in my own concern that I forgot. I did not mean anything by my comment; I was only trying to be humorous about something that is somewhat painful to me. Although why it should be after all this time, I don't know," she continued. "After all, I have always been aware that a young woman who has spent most of her time with the army is unlikely to receive many proposals, but I wouldn't trade my life for one in Society."

"I don't think you are overly tall. You are not, for instance, as tall as Mrs. Casey," he added with a devilish grin.

Elspeth started to laugh helplessly and he joined her. When she finally caught her breath, she looked at Val and said, "Oh, dear, Lieutenant, if this is the way you give compliments to young ladies, I am not surprised you are alone." When she realized just what she had implied, Elspeth blushed and attempted to stammer out an apology while Val just stood there grinning at her discomfort.

"You are just going to let me put my foot in my mouth even further, aren't you, Lieutenant?"

"I was just curious, Miss Gordon, about what you would say next. You are correct, though. I have no, uh, entanglements of the female sort."

Elspeth giggled. "No, uh, entanglements of the female sort! What a delicate way of putting it, Lieutenant," she teased.

"Miss Gordon, you know I shouldn't be having this conversation with a respectable young lady."

"Yes, and you can see why I don't belong in Society, Lieutenant. Because I find myself having conversations with men that young ladies do not have. I suppose it comes of growing up around soldiers. We become comrades and speak freely to one another, which does not happen at assemblies, I assure you."

They were halfway to the village at a place where the path stopped climbing and began to go downhill.

"Come, Miss Gordon, shall we sit down and catch our breath?" asked Val, gesturing to a large boulder beside the path.

Neither she nor the lieutenant was really out of breath, thought Elspeth as she sat beside him. But she was happy to have an excuse to prolong their conversation. She felt that she had finally broken through his reserve and was feeling quite comfortable with him. The rock had absorbed some of the heat of the afternoon sun, which was still high enough to keep them comfortable.

"I think it is a shame that you have resigned yourself to spinsterhood, Miss Gordon," Val said quietly, breaking their comfortable silence. Elspeth was suddenly very aware that they were sitting very close to one another, so close that their thighs were lightly touching. "A man would have to be a fool to overlook your courage and honor and honesty."

Elspeth felt a warmth radiating through her that couldn't possibly be from the late autumn sun.

"Thank you for those kind words, Lieutenant," she said softly. "I would think a woman equally foolish who did not value the same qualities in you," she added.

"I am content to live and die a soldier," Val said lightly.

"That does not have to preclude a wife and children, Lieutenant." Elspeth turned at the same time as he faced her.

"Of course not, but I doubt they are in my future. You, however, would make a wonderful wife for a soldier, Miss Gordon." He said it with a sweet smile that softened his face in a way that went right to Elspeth's heart.

"Has any one of your soldier comrades ever told you that you have a very . . . lovely mouth, Miss Gordon?" Val said softly.

Elspeth ducked her head and shook it. Val put a finger under her chin and lifted it. "A very . . . kissable mouth, in fact." He reached up and ran his thumb by the side of her mouth. They both sat very still and then Val traced her cheek with his finger.

Was he going to show her that she did have a kissable mouth? Elspeth wondered. Was she going to let him? Of course she was, she thought, as unfamiliar but somehow recognizable sensations flooded her. But just as they were leaning in to one another, they heard someone coming up the path and drew back.

Val stood up quickly. "Someone is coming, Miss Gordon. Ah, it is Private Ryan. Perhaps you can escort Miss Gordon the rest of the way, Private?"

Elspeth could do nothing but nod and stammer a "Yes, of course, Lieutenant Aston. I don't want to inconvenience you. Good afternoon."

"Good afternoon, Miss Gordon."

He *had* been going to kiss her, hadn't he? Or was he just being kind? Yet he seemed so eager to get rid of her that of *course* he hadn't been meaning to kiss her. Had she appeared to solicit a kiss? Was that why the reserved look was back on his face when he said good-bye? Elspeth blushed scarlet at the memory of their conversation. She had been much too frank. Perhaps he thought her free with her kisses because she was so free with words? But they had been so comfortable together. And then delightfully uncomfortable . . . delightful to her, at least. But she couldn't know what the lieutenant had felt and was unlikely ever to find out.

Val felt as though he had been ambushed by desire and was as shaken by it as by the French captain's attack. He had been sitting there, quite innocently enjoying his friendly conversation with Miss Gordon, not even aware that she had gotten underneath his guard, and then he had turned to face her. The sun had been on her hair, revealing the glints of red hidden among the strands of brown. Her lips had been parted and he realized that her mouth was wide and generous and as tempting as a ripe summer berry. He told himself he was only trying to reassure her when he told her of her kissable mouth. But if Patrick Ryan hadn't come up the path at that moment, he would have had to show her just how kissable she was, and that would have been disastrous.

But first it would have been delightful, he was sure, he thought with a sigh. And different. What would it have been like to share a kiss with a woman who hadn't experienced many kisses—perhaps none? Of course, he hadn't done a lot of kissing himself. Whores got right down to business. And he hadn't spent much time kissing the other women he'd had. It could be a new pleasure, gently exploring Miss Gordon's lips. Except that he would make sure it would never happen. They were unlikely to be alone together again, thank God. And he was off again tomorrow.

Chapter 10

The Light Horse Regiment arrived in camp two days later. As they rode in, Charles Faringdon, Viscount Holme, found it very difficult to keep his eyes front, he was so eager to see if he could spy Val. But his brother was nowhere in sight, and it was only hours later, after settling his men, that he was able to present himself at Captain Grant's tent and inquire after his brother.

"Captain Grant."

"Good afternoon, Lord Holme. Welcome to Portugal." Colquhoun knew something of Val's history after all their years of serving together and he knew the young man in front of him was responsible for Val's commission.

"I was wondering if you might know where I can find Lieutenant Aston, Captain."

"Sit down, Lord Holme. I have wanted to say thank you to the man responsible for giving me such an able officer."

Charlie gave Grant his warmest smile. "I tried to get Val to accept a commission for years, Captain. I finally convinced him it would be very bad for one brother to be serving in the ranks when the other was an officer, though I do think he was finally beginning to want it for himself. Is he in camp?"

"I am sorry to say he is away, and probably won't be back till tomorrow evening at the earliest. But I'll tell him you have arrived as soon as he reports to me."

"Thank you, sir."

* * *

It was hard to wait another day, but Charlie supposed he could manage after six years. The last time he had seen his brother had been when Val visited him in London before leaving for the Caribbean. Six years of keeping in touch by letter, and worrying from one missive to the next if he would hear his brother had been wounded or died of a tropical fever. Now, of course, he could worry about whether Val would make it back from his latest mission without being captured or killed. But at least they would *see* one another, face-to-face.

He was walking back to his quarters when he heard someone call him. It was George Trowbridge, who had been a few years ahead of him at school. George hadn't been a friend, but Charlie was happy just to see a familiar face.

"It's good to see you, George. I just arrived today and am all at sixes and sevens."

"This is your first time out, isn't it?"

"It is. I only received my commission last year and we've been posted in Sussex until now."

"You picked a good time to arrive, Faringdon. It looks like we're settled in for the winter and no fighting before the spring. Except for the cold and boredom, it isn't a bad billeting. Not a wide choice of women, but a few pretty baggages around the baggage, if you know what I mean," he added with a wink and a leer. "We lowly junior officers don't dine with Nosey and his family, of course, but Major and Mrs. Gordon have been very good to us poor 'orphans.' I am sure you will receive an invitation to dinner."

"Major Ian Gordon?"

"Do you know him?"

"I met him and his family a few years ago when they were on leave in London. He was at Assaye with Wellington, wasn't he?"

"He may have been. I know he and his daughter and his wife spent many years in the East."

"Is Miss Gordon here in Portugal also?"

"She's been following the drum for years, evidently. A good sort of girl, easy to talk to, but not really my type. Too tall and plain, for one thing. But she can put you at your ease, I must say that for her. I say, Faringdon, here comes Lucas Stanton. You remember him?"

Charlie turned and hoped that the smile on his face looked like a smile and not the grimace it felt like.

" 'Tis practically a reunion, isn't it, George?" said Lucas, clapping Charlie on the shoulder. "We've got Faringdon and you and James; oh, and Aston too, though he was hardly at school long enough to count . . . or learn to count," Stanton added derisively.

Charlie disliked very few people, but Lucas Stanton was one of them. "Dislike" was almost too mild a term. The winter would be very long indeed if he had to suffer the company of these men very often. He wondered how Val was coping with Lucas's presence.

"Oh, but, Charles, I am sorry." Lucas was offering him a patently false apology. "Aston is your half-brother, isn't he? Now how could I have forgotten that? You must excuse me."

Charlie was sure that Lucas Stanton had not forgotten a thing, but he accepted the man's apology as though it were sincere.

"Aston has turned out surprisingly well, after all, wouldn't you say, George?"

George, whom Charlie remembered as a weak-willed follower rather than an instigator of any bullying, tried to make up for the thinly disguised dislike in Stanton's voice. "Captain Grant thinks very highly of your, uh, brother, Charles."

"I am happy to hear it, but I am not at all surprised," Charlie replied. "Val was always good at fighting tyrants, as I recall," he said pointedly. "Well, gentlemen, I must get myself settled in. I am looking forward to a dinner at the Gordons.

No wonder Val had been happy to have been called away from his regiment, if it got him away from the likes of Lucas Stanton, Charlie thought as he walked back to his tent.

The next morning he attended a briefing for all the officers and after it was over, Major Gordon approached him.

"Welcome to the lines, Charlie."

"Thank you, Major. It is good to find a familiar face."

"Mrs. Gordon and I like to have the young officers in to dine with us occasionally. Will you join us tonight?"

"I would be very grateful, Major."

"We are hoping that your, er, brother will be back in time to make up one of the company."

"So am I, Major Gordon."

Charlie smiled as he watched the major walk away. No one seemed able to allude to his relationship with Val without some hemming and hawing, as though it were something to be embarrassed about. Well, he'd met with that attitude over the years and he hadn't let it bother him before, so he was damned if it would now.

He was out drilling his men when he spied the lone horseman coming down out of the hills. He hoped it might be Val, and as the rider got closer he was sure of it. Both man and horse looked exhausted. Charlie, whose hand was lifted to send his men off on another saber charge, kept it there while he watched his brother ride by. It was only when his own horse gave a little crow-hop that he realized his men had been awaiting his signal and as he swept his hand down and yelled, "Charge!" his feelings almost overwhelmed him. He had missed his brother for twelve long years. Oh, they had written and spent that lovely long day in London together. But he had hoped for something so different when he first had found him. He had hoped they would all become one family.

Well, he had been young and perhaps foolish to have hoped for that. He was older now and much more aware of the complexities of the situation. But at least they were together again and this time he wasn't going to let Val's ridiculous pride separate them.

Charlie cut his drilling short after warning his men not to be too eager. It was a hard balance to achieve, he told them. They needed to put everything they had into a charge and at the same time not let themselves get swept too far into enemy territory.

He handed his horse over to one of his corporals and hurried off to change. He was to dine at the Gordons' and so was Val. He wanted to be at his brother's tent before Val finished his report.

* * *

Charlie was coming down the row just as Val was lifting his tent flap.

"Val!"

Val let the tent flap fall and turned. The man who faced Charlie was not the youth he'd last seen, but a man. A soldier. His face was browned by the sun except for the places where it was reddened from the cold winds that blew through the Portuguese mountains. There was a thin scar that ran from his ear along his jaw and his face was thinner than Charlie remembered. But his eyes were the same clear gray.

"Don't you recognize me, Val?" Charlie asked with an endearingly diffident smile.

"Charlie? I knew you were to arrive soon. Was that your regiment I saw drilling when I rode in?"

"Indeed. With me in command."

"With you in command," Val repeated with a bemused smile. "How could my little brother be old enough to command a cavalry regiment?" Val stepped forward, his hand outstretched. Charlie grasped it and they looked into each other's eyes for a moment. Charlie could feel his own eyes fill, but he'd be damned if he'd let Val see the tears, so he pulled his brother by the hand into a back-pounding embrace. When they finally pulled away from one another, Charlie was surprised and moved to see the sheen of tears in his brother's eyes.

"It has been a long time, Charlie. I barely recognized you in your uniform, and with at least another inch of you! You practically tower over me—or is that the boots?" Val teased.

"It's all me. My mother's family ran tall. And it is barely an inch or two—"

"At least three, my lord," Val replied with mock servility.

"Don't you 'my lord' me, Valentine. And if it has been a long time, whose fault is that?" Charlie asked with a smile. Then, with a spark of real anger, he pulled himself away and said, "Damn it, Val, I've *missed* you. Why in God's name did you run off?"

"I've missed you too, Charlie," Val replied softly. "But you know why I ran off. I had no choice."

"You bloody well did. You could have stayed at school—"

"Hardly!"

"All right, then, you could have asked Father to send you to Yorkshire. Surely running the estate would have been preferable to a life as a common soldier?"

"We've been over this before, Charlie. It hasn't been such a bad life these past twelve years," Val replied mildly. "I've learned far more than I would have at Queen's Hall. And except for the commission, I did it all on my own."

"Oh, Lord, I don't want to quarrel with you, Val. I am just so happy to see you."

"And I, you, little brother. Though not so little and looking very handsome, I might add." Val gave a rueful grin. "I, on the other hand, look like hell," he said, looking down at his travel-stained uniform and dirty boots. "Come in while I clean up."

"I am dressed for dinner at the Gordons'," Charlie announced after he sat down on the edge of the cot. "Are you going?"

Val, who had his face buried in his washing bowl, lifted his head. "I don't know that I am expected . . ." He glanced over to the small table that served as his desk. "Perhaps I am. Pass me that piece of paper, will you, Charlie?" Val unfolded it and read it. "It appears I am, though I should excuse myself from this one," he said, looking down at his trousers in despair. "I think I have a clean uniform. . . ."

"Do come, Val. We don't have to stay late, but I've been looking forward to seeing you for days."

"Oh, all right, but if I fall asleep at the table, jab me awake, will you?"

Chapter 11

As they walked down to the village a half hour later, Charlie stole a glance over at his brother. He was dressed in a clean uniform and looked very handsome in a gypsyish way. His broad shoulders and muscled thighs gave him a solidity, a groundedness that Charlie did not think he himself possessed. But then, Val had been in the infantry these past twelve years. And though he himself was still slender, he filled out his tunic quite satisfactorily, he told himself.

When they passed two of the village women along the way, Charlie nodded and smiled. He could feel their eyes following and, when he turned, saw their appreciative glances.

"There are two women who will be dreaming of a handsome English lieutenant tonight, Charlie," Val joked as he followed his brother's glance.

"If they dream of anyone, it will be you."

"Me? Not with you next to me. Why, your hair matches the gilt on your epaulets, Charlie!"

Val meant what he said. His little brother had grown into a classically handsome young man who in almost every way resembled his father. But his nose and his height he got from his mother. It was ironic that the illegitimate son had inherited the earl's one distinctive feature, Val thought humorously.

And his father's pride and reserve, he admitted as he watched Charlie greet the Gordons. Charlie had never lost what had endeared him to Val in the first place: his warm and open nature, which was something else that must have come from his mother.

James, who had been standing by the fire, came over to greet Charlie after the Gordons' welcome.

"It is good to see you, Charlie," he said quietly.

"James! It is wonderful you are here," Charlie replied, taking his hand eagerly.

"This is the man who broke my sister's heart by taking a commission, Val," James teased.

"Don't you listen to him. I only danced with the chit twice, James, and you know it."

"Ah, but you took her in to supper."

"Yes, and bored her to death, I am sure."

"You made a great impression on her, Charles."

"Stepped on her feet three times if I did it once, James. That's the impression I made!"

"And here I thought it a match made in heaven," said James with mock sadness.

"Now, now, Lieutenant, Maddie told me about the handsome Viscount Holme who took her in to supper," said Elspeth, her eyes laughing.

"Did she also tell you, that in addition to breaking her arch—*arch*, James, not heart—I spilled punch on her gown?"

"She may have added a postscript about that, my lord," Elspeth admitted.

"It was a few years ago," protested Charlie. "My awkward period, don't you know!"

They all laughed and then Elspeth gestured toward the table. "Shall we, gentlemen?"

"Are Trowbridge and Stanton not expected, then?" James asked.

"Elspeth thought a smaller table would be nicer this evening, given that it is Lieutenant Aston's reunion with his brother," Mrs. Gordon informed them.

"I am very grateful for your thoughtfulness, Miss Gordon," Val said quietly.

"It is nothing, Lieutenant. Now, Jamie, you sit next to me. Lord Faringdon, you on my other side so Lieutenant Aston can talk to you more easily."

Val was touched by Elspeth's recognition of his and Charlie's relationship and thankful he didn't have to deal with Lucas Stanton tonight. Given how tired he was, it would have been difficult to keep his temper had the man delivered any of his subtle insults.

"Tell us, Charlie, what was the mood at home when you left?" asked the major.

"They are laying bets in all the clubs on the prince's loyalty to his Whig friends if he becomes regent, Major Gordon."

"Don't you mean *when,* Lieutenant? Surely a Regency is inevitable given the king's, uh, state of mind."

"I suppose so, sir."

"If the Whigs come in, then Wellington's campaign is doomed," continued the major. "Ach, 'tis a hard thing to be a soldier with Whiggish tendencies tha' now," continued the major, falling into the Scots vernacular.

"Surely you are not a Republican, though, Major Gordon?"

"No, no, Charles. I do not think changes brought about

by bloodshed ever last. Look what happened in France. In the end, they traded a king for an emperor."

"Although we must admit Napoleon kept most of the legislative reforms that came out of the Revolution," interjected James.

"But he plays puppet master with all of Europe, James," Val protested. "Setting his brother on the throne of Spain."

"I don't agree at all with his methods, Val, which is why I am here, but the reforms Joseph Bonaparte would institute in Spain are long overdue, don't you agree? The Bourbons were hardly a model monarchy," he added dryly. "What do you think, Charlie?"

"I am here because I believe that if Boney succeeds in Spain and Portugal, his next step will be to invade England. I confess I haven't thought much further. I've never considered myself a Tory, but if they are willing to stand behind Wellington, then I hope the king undergoes a miraculous recovery!"

"Well, I think it a shame that you men let yourself be bound by a system that leaves you no choice between Whig and Tory," said Elspeth. "There is some truth on both sides. Indeed, if I could vote, I'd want someone who could reach beyond party politics, someone who believed in reform, but also saw the necessity of stopping a man who wishes to impose equality by force," she continued passionately.

James lifted his glass and, leaning forward, touched it to Elspeth's. "Hear, hear, Miss Gordon. Perhaps someday women will have the vote and we might see a different society."

Elspeth's cheeks were flushed and a few strands of her hair had escaped as though they shared her passion for freedom. Val thought her fervor lit her from the inside out. The unconventional Miss Gordon was a passionate woman, he thought appreciatively.

"Shall we return to the parlor, Ian?" asked Mrs. Gordon.

Val was thankful for the interruption, for he could feel the stirring of desire.

"Only if you give us some music this evening, Peggy, to lighten our moods," said her husband. "My wife, who is very talented on the keyboard, has had to make do for these many years, haven't you, Peggy? Of necessity, she has become very versatile on various portable instruments," he added proudly, as Mrs. Gordon brought out a small guitar.

"Stringed instruments, yes, Ian. But Private Ryan is a maestro on the squeezebox. Will you join us later, Patrick?" she asked the orderly, who was in the middle of serving them port.

"Sure, and I'd be happy to, ma'am."

Mrs. Gordon strummed a few chords and then began to play. At first she offered them some plaintive Portuguese tunes, and then a Spanish waltz.

Val had loved music from childhood, for his mother had had a fortepiano and played regularly. But he hadn't had much music in his life since then. Pub songs, when George Burton had come home roaring drunk. The village carols. Hymns at Sunday services. And the usual marches and songs of war since he'd joined the army. The combination of the rich port and the sounds of the guitar strings relaxed and worked on him, opening doors that he had closed and locked long ago.

"I am very drawn to the music of Spain," Mrs. Gordon confessed, "although it is often in a minor key."

"Gi'e us some Bobby Burns, Peggy."

She smiled over at her husband. "Here is one that goes along with our dinner table conversation, Ian."

Major Gordon possessed a wonderful baritone voice and it was clear that the Gordon family sang together often, Val realized, when Elspeth joined in on the last verses:

> For a' that, an' a' that,
> It's comin' yet for a' that,
> That man to man the world o'er
> Shall brithers be for a' that."

"Another chorus, Mrs. Gordon," demanded Charlie, flinging his arm over Val's shoulder as they sang.

"I've never heard that sung before, Major Gordon," said James, after the last notes rang out.

"Oh, aye, amongst the Sassenach, Bobby is better known for his love songs, not that they aren't something to be proud of too."

Mrs. Gordon began to strum and nodded at Elspeth, who began in a rich alto voice "Ae Fond Kiss."

> "Had we never lov'd sae kindly
> Had we never lov'd sae blindly
> Never met or never parted—
> We had ne'er been broken-hearted."

Val couldn't close the door quickly enough. Before he realized it, he had been carried back to his mother's cottage and she was singing the same song as he lay in bed, unable to sleep. He had crept down the stairs, meaning to ask her for warm milk, when she stopped playing in the middle of the next verse. He'd sat down on the last step, realizing his mother was crying, very quietly, but as though her heart was indeed broken. "Oh, I thought I could bear it, could live the rest of my life on that last kiss," she was saying, her voice choked with tears.

She was crying about his father, Val had thought, as he crept very quietly back to bed. He'd seen the occasional tear in her eye when she spoke of him, but Val had never before realized the depth of her loss. Of course, now he knew it was the Earl of Faringdon's desertion that had broken her heart.

His eyes glazed with tears as he remembered. Dear God, he'd disgrace himself if he wasn't more careful, he thought as he quickly wiped the corner of his eyes.

Thank God Mrs. Gordon switched to a livelier song and by the time the chorus of "Green Grow the Rashes" came around, Val was able to join in. Then Mrs. Gordon looked over at her husband. "Will you gi'e us another, Ian?"

Major Gordon stood up and moved over to the mantel so that he was looking directly at his wife as he sang: "O, my luve's like a red, red, rose . . ."

What would it be like to love a woman like that? wondered Val as he watched the major and his wife. Some of his own sweetest hours had been spent "among the lasses, o," but friendly and playful lust could hardly compare to the devotion he saw between the major and his wife. Despite the gray in her hair and the lines on her face, Peggy Gordon was obviously still a newly sprung rose to the major, their love as rich and alive as those roses in Val's mother's garden.

Damn, he would *not* think of his mother, and he managed finally to close the doors that had begun to open inside himself.

"You and Mrs. Gordon are as excellent partners in music as you are in life," said James, breaking the silence that reigned when the last strains of music had died away.

"It was the luckiest day of my life when I met Peggy," said the major with a broad smile.

"The Scots are an interesting mix, Major Gordon," said Charlie. "I know that the Highland regiments are fierce fighters, but your countryman's songs go right to the heart."

"Oh, aye, laddie, we are very different from yer cold Sassenach: wild in war and warm in love."

"Now, Ian, don't start," warned Mrs. Gordon. "You are insulting our guests!"

"Ach, well, they can't help being what they were born," said the major, a teasing gleam in his eye. "And I confess I am thankful that Wellington is a cool and logical Sassenach, after all."

They all laughed at Major Gordon's seemingly grudging admiration for a man they knew he held in the highest esteem.

"Shall we have Patrick in, Mama?"

Mrs. Gordon looked over at Val, who was trying to hide a yawn behind his hand. "I think Lieutenant Aston has had enough, Elspeth. Another evening."

Val spluttered an apology. "No, no, bring in Private Ryan, ma'am. It is only the port."

"It is the hours you've been riding the hills, Lieutenant. No, we will call it an evening, shall we?" Mrs. Gordon said it so graciously and sympathetically that Val did not feel the least embarrassed.

As he and Charlie and James walked back to the camp, Charlie said, "What a lovely evening. I envy the Gordon family," he added with a note of wistfulness in his voice. "There is such obvious affection between them all."

"Yes," agreed James. "And I am always amazed that no one has had the sense to fall in love with Elspeth."

"Love has nothing to do with *sense*," Charlie told him

with a grin. "If men and women loved those whom it was reasonable to love . . . why, the human race would probably have died out by now."

James laughed, but Val thought he heard a trace of sadness in his friend's voice when he replied, "I suppose you are right, Charlie. Good evening to you both," he added as they came to his tent.

Val's quarters were next and he and Charlie stood awkwardly outside for a minute.

"I've read Burns, of course, but I've never heard 'A Man's a Man' sung before tonight," Charlie said.

"It's a good song for you to sing, Charlie, for it is who you are: a good, honest man, 'tho' e'er so rich,' " Val told him, smiling as he changed the verse. "You take everyone as he is . . . you took me as I was, and for that I was forever grateful. I am glad we 'brithers be'," he added, putting his hand on Charlie's arm.

"And so am I, Val, so am I."

Despite the fact that he was exhausted—or perhaps because of it—Val did not fall asleep immediately. He lay there on his cot while Burns' melodies played inside his head. What was it about music that touched the heartstrings? Val smiled at the aptness of the word. It was as though the strings of the fortepiano or fiddle or guitar caused a sympathetic stirring in the heart and aroused one's emotions to a depth that nothing else could. Oh, the drums could stir you and the Highlanders' damned pipers drive you to a fighting frenzy, but the music tonight made him feel what he hadn't felt for years.

Robert Burns believed in the equality of man no matter what his rank. No, the *brotherhood* of man. The Gordons and Charlie and James also seemed to believe it. Then why was it so hard for him?

Oh, at some level, of course, he knew he was the equal of any man; twelve years of soldiering had taught him that. He didn't think he regarded military rank or the lack of it as very important. Nor did he envy Charlie his viscountcy or eventual earldom. If he envied Charlie anything, it was his father. But damn it, he didn't want Faringdon for a father. He was so tired he was getting it all mixed up in his head. He guessed what he envied was that Charlie had

had a father and mother. Parents who were married and presumably faithful. All he had—and it was ironic, wasn't it?—was the same father, who had been outstandingly unfaithful.

But as James and Charlie had said, love never was reasonable. He wondered about James. Did that note of sadness in his voice mean that he had loved someone whom it made no "sense" for him to love? He hoped someone, someday soon, would have the sense to love Elspeth Gordon, was his last incoherent thought as he finally drifted off to sleep.

Chapter 12

Mrs. Casey was aware of the arrival of any new officers and presented herself at the earliest opportunity. She was at Charlie's tent the next afternoon, waiting for him when he returned from his duties.

"Good afternoon, my lord. I am Mrs. Mags Casey."

"Er, how do you do, Mrs. Casey?" Charlie was a bit taken aback by the woman in front of him, who didn't have to look up because she was almost the same height.

"I wanted to bid you welcome to Portugal, sir."

"Why, thank you very much," Charlie replied, wondering just what sort of welcome she had in mind. Surely the camp followers hadn't started drumming up business in such a direct manner?

"I was wondering if you have anyone to do laundry for you."

Ah, so that was what this was about. Charlie didn't like rejecting anyone, but the thought of taking this Amazon to bed would have driven him to it. He was happy to be able to employ Mrs. Casey in a different way.

"Why, no, I haven't had time, but I must confess my dirty shirts are piling up since I arrived in Portugal!"

"Just as I supposed, my lord. This is how I work . . ." Mrs. Casey told him matter-of-factly, and proceeded to explain.

"That seems all right and tight, Mrs. Casey," Charlie replied. "I can give you a bundle today. Do you do sheets too?"

"Yes, indeed, my lord. And if you want a reference, you can just ask Lieutenant Aston. I am sure he would vouch for me."

"So you take care of my brother's laundry too," said Charlie as he stuffed his shirts into a pillow slip.

"The lieutenant is your brother? Why, he doesn't look a bit like you, my lord."

"He is my half-brother, Mrs. Casey, and he resembles his mother. Except for his nose," Charlie added with a smile.

Mrs. Casey grinned and took the laundry from him. "I'll have this back to you in a few days, my lord. And if any other woman should approach you, you just tell her I've got your needs taken care of. At least as far as clean clothes are concerned," she added with a smile and a wink.

"Yes, well, er, thank you, Mrs. Casey," Charlie stammered as his face got red.

Later that evening, as she was getting ready to slip into Will Tallman's cot, Mags told him of her discovery. "If Lieutenant Aston is Lord Holme's half-brother, then he must be the by-blow of the earl, Will. And him a common soldier all these years!" she added with amazement.

"He doesn't like to speak of it, Mags," Will cautioned her.

"You knew about him all this time and never told me!"

"It was not my secret to tell, Mags. Of course, now that his brother's here, he'll not keep it such a secret, but there is no need to go gossiping about it."

Mrs. Casey left the buttons on her night rail undone and slipped under the covers. "Oh, your feet be cold, Will. And your legs too," she teased as she trailed her hand up his thigh. "And what's this between them? A block of ice?"

"It just needs the touch of your warm hand, Mags," said Will with a delighted groan as she stroked him.

"It was a pleasant surprise to find this on such a small man," murmured Mags.

"It is not that I am so small. It is just that you are a big woman, Mags."

"And don't you like big women, Will?"

"You know I do, Mags. Oh, you know I do," Will reassured her, as he rolled her over on her back and began to push her night rail up. His hands kneaded her buttocks and she drew her legs up to meet him.

" 'Tis only with a woman like you that I'm not afraid I'll hurt her, being so large and all," he teased.

Mags playfully cuffed his ear. "Oh, don't be so full of yourself, Will!"

"I want you full of me, Mags," he whispered as he thrust into her.

"Oh, yes, Will, yes," she moaned in delight.

They both lay there contentedly afterward, Will's arm around Mags and her head turned into his shoulder. It was one of the things she most liked about him, the way he was affectionate afterward, rather than just rolling over and going to sleep, or worse, sending her back to her own tent like some men might do.

"You are a fine woman, Mags," he murmured, stroking her hair.

"If I am such a fine woman and I satisfy you so well, Will Tallman, then why won't you make an honest woman of me?"

"Mags, let's not start. I am just not a marrying sort of man. I told you that in the beginning, and I haven't changed. Soldiers shouldn't ever marry," he added. "It leaves too many widows."

"Do you think I'd mourn you any less if you died tomorrow, Will, just because we aren't married?"

"Of course not, Mags," he said soothingly. "But that just proves my point. Why do we *need* to get married, if it won't change our feelings for each other? Now go to sleep, woman."

"I'll give it up for tonight," Mrs. Casey muttered, "but you'll be hearing from me again, Will Tallman."

"Aye, I'm sure I will, Mags," Will replied with dry humor.

He lay awake for a while after she fell asleep. Mags Casey was certainly not the first woman he'd had since he joined the army, but he did wonder if she might be the last. He took all the teasing about the unlikeliness of their coupling in good humor. He was himself rather amused by their difference in size. He'd always preferred small women before Mags, but from the first time he'd seen her, stirring a kettle full of officers' shirts and joking with the other women, he'd been attracted to her. Now all she had to do was walk into his tent and his cock stood at attention. He'd be happy to spend every night with her, and aye, most of the day too, if it had been possible. But he'd made up his mind a long time ago that he would never marry as long as he was a soldier. He had no objection to having the same woman every night. But if that woman were his wife . . . well, it would be a worry and a distraction when he went into battle, for one thing. And he needed to feel free, though whenever he tried to explain this to Mags, they quarreled.

"I just don't want to be tied down, Mags," he would say. "Nor to be worried about my wife while I am fighting."

"You want to be free for another woman, is that it? Maybe Lucy Brown, who's been twitching her bottom at you for months?"

"I don't want another woman, Mags. I'm very happy to have it be you in my bed each night. I just like knowing I *could* have one if I wanted to."

"You don't have to worry about Boney's soldiers, Will Tallman. I'll kill you myself before I'll let anyone else have you!" Mags said it so fiercely that Will believed her.

Well, it would likely be a Frog that got him, for all her threats, for he truly had no desire for another woman. Mags suited him just fine—as long as she was content to stay Mrs. Casey.

Over the next few weeks, the weather turned warmer, but since the milder temperatures were accompanied by rain, the men were made more uncomfortable. The paths were all mud, the tents were wet through and dripped constantly, and there wasn't a dry, much less clean, stitch of clothing in the whole encampment.

Val much preferred dry cold and snow to the incessant icy rain that pelted him as he rode through the hills. His only consolation was that the French had to be as miserable. Probably more so, since they had less food.

Of course, the British troops were doing more drinking than eating, but Val couldn't blame them for keeping themselves warm in any way they could. But quarrels broke out on the hour, or so it seemed, and at least twice a day some of them turned violent, which led to the perpetrators being flogged.

"It is two weeks to Christmas, Lieutenant. If this bloody rain doesn't stop, the men will be ready to swim back home for their holidays!" said Captain Grant. "I almost wish the damned Frogs would attack; it would give the men something to do!"

"If it makes you feel any better, the French have been doing their share of fighting and flogging," Val told his commanding officer with an ironic grin.

"Our troops' behavior only confirms Wellington's view of them. It is hard to convince him that not every British soldier is a drunken brawler."

"Perhaps if there was something to promise the men?"

"Dry clothes? Sun? Plum pudding for Christmas dinner?"

"If we are lucky, the weather will change and we will all dry out for Christmas. But what if His Lordship planned a holiday party? Or even a ball?" suggested Val.

"For the enlisted men?"

"A ball for the officers and for the local dignitaries. Music and feasting for the men. If we started now, we just might be able to round up enough chickens for a stew. Maybe even come up with a piglet or two! I think I can vouch for being more successful at that assignment than smoking out our spy, Captain," Val added.

"No luck, then?"

"Whoever it is, he's damn good. We know it is an officer. My guess is that it is one with Whig sympathies. But there are a few of them, and none strike me as a traitor." Val paused. "I would of course prefer it to be someone like Lucas Stanton, but he is constantly spouting Tory rhetoric."

"Which makes for a good cover," said Captain Grant.

"Indeed," said Val thoughtfully. "I have considered bringing in reinforcements," he added with a grin.

"Oh?"

"Mrs. Casey does some officers' laundry. She has regular access to their tents. But I hesitate to bring a woman into this."

"I agree with you, Lieutenant. We'll save Mrs. Casey for a last resort."

Chapter 13

Lord Wellington was easily persuaded to agree to a Christmas ball in Mafra, for he could see that even his officers' tempers were severely strained by the weather.

"And the men? What might we do for them, Colquhoun?"

"A double ration of rum on the day, sir."

Wellington snorted. "The last thing they need!"

"Not if you cut the rations slightly in the next few weeks with the promise of a Christmas feast at the end. Maybe even offer a few prizes for a marksmanship contest. Something to look forward to and focus their attention, my lord."

"And where is this feast to come from, Captain?"

"I thought I would utilize a few of my exploring officers, my lord. Perhaps send Lieutenant Aston back into the mountains. The guerrilleros are experts at foraging. I don't think the French will be going anywhere in this weather, my lord," he added reassuringly.

"Well, if anyone can find food in this country, it is you," Wellington told him with an approving nod.

Nine days before Christmas it stopped raining and in one afternoon the temperature dropped below freezing. Overnight, the ground, which had been ankle-deep in mud, froze into an uneven terrain of wheel ruts and bootprints. The tents were stiff with ice and on every puddle a silver skin of ice had formed.

Val rode out early in the morning and when he turned

to look back at the camp, he smiled. The ice on the tents and the few trees were lit by the winter sun so that everything sparkled. Even the ice in the wheel ruts and puddles were shining. "It is enough to fill a man with holiday spirit," he told Caesar as they rode into the hills. "Let's hope we're successful in finding food."

When he reached Sanchez's stronghold, he was met by Jack Belden.

"I am afraid you have ridden a long way for nothing, Lieutenant Aston," the captain told him. "The weather has kept the French quiet and we haven't a single dispatch!"

"My mission is far more serious than collecting the odd dispatch," Val said dramatically.

"Indeed?"

"I have been commanded to invite you to a ball on Christmas day," Val continued with a grin.

"A ball!"

"Lord Wellington believes that a holiday celebration is just what the men need to keep their minds off the discomfort of a Portuguese winter. Many of them are finding it far more difficult to sit still than to do a twenty-mile-a-day march."

"A ball, eh? Just whom will we be dancing with? Each other?" Belden asked with a wry smile.

"There are a number of respectable local women as well as some officers' wives."

"Well, you can count on me and the colonel."

"Good. But there is another task I've been set, Captain. Procuring provisions for the men's dinner."

"Now, that will take some doing, Lieutenant!"

"Captain Grant and a number of us are out foraging. I suspect he is hoping for a miracle along the lines of the loaves and fishes. If we all come back with something and the men contribute what they have, together with a double ration of rum, it should feel like a holiday feast."

"We do have a cache of potatoes, Lieutenant. We could spare you some of those. And there *are* the piglets, of course," he added with a twinkle in his eye.

"Piglets! A roast pig would be just the thing," cried Val.

"I don't know that I can get you more than one, for the cook has been planning to make sausage out of them.

Speaking of which, I can also send you back with some to flavor the potatoes."

The piglets were penned behind the small ruined house that served as a cook station. Val listened as Jack bargained with the cook. The viscount was so fluent and the bargaining so quick that he missed some of what was being said.

"He says you can have the runt," said Jack as the cook threw up his hands and retreated into the house.

It was easier said than done, Val realized as the two of them chased the piglet around the pen. Finally the viscount dove for him and managed to grab his hind legs.

"You had better save me a slice of pork loin," Jack threatened as he looked down at his jacket. "I'll have to settle for the feast, since no one will dance with me in this jacket!"

Val rode off that afternoon with a good fifteen pounds of potatoes and a dozen links of sausage in one saddlebag, and a squealing piglet in the other. It was only two days until the full moon, so he was able to pick his way down the track fairly easily until midnight, when he finally stopped to rest.

"All right, piggy," he crooned as he lifted the little animal out and tied him to a bush. He drew his blanket around him and, leaning back against a rock, closed his eyes. He was just nodding off when the squealing began.

He could hear the pig trotting back and forth and back and forth, and decided to try ignoring it. He's bound to exhaust himself, he thought. But the plaintive whining continued.

"Bloody animal! You'll bring someone down on us if you don't shut up." He walked over to the bush and the little animal pressed against his leg.

"It is company you want? You are missing your mother and brothers, I suppose." Val untied the rope and led the piglet over to where he had been resting. "All right, all right, if this will keep you quiet, you can sleep next to me, you wretched runt."

The piglet was not content to sleep outside the blanket, however. He lifted it up with his snout and scrabbled under it, giving a contented little sigh as he sank down next to Val.

"You are a *pig,* sir, not a dog," Val told him sternly. The pig only gave a little grunt and pulled closer. Val gave a helpless sigh and resigned himself to his fate.

The next morning he was awakened by a wet tongue scraping across his face. "Ugh, get down, you blasted pig, or I'll slit your throat right here!" The little animal just cocked his head to one side and gave Val such a bright-eyed, knowing look he had to laugh.

It was hard getting the squealing animal into his saddle-bag again, but he finally accomplished it and after a few minutes of squealing, the piglet was finally soothed by the rhythmic motion of the horse and remained quiet for the rest of the ride home.

Val unloaded the potatoes and sausage and carried them to Captain Grant's tent.

"Is the captain in?" he asked his orderly.

"Yes, sir. You can go right in."

"Welcome back, Lieutenant. I hear you succeeded in getting us some supplies."

"Potatoes and sausage, sir. And one more thing: a piglet."

"You have a butchered pig with you? We'd better get that over to the cook's at once," Grant told him.

"Not a dead pig, sir, though he was very close to death last night. A very alive one."

"A live piglet, eh? How big is he?"

"The runt of the litter, sir."

"We managed to procure a side of beef for His Lordship's table, Lieutenant. But roast suckling pig . . . that would do very well for you and some of the other officers. Bring him down to Major Gordon's, Lieutenant."

"Yes, sir."

When he reached the Gordons' house, Val tied his horse and lifted the piglet from his saddlebag. He was hoping just to hand the animal over to Private Ryan, but when the door opened, there he was, standing with a squealing piglet in his arms, facing Miss Elspeth Gordon. He lifted his shako awkwardly with one hand and gave a bow, and the piglet, taking advantage of the moment, wriggled free and ran into the house.

"You come back here, you bloody animal," shouted Val, as he pushed past Elspeth, who watched with astonishment and growing amusement as the normally reserved and dignified Lieutenant Aston got down on his knees trying to coax the pig from under the sofa where he had taken refuge.

"Damn you," Val growled as he thrust his arm under and tried to grab the elusive animal. Then his tone changed. "Here, piggy, piggy," he crooned.

"Perhaps I can shoo him down to you, Lieutenant," said Elspeth, her voice strained with her effort to keep from laughing. She knelt down at the other end of the sofa and gently batted at the piglet, who finally decided to take refuge with the human most familiar to him. As he stuck his snout out, Val grabbed him and stood up. The piglet wriggled around and began to lick his face.

"Is Private Ryan available, Miss Gordon?" Val asked in as dignified a tone as he could muster.

"Yes, he is, Lieutenant. Is the pig for him?"

"The bloody . . . I beg your pardon, Miss Gordon. The pig is for your family's Christmas dinner."

"I see. Let me get Private Ryan." Elspeth got herself into the kitchen as quickly as she could before she gave way to the laughter that she had heroically controlled.

"Are you all right, miss?" asked Private Ryan.

"Yes, Patrick," she finally answered, wiping the tears from her cheeks. "It is Lieutenant Aston. He is in the parlor in need of your assistance."

When Ryan saw the lieutenant holding the overly affectionate piglet, he had to smile. "Em, Miss Gordon said you had something for me?"

"Take him, Ryan," said Val disgustedly, thrusting the pig at him. "He is to be Christmas dinner."

"I see, sor. He seems quite fond of you, sor," added Patrick as the little pig struggled to get back to Val.

"The feeling is not mutual, I assure you, Private Ryan," said Val, as he looked down at his uniform, which was now missing several buttons due to the animal's sharp little hooves. He was trying to straighten out his jacket when Elspeth returned.

"Thank you for your contribution to our feast, Lieutenant. I hope you will enjoy the roast pork, sir. It appears you and the piglet became rather close on your journey here," she added, her eyes dancing.

"I assure you, Miss Gordon, I am looking forward to seeing him on a platter with an apple in his mouth."

"Poor little pig," Elspeth murmured.

"Poor little pig, my . . . Just look what he has done to my uniform."

"I see you are missing some buttons, Lieutenant," Elspeth replied sympathetically. "If you leave your jacket here, I would be happy to sew on new ones for you. It is the least I could do after the risk you have taken on your latest mission."

Elspeth's tone was all soothing flattery, but when Val looked down, he could see she was fighting to keep her face straight.

"I can see you are trying to humor me, Miss Gordon. Believe me, this was as dangerous a mission as any I've undertaken, with that bl—animal making enough noises to alert any Frenchman or bandit within twenty miles of me!" Val said with a grin.

"Whatever did you do?" asked Elspeth seriously.

Val hesitated. "I let the blasted pig sleep next to me," he admitted, his face growing red. "And I hope you will keep that information in confidence, Miss Gordon."

"Of course I will, Lieutenant," said Elspeth kindly, but with a spark of amusement in her eyes.

"Thank you. Uh, I had best get back to my quarters and start searching for buttons."

"Then you refuse my offer, Lieutenant?"

"I thank you for it, Miss Gordon, but I am quite good with a needle and thread, I assure you."

As he left, Val met Private Ryan coming around from the back of the house.

"I've got the pig penned up, sor, but he is whining like a bagpipe. 'Tis missing ye, he is, sor."

"Well, he can miss me till doomsday," said Val. "Which for him will be sooner rather than later."

Chapter 14

Two mornings later, just before dawn, Val awakened with a start. Someone was trying to get into his tent, he realized, and he grabbed his pistol from under his cot and waited for whoever it was pushing at the flap. A small gap opened at the bottom, letting in a shaft of early morning light, and in trotted the piglet, who stopped midway and cocked his head as if to say, "Well, here I am, and aren't you pleased to see me?"

Val swore fervently and fluently, but the little animal was not at all deterred. He trotted over to the cot and, putting his front hooves on the edge, hauled himself up.

"You are worse than any puppy, sir," complained Val, pushing him away from his face. "Indeed, though, you are as smart as a dog to find me," he added with a reluctant grin. "How did you do it?"

The pig only gave a contented sigh for an answer as he crawled under Val's blanket and snuggled next to him.

"Oh, no, not this time," said Val, jumping out of bed. "You go right back to the Gordons' pen."

Val dressed quickly, for he wanted to be out of camp and on his way to the village before anyone was awake. "I'm not carrying you this time," he muttered. "Not after I sewed new buttons on." He grabbed a length of twine and tied it around the piglet's neck.

He expected to haul the little animal all the way, but instead the piglet trotted along next to him. It seemed as though he was going to make it out of camp without anyone seeing him when, just as he passed the last officer's tent, James stepped out, his breeches half-buttoned, obviously intending to relieve himself.

"Uh, good morning, James."

"Am I dreaming, or is that a pig that I see before me?" James asked dramatically.

"If I told you you were dreaming, would you believe me and go back inside?"

"Actually, no, Val," said James with a grin. "The call of nature was too strong to let me go back to sleep. And my dreams are usually sweeter than this. So, is this our Christmas dinner?" James asked, leaning down and scratching the piglet's ear.

"He won't last till Christmas day if he doesn't stay out of my way," growled Val.

"Why, Valentine, it is only that he has developed a fondness for you, it would seem. Perhaps you took him too soon from his mother?"

"Go relieve yourself, James. And I trust you will keep this to yourself?"

"It will be difficult, but I will keep your little admirer a secret, I promise."

Val and the pig snorted together and James waved them on. "Get out of here, Val. You will have me pissing myself if I don't stop laughing."

When Val reached the Gordons', he took the pig around the back of the house and unceremoniously dropped him in the pen. The gate was swinging on its hinges and Val closed it quickly before the little animal could reach it.

"Now, just how did you manage it?" Val muttered as he inspected the gate. But he didn't have to wonder too long, for the piglet trotted over and, bracing himself on his hind legs, reached up and pushed at the latch with his snout. It only took him three or four tries to move it and if Val hadn't been there to stop him, he would have been free again.

"You are a smart little bugger, I must admit," said Val with an appreciative grin. "But I am going to tie this gate shut, my lad." Val drew the twine leash from his pocket and wrapped it around the gatepost several times. "There, now, I defy you to get out again!" As he turned his back and started to walk away, the piglet started whining and then letting out pathetic squeals.

"Damnation, you'll wake the whole bloody household!"

The only way to quiet the pig, of course, was to walk back, kneel down, and scratch around his ears.

"It seems as if you have missed him as much as he has missed you, Lieutenant," said an amused voice behind him.

It was Miss Gordon, in a blue flannel wrapper with a voluminous plaid shawl around her shoulders. The only thing she had on her feet were sheepskin scuffs and before he stood up, Val caught a glimpse of shapely ankles.

"He is an escape artist, this piglet. He ended up in my tent this morning," said Val disgustedly.

"I have heard that pigs are very intelligent animals, but I never believed it until now. It just goes to show you that you shouldn't judge anyone by his appearance, doesn't it, Lieutenant? However did he get out of the pen?"

"Lifted the latch with his snout," said Val with a grin, which he was horrified to realize was both disgusted and proud.

They both leaned over the fence and watched as the piglet rubbed his head against Val's boots.

"He won't bother you again, Lieutenant Aston. I'll make sure Patrick keeps the gate tied. And in a few days, he'll be—"

"Uh, yes," said Val, turning away quickly. "Which is all to the good, because I must confess I might find myself getting fond of the little bug—er, I beg your pardon, Miss Gordon."

Elspeth laughed. "I have heard the word before, Lieutenant."

"You had best get inside, Miss Gordon. You shouldn't be out on such a cold morning, bare-legged and all." Val only realized what he was saying after the words were out. He wasn't supposed to have noticed Miss Gordon's bare legs, much less comment on them. Damn, but he'd served as a common soldier too long. "I beg your pardon again, Miss Gordon. I shouldn't be commenting on your, er, limbs. . . ." Of course, here he was, mentioning them again, he thought, his face getting red.

"Lieutenant, I thought you knew by now that I am not easily embarrassed. I am not at all insulted, I assure you," replied Elspeth with a smile.

"Thank you, Miss Gordon. I'd best be off."

"Good morning, Lieutenant. I am looking forward to seeing you at Christmas dinner."

Val mumbled something about "And I too," but Elspeth thought that his backward glance at the pigpen did not come from anticipation of roast suckling piglet. "I think the lieutenant is fonder of you than he would like anyone to know, piggy," she said thoughtfully as she watched the little pig at his food.

Val got through the next few days with just a few pig jokes, and those referring only to his arrival with the piglet. He was grateful that neither James nor Miss Gordon had said anything about the little animal's early morning visit.

The laundresses' telegraph seemed to be quite efficient, however, for when Mrs. Casey delivered his clean shirts the day before Christmas, she was full of news about the piglet.

"Mrs. Ryan says he will not make a very satisfactory dish, Lieutenant, for he is wasting away from missing you," Mrs. Casey told him as she handed him his pile of newly laundered shirts.

"I am sure his lack of appetite has nothing to do with me."

"I wouldn't be so sure of that, sir. You did take him away from his mother. Why, I remember my uncle telling a story of a clutch of ducklings following his old sheepdog around for weeks because their mother died when they were very young."

"Well, there is no chance of the pig following me around, Mrs. Casey, for he is securely penned."

"He will be dead and stuffed tomorrow," she said matter-of-factly. "You will be fattening yourself on all that pork fat," she added cheerfully. "Though it is a little sad, him being such an intelligent piglet and all."

"Yes, well, thank you, Mrs. Casey. Here are the dirty sheets. I hope you will be enjoying a holiday feast yourself."

"Will and I are looking forward to it. Happy Christmas, Lieutenant."

"Happy Christmas, Mrs. Casey."

The closer it got, the less Val was looking forward to Christmas dinner. He awoke Christmas morning with a heavy feeling in the pit of his stomach and wondered if he might be coming down with something.

The early morning had been set aside for worship and Val hurried to shave and dress in his best uniform.

As he listened to the familiar Christmas day readings, pictures of that first Christmas formed in his mind: the exhausted Joseph and Mary who could find no shelter except in a stable, the miraculous birth, the shepherds coming to worship, the piglet peering over the top of the manger. . . . Damnation, that animal was turning up everywhere, even his religious musings, Val thought, groaning an audible groan.

James, who was standing next to him, peered over. "Are you all right, Val?" he asked anxiously.

"Yes, James. Just an unsettled stomach."

There was an officers' breakfast, but Val excused himself early and made his way to Will Tallman's tent, where a number of old comrades were breakfasting together in a tradition that went back several years.

" 'Ere 'e is, Will," announced one of them.

"Happy Christmas, sir," said Will. "We thought you might not make it to our little celebration this year."

"I was glad to get away, Will. Both the company and the food were too rich for me," he said with a wry smile.

"You are looking a little peaked," said Mags Casey. "Have a sausage," she offered, handing Val a plate.

"My appetite seems to have deserted me," Val confessed. "But I will take a bite or two of this, for it smells so good. However did you get the sausage, Will? It was supposed to go in the stew."

"Oh, I know the quartermaster's, uh, intended," said Mrs. Casey.

A few of the men smiled at Mags's characterization.

"Don't you be so quick to laugh," she said, waving her spoon at them. "She may have been his whore before now, but as of this morning, she is his fi-an-cée. And what do you think of *that,* Will Tallman?" she added angrily, giving him a sharp rap on the top of his head.

"Are any of you going to be shooting later on?" asked Val, trying to change the subject.

Mags's face softened and she laid the spoon gently on

Will's shoulder, almost as though she were dubbing him her knight. "Will is going to be taking the prize, aren't you?"

"I feel reasonable confident against my fellow footsoldiers, but the second half will be rifle against musket."

"How can that be done fairly?" asked Val. "Why, a rifle can shoot much farther than a musket."

"They will be setting up the targets at two ranges, sir," explained Private Murphy. "They will score the number of bull's-eyes."

"You had better not drink too much of Mrs. Casey's coffee, then," joked Val, for she had been most generous in lacing the coffee with rum. "I don't want to lose my month's wages, William."

The day was cold, but at least it was a dry cold and the sun was shining down on the parade ground as most of the camp gathered later that morning for the marksmanship competition.

It was close, but Will emerged the winner at the end of the first round, just as Val had expected. Then two new targets were set up.

"There's the rifleman you'll be shooting against, Will," said Private Doolittle. 'E's from the Ninety-fifth. David Hardin," he added, a note of awe in his voice. "Why, Oi 'ear 'e can 'it a man in the 'eart at two hundred yards.'"

Val watched as a tall, thin older man emerged from the ranks of green-jacketed rifles and positioned himself at the firing line. He clapped Will on the shoulder and said encouragingly, "Go on, Will, you can take him."

"I'd like to, Lieutenant, just to show up those riflemen."

"It will be the best three shots out of five, gentlemen," announced Lord Wellington himself, who had arrived in time to judge the final round. "Private Hardin will shoot first."

"That gives you the advantage of the last shot, Will," said Val.

Private Hardin bit off the end of his cartridge and poured the powder and rammed the ball down in a fluid series of motions. His rifle was up at his shoulder and his first shot fired in under twenty seconds.

"One inch to the left of the bull's-eye," the scorekeeper intoned.

Will wasn't as fast a loader and it seemed he brought his

musket up and aimed very slowly, although the reality was that it only took thirty seconds.

"One-half inch from the center," called the scorekeeper.

"First round to the Eleventh Foot," announced Lord Wellington to the raucous cheers of the infantry. But the next two rounds went to Private Hardin, whose expression had not changed since he took the field. His second shot was a bull's-eye and his third only a fraction from the center.

"Just a hair short of a bull's-eye," called the scorekeeper after Hardin's fourth shot.

"All right, Will," called Private Doolittle, "you can take this back."

"Half a hair," announced the scorekeeper with a grin after Will's shot.

"Fourth round to the infantry," he called out, after checking Will's shot.

It seemed to Val that Private Hardin made his next preparations a bit more slowly.

"Half a hair from the center!"

Val could see Will's hands trembling as he poured his powder down the barrel.

"Don't ye worry whether you win or lose, Will Tallman. You've always found *my* bull's-eye," Mags Casey stepped up and whispered in his ear.

Will gave her a grin and a hug. "Thanks, Mags."

He lifted the musket to his shoulder and sighted the target. Then he squeezed the trigger slowly, breathing a quick prayer.

"*Bull's-eye!* Marksmanship medal to Private Will Tallman of the Eleventh Foot."

The infantry went wild, while the green jackets stood around with dazed looks on their faces. David Hardin had never been beaten before.

"You do be a fine shot, Sergeant Tallman," said Hardin in his soft west-country voice. "Maybe you'd like to join the Ninety-fifth," he added with a grin.

"Thank you, Private. I was proud to be shooting against you. But I think I'll stick to my musket."

"Come on, Will, Old Nosey himself is waiting to give you your medal," said Mags, linking her arm in his and walking him toward the tall, austerely clad figure.

"Oh, my Lord, whatever will I say to him?" Will whispered.

"Don't you worry, you just bow and say, 'Thank you, my lord.'"

"So this is the man who outshoot Hardin," said Wellington. "Let me shake your hand, Sergeant."

Will bowed and then stammered out a thank-you.

"Give him your *hand,* Will," said Mags.

Will stuck his hand out and felt it pressed by cool, dry fingers. Wellington turned and took from one of his officers a small gold medal hanging from a red-and-white ribbon.

"Shall I pin this on you?"

"Not on me, my lord. If I won this—and I didn't think I would, you understand—I'd already decided to give it to Mags . . . uh, Mrs. Casey."

"So this is not Mrs. Tallman, then," said Wellington dryly.

Will blushed. "No, my lord."

Wellington turned to Mags. "Mrs. Casey seems a fine woman, Sergeant," he said as he pinned the medal on her gown.

"Indeed she is, sir," Will stammered.

"Perhaps you might consider the gift of this medal something like a statement of your honorable intentions toward her, then?"

"Like we are a-fianced, my lord?" asked Mags, tucking her arm through Will's and drawing him close.

"Something like that," Wellington responded with an uncharacteristic twinkle in his eye. "What do you say, Sergeant?"

"Er, yes, my lord. I never did have it in my mind to look elsewhere."

"Then it is settled. Mrs. Casey, you can consider yourself affianced. Sergeant Tallman, you have won yourself a medal and a fiancée today. Congratulations."

"Yes, my lord. Thank you, my lord," Will answered dolefully.

"That was very wicked of you, my lord," said Mrs. Gordon after Will and Mrs. Casey walked away.

"It was, wasn't it? But I couldn't resist it, Mrs. Gordon. They make such a delightfully odd couple. And who knows,

I might have done him a favor. Mrs. Casey may well be satisfied just with a betrothal, after all."

"Congratulations, Will."

"Maybe you should be offering me condolences, sir," complained Will a little later. "Mags has gone off to show off her medal and brag to all the women."

"I am almost disappointed in you, Will," said Val. "You've always said you were not a marrying man."

"Nor am I, sir. I didn't make any promises up there no matter what Mags thinks! I didn't have much choice about this affiancing, what with Old Nosey himself pushing it on me," he added disgustedly.

"Perhaps Mrs. Casey will be happier now that she can call herself your fiancée."

"I never said I wouldn't have a fiancée, sir. If it makes her happy, then I'll just have to hope it holds her for a long time!"

Chapter 15

The officers were expected at Major Gordon's by two and the closer it got, the less Val felt like feasting.

"I am ravenous," said James as they walked to the village.

"I think I have a touch of indigestion myself," said Val. "Too much sausage and rum for breakfast."

"Yes, of course, you ate with your old companions, didn't you?" replied James. "Well, it must be that."

"What else would it be?"

"Oh, perhaps a reluctance to feast on a little animal that was so fond of you?" asked James sympathetically. When Val looked over at him, however, he could see that his friend's mouth was twitching.

"Don't be an ass, James. It is nothing but a spot of indigestion."

Val had hoped that a glass of wine would make him feel better, but for some reason, sweet as it was, the red wine the Gordons served only left a sour taste in his mouth.

When Mrs. Gordon summoned them all to the table, he was tempted to excuse himself. But there had already been one snide comment from Lucas Stanton and he knew he'd make himself a laughingstock if he left. And, damn it, the state of his stomach had nothing to do with the main course, after all!

Val was seated opposite Elspeth and next to James and George.

"Doesn't Miss Gordon look lovely tonight?" asked George.

"Absolutely," agreed James, smiling across at Elspeth.

Val said nothing, but his eyes widened in appreciation as he took in Elspeth's appearance. She was wearing a dress of fine wool, so light it appeared to be another fabric altogether, and across her shoulders was pinned a wool sash in the Gordon tartan. The deep green of her dress brought out the green flecks in her hazel eyes. Elspeth, who had lowered her eyes in embarrassment at George's compliment, lifted them and found herself gazing directly into Val's admiring gray ones. The moment was brief, but she flushed with pleasure at the appreciative smile he gave her.

As Private Ryan removed their first course, Elspeth saw Val's expression as the others began to anticipate the main course.

"You are quieter than usual tonight, Aston," commented Stanton.

"Not mourning the piglet, are you?" said George with a jab in Val's ribs and a loud guffaw.

"Private Ryan," said Elspeth.

"Yes, Miss Gordon?"

"I believe you said you needed a little help in the kitchen?" Elspeth stared intently at him and then shifted her gaze across the table and back.

"Er, yes, miss. Lieutenant Aston, may I ask you to help me get the roast onto the platter?"

Until that moment, Val had not been able to admit where his discomfort was coming from. But as he rose, he realized he didn't know what would be worse: sitting there waiting for that damned little pig to be placed in front of him, or going into the kitchen and helping Ryan slide him out of the pan. He knew one thing: Not one bloody piece of pork was going to pass his lips. And at least in the kitchen he would have time to assume an air of indifference and think of some reason for not partaking of the main course.

When he got there, Private Ryan was already opening the oven door. "There is the platter, sor. I was afraid it would be too heavy for Mrs. Ryan to handle. Hold it steady, now, sor, while I slips the capon out."

Val almost dropped the platter in his surprise.

"Capon! I thought we were having roast pork."

"Roast that dear little piggy?" Private Ryan said sarcastically but with a sympathetic twinkle in his eye. "Sure and Miss Gordon and me wife wouldn't let me near him, sor. Though I have to confess I grew a bit fond of him meself," he added. "Here, watch yerself, sor, or ye'll be having both birds in yer lap."

As the private slipped the second fat fowl onto the plate, Val breathed a sigh of relief. "But where is the pig?"

"Traded to a family in the village, sor, for these birds. They needed a male for their sow, though it will take him some time to grow tall enough. He may end up on a dinner table yet, but at least you won't have to be eating him! Miss Gordon's a softhearted lass," he murmured appreciatively.

The smell of sage and thyme was filling the kitchen and the hall, and Val's stomach began to rumble as he returned to the table.

"The roast made it safely to the platter, I take it, Lieutenant," said Major Gordon with a sly smile.

"All right and tight," replied Val, and he winked across the table at Elspeth as he slipped into his chair.

There were a few groans of disappointment when the platter was set down.

"Why, wherever did the pig disappear?" asked George.

"Taken refuge with Aston, no doubt," replied Stanton.

"This is Elspeth's doing," the major informed them. "She was worried that the pig, being so small, wouldn't feed us all, so she did some hard bargaining for these birds."

"Sure and they'll make us a grand soup after, sor," Private Ryan chimed in. "Miss Gordon is a good, practical lass."

"Miss Gordon is a young woman with a soft heart," muttered James to Val as they started their dinner. "I am just not sure whether her sympathy was with you or the pig!"

"The pig, James, the pig," Val replied with a smile.

The table was very quiet, for the food was delicious and all of them were hungry for something different than the usual fare. After dinner, they made their way to the parlor, where a cheerful fire was burning and a decanter of port waiting.

"Thank God we have an hour or so before the ball to digest that wonderful dinner, Mrs. Gordon, for no one of us could be light on his feet after that meal!" James joked.

"Shall we have some music, Peggy?" the major asked.

They went through all the choruses of "God Rest Ye," "The Holly and the Ivy," and "Adeste Fideles."

"Now you, Lieutenant Aston. Surely you must have picked up a song or two in your travels," suggested Mrs. Gordon.

"What about the 'Boys' Carol'? " James suggested.

"You know my Spanish is far superior to my Latin, James," said Val with a smile. There was no chip on his shoulder when he said this, James realized. Something—perhaps it was simply the joy of the holiday—had allowed Val to be more himself, more open that his friend had ever seen him.

He sang them a Spanish carol from the hills, a shepherd's carol, and as he sang, James glanced over at Elspeth Gordon. She was sitting across from Val and she had an appreciative half-smile on her face and a dreamy look in her eyes. Sits the wind in that quarter? wondered James. Well, they would make a good pair, now that he thought about it. Val's birth made him ineligible for any young ladies in Society, but Elspeth Gordon and her parents were just unconventional enough to overlook Val's status. The question, James thought as he looked back at Val, was whether his friend would appreciate Elspeth, and if he did, would he allow himself to consider her as a possible wife?

They ended their festivities with small cups of Turkish coffee and then set out for the walk to the other side of the village.

"May I escort you, Miss Gordon?" asked Val, offering his arm.

"I would be delighted, Lieutenant."

Val made sure to hang back and let the others go a little way ahead before he turned to Elspeth. "I want to thank you for your softheartedness, Miss Gordon, for I think it was more than practicality that made you trade the pig."

"I had begun to grow quite fond of him, I must confess, and it seemed to me that you might find it difficult to eat the poor little thing after you'd shared a blanket with him."

"You are right, although I am ashamed to confess it."

"I don't think there is anything to be ashamed of, Lieutenant. I think it admirable for a soldier to be able to keep his heart open to the plight of a small animal even after the sights he sees on the battlefield," she added with a slight shudder.

"You may have seen more of those horrors than I, Miss Gordon. It was quiet in the Caribbean, with only a few skirmishes around a small mutiny. I was at Talavera, but now that I am in Captain Grant's service, I am unlikely to become involved again."

"I hope not," murmured Elspeth. "I have walked the fields the day after a battle. . . ." She was silent for a moment and without thinking, Val drew her arm closer to him. "I *do* believe this war is necessary," Elspeth continued. "We must stop Bonaparte. But sometimes the price is horrifying and exorbitant."

"I am surprised your parents let you walk the field."

"Oh, I convinced them a long time ago that if I was to follow the drum with my mother, I would not shrink from the realities of a soldier's life. And I had a purpose, Lieutenant. I was helping to identify the dead and make sure there were no living men amongst them."

It was Val's turn to shiver. "A gruesome task for a lady."

"But a necessary one and by now, Lieutenant, you must know I am no lady."

"You *are* the granddaughter of an earl, Miss Gordon."

"My mother's father was only a younger son."

Just then they heard someone coming up behind them and Val stepped protectively in front of Elspeth. "Who is there?"

"*Hola, amigo.* Is it Lieutenant Aston?"

"Captain Belden?"

"And Colonel Sanchez. We have just finished our supper with Lord Wellington and are on our way to the dancing."

"Bienvenidos, Capitan," said Elspeth.

"Habla español, Señorita Gordon?" Val asked with surprise.

"Un poco. A very little," she added with a soft laugh. "Will you introduce me?"

"Yes, I'm sorry. Miss Elspeth Gordon, may I present Captain Jack Belden and Colonel Julian Sanchez."

"I have occasionally seen you walking with Lord Wellington, Colonel Sanchez," said Elspeth. "I am honored to meet such a devoted patriot. And Captain Belden. I have heard of you from my friend Maddie Lambert," she added.

"And probably nothing good, Miss Gordon?"

Elspeth laughed. "You are right, Captain, your reputation has preceded you. Among other things, you *are* reported to be quite charming and an excellent dancer."

"I will admit to that, Miss Gordon," said Belden.

The four of them walked on together and before Val knew it, his place next to Elspeth had been usurped by the captain.

"Not for nothing do they call him the Jack of Hearts, eh, Lieutenant?" Colonel Sanchez said admiringly as they watched the other two walk ahead.

"Indeed," Val replied curtly.

"It means nothing to him, Lieutenant. The captain, he already has a beautiful señora."

"That doesn't seem to be stopping him!"

"No, well, he is an accomplished charmer, Captain Belden," Sanchez admitted with a grin. "But Señorita Gordon seems like a sensible young woman and not one to be taken in by charm."

"I hope not . . . for her sake, you understand," Val muttered.

"Of course."

Chapter 16

The largest house in the town was the mayor's and Wellington had commandeered it for the evening. The front parlor and dining room had been set up as a combination receiving area and card room. Several tables of whist were already in progress by the time they arrived. The mayor's "ballroom" was not very large, but it could accommodate two small sets for country dancing.

Val found Charlie waiting for him. "Happy Christmas, Val," said his brother. "It is good to be with family for the holiday."

"Happy Christmas to you, Charlie," Val replied and, surprising both himself and his brother, pulled Charlie close for a warm hug. He let him go almost immediately and quickly asked, "What was dinner like at the general's table?"

"Roast beef," groaned Charlie. "I'll not be able to dance for hours."

"Not even with that pretty señorita who is giving you come-hither looks when her parents aren't watching?" Val teased.

"Is she really?" asked Charlie, blushing with pleasure. "Well, I suppose I might be recovered in time for the next set. But what about your dinner, Val? I heard roast suckling pig was to be on the menu," he added sympathetically.

"Actually, it was roast capon, Charlie. Miss Gordon grew fond of the piglet and couldn't bear the thought of eating him."

"Miss Gordon, eh? And how much were you planning to eat?"

"If you must know, I was ready to excuse myself from the meal," Val admitted with a shamefaced grin. "I'd grown rather fond of the little runt myself!"

"I think Miss Gordon is a delightful young woman, Val. And I am sure she is looking forward to dancing with you tonight."

"Are you trying to play matchmaker, little brother?"

"Not at all," replied Charlie with great dignity. "I was merely suggesting that you and she might enjoy one or two sets tonight." Charlie watched as the next sets formed. "But I see you may already be too late for this one, Val," he added with a grin. "Jack Belden has got her and I've never seen a young woman able to resist him. He had all the young ladies in London sighing after him last Season."

"I am sure Miss Gordon is sensible enough to recognize a rake, no matter how charming."

"He's not really a rakehell, Val. He just possesses the deadly combination of that dark and brooding Spanish countenance, which is enough on its own to make women swoon, with unexpected humor and charm. And who could resist that dashing motley uniform?"

"I hear he already has an inamorata," Val replied stiffly. "A Spanish lady."

"Does he? Well, I am going to brave the señorita's parents, Val. Wish me luck."

Val watched as Charlie made his way around the room and introduced himself to the young woman and her parents. Within a few minutes they were all smiling and chatting away in what Val assumed was a combination of Charlie's meager Portuguese and their little English. Well, who could resist Charlie? He had his own charm, very different from Jack Belden's, but powerful in its own right.

Elspeth was smiling up into Belden's face when he led her off the dance floor and for a few moments Val was filled with a fury so sudden and strong that it took him completely by surprise. How dare the man flirt with Miss Gordon like that? And why was she giving him that simpering look back? It took Val a moment to realize that Miss Gordon was merely smiling, not simpering. Belden had only had one dance with the lady, after all, and he was bowing and moving off. Without making a conscious decision, Val made his way to where Miss Gordon was chatting with the surgeon's wife.

"Mrs. Clitheroe. Miss Gordon."

"Lieutenant Aston, how lovely to see you here tonight,"

said Mrs. Clitheroe. "I do think His Lordship was inspired, don't you? A dance was just what we all needed to lift our spirits."

Val smiled. "Lord Wellington is an incomparable commander. He knows just how to encourage his men, whether in battle or ballrooms."

The three of them chatted for a while and then Mrs. Clitheroe excused herself as she heard the musicians tuning up for the next set. "I am shameless, I admit, but I am going to drag my husband away from his cronies and make him dance with me. I hope you will not disappoint Miss Gordon, Lieutenant?" she added.

"Oh, dear, she didn't leave you much choice, did she?" Elspeth said with an apologetic smile.

"She only made it easier to do what I came over here to do, which was to ask you for the next dance," replied Val with a bow. "Will you join me in this next set?"

"I would be happy to, Lieutenant Aston," replied Elspeth.

The music was lively and the musicians went immediately into another tune, so Val and Elspeth had two dances together. When the music finally stopped, they looked at each other and laughed. "Thank you, Miss Gordon, that was delightful, but I am ashamed to confess I am out of breath," said Val with a smile.

"I too, Lieutenant. Oh, dear, and it is quite warm in here."

"Do you have a shawl with you?"

"A shawl! I would faint from the heat then, Lieutenant!"

"I was going to suggest that we step outside for a little fresh air, but I wouldn't want you to take a chill."

"A breath of air is just what I need," agreed Elspeth, "but if it is only for a moment, I won't need my shawl."

"You are sure?"

"I am," said Elspeth, placing her hand on top of his arm. "I don't believe we will make it out the front door, there is such a crush now, but there is a side entrance."

Elspeth's arm rested lightly on his, but Val was acutely aware of the slight pressure of her fingers as he led her out.

There was a small herb garden on the side of the house and the faded plants shone silver in the moonlight.

"It is too cold a night to stay long, Miss Gordon," he warned.

"I know, but it is so good to be able to breathe, and to look at the stars, Lieutenant. The Christmas star must have been very bright to stand out from all these and lead the Magi all the way to Bethlehem," she whispered.

Val could see her beginning to shiver. "Miss Gordon, I think I should take you back in."

"Oh, just another minute," she pleaded. "On such a Christmas night, one can almost hear the angels singing."

Val quickly unbuttoned his tunic. "Here, at least put this on, Miss Gordon," he said. As he draped it over her shoulders, Elspeth reached up to grasp the jacket and instead her hand touched his. He expected her to draw hers back, but she let it rest. He was surprised to realize that despite the cold, her hand warmed his, and when he brushed his thumb against hers, her fingers tightened around his.

"Glory be to God in the highest and on earth, peace. . . ." she whispered. "Will we ever see peace, Lieutenant?"

"Peace to men of good will is what they sang, Miss Gordon. I suppose we will have peace when men will each other good rather than harm." Val felt her shiver again and pulled his tunic a little tighter around her.

"You are freezing, Miss Gordon," he said, standing there, his hands resting gently on her shoulders. "We must go in."

"Yes, I know," Elspeth whispered. But she only turned her face up to his, and without thinking, he let go of the jacket and caressed her cheek with his hand.

"Your lips are turning blue, Miss Gordon," he said softly.

"I am sure you exaggerate, but perhaps you can warm them," she said as she turned her face slightly and pressed her lips into the palm of his hand. The intimacy of the moment gave Val such pleasure that he wanted it to last forever. But then he wanted more, and turning her face gently, he leaned down and pressed his lips against hers. "Is this better?"

"Oh, yes."

Val's tunic slipped off completely as they both let go of it at the same time. Elspeth put her hands on his shoulders and Val lowered his head again, but this time he urged her mouth open.

It was a kiss that shook both of them to the core and when Val finally pulled away, they stood speechless. Then Elspeth lowered her eyes in confusion and saw Val's tunic. "Oh, dear, your tunic will be ruined," she said nervously as she leaned down to pick it up.

"Please don't concern yourself, Miss Gordon. The ground is frozen and I doubt it could get very dirty," he reassured her as she brushed it off and handed it back to him.

He shrugged himself into it and buttoned it as quickly as he could with cold-stiffened fingers while she stood there, her arms wrapped around herself for warmth.

"I must get you inside," Val told her as he pushed the last button through. "Before you freeze." He didn't add what they were both thinking: "Before anyone notices our absence."

They managed to slip back in quietly and before Elspeth could say anything, Val led her over to a small group of officers and ladies, bowed formally, and thanked her for the dance. He was gone before she realized it, and it took her a minute until she could join the conversation with her usual enthusiasm.

Val wanted to excuse himself from the rest of the evening. He wanted never to have to face her again. He wanted . . . damn it, he wanted to be kissing her again. He wanted everyone else to disappear so he could walk over to her and take her in his arms and not have to worry about cold or scandal.

He had wanted to kiss her before, of course. Perhaps he had been wanting to kiss her since he'd met her. But wanting was one thing; acting on it was quite another.

It was that damned pig, he told himself. If she hadn't been so understanding, so attentive to his feelings about the little animal, maybe nothing would have happened. But she had shown both kindness and humor, which had completely disarmed him. His defenses might have been able to withstand one or the other, but with both, she had breached them. And then leveled them completely with her kiss.

He could still feel the imprint of her lips on the palm of his hand. It had not been a stolen kiss, but one freely given. And that's what made it so damnably difficult. He and Elspeth Gordon had begun a friendship. Now, clearly, their companionship was revealing some complications. And the attraction was mutual, since she had asked him to warm her lips. Were she any other woman, he would be happy. But where could these feeling lead them? Perhaps to a few more stolen kisses, but nothing more. Certainly not marriage.

Val had never pictured himself married. In the army, you lived from day to day, and he hadn't spent much time thinking of the future. If anyone had asked what he planned to do after the war, he wouldn't have known what to answer. He had never thought of his future, he realized, not since his mother died. He had lived in the present: He had had to survive George Burton, Queen's Hall, and the British army. Well, thank God, he had enough practice at it, for that was the way he would have to go on. Only now he didn't just have to survive a war, but his encounters with Elspeth Gordon.

By the time they returned home in the wee hours of the morning, Elspeth was dizzy from her efforts to focus on her dance partners, the social chatter, even a brief conversation with Lord Wellington, who jokingly warned her about Jack Belden and recommended she beware of all his exploring officers. "They are a special breed, ma'am, and adept at disguise and deceit. Eh, Colquhoun?" he added humorously.

"I think some of us can tell the difference between deceiving the enemy and toying with the heart, my lord. But I must agree with you about Captain Belden. He is one to guard your heart against, Miss Gordon," Captain Grant added with a teasing smile.

"You need not worry, my lord, Captain Grant. I have been in the army long enough to tell the difference between true and Spanish coin," Elspeth assured them dryly.

"Indeed you have," Wellington said to her approvingly.

It was true, Elspeth thought later, sitting in bed, her back against her pillows, her knees drawn up, her hands clasped around them as she gazed into the darkness. She had dealt with everything from flirting to outright seduction over the years. She had easily dismissed the intermittent attention paid to her as misguided efforts on the part of young officers to gain her father's attention. And as for someone like Jack Belden, well, charming women came as naturally to him as breathing. He was amusing company and a wonderful dancer and she only wished she had gone outside with *him,* for then his kiss would have been stolen, not given . . . and meaningless.

Her cheeks burned as she thought of how forward she had been with Lieutenant Aston. Not only had she pressed her lips into his hand, she had actually asked him to do more. What must he think?

But it had been a lovely kiss, she thought with a little sigh of remembered pleasure. "No, my lord," she whispered to an imaginary Lord Wellington, "you need not worry about me with Jack Belden. It is Lieutenant Valentine Aston who endangers my heart." She feared it was true. Valentine Aston was different from any man she had ever met. He had little obvious surface charm. Indeed, she thought, smiling into the darkness, he seemed most of the time to be too grimly intent on carrying that damned chip on his shoulder to give much thought to pleasing a lady. But when one caught glimpses of the man he was underneath, as she had, well, then, he was hard to resist. For much of this evening she had felt she was in the presence of the real Val, a man of hidden warmth, who could share her humorous view of the world. He would not have eaten a morsel of that roast pork, yet he saw the irony in his tenderheartedness toward a small animal with all the devastation going on around them.

He was a solid man, Lieutenant Aston, and she appreciated solidity. He had the capacity for love, for she could see what he tried to hide, his love and admiration for his brother. He was a lovable man too. Charlie admired him and from what she knew, his former comrades held him in great affection. He was handsome, though not with the Byronic looks of Jack Belden or the sunnier handsomeness of his brother. Elspeth could see his face looking down at hers, and imagined herself tracing the thin scar that ran down his jaw. His lips were full and generous, and as she pictured them touching hers, she felt the same liquid warmth spreading through her as she had earlier this evening in the garden.

"I have never felt that way before," she whispered to herself. "Or perhaps I have never *let* myself feel that way."

She had come to realize, when she had looked around at the girls at school, that her appearance and her background made her very different from them. She was tall and although her features were pleasant, she knew she could never lay a claim to beauty. There were other girls who were not beautiful, of course, but each had something else to recommend her: petite stature combined with a generous figure, or perhaps a graceful femininity. It was not only her appearance. It was who she was. Or perhaps who she wasn't. She wasn't sheltered. She wasn't fluent in French, although she could speak fluent Hindi. She wasn't soft; she was strong, independent, and said what she meant. Above all, she was not self-deceptive. It became clear, after a few visits to the homes of her classmates, and a few local assemblies, that their brothers and friends considered her a great confidante. But to any of the men she found attractive, she remained invisible. So she had early on accepted what seemed to be her fate.

Truly, she thought, it was not such a bad fate. She had been honest about not wanting a Season. She loved the freedom and adventure her life gave her, despite the lack of comforts that most young women took for granted. She knew she could not have tolerated the boredom and constraint that a life in Society would have forced upon her. In that respect, at least, she was her mother's daughter.

Of course, being her father's daughter, she had a romantic and passionate side to her nature, but she had kept it hidden away from others, and almost from herself, until now. She gave a little gasp as the full realization hit her. And the pain. She wasn't as happy as she had thought herself. She hadn't resigned herself completely to her solitary state. She *wanted* love. How had she ever convinced herself otherwise? She wanted a strong man's arms around her, making her feel cherished. She wanted his lips on hers, making her feel loved. She wanted his body pressed against hers, making her feel desired.

She thought she might hate Val Aston for waking her up to herself. A little sob escaped her. And what was even worse, maybe she was beginning to love him.

Chapter 17

Charlie always enjoyed himself at a dance and last night was no exception. He had managed to partner almost every woman present, he thought with a smile as he dressed the next morning. Except for Elspeth Gordon, whom he couldn't get near, between Jack Belden and Val.

He had actually been a little concerned for her when he saw how Jack was monopolizing her, for very few women could resist him. I wonder what it is about a melancholy countenance that captures the ladies? he asked himself as he gazed at his own open, cheerful face in his shaving mirror. You would think they would be drawn to one who looked more acquainted with joy rather than sorrow. Perhaps it was the challenge. Perhaps each lady hoped to be the one woman who could lift that melancholy.

Of course the irony was that Jack merely appeared melancholy. He had a changeable temperament, that was true, but enjoyed life far more than his face suggested.

Then there was Val. Jack's looks drew women like moths to a flame, but his brother too often looked forbidding. Perhaps forbidding was too strong a word, but he was expert at keeping his face expressionless and his eyes shuttered. Very few people knew the real Val, as he did. His brother had a great capacity for love, though he had a hard time showing it.

He had seen Miss Gordon and Val dance their two sets and then disappear into the garden. Elspeth Gordon had not let Jack Belden maneuver her anywhere in private! He didn't know how long they had been outside, but certainly long enough for a kiss?

Charlie hoped so. The more he thought of it, the more he liked the idea. Elspeth Gordon would be perfect for his brother. She was too strong-minded to be daunted by Val's ridiculous pride. And she was independent enough not to mind about the circumstances of his birth. She *was* the granddaughter of an earl, Charlie mused, but Mr. and Mrs. Gordon had married despite some disparity in their stations. He didn't think that Val's background would weigh much with them. Perhaps he could do a little matchmaking to help things along. It certainly would relieve the boredom of sitting around waiting for Massena to make his move!

As Charlie emerged from his tent, he saw James a few steps ahead of him and called out, "Is there any mail today, James?"

"I am on my way to find out."

"I'll go with you. I haven't heard from my father in an age. Did you enjoy the ball, James?" he asked as they made their way down the row.

"It was an excellent diversion for us all. And you, Charlie?"

"Danced with every lady except one."

"And who was that unlucky woman?" replied James with a grin.

"Miss Gordon's time was quite taken up by Jack Belden and my brother."

"Indeed, I had noticed that myself," said James with a knowing smile. "I think that your brother was the one who brought her in from the garden most becomingly flushed despite the cold?"

"So you saw them come in too? Well, I have become convinced they are made for each other."

"Really?" said James with a raised eyebrow.

"Oh, don't be so stiff, James! Don't you think that Miss Gordon would be perfect for Val?"

"I am only teasing you, Charlie. I admit the same thought struck me when I saw them last night. You know, neither of them is likely to make a conventional match, what with Elspeth's upbringing and Val's birth.

"You know, my father told me that it was Val's mother who refused to marry him. She knew that there had been a long-standing agreement between my parents and she felt that a marriage between social equals had more of a chance at success."

"She must have loved him very much to give your father up," James commented softly.

"Yes, and she had a strong sense of honor. I suppose that is where Val gets his!" Charlie was quiet for a moment. "I think he would have been very different had she lived."

"Does he know the story?"

"It is my father's to tell and Val has always refused to listen," Charlie replied sadly.

"Typical!"

"Oh, yes!" They both laughed.

"So will you help me, James?"

"You know, I think I might enjoy a taste of matchmaking very much, Charlie."

There was mail for both of them.

"Two letters from my father! The mails are so slow."

James had two letters also. "From my sister Maddie," he announced with a smile. "It will take me hours to decipher it, for she crosses and recrosses in her eagerness to tell me all the gossip from London. Unfortunately, the other will be easy to read," James said with a heavy sigh. "A letter from the family solicitor, who no doubt has discovered another debt for me to settle."

Charlie was quickly scanning his father's letters.

"What does your father have to say, Charlie?"

Charlie frowned. "It seems the king had a relapse at the end of the month. My father was writing this the first week of December. It is very bad, James. Evidently he was quite out of control and they had to put him in restraints for a time."

"Then a Regency will be necessary. . . ."

"And we know what that will mean, James. Prinny will bring in the Whigs and we'll all be ordered home. No one in the Opposition believes Wellington can hold Portugal, much less succeed in Spain." Charlie snorted with disgust as he read further. "They are laying bets for and against him, it seems. Some believe that Massena will be driven to retreat by February, but others think he is in a better position than we are and that the Whigs will call for an evacuation."

"It *is* surprising that Massena has made no move."

"But if he can sit tight, and if the king does not recover . . ." Charlie's face brightened. "But he'll never make it through the lines, James. That's what those fools in London can't see. Now, what does your sister have to say for herself?"

"She is full of excitement over the holidays, even though the family celebrations will of necessity be spare this year. And of course she is beside herself about the coming Season. She had to put her come-out off for a year because of my father's death. And then another year because of the lack of funds. But between my great-aunt, who offered some help, and some funds I was able to set aside, she will have a chance to find a husband after all. My sister, of course, is hoping for a full retreat so that I can attend her come-out ball. I must admit, I would like to be there for her as head of the family."

"Surely you are due a leave, James?"

"Wellington doesn't like his officers flitting back and forth on flimsy excuses, Charlie."

"But this isn't flimsy, James. You do need to be there for Lady Madeline. You should at least try him."

"I will, Charlie, I will."

The day after Christmas, Val rode back to the border with Colonel Sanchez and Jack Belden to see if there was any news about Napoleon's intentions. But none of the captured dispatches revealed any plan to reinforce Massena's army.

"If he doesn't send more troops, then he will lose Portugal," said Val.

"And eventually Spain," said Sanchez with a satisfied grin.

Halfway back to camp, Val ran into a mountain snow-storm and it wasn't until a week after Christmas that he stumbled into his tent and collapsed. He was awakened midafternoon the next day by Mrs. Casey, who was bundling up his laundry.

"It looks like I should be washing the sheets you're lying on, Lieutenant," she said, frowning down at his dirty boots, which he had been too tired to remove. "Not to mention

mending them!" she added. "You could at least have un-
buckled your spurs."

"You are a hard woman, Mrs. Casey."

"Oh, aye, some would say so, Lieutenant," she responded with a grin.

"And an engaged woman now, I hear."

Mrs. Casey patted the marksmanship medal, which rested
on her bosom. "Hung on me by Lord Wellington himself,"
she said proudly.

"So Will Tallman is now your fiancé."

"He is, and a lucky man too, though he doesn't seem to
know it."

"I will just have to have a talk with him," said Val, disen-
gaging his spurs from the bed linen and swinging his legs
over the side of his cot.

"You do that, Lieutenant, and I'll do this bit of mending
for nothing."

A few hours later, after a bath and something to eat, Val
went in search of Will. He found him huddled over a small
camp stove with a few men of the Eleventh Foot, playing
at hazard.

"Good afternoon, Will," said Val. "I haven't seen you
since the match. Congratulations."

"Thank you, Lieutenant," said Will glumly. "I hear they
spared your little piggy after all," he said with a grin.

"So they did, Will. But why are you looking so cast down
when you won both the contest and a betrothed?" asked
Val, keeping his face straight with difficulty.

"And that was none of my doing," grumbled Will. "What
the bleeding hell was I supposed to say when His bleeding
Lordship himself declares us engaged!"

Val couldn't look sympathetic for the life of him and a
broad grin split his face.

"Oh, so you think it is funny, do you, sir?" said Will.
"And just how would you feel to find yourself with a fiancée just because you hit the bull's-eye? I tell you, if I'd
known, I'd have shot different that day."

"But doesn't being affianced satisfy Mrs. Casey, Will?"

"Not that auld besom," pipped up one of the men. "She
be after him to set the date now!"

"She was happy for a few days. Strutting about and lording it over the other women. Although it's true that not many get betrothed by Lord Wellington himself," admitted Will. "Then I told her not to be getting any ideas about the wedding and that tore it," he said disgustedly.

"Oh, Will, you could have gone on for years as her fiancé," groaned Val. "Why ever did you open your mouth?"

"I'm sure *I* don't know. 'Twas just that I got tired of her never being able to be *quiet* about it. And I felt honor-bound to let her know that, despite a betrothal, I am still not a marrying man," Will said righteously.

"Of course, you have always been an honorable man, Will," Val agreed solemnly, but with a betraying gleam in his eye.

"By God, Lieutenant, I was right terrified," confessed Will with a shudder. "But now she's saying I'll be sleeping alone until I set a date! I'm praying Massena makes his move soon. I'm ready to put myself on the front line, sir. Then she'll see that she is better off as a fiancée than as a widow again!"

"Don't even joke about it, Will," Val said seriously. "We'll see action soon enough, and you are too good a friend to lose."

"Do you think we will, sir?" asked Private Murphy. "Here we sit behind the lines with the Portuguese manning the barricades and one in ten of us dropping from fever every day. At least you get a chance to go off on your exploring, sir."

Val realized that Murphy was right. He was able to feel active and to experience pride that occasionally his missions bore fruit. It must be difficult for the men to be sitting around doing nothing but freezing their bums off and facing no greater excitement than whether Mrs. Casey would get Will to the altar or not.

"Of course, we get to do double drills," Murphy complained bitterly. "The lieutenant makes sure of that! If I have to march one more bloody time from line to square to line, I swear I'll desert."

Val could sympathize, for he remembered how bored he had been in Kent when life had seemed one long drill parade. "I know what it is like, Private, but you'll be grateful to the lieutenant someday. It may all seem pointless now, but in the middle of a battle, it may very well save your life."

"We'll not see another battle, sir. Massena should have pulled back weeks ago. Boney must have promise him reinforcements. We'll be giving Portugal over to him by spring."

"I wouldn't be so sure," Val answered sternly. "I haven't served under him for very long, but from what I've seen, Lord Wellington is the man to drive the French out of Portugal . . . and Spain," he added as he stood up. "I'll talk to you later, Will. Maybe I can help you to a cease-fire with Mrs. Casey."

Mags Casey had certainly set her heart on marriage, Val knew, but it wasn't until she got "a-fi-anced" that her arrangement with Will wasn't enough for her. And Wellington certainly hadn't helped any, thought Val with a smile. Will would just have to give in or give her up, it seemed. Maybe he could convince his friend that a wedding date, far enough in advance, did not necessarily mean he would end up a married man. A lot could happen in a year. Mags Casey might change her mind. Her affection might fade. Or Will Tallman could be killed, as he himself had reminded Val.

"You are looking very preoccupied, Val."

"I didn't even see you, James," Val said apologetically.

"Your last reconnaissance quite distracting you, eh?"

"No, not that at all, James. I am just trying to come up with a strategy to save Will Tallman from Mrs. Casey."

James laughed. "I think that is hopeless, my friend. All Mrs. Casey has to do is sit on Sergeant Tallman while the parson closes the mousetrap!"

"I can't tell whether Wellington did Will a favor or not," admitted Val. "They are an odd couple, but do very well together when they are not at odds over this one thing."

"My money is on Mags Casey, Val. Once a woman has the ring—"

"Or medal," Val reminded him with a grin.

"Or medal. Once a woman has the status of betrothed, why, 'tis the devil to get rid of her. Especially a woman of Mrs. Casey's stature and determination!"

"I like Mags Casey," Val declared warmly. "But Will

Tallman is one of my oldest friends and he does not believe a professional soldier should take a wife."

"But do you think they would be happy together?"

"I am sure of it, once Will got used to it."

"Then maybe it is a friend's place to help things along."

"I'll have to think about it, James. Speaking of marriage, how is your sister doing? Have you heard from her recently?"

"In the last mail. She is beside herself with excitement."

"As she should be. Are you planning to be there for any part of the Season?"

"I've requested a short leave. It remains to be seen whether Wellington will grant it."

"Perhaps *you* will meet someone yourself, James. As Marquess of Wimborne, you will need to be thinking of marriage and producing an heir soon. Is there some young lady you have a preference for?"

"No young ladies have captured my heart, Val," replied James. "And despite the title, the finances are in such a state that I doubt a parent would welcome my suit," he added with a smile. "But enough of my affairs. Are you in camp for a few days?"

"As far as I know."

"Then what about an early morning ride together? Charles and I were planning to meet tomorrow. Will you join us?"

"I would be happy to, James."

"Till tomorrow, then," said James as he bade Val good-bye. "And we'll see if this friend can help things along with you," he added sotto voce as he watched Val walk away.

Chapter 18

The next morning a heavy mist hung over the countryside and Val and his horse were covered with fog droplets after only a minute. He had decided to give Caesar a rest and had chosen a rangy bay from the stables, one he'd never ridden before. The animal was high-strung and the slightest thing spooked him, like a tree appearing suddenly out of the mist, and Val had to concentrate on keeping his seat. When he reached the edge of the camp, he was almost on top of James before he saw him.

"What a morning," Val exclaimed.

"But the sun is already breaking through," said James, pointing to the ridge that bordered the camp on the east. "In fifteen minutes we will be exclaiming over the beauty of the day."

"I hope so. Where is Charlie?"

"I'm sure he'll be here any moment. There, I can see them . . . er, him."

Val did not catch James's slip of the tongue and when two riders emerged out of the mist, he looked over at his friend in surprise. "He's brought someone with him?"

"Why, so he has," said James cheerfully.

"Good morning, Val," Charlie called out. "Miss Gordon often rides out in the morning, so I asked her to join us. You don't mind, James?"

"Not at all. In fact, I am delighted. Aren't you, Val?"

"Of course." Well, what else could he have said? That he was dreading his next encounter with Elspeth Gordon?

She looked as embarrassed and uncomfortable as he felt. When he glanced over at Charlie and James, he saw his brother and his friend exchanging self-satisfied grins. So this wasn't really a delightful surprise to them, eh? Only to Miss Gordon and himself!

They rode slowly, James and Val in front and Charlie and Elspeth behind for a few minutes, and then, as if a giant hand had pulled aside a gray veil, the sun broke through the fog.

"There, didn't I tell you, Val?" said James. He turned in his saddle. "Why don't we try a nice long canter, Charlie? Elspeth?"

They spurred their horses and galloped across the valley. It *was* a glorious morning, Val had to admit as his horse finally settled down. Now that the animal was warmed up and the mist was gone, he realized the horse had a very comfortable gait and he relaxed into it, almost forgetting that Miss Gordon was a member of their party and he would have to converse with her sooner or later.

It became clear that it would be sooner rather than later, for as they pulled their horses to a trot and then a walk, Charlie ended up next to James and Val was side by side with Elspeth. "It has turned into a lovely day, hasn't it, Miss Gordon?" Val said politely.

"Yes, it has, Lieutenant. The sun is most welcome after the gray days we have had this week," Elspeth responded with equal formality.

Val turned in his saddle to face her. The sun was shining directly behind her and all the fog droplets that clung to her jacket had turned to diamonds. Her hair burned with reddish-gold lights and her face was flushed from their ride. She was dazzling and Val could think of nothing to say.

Finally Elspeth broke the uncomfortable silence. "I did not know that you were of the party, Lieutenant."

He supposed that after the other night, she hadn't wanted to see him again.

"I hope I have not spoiled your morning," Elspeth continued apologetically.

"And I hope I did not spoil yours . . . or your evening at the dance," he added, finally finding his voice.

Elspeth blushed. "I . . . enjoyed our walk in the garden, Lieutenant," she said.

"But had we been seen, it would have been awkward."

"Certainly not more awkward than the circumstances when we met," said Elspeth with a slight smile. "You have already compromised me and we agreed that was nothing to worry about."

"I think that you dismiss yourself too easily, Miss Gordon," Val said quietly. "You are an attractive woman and I could not help but respond to that the other night. But I should not have, for it would be both unfair and unwise to create expectations in, uh, either of us, that it would ever happen again."

"What sort of expectations, Lieutenant?" Elspeth asked brashly.

"We have agreed to be friends, Miss Gordon. But there could be no future for any other relationship between us. It was wrong of me to kiss you," he added.

God, but he sounded stiff and pompous. But what else

could he say? That the more he was with her, the more he was drawn to her? That he wanted to lean over and kiss her right now? They had both pulled their horses up and she was looking up at him, her lips parted, her eyes made almost green by the dark green jacket she was wearing.

"Why was it wrong, Lieutenant? After all, I practically asked you to. And you enjoyed the kiss, didn't you?"

Val groaned. "Of course I did. I didn't want it to end, damn it. I want to kiss you right now, and I would if Charlie and James weren't right ahead of us. Does that satisfy you, Miss Gordon? To know that I want you?" he added angrily.

"Not if it makes you so unhappy," Elspeth told him quietly.

"I am not unhappy, just frustrated. I am not used to wanting a respectable woman," he said bitterly. "Nothing can come of our kisses, Miss Gordon."

"And why is that, Lieutenant? Remind me," Elspeth said tartly.

"You know why."

"Oh, yes. Because I am the granddaughter of an earl and you are the bastard son of one. Of course, I am not asking you to *marry* me, Lieutenant. Just to kiss me, since we both find it mutually satisfying," Elspeth continued with dry humor.

Val laughed. He couldn't help it. Damn the woman. Here he was, trying to do the honorable thing, and here she was, deflating his heroic effort. And that was why he liked her so much: her sense of humor.

"I can't help it if you are determined to do the honorable thing, Lieutenant. But I don't have to pretend to like it," Elspeth added.

They were both smiling now. "Miss Gordon, whatever you think of yourself, you are an attractive woman and you will, I am sure, meet someone who will be free to woo you with kisses. But since that cannot be me, let us agree again to stay friends. Truly, I think we make very good friends if we can navigate such dangerous waters and end up smiling at one another."

"Oh, I suppose I shall have to agree with you, Lieutenant Aston, for clearly there is no hope of you ever coming down from your high horse."

Val was just about to offer her his hand to seal their

bargain when Charlie, who had turned around and was riding toward them, gave a loud hallo. Val's horse shied suddenly and then bucked, tipping him neatly out of the saddle.

"Oh, I say, Val, are you all right?" asked Charlie.

"Only my dignity is hurt, Charlie. It was not the best moment to be thrown," he added, grinning up at Elspeth.

"On the contrary, Lieutenant," said Elspeth, smiling back, "it was most appropriate."

"It is these foot soldiers," teased Charlie. "Give them a horse and they can barely stay on."

Val stood up and rubbed his hip. "And your light horsemen wouldn't last more than an hour of a day's march, Charlie."

"Come, Elspeth, we will leave them to their bickering," said James, who had ridden up in time to hear their interchange.

Val glared at Charlie and when James and Elspeth were out of hearing, said, "Now what was all this about, Charlie?"

"All what?"

"Don't play innocent with me, Charles," said Val, sounding so much like their father that Charlie grinned. "And don't be grinning at me like a monkey. What kind of scheming are you and James up to?"

"It was not a *scheme,*" Charlie responded indignantly. "You and Miss Gordon are friends, are you not? Why shouldn't I invite one of your friends on a morning ride?"

"And that was all there was to it?" Val said skeptically.

Charlie gave him a sheepish smile. "Well, both James and I had noticed when the two of you disappeared into the garden on Christmas night. She would make a wonderful wife for you," Charlie added in a burst of enthusiasm.

"You always did rush in, Charlie—"

"Are you calling me a fool, Val?"

"No, but can't you see that Miss Gordon and I can be no more than friends?"

"Oh, yes, I can see it very well, Valentine. It is your stubborn, bloody *pride.* Elspeth Gordon would not have spent a minute alone with you if she wasn't interested in something more than friendship, so it is not she who is putting up a barrier, is it? It is you and that damn plank you carry around on your shoulder. It is you who runs away when someone offers you acceptance and affection. Look what you did with Father. You would have run away from me too, if I'd let you. Because you consider me and anyone who cares about you a fool, don't you? For how could anyone love a bastard? Actually, Valentine, the question you should be asking yourself is how could anyone love such an arrogant, muddleheaded idiot!''

Charlie spurred his horse and cantered off without a backward look, leaving Val openmouthed in amazement. Charlie had never criticized him, had never really been angry with him before. Charlie had always loved him and admired him unconditionally.

Charlie was wrong, he told himself stubbornly. He had run from school because he didn't belong, and from the earl for the same reason. And pride? Why, he had no pride; he only carried the everlasting shame of his birth.

He mounted the bay carefully and held him down to a walk as he rode back to camp. He wanted to dismiss all of Charlie's charges as foolish, but what if he was even partially right? James had also accused him of having a chip on his shoulder, of looking for insult when there was none. But damn it, why shouldn't he? There had been plenty of insults offered him over the years. He had learned to wear an armor of pride, for he would never have given his tormentors the satisfaction of knowing that they had hurt him.

Yet there he was, using the word himself. But how, Charlie, could someone who was proud (not that he was admitting it, mind you) also feel that those who loved him were fools? You can't have it both ways, brother!

But Val was nothing if not honest and as his anger faded away, he thought about Charlie. His younger brother had offered him love almost immediately, an openhearted, unquestioning love. Val had responded to it. How could he not, for he was so starved for affection? He remembered that instant feeling of sympathy when Charlie spoke of losing his mother. That had forged the bond between them.

But admit it, Val, he told himself as he searched his soul. There has always been something in you that has held back from Charlie. You *do* think him a little foolish for loving you and idealizing you. It was a dark corner of his heart that he was holding a lantern to and he didn't like what the light revealed. Huddled in that corner was a young boy who had been exiled from Paradise and exposed to the shame of illegitimacy. That boy had felt unlovable; that boy . . . But before Val could see his face, before he could feel as he had felt, he shuttered the lantern.

The sun was shining and he was almost back at the encampment. He had only been in that dark corner for a moment, but that had been long enough to know that he didn't want to go back anytime soon. Going back would mean looking into that boy's face and feeling his heartbreak and Val was not ready or willing to do that. He wasn't sure he ever would be.

"Charlie did not tell me that we were going to join you and Lieutenant Aston, James. I would not have come if I had known," Elspeth said as they rode back.

"I suppose I owe you an apology, Elspeth," admitted James. "I confess that Charlie and I were playing matchmakers. You and Lieutenant Aston—"

"Are good friends, James," Elspeth said firmly.

"And nothing more?"

"Not according to Lieutenant Aston."

"And what about you, Elspeth?"

"I am happy to have him as a friend. I admit he is a very attractive man . . . but then so are you, and that has never gotten in the way of our friendship. Indeed, I have always wondered why."

"Perhaps it is because I am Maddie's brother and therefore something like a brother to you," he replied easily.

"You are probably right," she agreed with a fond smile. "Whatever it is, James, I am glad of it, for it is good to have an uncomplicated friendship with a man you care for."

"I cannot agree with you more, Elspeth. Romantic feelings complicate things, don't they?" he added with pointed humor.

Elspeth was happy to find that her father was already up and away and her mother still asleep when she returned to the house. Private Ryan had a bath waiting and after she added a few pitchers of hot water she sank down into the copper tub gratefully and let the heat soak the stiffness out of her muscles.

As she relaxed, she thought back on her conversation with Lieutenant Aston. At first he had been stiff and unbending: They could only be friends, he was sorry for their kiss. She had never felt so embarrassed in her life until he had admitted he wanted to kiss her again, right then and there. She felt herself grow warmer than the hot water warranted as she imagined what a second kiss might have been like. She wanted him as much as he seemed to want her, she realized as she closed her eyes and felt herself dissolve away, until she was all desire.

Despite her heated state, she realized after a few minutes the bathwater was growing cold. What do I want from Valentine Aston? she wondered as she stood up and wrapped some toweling around her. Certainly she wanted another kiss. But was there more? She certainly wanted their friendship. They shared too much to give it up: the danger that had brought them together, the experience of not quite belonging, and a sense of humor. Thank God for that, or their conversation could have led to disaster.

He had said he could not marry her. But might he want to marry her? she wondered as she stared into the small mirror hung on the wall. She wasn't beautiful. He was more beautiful than she, Elspeth thought, despite the scar running down his jaw and that very noticeable nose. She knew most women would have found Charlie or James more attractive. Perhaps it was the juxtaposition of hard and soft, guardedness and tenderness, strength and vulnerability that drew her.

No other man of her acquaintance had stirred her this way. But she had guarded herself for so long from any dream of love that she was almost afraid to look at her own feelings. What *did* she want from him besides his kisses and his friendship? She wasn't at all sure, but was beginning to think that it might be his love.

And wasn't that a pity? Elspeth told herself. For even if she were to inspire it, which was unlikely, Lieutenant Val Aston was so proud that he would never admit to it.

Chapter 19

Val had given a brief report to Captain Grant when he returned from the mountains, but he was again summoned to Grant's tent a few days after his morning ride.

"Good day, Lieutenant. I read your report."

"It wasn't much of one, sir. Colonel Sanchez has not been able to gather any information about Bonaparte's plans. But at least we know that for now there are no reinforcements on their way to Santarém. It still appears a stalemate."

"But a calculated one. Massena is holding out despite his lack of supplies. Someone is feeding him very accurate information about the political situation at home."

"How is the king's health?"

"Not improving. We are very close to a Regency being declared. We have to catch this traitor, and fast, Lieutenant. We cannot keep general news from reaching the French, of course, but Massena is receiving information before it is widely known, which tells him it is worthwhile to wait. We had some luck while you were away, however. I captured a French "deserter" on my last ride out. He claimed he was starving and that is why he left."

"We have had other deserters, sir."

"Yes, but none with a hollow boot sole, Lieutenant," said Grant with a satisfied grin.

"Was he carrying anything?"

"No. We searched him thoroughly and once he knew he was well and truly caught, he admitted he was to meet an English 'milord.' " Grant looked at Val with raised eyebrows. "We have narrowed it down to three: Lucas Stanton, George Trowbridge, and James Lambert."

"Well, we know it can't be James. George is too stupid.

I have always suspected Stanton. The Frog wouldn't tell you his name?"

"He didn't have a name or a description. Only a password and a rendezvous."

"The mail arrived a few days ago," mused Val.

"Yes, it is likely that our man received news from his contact at home that he was intending to pass on."

"So we need to determine who received mail."

"I wish it was as easy as that. All three of them did."

Val frowned. "I mentioned Mrs. Casey to you before, Captain Grant. She does have easy access to all their tents. It wouldn't be hard for her to search their belongings for any recent letters."

"I don't like to put a woman in danger, Aston."

"Mags Casey is a tough woman, Captain. And right now it might be good for her to have a sense of purpose other than getting Sergeant Tallman to the altar, sir," Val replied with a twinkle in his eye.

"All right, Lieutenant, you may employ Mrs. Casey. But she is not to take any unnecessary risks, mind you."

"Don't worry, sir, I will tell her in no uncertain terms."

Val found Mags standing in front of her washtub, stirring sheets and looking uncharacteristically gloomy.

"Your bed linens are clean and dry, Lieutenant," she told him. "But I haven't had a chance to mend them yet, sir."

"That is all right, Mrs. Casey. I've come to talk about something else. Is there someplace private where we could talk?"

"We can use the tent, sir," said Mags, putting down the stick she was using to stir the sheets and wiping her hands on her voluminous apron. When they were inside she gestured toward one of the cots. "I'm afraid that is the only seat I can offer you."

"This is fine, Mrs. Casey. Please sit down."

She sat herself on the edge of the opposite pallet. "Now, Lieutenant, if this is about Will Tallman . . . I would be disturbed to think he would send you to me. But I am not going to end our betrothal and I *do* want to know when he intends to marry me," she added in a rush.

"It has nothing to do with Will, Mrs. Casey," Val reas-

sured her. "It is something far more important. Captain
Grant and I have a request to make of you. But I want
you to know that you are at liberty to refuse if you want."

Mrs. Casey's eyes lit up. "You need my help snooping
around, do you, Lieutenant? Well, I am right happy to do
it for you. Why, who else could do it as well as I?"

"That is what I told Captain Grant. You are in and out
of officers' tents and could easily look through their things.
Do you read, Mrs. Casey?" Val asked hesitantly. He suddenly realized that the whole scheme might collapse right
then and there.

"I can, Lieutenant," Mrs. Casey answered proudly. "I
have enough reading and figuring to keep my own accounts," she added, pulling a small tattering book out of
her pocket. Thumbing through the pages, she read slowly,
"Lieutenant Trowbridge, two shillings."

"Then you will be perfect," said Val with a relieved
smile. "We need you to read through any letters recently
arrived from London. Someone is keeping the French well-
informed about the political situation at home, so you
would be looking for any information about the king's
health and a possible Regency bill."

"Is the old king gone mad again, sir?"

"He has had another episode. At first it seemed he had
recovered, but then he suffered a relapse."

"Dear me, then his foolish son would be in charge,
Lieutenant?"

"Er, the prince would become regent, that is true."

"I don't think much of him, sir. There he was, married
to that lovely lady, even though she was a Papist. Mr. Casey
was a Papist, you know, and they are not all devils, though
the ministers would have us believe so."

"His position demanded he marry royalty, Mrs. Casey—"

"Oh, aye, but I lost all respect for him, Lieutenant. He
gave her his hand and his heart and then he abandoned
her."

"I must confess I sympathized with Mrs. Fitzherbert myself, Mrs. Casey," Val replied honestly. The prince's behavior, necessary though it was, reminded him too much of the
earl's treatment of his mother. "But unfortunately, he is
the eldest son and heir . . ." Val ran his hand over his face.

"I shouldn't have said that. Of course we are lucky to have him there to assume the Regency."

"Now, that is a load of codswollop, Lieutenant. He is a frivolous and foolish man, from what I have heard, spending money on foreign-looking buildings while people are hungry."

"I didn't know you were a Republican, Mrs. Casey."

"I am not one for chopping peoples' heads off, no matter if they deserve it. But I am a woman of common sense, Lieutenant, and I say you don't leave your soldiers who fought for you begging in the streets!" Mrs. Casey took a deep breath. "But much as I don't care for the prince, I would do anything I could to beat Boney."

"I am sure you would."

"Now, just who am I to be spying on?" asked Mrs. Casey with a gleam in her eye.

"We have narrowed it down to three suspects: Lords Stanton, Trowbridge, and Wimborne."

"Never! The marquess is a real gentleman."

"And a good friend of mine, so I must agree with you. But everyone else has been eliminated for one reason or another."

"I would bet it is that Lord Stanton. He's a mean one, Lieutenant. I've seen more than one girl come back from a night with him bruised and crying."

"I must confess that I have my own reasons for hoping it is Stanton," admitted Val. "But you must search all three carefully. And Mrs. Casey, I would not accuse you of being a gossip, but I know you love to talk . . ."

Mags laughed. "Don't worry, Lieutenant. Nothing will pass my lips."

"Not even to Sergeant Tallman," he cautioned.

"Him! He's lucky I am talking to him at all."

"We will pay you well, Mrs. Casey."

Mags looked shocked. "Why, I am a hardworking woman and proud of it, Lieutenant. I would be ashamed to take any money for helping Lord Wellington win the war."

"You have my sincere admiration, then, Mrs. Casey," said Val as he stood up to leave. "And mind that you take care."

"Don't worry. Not many men would mess with Mags Casey!"

* * *

Will Tallman had felt so badgered by Mags that at first
he was relieved when she adopted a new tactic and feigned
indifference. After a week of a cold and empty bed and
dirty laundry, however, he admitted to himself that life with
Mags even if she was constantly nattering on about marriage was preferable to life without her. He began to make
sure their paths crossed at least once a day and would stop
and chat with her. But she remained cool, barely giving
him the time of day. At first her attempt to show him that
he didn't matter to her amused him. But then, as days went
by, he became a little angry. She was beginning to seem
perfectly able to do without him. It just went to prove the
fickleness of women, he thought. After you for years to
marry them and then, all of a sudden, you were dirt under
their feet. And having to pay if you wanted your laundry
done or a woman in your bed! Not that he *wanted* another
woman in his bed, damn it. He wanted Mags Casey.

Mags was well aware of Will's reaction.

"He don't look happy, Mags," Lucy Brown told her after
Will brought her his dirty sheets.

"As well he shouldn't."

"But you are looking chipper enough!"

"I have more important things to do than to mope
around about Sergeant Tallman!"

She had been able to think of little else than Val's proposal as she washed and folded and mended the weekly
laundry. And after the next mail, she would begin her ca-
reer as a spy.

There was another mail delivery only a week after the
last, and when Mags made her rounds the day after, she
made sure to wait until afternoon when all three officers
were out.

Lieutenant Trowbridge's tent was first and her hands
were shaking as she picked up the letter that had fallen on
the floor next to his bed. She read it as quickly as she
could; it proved to be a letter from his younger brother,
who was mainly interested in the successes of a popular
pugilist and his own luck or lack thereof at the gaming
tables. "There is nothing for you here, Mags," she whis-

pered to herself as she put the letter back where she found it. "Unless this is some sort of code."

Lord Stanton's tent was next and Mags glanced over her shoulder somewhat fearfully as she entered. She didn't like Lieutenant Stanton any more than Lieutenant Aston did and she was convinced that if any one of these men was a spy, it must be he.

Stanton kept his tent very neat and there were no papers scattered about. Mags put her pile of laundry down and went over to the table Stanton used as a desk. There were two books, an inkwell, and a quill pen on the left-hand side, and on the right, three letters refolded and held down by a stone. "Now put things back as you find them, Mags," she reminded herself as she lifted the makeshift paperweight and began to unfold the first letter.

It was from Lord Stanton's mother, who seemed much more concerned with the latest society scandal than the political situation in London. The second one was from an old school friend, who also reported on the latest prizefight and the sales at Newmarket. There was nothing remotely suspicious about the letter, although the last paragraph was puzzling. The writer congratulated Lord Stanton on his successful "squeezing" of someone who was obviously another of their old schoolmates, but was not named. "Get as much as you can out of him now, Lucas. Indeed, I am surprised you've had anything from him, for rumor has it that he is pockets to let. But it is, after all, a capital offense."

"He must be blackmailing someone," Mags muttered. "He's a right nasty one, Lord Stanton."

She was just opening the third letter when she thought she heard a movement at the back of the tent. She froze, but heard nothing more, and decided she had been imagining things and quickly scanned the third letter, which was from a Lady Louisa, and obviously one of Lord Stanton's paramours. The writer did mention the king's illness in passing, but so briefly that Mags knew it could mean nothing. She carefully refolded the letters and placed them in their original order underneath the stone.

She was very proud of herself for being so careful. She made a bloody good spy, if she did say so as shouldn't, she thought.

The marquess's tent was farther down the row and Mags

was hurrying along when she heard a hiss from behind one of the tents. "Madame," came a whisper. She responded automatically, wondering who would be calling her, never even realizing it was a French form of address. As she stepped between the tents, all she was aware of was that the man who had summoned her wore a very dirty and tattered uniform of a voltigeur. One of the Frog deserters, who thinks I am going to do *his* laundry! was her last thought before she saw the pistol butt descend on her head.

"Have you seen Mrs. Casey, Val?" James asked later that evening after supper. "She was to have brought me my clean shirts this afternoon, but when I got back to my tent, the dirty laundry was still uncollected."

Val frowned. "Are you sure this is her laundry day, James?"

"She is usually as regular as clockwork. George," he called out to Lord Trowbridge, who was just passing by. "Did Mrs. Casey deliver to you today?"

"She did, James."

"That's very odd, then, isn't it, Val?"

"Perhaps she just had too much to carry, James. She'll probably be there tomorrow."

"You are likely right."

"Well, I must excuse myself," said Val. "I promised Will a game of hazard."

Val was hoping that Mags would be sitting in front of Will's fire, but it was only Murphy and Doolittle, throwing the dice.

"Have you seen Mrs. Casey anywhere, Will?" Val asked as casually as he could.

"I haven't seen her all week," Will replied.

"She's finally given up on him," teased Private Murphy.

" 'E's won and I've lost," confessed Doolittle. "I bet two shillings that she'd wear 'im down. Maybe I can win something back from you, Lieutenant," he added, rolling the dice.

"Uh, I just realized that there is something I need to take care of," stammered Val. "I will be right back."

Val told himself that nothing was wrong. Mags Casey had obviously decided to ignore Will. She had more laundry than she could handle, was all. But the mail had arrived yesterday, damn it. When he got to the tent she shared with Mrs. Brown, he found it dark and Mrs. Brown outside, drinking with the other women.

"Have you seen Mrs. Casey, Lucy?"

Mrs. Brown frowned. "Not since this afternoon, now that you ask, Lieutenant, but she had her deliveries to make, you know."

"She didn't finish them, it seems."

"Well, she had all her officers' linens done," Lucy responded with a puzzled look on her face. "Have you tried Will Tallman? I know Mags was bent on ignoring him this week, but maybe they've made it up."

"Uh, no," lied Val. "But I'm sure I'll find her there, Mrs. Brown. Thank you." Val kept a smile on his face, for he didn't want to start any rumors, but he hurried back to Will.

"Can I talk to you alone, Will?"

"Of course, sir."

"Let's walk for a few minutes," suggested Val.

"What is it, Lieutenant?"

"You must keep what I tell you absolutely secret, Will," Val warned him.

"You can trust me, sir," said Will, a puzzled look on his face.

"There is certain information that we needed about one of the officers, Will. I can't tell you more than that. But it seemed the best way to get it was to have someone who was always in and out of their tents to obtain it for us, so I asked Mrs. Casey if she would be willing to help us out."

Will grabbed Val by the sleeve. "You got Mags to spy for you?"

"I didn't think there would be much danger, Will, or I wouldn't have asked her. It's just that the mail came yesterday and she never finished her laundry rounds today."

"And Mrs. Brown?"

"I was just there. She hasn't seen her since this afternoon."

Like most redheads, Will Tallman was a pale man, but he grew even whiter at his news. "Do you think something has happened?"

"I don't know, but we need to find her, Will."

*   *   *

They found her outside the camp behind a clump of rocks.

"Mags," cried Will, falling on his knees beside her. "Oh, my God, look at her head."

Van knelt down and felt for a pulse. "She's alive, Will, but just barely. Go for the doctor."

"I can't leave her, sir, not like this."

"We need him quickly, Will. I'll stay with her."

Will touched Mags's cheek gently with his hand. "I'll be right back, Mags."

"And Will, get hold of something to carry her on and a few men to help us."

The left side of Mrs. Casey's face was covered with blood and her eye was swollen and protruding. Val took one of her hands in his. "I am sorry, Mags," he whispered. "I never would have asked you to do this had I thought there was any real risk."

Doctor Clitheroe was there in minutes. "Private Tallman is getting a pallet and will be here in a minute, Lieutenant Aston. Let me take a look." He lifted her uninjured eyelid and probed her head gently. "She appears to have been severely beaten."

"Will she live?"

"There is extensive damage to the skull and she may well lose that eye, Lieutenant. But her pulse is steady and she is a strong woman, Mags Casey, so she may very well come through. I just can't imagine who would do this to her."

When Will arrived with his small brigade, they lifted Mags carefully onto the pallet and carried her back to the hospital tent, where the doctor gently cleaned the blood off her face.

"I will kill the man who did this," Will said quietly but with such ferocity that the doctor looked up at him.

"Then I am glad I am not he."

"Look at her poor eye," whispered Will.

"Indeed, there is a lot of swelling on that side, both internal and external. She may well lose it, or at least the use of it."

"But she will be all right, Doctor?"

"I don't know, Sergeant Tallman. Only the next few days will tell. The sooner she regains consciousness, the better, of course. I'll send for you if there is any change."

"No, sir, you will not send for me, for I will be right here next to her."

"You can't stay here, Will," Val told him gently.

"I'll be here when I am not on duty, sir," Will replied firmly.

Val looked over at the doctor, who shrugged and said, "It is your choice, Sergeant Tallman. I'll have my orderly set up a cot."

Chapter 20

The news was all over the camp by morning and speculation ran wild as to who was responsible. Mags was popular with all who knew her and even Lord Wellington, who remembered her from Christmas Day, showed his concern by sending his orderly over with some oranges.

Two days later Mrs. Casey had still not regained consciousness, although the swelling had gone down and she looked more herself.

"It looks like she will keep the eye," the doctor told Will. "Though whether she will be able to see out of it is another question."

"When do you think she will wake up, Doctor?" Will was afraid to ask if the surgeon thought she ever would.

Clitheroe patted Will's shoulder reassuringly. "I've seen many a man unconscious longer than this, Will, who made a complete recovery. Now why don't you go back to your own tent and get some sleep, for God's sake? You are beginning to look worse than Mags."

"You do look exhausted, Sergeant Tallman," said a voice behind him. It was Elspeth, who had visited once already. "I will sit with Mrs. Casey awhile if you wish."

"Thank you, Miss Gordon, but it isn't the waiting I mind," said Will, looking at Elspeth with tortured eyes. "I didn't give her the one thing she wanted from me. I didn't make her my wife."

"I am *sure* Mrs. Casey will recover, Sergeant."

"I am not, miss," Will confessed quietly. "May I ask you something, private-like?"

"Of course, Sergeant," said Elspeth. "Come, we can step outside for a minute."

"I was wondering if you could talk to the chaplain for me. I was thinking that the one thing I could do for Mags . . . if she doesn't recover, you see . . . I'd like to marry her."

"But she is not able to take part in the ceremony, Private Tallman. She can't say her vows."

"No, miss, but I was wondering if you would take her part. Do it proxy-like."

Elspeth frowned. "I don't know, Sergeant Tallman. I have heard of proxy weddings, of course, but they usually take place when the bride or groom is far away."

"Well, Mags is far away, in a manner of speaking, but there is no doubt in anyone's mind that she wished to marry me."

Elspeth smiled. "No, Sergeant, there certainly is no doubt. I will talk to the chaplain. If he agrees, I would be honored to say Mrs. Casey's vows for her."

"Thank you, Miss Gordon."

"The poor man is utterly exhausted and beside himself with grief and regret, Reverend," Elspeth told the chaplain.

"It is rather unorthodox, my dear."

"But it *is* done."

"Why, yes, but under very different circumstances. What if Mrs. Casey were to awake and not wish to have been married?"

"Reverend, the whole camp has been gossiping for months over her campaign to get Sergeant Tallman to the altar. And Lord Wellington himself witnessed their betrothal."

The chaplain hesitated and then, with a sigh, gave in. "All right, my dear. We can do it this evening."

*　　*　　*

Elspeth sent Private Ryan off to inform Will of her success and went home to make sure that her second best gown was clean and pressed. "For I am to say wedding vows this evening," she told Mrs. Ryan with twinkling eyes.

"Why, you never told me, Miss Elspeth," said Mrs. Ryan with great astonishment. "Is it that handsome Lieutenant Aston? Patrick and I have been wondering ever since you disappeared into the garden with him."

Had everyone in the camp seen her go out the door with Valentine Aston? "I am funning you, Mrs. Ryan. I am not going to be saying my own vows, but Mrs. Casey's."

"God and his Holy Mother be praised, has she recovered?"

"No, she has not," said Elspeth sadly. "But Sergeant Tallman is feeling very bad that he never married Mags."

"As well he should!"

"They will be wed by proxy and I will stand in for her."

"So ye'll be almost a bride, darlin'," said Mrs. Ryan with a smile. "Give me your dress and I'll make sure it is perfect."

The hospital tent was bright with candle and lantern light when Elspeth arrived after dusk, accompanied by Private and Mrs. Ryan. When she stepped inside the tent, she was surprised to see Captain Grant looking stunningly handsome in his dress uniform. Mrs. Casey wasn't even his laundress, she thought inconsequentially. Then the tent flap lifted and Sergeant Tallman and Lieutenant Aston, also in their best uniforms, walked in. Elspeth remembered that they had both served under Captain Grant in the Caribbean.

The chaplain was standing at the foot of the bed, his prayerbook in his hand. "Who is the groomsman?" he asked. "I am, Reverend," said Val quietly.

"You and Sergeant Tallman stand over there, then," he said, motioning them to the opposite side of the bed. "Miss Gordon, you may stand beside me."

He began to read: "Dearly beloved, we are gathered here together to join in matrimony this man and this woman. . . ."

Will had told him that Elspeth would be saying Mags's vows, but Val had not realized what it would be like to see her as a proxy bride. She was dressed in an ivory wool gown and her plaid shawl was pinned to her shoulder. She looked pale, as though she were there to be married herself, but when she felt his eyes on her and looked up, she blushed a becoming rose.

For some reason the words of the Burns' song her father had sung came to Val's mind. "My love is like a red, red rose, that's newly sprung in June." It was winter, they were in a drafty hospital tent taking part in a most unusual ceremony, but Val felt his heart open in appreciation for her. The poet may have been saying two different things, he realized: that the woman he loved was as beautiful as a rose or that his own feelings were flowering as richly and strongly as that June flower. As he looked over at Elspeth, Val knew for him the song meant both. She had all the depth of a red rose, and his love for her, for that was what he felt, was as new and fresh as an opening flower.

As Elspeth quietly repeated Mags's vows for her, Val let himself imagine, just for a minute, what it would have been like were she saying them to him. He was so dazed by it all—the golden candlelight that lit her face, the soft voice in which she said the age-old words—that Will had to jab him twice in the ribs to remind him that he was holding the wedding ring.

They had managed to buy a battered old silver ring in the village and as Val handed it over, he was terribly moved by the look in Will's eyes. For all his complaining, for all his aversion to marriage, Will cared for Mags Casey, and it shone very clearly from his face as he lifted her left hand and slipped the ring on. "With this ring, I thee wed," he whispered brokenly. "And I wish I'd given in to you sooner, Mags," he added as he leaned down to give her a light kiss on the lips.

There was a moment's silence, which was broken by a concerted clearing of throats. Elspeth took the opportunity to wipe the tears from her cheeks. Sergeant Will Tallman was not a romantic figure, with his receding red hair and his weatherbeaten face, and Mrs. Casey was nothing but a common woman in some eyes, but Elspeth was very moved by the love that was so present.

Captain Grant cleared his throat a second time. "I brought a wee bit of brandy so that we could toast the bride and groom," he announced. He poured a small amount into the tin cups the doctor had provided. "To Sergeant and Mrs. Will Tallman, two fine soldiers in Lord Wellington's army."

"To Will and Mags," said Val, lifting his cup.

Elspeth was grateful for the warmth of the brandy, for it was chilly in the tent. After she drained it, she put her cup down and, unhooking her brooch, shook out her shawl.

"Here, let me help you with that, Miss Gordon." She handed the plaid over to Val, who carefully draped it over her shoulders.

"You said your vows . . . or rather, Mrs. Casey's vows . . . very well, Miss Gordon," he told her, with a look in his eyes that warmed her right down to her toes.

"Mrs. Tallman now, Lieutenant," she reminded him.

"Ah, yes, it will be hard to think of her as anything but Mrs. Casey, won't it? And even harder to think of Sergeant Tallman as a married man. You have forsworn yourself, tonight, Will," teased Val as Will approached them.

"But sworn yourself to a better fate," added Elspeth.

"I wanted to thank you, Miss Gordon. You said the vows so lovely it made it a real wedding."

"I felt privileged to be here, Sergeant Tallman. I have been to a few weddings before, but never one at which I felt the presence of such real affection."

"Oh, aye, I love Mags. I always have," admitted Will. "Thank you again, Miss Gordon. I am going to sit by my wife."

He said the word with such pride that Val had to smile. "Sergeant Tallman makes a very good Benedict, don't you think, Miss Gordon? Swearing never to marry for years and he says the word 'wife' so proudly. As well he should," Val added more seriously.

"Is there any reason Captain Grant called them both 'soldiers,' Lieutenant? Indeed, aside from his being your commanding officer, I could think of no reason for him to be here."

"I cannot say very much and I need you to keep what I do say in confidence, Miss Gordon."

"Of course."

"Mrs. Tallman had taken on a small job for us. You

might say she was injured in the line of duty," Val said seriously.

"That explains what has been puzzling me," said Elspeth. "Mrs. Casey is such a popular woman and I have not been able to figure out who in the camp would have wanted to harm her."

"We have put it around that the motive was robbery, for she had her laundry money on her."

"What was she investigating?" Elspeth asked without thinking.

"I cannot tell you that, Miss Gordon."

"Of course not, Lieutenant. I shouldn't have asked."

Val was quiet for a moment. "Sergeant Tallman was right, you know. You said your . . . her . . . vows very beautifully. When you say them for yourself someday, it will be to a very lucky man," he added.

"Thank you, Lieutenant," Elspeth replied after an awkward silence. "I only hope that Mrs. Tallman will be able to repeat her own vows soon. Oh, here is Private Ryan," said Elspeth brightly, as her father's orderly approached them. Goodness, she sounded like a ninny, announcing the obvious. But there was a feeling in the air that was making her very nervous.

"Ye did us all proud, Miss Gordon," said Private Ryan.

"I was just telling her that, Private."

"I was wondering if I might ask you a favor, sor. The missus and I would like to spend a little time with Will to keep him cheery. Would you be able to give Miss Gordon an escort home?"

"Er, I would be happy to, Private Ryan."

"Really, there is no need," Elspeth protested. "I can make my way back alone."

"Nonsense, Miss Gordon," Val said sharply. "It is unthinkable while Mrs. Tallman's attacker is still roaming free."

"You are right, Lieutenant," Elspeth admitted, "but that is no reason to take my head off," she added coolly. "Let me just say my good-byes."

They were both silent as they walked down the row, and then Val said stiffly, "I am sorry I snapped at you, Miss

Gordon. I know you are used to your independence, but I was concerned for your safety."

"I understand that, Lieutenant, and I appreciate it."

Of course, what she wouldn't have understood, thought Val as they both relaxed a little, was the other source of his tension. It was true, he *didn't* want her walking back alone, but he certainly hadn't wanted to be her escort. Not tonight, of all nights.

"Do you think Mags will recover?" Elspeth asked.

"The surgeon seems to think there is a good chance."

"If Mrs. Tallman was helping you in your investigation, then might you not be in similar danger?" asked Elspeth.

"I don't think so, or no more than usual," Val replied with a smile. "As far as we know, the person concerned is ignorant of our investigation."

"But Mags's attacker . . . ?"

"Most likely thought she was being nosy and was worried she might discover something by chance."

"I hope you are right. And I hope you will take care."

They were just starting downhill toward the village when Elspeth tripped over some loose rocks. Val instinctively reached out for her and they stood there for a moment, his arm around her waist and Elspeth leaning into him.

"Would you care if I were in danger?" he whispered, aware that being close to this woman was as great a danger as he ever faced as a soldier.

"Of course I would," Elspeth replied, attempting to make her tone matter-of-fact.

"Why?"

"Because we are good friends," she said, lowering her eyes.

"Of course. Just good friends," he added with a touch of irony. But a friend would not keep his arm around her slim waist. A friend would not pull her closer as he was doing now, so that he could feel the soft rise and fall of her breasts against his chest. And a friend would certainly not lower his head and capture her mouth with his.

As soon as his lips touched hers, Elspeth responded. Her arms went around his neck and she opened her mouth under his. After a deep kiss she turned her face away and buried it in his neck, but his collar was too stiff and so she rested her cheek on his chest, loving the feel of the rough wool and the smell of soap and healthy male. After a minute she became conscious of his buttons pressing into her cheek and she pulled back.

"Your tunic is not the most comfortable piece of clothing, sir," she said with a shaky laugh.

Val brushed her hair back gently and leaned down for another kiss, and Elspeth, heedless of the buttons, pressed herself against him. This time, she was more conscious of his trousers than his tunic, for she could feel him hard against her. She longed to have nothing between them—not the rough wool or the soft merino of her dress—and then had to laugh when he finally let her go, for it was a winter night and here she was imagining them both naked.

"I was just thinking how lovely it would be not to have so much between us," she explained when he gave her a puzzled look.

"I was thinking we need something more between us," he answered.

"Oh," she said softly.

"Miss Gordon, it is clear that our feelings go beyond friendship," he said with a note of despair in his voice.

"Yes, they do," she admitted.

"I am not going to apologize again. . . ."

"Well, thank goodness for that," she replied tartly. "I would be most insulted if you were sorry for such a lovely kiss!"

He put his hands on her shoulders and gave her a little shake. "Elspeth . . ."

"Yes, Valentine?" she whispered.

"When I looked across at you tonight, I let myself imagine . . ."

"What, Val?"

He let her go and said sadly, "Something that is quite impossible, my . . . good friend. Come, I must get you home."

By the time they reached her door, Val had himself under control. "Good night, Miss Gordon."

She lifted her face to him.

"No, Elspeth," he whispered fiercely. "Don't tempt me, for it must never happen again."

"Then good night, Lieutenant Aston," she said sadly and was inside as soon as he opened the door.

Chapter 21

Mags did not open her eyes until the middle of the next day, and when she did, she groaned as light translated itself into pain. The surgeon hurried over. "Are you awake, Mrs. Tallman?"

Mags opened her eyes halfway and this time the pain was not so bad. "Where am I?" she croaked.

"You are in the hospital tent, ma'am. You were attacked three nights ago. Do you remember none of it?"

Mags frowned and tried to concentrate, but it only made her headache worse. "My head . . . my eye . . ."

"The left side of your head was severely beaten, Mrs. Tallman. I think you will keep the eye, though I am not sure how much sight you will retain," the surgeon told her. "Here is a little laudanum for the pain."

She was asleep again shortly and didn't awake again until nearly midnight. There was a lantern next to her and this time, when she looked at the light, it was not so painful. It took a minute, but finally the shapes around her began to make sense, to her right eye at least. Her left saw only a blur. As she tried to lift herself up from her pillow, she heard Will's voice.

"Now, none of that, Mags."

"Will?"

"I'm here, Mags."

And there was his face, leaning over hers. "You look awful, Will," she exclaimed. "I can see that, even with only one eye."

Will laughed. "I am sure I do, since I have not had much sleep lately. You don't look so good yourself, woman."

"I don't feel so well, Will," she said as she lay back, her head throbbing.

"I am not surprised, after the beating you took," he replied, taking her hand in his. "You are lucky to be here, Mags."

She closed her eyes and frowned. "I am trying to remember, Will, but I can only remember going into Lieutenant Stanton's tent."

"The doctor says that happens, Mags. You may remember more in a few days, but it's possible you never will. Now go back to sleep. I'm right here with you."

"I'm glad, Will," she whispered and she squeezed his hand.

The next morning she felt more like herself, although the headache was still there and her left eye was not seeing much.

"Where is Will?" she asked plaintively when the doctor came.

"He's drilling his soldiers, Mrs. Tallman. We can't have him called up for desertion, now, can we?"

This time it penetrated. "Why do you keep calling me that?"

"What?"

"Mrs. Tallman. I'm Mags Casey, though I've been wanting to be Mrs. Tallman for a long time," she said with some of her old energy.

"Oh, dear, I wasn't even thinking," said the doctor. "I should have had Sergeant Tallman tell you."

"Tell me what?"

"There was a possibility that you would never . . . er . . . regain consciousness, Mags. Will knew that and he felt terrible he hadn't married you. So he did."

"Did what?" asked Mags, thinking that the beating must have been worse than she thought, for she wasn't understanding a word the doctor said.

"Married you."

"Married me? How could he marry me if I was not awake?"

"Well, it was what is called a proxy marriage. You were betrothed and everyone knew that you wished to marry Sergeant Tallman. So he asked Miss Gordon to speak your vows for you."

For one of the few times in her life, Mags was speechless.

"It was a lovely ceremony, Mrs. Tallman. Lieutenant Aston stood up for Will and Captain Grant looked splendid in his uniform," the doctor told her reassuringly.

"A lovely ceremony," she whispered.

"Now," said the doctor, sitting down next to her, "I want you to tell me how your head feels."

"Like I was kicked by a mule. And I can't see much out of my left eye."

"You may never again, Mrs. Tallman, but it was a miracle I could save it and that you see anything at all. Now the orderly will serve you some gruel and then I want you to get some sleep."

"Some sleep? It seems all I have been doing is sleeping," grumbled Mags, but after a bowlful of gruel and some barley water, she went right off.

It was only a few hours later that she awakened and this time she felt much more herself. Her head was still throbbing, but now it was only a distant drumbeat rather than all the drummers in the army taking up residence in her head. She made the orderly give her an extra pillow, so she was sitting when Will walked in.

His smile was radiant when he saw her.

"Will Tallman, you come right here," she said sharply.

"Are you all right, Mags?"

"Mags! You mean Mrs. Tallman, don't you?"

Will gave her a sheepish grin.

"After all these years of trying to get you to the altar, Will, and I wasn't at my own wedding," she scolded.

"I'm sorry, Mags—" he started to say.

"Sorry, Will?" she asked, the tears slipping down her cheeks. "Sorry, when you gave me something I wanted for so long? The right to call you mine." She reached out her hand to him and he took it in his.

Mags cleared her throat and tried to keep her voice from shaking. "Will Tallman, you are a good man and I love you for this. So much that I'll let you out of it if you are sorry for any other reason. I never heard of this proxy business and I am sure you could have the marriage annulled if you wanted. Though we have consummated it enough in advance," she added with a grin.

"You would do that, Mags?" he asked wonderingly.

"You never wanted a wife, Will. I shouldn't have kept at you. You only did it because you thought I was dying."

"Let me tell you, Mags Casey . . . I mean Mags Tallman . . . I did it because I love you and because it was the right thing to do. I've been thinking like a soldier for too long. It was time I acted like a man. So you are my wife, Mrs. Tallman, whether you want to be or not."

"Oh, I want to be, Will," said Mags with a little sob. "And that is your one and only chance to get out of it," she added.

"I don't want to, Mags."

"Nor do I, Will Tallman, and I take you as my husband to love and to cherish . . . I don't remember all the rest," she said with a blush, "though I've done it before!"

"Till death do us part, Mags," he whispered.

"Till death do us part."

As Val had told Elspeth, everyone believed Mags's beating had been part of a robbery. Sunday he was invited by the Gordons to dinner. As reluctant as he was to face Elspeth again, he knew that all three suspects would be there, and he was very careful to observe George, Lucas, and even James when the subject came up.

"I hear that Mrs. Casey has regained consciousness," said George.

"Thank God for that. She is the only one who does my shirts satisfactorily," complained Lucas Stanton. "But she is Mrs. Tallman now, or so I hear," he added sarcastically. "Setting herself up to become a widow again."

"Sergeant Tallman is a good soldier and has come through safely all these years," James commented. "I found the story of their marriage quite touching myself. I have always enjoyed Mags and I am very glad to hear she has not only recovered but has got her heart's desire," he added emphatically.

George's face had its usual dull look and Stanton seemed most concerned about the state of his laundry, thought Val. James? James, of course, would think of Mags, good fellow that he was. Well, he and the captain had concluded that it was most likely the contact who had attacked Mags, for not even Val could believe Stanton would attack a woman so brutally.

During dinner, Elspeth tried very hard to keep her eyes off Val, but it was almost impossible, for her gaze was drawn to his face more than one. She thought how ironic it was that the legitimate gentlemen were so ignoble-looking: George with his pasty round face and Lucas, whose eyes were narrow and mean and whose thin lips she would never have wanted on her own. Lieutenant Aston's mouth . . . no, it wouldn't do to look at his mouth or even think of it. Now, James, at least, looked and acted as a marquess should, if a title meant anything about the man who carried it. He was handsome, athletic, intelligent, and, most important of all, kind. When she had been at school with Maddie, half of the girls had fallen in love with him on his regular visits to his sister. Elspeth wondered again why he had not found anyone. He seemed to live an ascetic life, for she had never heard any gossip about mistresses and there had never been even a hint of a liaison here in Portugal. She knew that he was greatly burdened by his debts. Perhaps he could not afford a mistress. Perhaps he had put off his own need to marry until he got his sister settled. Well, good luck, James, she thought with some amusement, for Maddie's letters sounded like she was intent on enjoying her first Season to the hilt and did not sound at all ready to settle down.

After dinner and a few glasses of port, all of the guests except James took their leave. James lingered by the fire, chatting with Major and Mrs. Gordon about this and that, but all the while watching Elspeth out of the corner of his eye. When the Gordons excused themselves, he sat down opposite her.

"I heard from Maddie this week, Elspeth."

"Did you, James? And how is she? The last letter I received sounded like she was spending all her time at the dressmaker's."

"Her wardrobe seems to be almost complete and she will be leaving for London in a fortnight."

"Will you be able to join her for any part of the Season?"

"I am hoping to."

"It might be wise, James, if you want her future to be settled sooner rather than later. I rather suspect Maddie wishes to enjoy herself before choosing a husband," Elspeth said with a smile.

"I am afraid you are right," James agreed. "Not that I can blame her, for there may be very few choices in the end. I have only been able to squeeze out a small dowry for her. What she needs is for a rich man to fall madly in love with her, so that he doesn't care about her lack of fortune."

"And what do you need, James? I was thinking about you during dinner."

James lifted his eyebrows and gave her a quizzical grin. "Oh, I rather thought you were thinking more about Lieutenant Aston, judging by the way you were stealing glances at him," he teased.

Elspeth blushed. "Was I so obvious?"

"Only to me, Elspeth, for I know you well. But I shouldn't tease you, my dear. It is kind of you to be concerned about me."

"I was thinking of nobility and titles, James, and how well they fit some and how ill others. You, for instance: You are a true gentleman and deserve a loving woman."

"We all deserve love, Elspeth, but not all of us find it. Or have it find us." James hesitated as if he wanted to say more in an intimate vein, but then he continued humorously, "I suppose I will settle for any woman who will have me and my tarnished title. I suspect it may well have to be a wealthy cit's daughter. But I have been wondering, Elspeth," he continued more seriously, "has love found you?"

"I don't know, James," she answered simply. "I have been so long resigned to the fact I would likely never marry that I have guarded myself well against the possibility of love. I've never really believed I would inspire romantic feelings in another, but it could be I have been taken by surprise," she admitted with a blush.

"I have no way of knowing his feelings, but Valentine Aston is well worth loving, if you have any doubts," James said quietly. "If you do love him, it may be a long siege, my dear, trying to breach the wall of pride and insecurity he has constructed around himself."

"But what if I send my love out like the Forlorn Hope and I can't get through, James?" she asked with a rueful smile.

"Like any soldier, you must keep trying, no matter how hopeless it looks."

"Has love ever found you, James?"

James lifted his eyes to her and for one moment Elspeth thought she saw a soul in torment, but he lowered them so quickly, and his face was so calm, she told herself she had imagined it.

"Once," he said quietly. "But like many first loves, it was doomed to be unrequited," he added lightly.

"I hope loves come to you, James," said Elspeth, as she put a hand comfortingly on his. "You are a good man and dear friend."

"You think so, do you? A good man?"

"Of course. All who know you think so. How could they not?"

"Thank you for your trust in me, Elspeth," said James as he got up. "I must be going now or your father will be out here wanting to know what my intentions are," he joked.

As James walked back to his tent, he smiled a bitter smile, and had Elspeth been able to look into his eyes at that moment, she would have had no doubts about the unhappiness she had seen.

Chapter 22

Mags was released by the doctor at the end of a week on the condition that she rest for at least another two. She and Will settled in together, and Mrs. Ryan came to look in on her when Will was on duty.

She had not made any efforts to remember while in the doctor's care. Her head had hurt too much and her waking moments had been clouded with the laudanum he had given her for the pain. But now that the headaches were almost gone, she tried, unsuccessfully, to summon up the face of her assailant.

"I could be walking right past him, Will, and never know it," she said one night.

"Now, Mags, I don't want you making yourself sick trying to remember. One of the French deserters disappeared a few days after it happened and Captain Grant thinks that he was likely the villain."

Mags sighed with relief. "I am happy to hear he is gone, but what about the officers? I can't remember if I found anything or not," she added with a pained frown.

"The doctor said it may come back to you. Now lie down and get some rest."

"There's something else I am needing besides rest, Will Tallman. You haven't touched me since I'm home."

"Now how could I, and you still weak?"

"I am feeling so much better, Will," Mags whispered as she pulled him down next to her.

"Are you, Mags?" he said as he stroked the curve of her breast and pulled the blankets over both of them.

Mags swore it was their lovemaking that was responsible. She had awakened the next morning and, glancing over at the small table that Will used for a washstand, she saw a few pieces of paper lying next to his razor and it all came back. Or almost all. She remembered leaving Stanton's tent and the sense that someone had been lurking, but the memory of the actual attack still eluded her.

"You must get Lieutenant Aston," she told Will.

"I will, Mags, so long as you promise not to be talking of intimate things. I don't mind hearing that my knowing how to pleasure a woman brought your memory back, but you don't need to go spreading the news around!" he added with a sheepish smile.

When Val arrived, Mags was sitting in front of Will's tent, brewing coffee in an old tin pot.

"Shouldn't you still be in bed, Mrs. Tallman?" he scolded.

"I am feeling much better, Lieutenant, as I am sure Will told you," she added with a gleam of mischief in her eye.

"He told me that your memory has returned."

"Much of it, Lieutenant."

Val looked around, but they seemed to be alone and safe from anyone overhearing. "Tell me what you remember, Mrs. Tallman."

"I had gone to Lieutenant Trowbridge's tent first and I was just leaving Lieutenant Stanton's when it happened."

"Then you never got to Lord Wimborne's?"

"No, not that I recall."

Val looked thoughtful. "Then the likelihood is the attack was because of something you might have seen in one of the others'."

"Or to keep her from getting to the marquess's tent," said Will.

"I suppose so. What did you find in the others' quarters?"

"There was a letter from Lieutenant Trowbridge's brother on the ground next to his cot. Nothing but news about the latest prizefight, I am afraid."

"And Lord Stanton's?"

Mags frowned and closed her eyes, trying to picture things accurately. "There were three letters on his table. I remember I was being careful to fold them up just the way they had been. He's a very orderly man, is Lord Stanton."

"Can you remember what was in the letters?"

"One was from his mother," Mags hesitated. "There *was* something in one of them, Lieutenant. Just wait a minute and it will come to me."

Val sat there, praying that it would be the conclusive evident they needed, and when Mags put her cup down with a satisfied grin and said "Aye, now I can see it as clear as if I was standing there," he had a hard time not jumping up and throwing his arms around her.

"He had a letter from an old school friend. The man was congratulating him on squeezing someone."

" 'Squeezing' someone?"

"For something that was a capital offense."

"Do you mean to say that Lord Stanton is blackmailing someone?"

"Yes, and it was clear it was another old schoolmate."

Val rubbed his eyes. "Do you remember anything in any letters about the political situation at home, Mags?"

"Nothing more than what we all know, sir. But I thought

it was interesting, the 'squeezing' part," she added hopefully.

"But you never got to James's tent?"

"No, sir. I thought I heard something in the back of Lieutenant Stanton's tent, but I figured it was a small animal. I went out and looked around me, I think." Mags closed her eyes. "I'm sorry, Lieutenant, I can't remember anything else."

"Now, Mags, don't strain yourself," said Will, putting a hand on her shoulder.

Val sat quietly, trying to make sense of what he had heard.

"Whoever attacked you saw you coming out of Stanton's tent."

"I am sure of it, sir."

"Perhaps you missed a letter?"

"I might have done so, sir. I suppose he might have hid one. Of course, like Will said, whoever was watching might have been trying to keep me from the marquess's tent," she added thoughtfully. "Not that *he* could ever be the traitor, Lieutenant."

"A capital offense, the letter said?"

"Squeezing him for it."

Val's face lightened. "You know, Mrs. Tallman, much as I would like the villain to be Lucas Stanton, it may be you have solved this for us."

Mags's face lit up. "But how, sir?"

"George Trowbridge is Stanton's old schoolfellow. And treason is a capital offense. It just may be Stanton is blackmailing him."

"And Stanton not reporting it?"

"Yes, and that makes him as much of a traitor."

"But Lieutenant Trowbridge is so . . ."

"Stupid?"

"Well, I hate to be the one to say it, but he is a bit dim, sir."

"He doesn't have to do much. Just pass on information."

"But there was nothing much in his letters," Mags protested.

"No, but perhaps he had the information hidden somewhere else. Thank you, Mrs. Tallman. We will watch both of them carefully."

"Well, I am feeling better, sir, for I have been thinking myself a very poor spy indeed."

"Nonsense, Mrs. Tallman. You were a good soldier."

"I'll be back at my laundering in a week or so, Lieutenant."

"You are not getting involved again, Mags," protested Will.

"I *could* keep on looking, Lieutenant Aston."

"No, you can't ask that of her, sir, not after such a beating."

"I won't, Will, don't worry," Val reassured him. "I am sorry, Mrs. Tallman, but you are a retired spy," Val told her with a smile. "Captain Grant will have someone watch Stanton and Trowbridge coming and going. We don't want to risk you again."

"But there was nothing in either of their letters about the government?" asked Grant when Val reported Mags's news.

"No, but it is possible it had been hidden or destroyed."

Grant frowned. "It is possible, Lieutenant. It is possible that you want Stanton to be the traitor a little too much. He could very well be blackmailing someone at home for something completely different."

"But the writer of the letter called it a capital offense, sir. While there are all too many of these, I cannot imagine Lucas Stanton blackmailing someone for stealing a sheep, sir."

Captain Grant smiled. "I suppose you are right. There is then a strong possibility that George is our traitor and Stanton is using this for his own advantage."

"Which makes him a traitor too. I think we should have them both watched, sir."

"I will see to it, Lieutenant. I must admit I am glad we have something pointing us in a direction other than Lord Wimborne."

"I would vouch for James's loyalty to his country with my life, sir," Val declared.

"And I for your loyalty to a friend, Valentine," Colquhoun Grant murmured after Val left.

"You are looking very pleased with yourself, Val," said Charlie after he encountered his brother outside of Grant's tent.

Val turned and gave Charlie one of his rare open smiles. "I have not done anything, Charlie. Mrs. Tallman has."

Charlie looked at him with a questioning frown.

"Come, let us walk out of camp a ways," said Val and they took the path to the village. "May I rely on your discretion, Charlie?"

Charlie grinned. Whenever Val got serious, he sounded so like the earl that anyone would have known them for father and son.

"This is not a laughing matter, Charlie."

"Of course not."

"Mrs. Tallman was not attacked for her laundry money, Charlie. She was attacked because she was spying for us."

That wiped the smile from Charlie's face.

"Someone is getting word to Massena about the political crisis at home. It is why he has dug himself in, despite the lack of food and the illness plaguing his troops."

"He's hoping the proposed Regency will mean the Opposition will pull Wellington out of Portugal?"

"Exactly."

"Do you have any ideas who would be passing on such information?"

"We have three suspects: George Trowbridge, Lucas Stanton, and James Lambert."

"James!"

"That is why I am so pleased, Charlie, I knew it was ridiculous to suspect him, but anyone who had connections in Whitehall had to be considered. But Mrs. Tallman found us something that points in the direction of George Trowbridge."

"George is a hen-wit, Val."

"Admittedly," Val replied with a grin. "But he doesn't need much in his upper story merely to pass on information."

"What evidence do you have?"

"Mrs. Tallman discovered a letter in Stanton's tent that indicates he is blackmailing an old schoolfellow over a capital offense. We think he is on to George and making money off his treason. So James is cleared."

"Well, not precisely, Val," Charlie said hesitantly.

"You can't consider James capable of this?"

"No, but there might be another schoolfellow in England."

"That would be too much of a coincidence, Charlie. If Mags hadn't been attacked . . . But she was, and right after coming out of Stanton's tent."

"There are other capital offenses beside treason, Val," Charlie said thoughtfully.

"Too many to count," said Val, smiling at his brother.

"Unfortunately that is true," said Charlie. "Well, if you are right," he continued, "then Mrs. Tallman deserves a medal."

They had reached the top of the hill overlooking the village and, since it was a sunny day, sat down on the rocks. "Your troops are looking good, Charlie."

"I feel lucky to be here, working with men and horses."

"You are inspired with horses, Charlie. If you do as well with your men, you will have a crack troop."

"Thank you, Val," Charlie replied with a pleased blush. "I can't wait to see how they do in their first battle."

"Don't be so eager for that, little brother."

"Is it so awful, then?"

"I have only seen the one and that was awful enough."

"Well, it is what we are here for."

"Indeed it is. But don't be too eager to rush into the middle of the enemy. I would hate to lose you," said Val, keeping his tone light.

"Or I, you," replied Charlie. Their glances met for a moment and then both lowered their eyes in embarrassment at the strong emotion revealed there.

Later, when he was sitting in front of his mirror, unbuttoning his stock, Charlie thought about what Val had told him. He despised Lucas Stanton as much as his brother did. His feelings about George were not as strong, but he certainly could believe him weak enough to consider passing on information.

And James? Like Val, he would have thought any suspicion against him ridiculous. It was interesting, however, that the thought had never occurred to his brother that James was also an old schoolfellow. And Val seemed unaware that there was a capital offense aside from treason that James might be blackmailed for.

Chapter 23

January was a cold, gray month, but the news that finally arrived from England was bleaker than the weather. It had been decided that a Regency was necessary, given the king's continued state of delusion.

"Lord Wellington has received word from home that the prince and the Whigs are planning a ministry," Colquhoun Grant told Val.

"No wonder he has been looking so blue-deviled."

"If the Opposition indeed takes office, then it is safe to say that we will not remain here long."

"You don't think His Lordship can convince them that he can drive the French out of Portugal?"

Grant laughed bitterly. "Lord Wellington has enough trouble with the government that is favorable to him when he asks for supplies and troops. If the government is slow to supply us, I hardly think that the Opposition will."

"So Massena waits. . . ."

"Hoping for the new cabinet. Or reinforcement from Boney. Damnation, I wish we could ferret out this traitor so at least Massena's information would be less current than ours."

"You said someone has been working on this in London?"

"Yes, and has narrowed down the possibilities some, but the range of potential traitors is almost as great there, Lieutenant," Grant admitted with a despairing sigh.

"You know that Lord Wimborne has requested a leave, sir?"

"Yes, and Lord Wellington has granted it. He departs for England in less than a month."

"Perhaps he could be persuaded to act for us there?" Val suggested tentatively.

"No, Aston. The marquess is still a suspect. Not a prime suspect," he added as Val began to protest. "But not some-one we can ask for help. We will have to keep a close watch on Trowbridge and Stanton. But the other news from home might cheer you up," he added with a broad smile. "It is so cold that the Thames has frozen over, so we have the satisfaction of knowing that those at home are colder than we are!"

The winter behind the lines might not have been as cold as England's, but when he looked back on it, Val remem-bered it as the longest. News arrived steadily but slowly from home and it wasn't until late February that they dis-covered the prince had decided to retain Lord Percival's government. The king, while by no means recovered, had improved slightly and the prince, with uncharacteristic pru-dence, had decided to keep his father's ministers. Although many of the Whigs considered it a betrayal, it was generally agreed that the prince had acted wisely.

In the meantime, Grant, Val, and the other exploring officers continued their reconnaissance forays into Portugal and Spain. More of the French grew sicker every day, but Massena stubbornly held on.

James left for London in mid-February, which made the winter seem even longer to Val.

"By the time you return, James, I hope we will be in Spain, or at least on our way," he told his friend before James set out for Lisbon. "I will miss your companionship," he added wistfully.

"And I'll miss yours. But you will still have Miss Gor-don's company," he added with a teasing grin. "At least for a while. My sister writes that she has convinced Elspeth to come to London in time for her come-out ball."

It may be true that he had Miss Gordon's company, Val thought after waving James off, but the strain of keeping his deeper feelings leashed only added to his feeling that the winter would go on forever, spring would never come, and both armies would sit and rot in place, and be found, many years later, dry bones, the British behind the lines and the French at Santarém.

Val was not the only one feeling the almost unbearable

tension. Whenever the officers came for dinner and Lieutenant Aston was available to join them, Elspeth found herself longing for a glance, a smile, anything that would indicate that he remembered the feelings that had arisen between them. But his profile was forbidding, and once, when Val turned suddenly to look at her, as though he felt her gaze, she realized he reminded her of nothing so much as a raptor, a gray-eyed hawk.

But when he talked to Charlie, Elspeth saw the glimpses of warmth and affection that he was keeping so well from her.

One night after dinner, while the others lingered at the table, Elspeth joined Charlie and Val, who were sitting by the fire.

"Come, sit down here, Miss Gordon," said Val, getting out of his chair and settling himself on the small hassock next to it, his knees drawn up.

"Surely that is too uncomfortable, Lieutenant," she protested.

" 'Tis a lot more comfortable than the desks in the lower form, eh, Charlie?" he replied, smiling over at his brother.

"I wouldn't know, Val. You were the one who had to do Latin with them." Charlie turned to Elspeth. "He did look funny, Miss Gordon. He couldn't get his knees under the desk, so he just sat there on one of those little benches. . . ."

"How long were you at school together?" asked Elspeth.

"Not very long," said Val.

"Not long enough," scolded Charlie.

"Now, Charles, I was essentially sent down. . . ."

"Father could have had that reversed and you know it."

Elspeth could tell this was a familiar quarrel. "What did you get in trouble for, Lieutenant Aston?"

The brothers gave each other a quick glance.

"Fighting," Val replied curtly.

"Beating Lucas Stanton to a bloody pulp," elaborated Charlie.

"Well, that explains why there is no love lost between you," exclaimed Elspeth. "What did you quarrel over?"

Charlie and Val looked at each other again. "Not something that could be shared with a lady," replied Val, his gaze shuttered.

"Lucas could be very . . . cruel to the younger boys, Miss Gordon. Val came to one boy's defense."

"And for that you were sent down!"

"It was not a very sporting fight, Miss Gordon."

"And you didn't ask your father to help you?"

"He went off and took the king's shilling instead, Miss Gordon," Charlie said with a wry glance at his brother.

"But you couldn't have been more than seventeen!"

"Sixteen, to be precise," Charlie informed her while Val was silent. "He might have gone home to Faringdon, of course."

"The recruiting sergeant was very persuasive, Miss Gordon," Val said mildly, pointedly ignoring his younger brother. "I daresay it was likely the song that got me."

"The song?"

" 'The King's Drum.' The tune reminded me of one my mother used to sing me, about Tom the piper's son."

Elspeth smiled. "Why, you are right. I had never connected them before."

"I wanted nothing more than to be over the hills and far away," confessed Val.

"Leaving me behind," said Charlie and Elspeth could hear the sadness underneath.

"If I am not prying into private matters," Elspeth asked hesitantly, "I think you were not raised as brothers?"

"I didn't know I had a brother until I was eleven," Charlie said without thinking. Then he blushed and, looking over at Val, said, "I am sorry."

"Miss Gordon knows something of my background, Charlie. 'Tis no matter."

"I beg pardon; I should never have asked," Elspeth apologized.

"Not at all, Miss Gordon. We are all friends here. Charlie found out he had a brother after his mother died and straightaway went looking for me. Found me too, though I wager he may have had a few moments of doubt as to whether he'd done the right thing, when he saw me, a rough lad in a blacksmith's apron."

"You looked like you could take my head off with one swing of your hammer, Val," Charlie teased. "I thought you *would* take it off when I told you who I was." He reached out and punched Val's arm and both men laughed.

It always amused Elspeth that men so often resolved tension-fraught moments with physical contact and mock violence.

"You certainly did appear the 'husky, dusky coal-black smith,' " teased Charlie.

They sang the chorus of the old song, smiling at each other and completely forgetting Elspeth's presence until they came to the end and realized they had been singing about a man pursuing a young woman for her maidenhead.

"I do beg your pardon, Miss Gordon," they both said at the same time.

"Pray do not mention it, gentlemen," said Elspeth in a "my lady" tone so unlike her that they all burst out laughing.

"What is so amusing?" asked Lord Stanton as he came in to stand by the fire.

"Nothing, really, Lucas," said Charlie.

"Surely it must have been something," he pressured.

"We were merely reminiscing about our school days, Lucas," replied Val with a seemingly innocent smile.

"Auld lang syne and all that," Charlie added.

"You were there for such a short time, Aston, I am surprised you remember any of it," Stanton said sarcastically.

"Ah, but I have such a good memory, my lord," Val replied provocatively.

"We were also remembering songs from childhood," Elspeth quickly interjected. "Are there any you remember, Lord Stanton? Or you, Lord Trowbridge?" she added as the rest joined them.

" 'The Frog he did a wooing go,' " sang Charlie, and Elspeth silently blessed him for defusing the tension.

" 'Hey, ho, said Rolly.' " Her father came over and led them through the whole song as well as a rousing rendition of "The Fox Went Out on a Chilly Night."

"I had forgotten how enjoyable the old songs are," said Charlie with a smile after they finished. "Val was reminding us that one of our recruiting songs comes from an old Mother Goose rhyme," he added and started "Tom the Piper's Son," in his appealing tenor. When Elspeth glanced over at Val's face, she realized she would give anything to have him look at her with the same loving affection in his eyes he had for Charlie.

*   *   *

The end of February finally brought more sun and as its warmth hit the cold ground and half-frozen rivers, they awoke to mist-enshrouded mornings and whole days of fog, which made Val's reconnaissance missions more difficult.

One morning in early March he approached the French camp on foot, having left his horse some distance behind due to the heavy fog. He could barely see a foot in front of him and he climbed to his familiar lookout post by feel rather than sight. As he lay on his stomach, waiting for the fog to clear, every sound seemed magnified: the squawks of a crow, the small avalanche of pebbles when he moved the toe of his boot, even a slight rustling in the patch of grass next to him. It took him a few minutes to realize that none of the sounds he was hearing came from the French camp.

It was by now late morning and there should have been the usual sounds of camp animals and men drilling, but the fog was still so thick that he couldn't see through it. He lay there for a while, hoping that the sun would finally burn through the mist, but when the visibility didn't improve, he realized he would have to make his way closer to the French camp.

He crept down the side of the hill at a snail's pace, flattened against the rocks, fearing that every time he made a sound a French rifleman would find him. Halfway down, he drew out his field glass and peered through till his eye was aching.

It was deathly quiet: too quiet. As the mist swirled around him, Val felt he was suspended in time and space. He'd have to go even lower.

He considered himself a man of some courage, but he felt he was using up a lifetime's store as he lowered himself backward toward the site of Massena's camp. When he was finally only a hundred yards from where the sentries would have been posted, he plastered himself against the ground and inched closer.

Where there should have been tents, there were none. Where campfires had burned, there were blackened pits, and through the mist Val could see nothing else. He lay there for a minute or two and then realized that he was looking at the empty site of the French camp. Massena was finally on the move!

Or he was totally disoriented and would bump into a sentry who would shoot him on sight, he thought with ironic humor as he stood up slowly and walked into the center of the encampment. There he could see the detritus of a departed army: a few discarded tents, the empty corral, and piles of abandoned clothes and pots and pans. The French were truly gone. It took him a few minutes to determine the direction of their retreat. They were heading north, much as Wellington would have expected them to.

The fog didn't lift and Val made an agonizingly slow journey back to the lines. Massena had at least a thirty-mile start. The quicker Wellington received the news and mobilized his army, the sooner he could catch the French.

Speed was of the essence, but Val had to lead his horse for part of the way back, and when he reached the River Mayor, he realized that if he thought his vision useless before, crossing the river he felt like a blind man. He had to stop and feel the current of the river every few minutes and turn himself in what he thought was the right direction. Halfway across he had to swim and it took all his strength not to get swept downstream. When he finally reached the shore, he collapsed. But he roused himself a few minutes later, not only because of duty but because he knew he would freeze if he stayed there any longer.

He reached camp after dark and stumbled into Colquhoun Grant's tent, filthy, wet, and exhausted.

"My God, Aston, I came in today looking like I'd been put through a mangle, but you look like hell!"

Val gave him a wan smile and sat down at the edge of his cot. Despite the mess he was making of it, Grant didn't have the heart to move him. "Just don't lie down," he warned with a smile.

Val was too exhausted to respond to his teasing. "The French are finally on the move, Captain."

"Bloody hell! And in this weather. Where are they headed?"

"North."

"Yes, yes, just what we expected. When did they leave?"

"I would guess they have no more than a day's lead, sir. But they had thirty miles on us already, of course."

Grant grabbed his cloak. "Get yourself a hot bath and an extra ration of rum, Lieutenant. You've earned it," he said as he rushed out.

Val just sat there in a daze. It felt to him as though the mists he had fought with for hours had somehow rolled into his head. He finally got to his feet and stumbled to his own tent, where he stripped off his wet uniform and crawled under the blankets, falling asleep immediately.

He was surrounded by fog again, only this time it felt almost like a living energy swirling past him, enveloping him and then parting for just a second or two, as though teasing him and leading him on. When the mist would clear for those brief moments, he would see a vaporish figure in front of him, as though he were walking down the aisle of a mist-shrouded museum and every now and then one statue would appear and then another. One was little Gillingham from the barracks in Kent and another, Private Moore, whom he'd had flogged many years ago. Then, all of a sudden, there was his father. He stopped in front of the earl, trying to get his attention, but then saw that his father was gazing off into the mist with a look of such longing on his face that even Val felt pity. He peered into the shifting vapor, trying to make out what the earl was seeing. Finally, as though someone had exhaled a quiet breath, the fog was blown away and there stood his mother.

He had never felt such a combination of joy and pain. On her face was a smile so full of love that Val could not bear it. Then he became aware that her smile encompassed both father and son and he was incensed. How could she bear to look at, much less smile upon, the man who had abandoned her?

As though she could read his thoughts, his mother's face changed. The smile faded and her eyes filled with tears. "Sarah," called the earl and the mist came back and she was gone.

"Don't go, Mama," Val awoke just as his dream-self spoke those words.

He hadn't dreamed of his mother for years, not since the early days with George Burton. He became conscious as he lay there that his chest was tight with unshed tears.

Damn his father! He'd driven her away before Val could reach her.

It took him a few minutes to wake up to everyday reality and when he realized he was in his cot and it was early afternoon, he laughed. Here he was, blaming his father, even in his dreams.

There was quite a stir going on around him and then he knew that the army was getting ready to move. He draped his blanket around his waist and walked out of his tent. Men were running to and fro, tents were being taken down, and way at the end of camp the baggage carts were being loaded. Val could feel the energy of the chase in the air and when Charlie ran by without even seeing him, he called out a teasing, "View hallo!"

"Val! Massena's on the move!"

"I know," said Val. "I brought the news."

"I'm off to muster my men," said Charlie. "We have been assigned to General Erskine," he added with an eloquent shrug of his shoulders.

"Oh, God, don't do a thing he says, Charlie, for it's bound to be wrong. Just make your own judgments," replied Val with only partly mock despair as he waved Charlie off.

The chase was on, and Wellington, the old fox, was on the move, thought Val with a satisfied smile as he went in to pull on a dry uniform. "The fox went out on a chilly night, and he prayed to the moon to give him light, for he'd many a mile to go that night before he reached the town-o, town-o, town-o . . ." As he sang the old song again, he was reminded of their last evening at the Gordons' and he wondered whether Elspeth and her mother would be following Major Gordon into Spain.

Chapter 24

"I would prefer it if you were safe in Lisbon, Peggy."

"And I would prefer being with *you,* Ian. If only Elspeth weren't returning to England in a month . . . I can't leave her alone," replied Mrs. Gordon. "But this is the first time we have been separated in years, my dear. I couldn't bear waiting in Lisbon for news. At least if we remain in Pero Negro, I can receive word through the Ordenanza. And this house is quite comfortable."

"Oh, Peggy, ma dear," laughed Major Gordon, "ye are the only earl's granddaughter who would consider this comfortable! I have asked Private Ryan if he can spare his wife for a few weeks," he added.

"That wasn't necessary, Ian, but I must admit that we will appreciate her company."

"Good morning, Mama, Papa," said Elspeth, who had slept late.

"Good morning, dear. Your father and I have just been talking and I am happy to say he has agreed to let us stay here."

Elspeth gave her father a grateful smile. "I know you wanted us in Lisbon, Papa, but we would both have gone mad awaiting the news of the campaign. This way we are a little closer to the lines of communication."

"Mrs. Ryan will be staying with us, Elspeth," her mother informed her.

"Why, then, you could go with Papa."

Mrs. Gordon's face brightened for a moment, but she immediately replied, "Of course I can't leave you alone, Elspeth."

"Nonsense, Mama. I will have Mrs. Ryan and it is only for a month."

"Your father would be returning on leave to take you to Lisbon, Elspeth, and I can return to the army then."

"But you would rather go now, wouldn't you?"

"Yes," her mother admitted simply.

"Then I want you to," urged Elspeth, placing a hand on her mother's. "Truly, Papa," she added, turning to him, "I will feel less concerned for your safety if I know Mama is with you."

Major Gordon made one more protest, but then gave in to his daughter's request. "I want you to promise me that you won't do anything foolish, Elspeth. You will not be riding out of the valley."

"I will busy myself with mending and packing and reading, Papa," she reassured him.

Elspeth had been determined to make sure her parents were not separated, but as she watched the army begin its long march north, the regimental colors snapping in the breeze as the troops walked by, she was ready to cancel her trip to England and go with them. She felt the same restlessness that came over her whenever the army marched, a restlessness and longing that made her wish she were a soldier and not the daughter of one, whose place was always in the rear. Today it was worse, of course, because she wouldn't even be riding with the other women.

"Good day, Miss Gordon." The Light Horse troops were passing and Charlie had pulled his horse over to greet her. "I hear that you will be remaining in Pero Negro. We will miss your company."

"Oh, and I will miss the army, Lord Holme. My ship doesn't sail from Lisbon until April."

"Give my best to James and Maddie when you see them."

"And mine to Lieutenant Aston, my lord. I wish you both a safe return," she added.

"Thank you, Miss Gordon. It is always good to know a pretty woman cares," said Charlie with a grin. "I will tell Val."

He had taken his shako off in greeting and the sun shone down on his bright curls, turning them as gold as his epaulets, and not for the first time Elspeth thought what a handsome man he was.

Later, after the army had passed and she walked back to the village, she found herself singing:

> "You should see my light horseman
> On a cold winter's day
> With his red and rosy cheeks
> and his curly blond hair . . ."

It was a song she had recently learned and they had sung it a few times this winter, her mother and she. She had never thought of Charlie in connection with it before, but it was a wonderfully apt verse, she realized with a fleeting smile. Except it was not a happy song, but a lament for the lady's light horseman who "in the war had been slain." Elspeth shivered as a picture of Charlie leading a cavalry charge came to her mind. Sing a happier song, she told herself and hummed a few of the children's songs they had sung by the fire that last night after dinner. But it was hard to get the plaintive tune out of her head and over the next few days the music kept coming back to haunt her.

The first weeks Massena was on the move, it was clear from the way he was traveling that his initial intention had been to find a place where he could feed his starving army and make an attempt on Lisbon. Val and his fellow exploring officers sometimes found themselves in the middle of the rear-guard attack as Wellington sent troops to push Massena toward Spain. Finally the French gave up and went into a full retreat and Wellington felt confident enough to send his empty troop ships back to England. There would be no leaving Portugal now, by the back or front door!

One evening in late March Val returned to camp and walked restlessly to Will Tallman's fire.

"May I join you all, Will?"

"Sit down, Lieutenant, sit down and have a drink," said Private Murphy in a voice slurred with rum.

Val sat and drank down the offered ration in a few swallows, which made Will lean forward and take a closer look, for Val was usually an abstemious man.

"You look fair worn out, Lieutenant," he remarked. "Is it as bad up ahead as it has been here the last few days?"

"Worse, Will," said Val, holding out his cup to Murphy for another drink.

"More grave pits, sir?" asked Private Doolittle.

Val wiped his mouth with the back of his hand. "Oh, always those. We haven't got away from them yet, Private. Can you spare another dram?"

"Haven't you had enough, sir?" Will asked quietly.

"There isn't enough rum in the whole bloody army to make me forget what I have seen today, Will," Val said slowly, as though by pronouncing his words carefully he could prove he had nowhere near drunk enough.

Will waved away Private Doolittle's offer of rum. "Go on to your beds, lads," he said. "It's getting late."

The men stumbled off and when Will turned back, he saw Val sitting there, his head in his hands.

"What is it, sir?"

"What is it? It is this damned war, Will. I'm already sick of it and I've seen nothing at all. You expect to see casualties, of course," he continued in a voice that was now calm, as though he were instructing a group of raw recruits. "We all know war means fighting, and fighting means dead and wounded men. There are enough of them out there, Will," he said in an ironic aside, "with a sortie from Napier here and a rally from Massena there. But they don't tell you about the smells. . . ."

"The pits have been something awful, sir, what with new bodies piled on top of old."

"I know the French were starving, Will," Val continued, his tone changing again to an agonized whisper. "But to hang up a mother and child and burn them alive, hoping that they would reveal some small cache of food . . . my God, I wouldn't have thought even a Frog capable of that."

"It has been that kind of war, Lieutenant," Will replied softly. "With the civilians suffering as much as the soldiers."

"I am sorry for ruining your evening, Will." Val stood up and swayed a little as the ground seemed to dissolve and form again under him.

"I would have seen it tomorrow or the next day, sir."

"I'll leave you, then, Will. Good night." But Val just stood there, swaying as though he were caught in a heavy wind.

"Why don't you stay here tonight, sir."

"Couldn't do that, Will," he mumbled.

"Of course you can, Lieutenant." Will took Val's arm and led him into his tent. "Just lie down on my bedroll, sir."

"Not big enough to share," protested Val.

"I'll use my extra blanket, sir." Will guided Val down and then went back to the fire. He had lied. He had no extra blanket. But he could sleep sitting or standing after twenty years in the army and the lieutenant didn't need to be alone tonight.

Val awoke late with a thundering head and a sour stomach. Someone was shaking him and it felt like an earthquake.

"Get up, sir. We're out of here in half an hour."

He sat up and Will thrust a cup of coffee into his hand. "Here, sir, this should help."

It did, somewhat, and he was finally able to stand up.

"You'd better get back to your own tent, sir. Can you make it?"

Val nodded. "Thank you, Will. I wasn't good company, I know, but I was glad not to be alone last night."

"It was nothing, sir."

"You are a good friend, Will. You make sure you take care when we finally catch up to the Frogs."

"Don't you worry. I am an old soldier and I know how to stay alive. I'd better, or Mags will kill me," he added with a laugh.

Val walked back to his tent very slowly and carefully, not wanting to jar his head. He didn't even notice Major Gordon approaching him until the major reached him and said good morning.

"Good morning, sir."

"Ye look like hell, laddie," the major said bluntly.

"I've *been* in hell, Major," Val replied, "so it is not surprising I look like an inhabitant."

The words were ironic, but the major heard the agony underneath them. "Aye, laddie, 'tis worse than anything I've ever seen and I have been to my own share of hells."

"I hope we can push them into Spain quickly, then,

Major, for I want nothing so much as to be away from all this."

"Don't worry, Lieutenant. We have turned them and now the bloody croakers at home will see just what Old Hooky can do."

"How are your wife and daughter doing, Major?"

"Oh, Peggy is an old trooper, ye know. As is Elspeth, but I am glad she is not here to see this."

"She didn't follow you, sir?"

"She is committed to return home for Lady Wimborne's come-out."

"Ah, yes, I remember. So she is in Lisbon?"

"She wouldn't go that far. No, she is waiting in Pero Negro. I'll be back to escort her to Lisbon in a few weeks. But for now, I'm enjoying chasing Massena over the mountains."

As Val packed his knapsack and rolled up his bedding, he pictured Elspeth riding by the mass graves or seeing what he had yesterday. Thank God for Lady Madeline. He couldn't bear the thought of Elspeth in this place. She was strong, he knew, but even the most seasoned men had been horrified. It was a good thing she was out of it.

Val had been sent to the guerrilleros encampment, and by the time he returned, Massena, after a brutal march through the mountains, had turned east again.

"It looks like he intends to face us at the Coa," said Captain Grant, after Val gave him his report.

"Can we break through?"

"I certainly hope so, since Sanchez can keep him busy all the way to Salamanca. Thank God for that old fox," he added with a grin. "And how was Jack Belden?"

"I didn't see him this time, sir. Evidently he was visiting his lady."

"She is a lovely woman, Maria Elena. Have you met her?"

"Never had the pleasure, sir."

"Widow of a local mayor. I wonder if he means to marry her and bring her home," mused Grant.

Val wondered about that as he washed and dressed for dinner. An Englishman of respectable background to marry a local alcalde's widow? It didn't seem very likely. On the other hand, he had heard Jack speak of her very fondly.

When he spied the other officers in Major Gordon's tent, he was happy to see that Charlie made up one of the party. But it wasn't until the major proposed a toast to the next day's engagement that he realized that his brother was to be part of the attack at Sabugal.

"Here's to the Light Horsemen!" said the major. "May they ride right over Reynier and his Second Corps."

"Hear, hear."

Val only lifted his glass and gave his brother a worried glance, when Charlie answered with a bright smile.

"Will you walk with me a little, Val?" he said after dinner.

"Of course."

They were both silent and then both spoke at once:

"So, tomorrow is your first engagement . . ."

"Tomorrow will be my first time in the field, Val . . ."

Charlie laughed and then, turning serious, said, "I am a bit anxious, Val. Not at all about my men," he added. "They are excellent troops," he said warmly.

"Because of you, Charlie. You don't have to be anxious about them. It's your commanding officer you have to worry about!"

Charlie punched him in the arm. "Hush, Val, someone might overhear you."

"Oh, everyone knows Erskine is a fool. Especially Wellington. I wish Crauford was not on leave," he added.

"I must confess, so do I," said Charlie with a sigh. He hesitated and then said, "Val, I want you to promise me something."

"Anything, Charlie."

"If anything should happen to me—"

"Nothing will happen to you, Charlie," Val said fiercely.

"Of course not . . . but on the off-chance that it should, I want you to bring this home to Father for me." Charlie pulled at his finger and held out his battered gold signet.

"Put it back on, Charlie. I can't take it."

"Just hold it for me, then, Val. Until I come back," his brother said gently. "It has been handed down for the past three hundred years and I would hate to have a . . . hate to have it slip off in the battle. Please."

There was a three-quarter moon and Val could see the same look on his brother's face as had been there so many years ago when he had come to find him. He stopped and faced him.

"Charlie . . . I don't know that I have ever said . . . it is just . . . I am very glad you came to find me. . . . It is good to have a brother. . . ." Val's voice broke and he stood there, trying to regain control.

"I am so glad I found one, Valentine," replied Charlie with one of his warm smiles. He held out the ring and Val took it. "Promise you will take it to Father yourself."

"I promise, but only because I know I will not have to. You will come galloping back the hero tomorrow, Charlie, having chased the French halfway into Spain!"

They were quiet for a few minutes as they walked on, and then Charlie broke the silence.

"Have you ever determined who was sending information to Massena, Val?"

"No, and once he was on the move, it didn't matter. But we have finally pinpointed the traitor at home."

"You know that James—"

"James is out of it, thank God," Val told him. "And he is probably charming all his sister's friends. Perhaps he will use this opportunity to find himself a wife."

"Yes, indeed," Charlie replied blandly.

The next morning, one of the persistent fogs that seemed to characterize spring in Portugal was swirling in and the jingling of bits and spurs that marked the cavalry's departure was muted. Val could barely make out his brother's troops and almost missed them until Charlie was almost on top of him.

"Take care of yourself, Charlie," he said as he walked a little way beside him.

"I will, Val," said Charlie, reaching down and grasping his brother's outstretched hand. It was only a quick handclasp, for Charlie's horse, full of energy and taking little dancing sidesteps, pulled them apart.

Chapter 25

Val's orders were to ride across the Coa at a point south of Sabugal and determine if Massena's troops had crossed. As he made his way downstream, he could hear the French calling out to one another and when he crossed a few miles below Reynier's troops the fog was still heavy. But there was silence on the other side, which meant that Massena intended this as an attempt to hold the line and prevent Wellington from crossing the river.

By the time he recrossed the river, Val could hear the sound of muskets and knew the engagement had begun. He found Captain Grant and Wellington watching from the top of a nearby hill.

"So they mean to make a stand?"

"It would seem so, my lord."

Wellington offered Val his field glass. Without it, he could see only swirling mist and flashes of red and blue, but when he held it to his eye, he could make out the cavalry very clearly.

"The cavalry seems to be very active, my lord."

"You mean that Erskine is sending them every which way, don't you, Lieutenant? Between him and the damned fog I am surprised we are holding them."

But holding them they were. Even Val, through all the confusion of smoke and fog, could tell the French losses were higher than the British. When one of Wellington's aides climbed the hill an hour later, it was confirmed: The French were in full retreat.

"We almost wiped out Reynier's Second Corps, my lord," announced the aide.

"Yes, I could see that, and we would have done it completely if it hadn't been for that bloody Ers—the bloody fog."

The aide gave Val an amused glance.

"Come, Captain Grant, let us get back to camp and prepare our dispatches," said the duke.

Val watched Wellington down the hill. He was dressed, as usual, in a plain blue jacket and looked quite unprepossessing, in contrast to the French officers Val had spied through the glass. But he had done it! He had accomplished what no one thought he could do: He had driven the French out of Portugal! With a sudden spurt of energy, Val scrambled down the hill, eager to congratulate Charlie on his troops' part in the victory.

When he reached the camp, the dirty and exhausted troops were straggling in. At first it seemed they were all foot soldiers, but after a few light horsemen went by, Val stopped a young lieutenant who was cradling his arm in front of him.

"The Sixth Light troops, where are they?"

The young officer only gestured toward the rear. Val couldn't wait for everyone to file by, so he started off, slowly at first, and then faster, as he made his way through more and more riders with no sign of Charlie. As he drew closer to the river, the fog was beginning to burn off, and as it lifted, the sun glinted on a gold epaulet here, a sword hilt there as it shone down on the scattered dead and wounded.

Val froze. Surely he had missed his brother, he told himself, as he watched the surgeons and their assistants begin their search through the wounded. He should just make his way back to camp and there he would find Charlie and give him back his ring and have a stiff drink. Suddenly returning the Faringdon crest seemed critical. Charlie must have it back.

As he stood there, unable to move forward or turn back, he heard a groan and saw one of the men from Charlie's company pulling himself up on one elbow. "Water," the man whispered, looking pleadingly at Val. Val's canteen was only half-full, but he knelt down next to the wounded man and held it to his lips.

The man's thigh had been sliced open to the bone by a French saber and Val winced as he looked at it.

"Looks bad, don't it?" said the soldier, grinning at the

look on Val's face. "But if the bloody sawbones gets here soon enough and sews it up, I'll keep it. Better a saber cut than a musket ball any day, is what I say."

"I am looking for my brother, Lord Holme."

The man looked at Val thoughtfully. "Your brother, eh? A good man and a good soldier," he added sadly.

"He is," Val agreed. "Now, where did you see him last?"

"He and two of his men were inside the French lines the last time I saw him. Down close by the river."

Val left his canteen and made his way to the river. "Oh, God, Charlie, where are you?" he muttered as he walked the muddy riverbank, stepping over the dead and wounded as best he could.

He found Charlie's bay first, standing head down, his rear leg hamstrung. Val gently stroked his neck and looked around. Then he saw his brother twenty yards away, lying on his back as though he were napping by the river. The sun gilded his hair and the buttons on his tunic glittered. The buttons that were clean of blood, that is. Val knelt beside him and gently closed his eyes with the palm of one hand. "You shouldn't be looking directly at the sun, Charlie," he whispered. There was a froth of blood around his brother's mouth and Val pulled a linen square out of his pocket and carefully wiped Charlie's lip clean. When he looked down, he saw the wound: a saber thrust had pierced his brother's lung. "Please God, you died quickly, Charlie," he said, smoothing his brother's hair back from his brow. He picked up Charlie's hand and sat down on the blood-stained grass.

"You did well, little brother," he said as he stroked Charlie's hand. It was still warm and Val could imagine that Charlie was only unconscious. "Despite that fool Erskine, we won, Charlie, and the French are on their way out of Portugal."

He looked down. There on his brother's third finger was a white stripe in the shape of the Faringdon ring. "Charlie, I kept the ring safe in my kit," Val reassured him. "I was afraid if anything happened to me . . . well, you must have it back, Charlie."

Oh, God, his brother wasn't listening, couldn't hear him, would never smile at him again. Val felt a great emptiness. Charlie had loved him, God alone knew why, but Charlie had loved him. And he had loved Charlie. Had he ever told him? Never in so many words. And now it was too late. "I love you, Charlie," he whispered. Surely his brother could hear. Surely his hand would stir and he would give Val a sign. But the sun shone down on them both and the flies and mosquitoes buzzed and settled on Charlie's bloody uniform, and the day became warmer as his brother's hand grew colder and colder.

Val didn't know how long he sat there before the surgeon reached them.

"He's gone, is he?" The doctor patted Val's shoulder. "Is there anything you want, Lieutenant?" he asked awkwardly. "A keepsake? The burial detail will be around soon."

Val shook his head and then watched as a small breeze lifted a lock of Charlie's hair. "Do you have a knife with you, Doctor?"

"A scalpel, Lieutenant." The surgeon handed it to him, a puzzled look on his face, which became a look of compassion as he watched Val cut off a few thick curls and tuck them into his tunic pocket.

"Where is the burial crew, Doctor?"

"Back up the hill, Lieutenant. They are digging a pit . . . er, a grave . . . and soon will start hauling the bodies."

"I will wait, then. I don't want him to be alone. Nor do I want the battlefield buzzards going through his pockets or cutting off his buttons," Val added bitterly. "I will wait with him."

It took an hour, but they finally came to carry Charlie to his final resting place in the soil of a foreign country. Val watched as they shrouded the body and placed it next to one of his fellow light horseman. Charlie was one of the last and as the dirt was piled up on top of them, the chaplain recited the burial service.

"You should lie at Faringdon, Charlie," Val whispered as he dropped a handful of dirt on top of the mass grave.

When he returned to camp, it was dark and he went straight to his tent. He had wrapped Charlie's ring in a piece of linen and pushed it in the back of his kit. He lit a candle and pulled the kit out of his knapsack.

He sat there, looking at the battered gold ring. The Faringdon crest, passed down from generation to generation. He had promised to return it. He drew an old brass chain out of his kit and, threading it through the ring, hung it around his neck. It lay there, heavy over his heart.

"It should have been me, Charlie," he whispered as he fingered the ring. "You were the son he loved."

The ring was gold, but might have been lead for all its lack of luster. He carefully pulled out the curls from his pocket. "For a' that and a' that, the man's the gowd for a' that," he half sang, half spoke. "You were golden, Charlie. Not because of your title, but because of your loving heart." There was a small book in his knapsack that he had carried for years, and he drew it out and opened it to where a faded, brittle rose was still pressed between its pages. There he placed the locks of hair and carefully closed the book. He held it on his lap for a long while before repacking it carefully, for in it lay the only reminders he possessed of the two people who had truly loved him.

Chapter 26

For the next two weeks, Val was so busy reporting on the French retreat and Massena's arrival in Salamanca that he had little time to think of Charlie, much less mourn him. He slept little and ate only enough to keep him going.

"You look like hell, Lieutenant Aston," Captain Grant told him bluntly after his last foray into Spain.

Val rubbed his hand over the bristles on his face. "I apologize, sir. I didn't take time to shave—"

"Do you think me offended by your whiskers? I am worried about you, Aston. I've had to send you out, but you have only just lost your brother."

"I assure you, I am well, sir," Val said stiffly.

"Yes, of course," said Grant, not willing to push where

a man didn't wish him to go. He fingered the papers on his desk. "We have finally discovered the informant at Whitehall, Lieutenant."

Val's eyes showed the first interest in anything since Charlie's death.

"Congratulations, Captain."

"He is the younger son in a well-known family, Aston. Possessed by a great enthusiasm for radical ideas. Didn't really *see* it as treason, mind you," Grant continued with heavy sarcasm. "He thought it would help to bring about a stalemate, Napoleon would send in more troops, Wellington would retreat, and the war would be over. I think he really believed he was contributing to a sort of bloodless revolution."

"A revolution in which one man tyrannized all of Europe!"

Grant lifted his eyebrows and gave Val an ironic smile. "The thing is, Lieutenant, in return for a pardon—"

"Pardon! But he's a traitor, Captain."

"He is also the scion of a noble family. In return for not being put on trial he has revealed the name of his accomplice."

"Lucas Stanton," said Val with great satisfaction.

Colquhoun Grant looked up at Val and shook his head. "It would be so much simpler if it were so, Lieutenant. No, the man to whom he passed the information is the Marquess of Wimborne."

"James? No, I'll not believe it!"

"The marquess was one of our original suspects, Aston," Grant said quietly. "And he was an old schoolmate of Stanton's."

"So you are saying that Stanton was blackmailing James?"

"It would seem so. It all fits: Treason is a capital offense. Lucas discovers him and then blackmails him."

"But *why* would James turn traitor in the first place?"

"Because he needs the money. His father pretty well bankrupted the estate, as you know. And the marquess's sympathies have always been with the Whigs. He was known to hold rather radical opinions at university."

Val shook his head. "I still can't believe it. But whomever Stanton has been blackmailing, then he is as much a traitor."

"We have nothing but Mrs. Tallman's memory of that letter, which is hardly the evidence we need. Someone must confront Wimborne." Grant hesitated. "I was hoping that someone would be you, Lieutenant."

Val looked at him blankly. "Me? Why, you need every exploring officer you can get, Captain, now that we are going into Spain."

"Especially one of my most capable ones, Lieutenant. But we must avoid a public scandal at all costs," he added with regret. "And the marquess cannot return to his position here."

"He was my only friend at school," Val said almost to himself. "How can I accuse him of this?"

"You will have a chance to question his young confederate first, in order to satisfy yourself of the truth of his statement. If you are satisfied, then your duty will be to question Lord Wimborne."

"And if he admits to it? What will happen to him?"

"The authorities may also want to avoid a trial in his case. Perhaps exile to the colonies."

"Exile? What of his sister?"

"The decision will be made by those above you, Lieutenant. Your job is only to determine the truth of these accusations. You will leave as soon as possible, but not before you eat and sleep, Aston, and that is an order."

Val was so upset when he left, he almost ran into Major Gordon.

"Ye look a fair sight, laddie."

"So Captain Grant tells me, sir. I confess I haven't looked in a glass for a week."

"If you have time tomorrow evening, we would love to have you dine with us."

"I would be happy to, sir, but . . ." Val hesitated. He didn't think he could stand an evening with Lucas Stanton.

"But what, laddie?"

"I don't wish to be rude, but I would rather not come if Lord Stanton is invited."

"Lord Stanton is not one of my wife's favorites. Or mine," he added, "though I shouldn't confess it. Do come, laddie," he added gently. "Ye've had a terrible loss and we wish to express our sympathy in some way."

"Thank you, sir. I will."

When he got back to his tent and looked in the glass, Val laughed. He looked like one of the bandits who had abducted Elspeth. If she could see him, she wouldn't come close enough to smell him, much less kiss him.

It was the first time he had let himself think of her in days. After the army had left Pero Negro, he had exercised great discipline, banishing her face from his mind whenever it came to him. He hadn't been able to keep her out of his dreams, however, and he awakened many a morning hard with wanting her. But since Charlie's death, he had not dreamed at all or had time to dwell on anything but getting information back to Wellington.

He stripped off his filthy uniform and shivered as he washed himself with water that was unheated. He *had* lost weight, he supposed, for he could feel his ribs under the washcloth. As he toweled himself dry, memories of Elspeth's kisses came flooding back and he was amazed, given his state of exhaustion, that he could feel aroused.

He would *not* think of her, he told himself. They were pointless fantasies and he tried to turn his mind to something else, anything else. But all that came to him was Charlie . . . and James. He sank down on his cot and stared blankly at the wall of his tent, which was moving in and out in the light wind that was blowing. He had survived on so little over the years: The memory of his mother's love, the knowledge of Charlie's affection, and the thought of James's friendship had sustained him. He was proud of his ability to live with so little. But now the little had become nothing and he wasn't sure he could survive that. His brother was dead, his friend not the man he had thought him to be, and his love someone he could never marry. As he sank back upon his cot, he wondered how he would make it through the years that stretched ahead of him, empty of love and affection.

He slept through the night and half the next day and looked considerably revived when he presented himself at the Gordons'.

"Good evening, Lieutenant," said Mrs. Gordon with a warm smile. "I was so glad that Ian invited you. I have had few opportunities to dine with him, much less anyone else this last week."

The food and the table were much plainer than in Pero Negro, but the warm welcome and the informal family atmosphere was the same and Val found himself relaxing for the first time in days.

"So Massena is in Salamanca?"

"For now, sir. But there is the possibility that he might make a last-minute attempt to save Almeida. It is the last piece of Portugal in French hands and Captain Grant intercepted a dispatch which indicates that Napoleon would very much like to see Massena push back."

Major Gordon frowned. "I don't like it, laddie. I wouldn't want to face the French without Wellington."

"Without Wellington?"

"Didn't you hear? He left with only a few officers and rode south to see how Beresford is doing outside of Badajoz."

Val grinned. "I haven't heard anything today, not even reveille, I was that tired, sir."

"We were very sorry to hear of your brother, Lieutenant Aston," said Mrs. Gordon, after a few moments of listening to the men discuss strategies to outwit the French. It was the first time Charlie had been brought into the conversation.

"Thank you for your kind sympathy, Mrs. Gordon," said Val. The expression on his face kept his hostess from saying anything more, but Ian Gordon did not share his wife's reserve. "It will be a dreadful blow to your father," he said. "I hope he receives the news privately and not from the casualty lists." The major looked over at Val. " 'Tis a shame he is not able to make you his heir."

Val's hand automatically went to his chest, as though to finger the ring that was hanging around his neck, reminding him of the promise he had made to Charlie. "I doubt that he would wish to even if he could, Major," he responded coolly.

"It's a damn shame a man has to settle for a second cousin or whoever the heir is, when you are his own son, laddie."

"Ian!" his wife protested.

"I am just telling the boy what I think, Peggy."

"He is hardly a boy, Ian."

"Thank you, ma'am," said Val dryly.

"It is none of our business, Ian."

"It is all right, Mrs. Gordon. You both have been very kind to me and you knew I loved Charlie. It is only natural Major Gordon would speak as a friend."

"I hope you know I am your friend, laddie," said the major.

"I am honored, sir."

They were all quietly eating dessert when the major declared, "But I wish, Peggy, that Old Hooky hadn't gone haring off. It means I will have to stay here and send someone else to escort Elspeth."

"Perhaps we could send Private Ryan back?"

Major Gordon frowned. "Perhaps."

Val cleared his throat. "You may not have heard, Major, but I am being sent back to England on a mission for Captain Grant. I would offer myself as Miss Gordon's escort, if you thought it not improper."

Both the Gordons' faces lit up. "Mrs. Ryan will be there to go with her to Lisbon, Lieutenant," said the major.

"But will it slow you down, Lieutenant?" asked Mrs. Gordon.

"Pero Negro is not that much out of my way, ma'am," Val reassured her. "But I am leaving early tomorrow, so you will have no time to get word to your daughter about the change in plans."

"Elspeth is a soldier's daughter and a good campaigner. She knows things change weekly in the army," said Major Gordon with a proud smile. "But you must give the lieutenant a note, Peggy, explaining the situation."

"I will, Ian, right away." Mrs. Gordon went over to her husband's table and penned a quick note.

"There you are, Lieutenant," she said, handing Val the folded paper. "I cannot thank you enough."

"It is the least I can do in return for your generous hospitality over these last months, Mrs. Gordon."

*   *   *

"Well, I think that turned out well, Peggy," the major said, turning to his wife after Val left.

"What a lucky coincidence Lieutenant Aston was returning home."

"Indeed. They will have a good three weeks together, Peggy," he said, pulling his wife to him. "I hope Elspeth puts it to good use."

"Ian!"

"She is half in love with him already, I am convinced, whether she knows it or not."

"Do you think so?"

"Don't you? You have seen the way she looks at him."

Mrs. Gordon nodded.

"And whether Valentine believes it or not, I know enough about Charles Faringdon to know that he will publically recognize Lieutenant Aston as his son. Perhaps that will remove some of the lieutenant's stubborn insistence that he is unworthy of ma wee lassie," he concluded with great satisfaction.

"Do you think *he* has affection for her, Ian?"

"I cannot be sure, Peggy, but I am willing to wager that there is something between them, and that is at least a beginning."

"What if he remains alienated from the earl, Ian? Would you feel the same about a match between them?" his wife asked.

"Of course I would. 'A man's a man.' You know I believe that, Peggy."

"Yes," she said with a warm smile, "and that is why I love you, Ian Gordon, even though you do go rushing in where even an angel wouldn't."

"I am no angel, Peggy," he answered, leaning down and muzzling her neck.

"Oh, I know that and am very glad for it!"

Val had volunteered his services without thinking. Or rather, only thinking about it as a way to show his gratitude to the Gordons for their kindness to him. How could he not have volunteered? he asked himself as he prepared to ride out the next morning. He was going to England; it would have looked odd *not* to have offered.

He stopped at Will Tallman's tent on his way out of camp and found Mags just setting the coffeepot on the fire.

"Will you have a cup with us, Lieutenant?" she asked.

"I can't stop that long, Mrs. Tallman. I just wanted to say good-bye and wish Will luck in the coming weeks."

Will pushed open the tent flap and stumbled out. "Good morning to you, sir."

"Good morning, Will. I can't stop, but I wanted to tell you both good-bye."

"You will be missed, Lieutenant," said Will, extending his hand. Val took it and held it for a minute. "You make sure you don't do anything foolish, Will. You are a married man now."

"Mags won't let me forget it, sir!"

"When will you be back, Lieutenant?"

"I have to resolve this situation you were caught up in, Mags. I don't suppose you've remembered anything further? Perhaps Stanton's letter gave a name to the man he was blackmailing?" Val asked hopefully.

"I can't swear to it, of course," said Mags, "but I'm sure as sure that what I do remember is right."

Val sighed.

"Which way do you ride, Lieutenant?" Will asked him.

"Straight south and then west, Will. I am stopping in Pero Negro to escort Miss Gordon to Lisbon and then to London."

"Have a fine time at all those balls and musicales, Lieutenant," said Mags with a teasing smile:

"I doubt if I will have much time for that, Mrs. Tallman," Val replied, grinning back.

Mags and Will watched as he rode off.

"He looks right hagged, your lieutenant," said Mags.

"He took his brother's death hard. And I am sure he wishes he was riding north into Spain. The action would keep his mind off of Lord Holme."

"Maybe Miss Gordon can help with that, Will."

"Do you think so, Mags?" Will asked speculatively.

"I think they would make a good pair. Almost as good as you and me, Will," she added, planting a kiss on top of his head as he sat there by the fire.

Chapter 27

Elspeth had spent her time trying to keep herself occupied with sewing and the few books that were available, but nothing except a long walk every afternoon could cure her of her restlessness. It was frustrating to be betwixt and between: not with the army and not yet on her way to London. By the time her father was due to arrive, she found herself jumping up and peering out the window at every unfamiliar noise.

"Ye must calm yerself, Miss Elspeth," Mrs. Ryan gently scolded her late one afternoon after Elspeth had jumped up three times.

"I know, Mrs. Ryan. But I just want to be *off*." Elspeth put down the night rail she was mending and, pulling a shawl off the hook by the door, said, "I *must* walk, but I will be back shortly."

"Ye take care, Miss Elspeth. It will be getting dark soon."

"I will, Nelly, don't worry."

Sometimes Elspeth walked south out of the village, but today she felt pulled north up the hill and then down into the valley where the army had camped. She tried to tell herself it was because she wished herself with them, but she suspected it was because the place held memories of Lieutenant Aston. Somehow she felt closer to him when she walked out toward the valley.

It had been a warm day, but as the sun went down, Elspeth had to pull her shawl tight around her to keep out the chill. She was just about to turn back when she saw a rider approaching. He'd obviously come from the northern track out of the mountains and she had a moment of fear until she realized that he wore red. Her father at last, she thought, until she realized he was riding a chestnut and not her father's gray. Her hand went automatically to her heart. Please God, nothing had happened to her father. She had had no word at all about the army's journey north, but there would have been skirmishes and perhaps even a battle by now.

It was only as the rider come closer that she recognized him. It was Lieutenant Aston. She gave a sigh of relief. Surely he was only on mission for Captain Grant and had no bad news for her. When he pulled his horse to a walk, she started out to meet him.

"Lieutenant Aston! I am surprised to see you," she called, shading her eyes as she looked up at him.

"And I, you, Miss Gordon. Surely you should not walk so far from the village?"

"It is perfectly safe and I never go farther than that tree," Elspeth reassured him. "But what brings you to Pero Negro? I hoped you were my father. Do you have any news of him?" she asked with a trace of anxiety in her voice.

Val dismounted and, looping the reins over his arm, walked beside her.

"I have a note from your mother, Miss Gordon, which I will dig out of my pack when we get to the village."

Before he could finish, she turned and asked fearfully, "Nothing has happened to my father?"

"No, no, not at all. But Major Gordon was required to stay with his troops. And since I was on my way to England, I, uh, offered to be your escort."

"Oh," said Elspeth, a bit taken aback by the change in plans.

"I hope you have no objection?" Val asked formally.

"Why, of course not, Lieutenant. It is just that I have not said a real good-bye to my father, assuming I would see him in a few weeks," she replied wistfully. "But if there is anything that does not change, it is the army," she added with a smile. "Whenever you think things will go one way, then inevitably they will go the other. When do we leave?"

Val laughed. "Your father promised me you were as flexible as any soldier. But you will have a whole day to get ready, Miss Gordon," he joked, "for my horse could use a day to rest."

"It looks like you could too, Lieutenant Aston," Elspeth told him, noticing for the first time how haggard he looked.

"I wouldn't mind a good night's sleep."

"You can have my parents' bed. And a good supper tonight," she added, noticing that his uniform was fitting very loosely.

As they made their way back to the village, each became aware of a certain familiar tension between them. After the first shock was over, Elspeth realized how happy she was to see Lieutenant Aston. It was a good thing she had Nelly Ryan for company, she thought, as she glanced over at the man walking beside her.

When they reached the house, Elspeth showed Val where he could stable his horse and told him that she would see to getting him some hot water for a bath.

She was gratified to see his eyes light up for a moment at the thought of that luxury, for he looked careworn and exhausted. She imagined that he had been hardly out of the saddle as the French moved north.

She and Nelly set the tub up in the kitchen and she told her companion that she would have to interrupt her supper preparations for a while so that the lieutenant could bathe.

"There you are, Lieutenant. I've hung a piece of flannel on the over door so you will have a warm towel, and there is a piece of soap in the tub."

"Thank you, Miss Gordon," Val said with a grateful smile.

"Nelly has a stew on the stove and some bread in the oven, so you only have ten minutes for your bath," Elspeth told him apologetically.

After stripping off his uniform, Val sank gratefully into the copper tub and felt around for the small fragment of soap. It did not produce much lather, but did the job well enough, and after he had washed, he rested his head against the back of the tub and automatically fingered Charlie's ring. His neck and chest were green from the brass chain, but he hadn't taken it off since he had slipped it over his head. Holding on to it like a child, and relaxed and warm for the first time in days, he fell asleep.

"I have to get into the kitchen to see to the stew, Miss Elspeth," Nelly said anxiously. "How much longer do you think the lieutenant will take?"

"I'll call and remind him, Nelly, while you draw water

from the pump," Elspeth reassured her, going to the kitchen door and calling softly, "Lieutenant Aston, Nelly needs to check on supper."

There was no answer. "Lieutenant Aston?" He must have fallen asleep, she realized. She smiled and then sniffed. The stew was beginning to smell scorched. Oh, dear, she was going to have to go in and wake him.

He *was* asleep, just as she had guessed. Keeping her eyes averted, she took the flannel off the oven door and, using it as a pot holder, took out the stew. "Just in time," she whispered. But the flannel was not thick enough to protect her hands for long and she let the pan slip onto the counter.

She glanced over worriedly just as Val opened his eyes and, startled by the thunk, began to pull himself up.

"I—I am so sorry, Lieutenant," Elspeth stammered, "but I had to rescue Nelly's stew, and you had obviously fallen asleep. . . ."

Val had sunk down again as soon as he realized where he was. They were both flushed from embarrassment and the heat of the kitchen and from something else too, he realized as he felt himself grow hard.

Elspeth was standing frozen as though she had been caught in a child's game of statues. He didn't want her coming closer, but he did need the toweling she was holding.

"Miss Gordon."

"Yes, Lieutenant?"

"Perhaps you could place the towel on the edge of the tub as you leave?"

"Oh, yes, that is a good idea, Lieutenant," Elspeth said, cursing herself for acting like an idiot. Averting her eyes, she lay the flannel on the edge of the tub and left the kitchen.

"I must have sounded like a complete widgeon," she muttered as she shut the kitchen door behind her. But it had been more than embarrassment that had shaken her and more than the sight of Lieutenant Aston's broad chest covered in wet brown curls. It was the way his face had looked in sleep. He had seemed so much younger and more vulnerable to her. She had wanted to reach out and smooth his hair back from his brow. They were dangerous, such thoughts, and she had better banish them, for she and Val would be facing one another over dinner very shortly.

At first there was an awkward silence as Nelly served the stew, but as she sliced the bread, Val, knowing that someone would have to break it, said, "Miss Gordon rescued that stew just in time, Mrs. Ryan." Elspeth looked up and, seeing the twinkle in his eye, knew that things were all right.

"You must tell me what has been happening, Lieutenant," Elspeth demanded as they finished their supper. "I know Massena has gone north, but we have had little further news here."

"There were a number of skirmishes and rear-guard actions as he retreated," Val told her. "I was ahead of the army much of the time and it was the first time I have wished to be back with my regiment," he added. "What the French did to the countryside and the people . . . well, I am glad you were here and did not see it."

"I can imagine it must have been bad, considering the French troops had been sitting and starving for months."

"You cannot imagine, thank God," Val replied with such finality that Elspeth did not have the courage to ask any more questions until they were seated by the fire in the parlor, each with a small glass of port.

"Are the French out of Portugal, Lieutenant?"

"They are, Miss Gordon, except for the small garrison at Almeida. They tried to hold the line at the River Coa, but we drove them off in Sabugal."

"Did we lose many men?"

"More theirs than ours." Val was silent for a moment and then said, "Charlie fell at Sabugal."

He said it so softly that Elspeth wasn't sure she had heard him correctly. "Fell? Charlie?" She looked over at him and then she knew. "Oh, no, not Charlie," she said in an agonized whisper.

"If Crauford had been there . . . But that damned fool Erskine had the cavalry going in every direction," Val told her bitterly.

What could she possibly say to him? Elspeth wondered. He had lost the person closest to his heart.

"I'll be going off to bed, then, Miss Elspeth," said Nelly, who had come in without either of them noticing her.

"Oh, yes, of course, Nelly."

When they were alone again, Elspeth reached over and put her hand over his. "I am so sorry, Lieutenant Aston. . . . We all loved Lord Holme," she added, her voice quivering. Val gripped her hand convulsively. "Everyone loved Charlie," he said hoarsely. "He should not have died. If anyone had to, it should have been me."

"Oh, no," cried Elspeth. "You must not say that."

"Why not? It is true." He looked over at her, his eyes despairing. "He was so *loving*."

"He was," Elspeth whispered.

Val dropped her hand and, opening the neck of his tunic, drew out the ring. "He gave me this before he left. The Faringdon crest," he explained. "To keep safe until he came back. To return to his father if he didn't. . . ." Val fingered the ring and said brokenly, "It is all I have of him and I never really told him what he meant to me."

Elspeth had been in the presence of grief often in the army and knew how necessary it was to mourn in order to come to terms with one's loss. But there was nothing healing in this grief. There was agony over losing his brother, but there was more than that and it seemed as if it was tearing him apart.

She rose and knelt beside him. "Oh, my dear," she said without thinking, "you must not torture yourself. Your brother knew you loved him; I am sure of it." She reached up and touched his cheek.

Her soft touch released something in him and Val caught her to him as though he were drowning and only she could save him. He captured her mouth with his and she opened hers willingly. The kiss left them both breathless when he finally released her.

He slipped off the chair and was down on his knees before her, one hand cupped behind her head as he bent down for another bruising kiss, the other caressing her breast.

At first Elspeth pushed his hand away, and he pulled back instantly. But the look in his eyes was so desperate that she forgot everything in her desire to comfort in what seemed the only way she could, and so she put her arms around his neck and pulled his mouth against hers again.

This time, when his hand slipped under the bodice of her dress and his thumb began to circle her breast, she only gave herself over to the sensation.

Val was beyond being aware of where he was and who she was. He only knew that he wanted her, that no one in the world could comfort him but Elspeth. As soon as he felt her willing response he lifted her up.

"Where is your room?" he asked hoarsely. "I can't take you here on the floor."

Elspeth took his hand in hers and led him into the bedroom.

He unpinned her dress with shaking fingers and, after she crawled under the covers, pulled off his boots and uniform. Then he drew the brass chain over his neck and dropped the ring on the small table beside the bed.

"Do you want me to turn the lamp down?" he asked her.

Elspeth nodded and he turned the wick until the lamp flickered out, and crawled into the bed.

She still had her shift on and he slipped his hand underneath and sought her out, groaning with pleasure at the moistness that met his fingers. Then he was over her, his hands woven through her hair. He claimed her mouth and thrust with his tongue, and she arched up and felt him hard against her belly.

"I can't wait," he groaned and, slipping his hands under her hips, he lifted her up to meet him.

He was beyond thought, beyond care, beyond anything but his need to bury himself in her. Elspeth felt a searing pain at his second thrust, but as he filled her, she began to move with him.

Oh, God, he wanted to go deeper. He was already lost, so why not truly lose himself in her? He cried out at the moment of his release and then collapsed next to her, leaving Elspeth as full and as empty as she had ever felt in her life.

Elspeth lay there, waiting for him to say something, anything. Not that he loved her. She didn't expect that, for she knew this had not been about love, but grief. But she needed to hear that she meant something to him, that she had at least been able to ease his pain. But he was silent and she was afraid to move or speak. After a few minutes, however, she gathered up her courage and, raising herself on one elbow, looked over at him.

He had fallen asleep almost instantly, it seemed. Elspeth didn't know whether to laugh or cry. He *was* exhausted, she told herself. But he had turned away and left her there hoping that he would pull her close, wishing for words of affection, if not love. She slipped out of bed and, holding her gown up against her, crept down the hall to her small bedroom, where she crawled under the covers and cried herself to sleep.

When Val awoke the next morning, he felt rested for the first time in weeks. It took him a minute to realize where he was and to remember what had happened the night before.

He had taken Elspeth Gordon to bed. She had not been unwilling, but he had used her, he realized as he tried to reconstruct the evening. Used her for release and to assuage his grief. He hadn't used a woman so selfishly since he was eighteen. And this was the woman he loved. My God, what was he going to say to her?

He pulled himself up and looked at the crumpled bedclothes. There were a few bloodstains, reminding him that it was the first time for Elspeth. He ran his hands over his face. Had he hurt her badly? He had certainly not given her any pleasure, but he hoped he had not given her too much pain.

He would have to marry her this time and he felt a sinking sensation as he realized that he had not only taken her maidenhead but also her freedom to choose. She would have to wed him. This wasn't like before. It had nothing to do with satisfying external appearances. This had to do with honor. He could not look her father and mother in the face if he failed to marry her.

The irony of the situation was not lost on him. He loved her and therefore would never have proposed, to save her from the dishonor of marrying a bastard. But he had dishonored her, and therefore he had to propose.

The sun was just coming up and he hoped that Nelly was not an early riser as he walked quietly down the hall. He could not face Elspeth over breakfast without talking to her. Without letting her know that he would make things right. Or very wrong, depending upon how you looked at it.

He opened her door quietly and walked the short distance to her bed. She lay sleeping, her hair spread out on the pillow, and he wished he could let her sleep, could just leave her to her dreams rather than waking her to the harsh reality that faced them.

"Elspeth." She stirred a little at his whisper, but her eyes remained closer. He reached out and gently shook her shoulder.

Her eyes opened and she looked at him with a puzzled frown as she tried to make out what he was doing in her bedroom. Then it all came back, and drawing the covers around her, she sat up.

"Lieutenant Aston . . . ?"

"Elspeth, we need to talk. It must be clear to you . . . after last night and my shameful behavior . . . that we must wed."

Elspeth just sat there as though waiting for something from him, but he didn't know what.

"I know that you cherish your independence and would not have given it up except for love. . . ."

"Yes," she whispered.

"We have no choice. You can see that, I am sure. But we are friends and there is also an attraction between us. I am just sorry I did this to you."

"I see," Elspeth replied, her heart sinking.

"My concern is the same as it was in the fall, Miss Gordon. But not to marry you after last night would be to dishonor both you and your parents, who trusted me."

Elspeth thought that if hearts could break, now would be when hers would crack. He was *sorry* he had to ask her. Of course, part of his reluctance was his ridiculous combination of pride and shame about the circumstances of his birth. But if he had cared for her at all, surely there would have been some joy in his offer.

"I cannot marry you under these circumstances, Lieutenant Aston," she answered calmly, although it was difficult to keep her voice steady.

"It is precisely because of these circumstances that you must, Miss Gordon." His tone was that of a man used to being obeyed.

"I am not one of your foot soldiers, to be ordered around," Elspeth responded sharply.

Val took a deep breath. "Of course not, Elspeth. I apologize for barking at you. But there really is no choice, so we must both resign ourselves to that."

She knew he was right. And after all, there was no man she would rather marry. But not like this. Not like this.

"We will have to wait until Lisbon, where we can find a clergyman. I am sorry your parents will not be present. It won't be the wedding you must have dreamed of," he said regretfully.

"I put away my girlish fantasies years ago, Lieutenant," Elspeth replied tartly. She would be damned if she would let him see how vulnerable she was. "And Nelly will be awake soon, so you had best get yourself out of my room. Or she'll think you have to marry me," she added with bitter irony.

After he had bowed himself out, Elspeth sat there, the covers pulled up around her. She had lied, of course. She had not let go of all her girlish dreams. Hers were different from other girls'; she had never desired a large Society wedding. She had never dreamed of marrying an earl or a duke. But she had hoped one day a man she loved would acknowledge his love for her. She had wondered, of course, what joining physically with a man would be like and had pictured it as a union of hearts and souls as well as bodies.

"Well, lassie," she told herself as she got out of bed and began to dress, "last night was certainly different from anything you ever dreamed." She blushed as she recalled Val's urgency and her own response to it. She had wanted him as much as he wanted her; she couldn't deny that. Her body had responded to his desperate need for comfort. She could only hope he had found some.

Chapter 28

They made the journey to Lisbon quickly and as soon as Val got the women settled, he went out to find an English clergyman. He was directed to a Reverend Arthur, who at first protested that without a special license he could do nothing.

"We sail in two days, Vicar. We are in the middle of a war. And it is *necessary* that we marry. Surely under those circumstances an exception can be made."

"The lady is in a delicate condition?"

Val almost smiled. Elspeth was anything but delicate. Of course, he had hinted she might be increasing to get the man to perform the ceremony. He nodded and tried to look desperate. For all he knew, it could be the truth. That thought suddenly shook him, for he had never pictured himself becoming a father.

They arranged a private ceremony for the next day, and after Val left, he wandered the streets, thinking what a disservice he was doing to Elspeth. She should have a wedding dress, flowers . . . why, he hadn't even a ring to give her. He could at least remedy that.

He found a street with three jewelers' shops. The first two had nothing that appealed to him. Elspeth was not the sort of woman to wear gaudy diamonds even if he could afford them. He was about to give up hope of finding anything when the third jeweler pulled out a tray of antique rings. There, in the middle row, was a ring of matte gold set with a small, dark emerald. It was simple and elegant and Val knew he had found Elspeth's wedding ring. He was able to bargain the jeweler down to an affordable price and he pocketed the box and returned to their apartments feeling better than he had in days.

The next morning was cloudy as they set off for the small

chapel. Elspeth had gone shopping too and she wore a new silk shawl over her shoulders and her hair was held back with a silver and abalone comb. Val stole glances at her as they walked. She looked lovely, he thought, but also pale and serious.

Nelly acted as one witness and the sexton of the church another. When the vicar asked Val for the ring, Elspeth looked surprised when he pulled out a square of tissue paper and unwrapped it to reveal her ring. She offered Val a shaking hand and he slipped on the ring. It fit perfectly and she gave him a quick, delighted smile.

Val had arranged for a wedding breakfast in their apartments and he invited the vicar and the sexton to join them. He didn't know if he was relieved or disappointed when they refused. Nelly sat with them for a while and exclaimed over the tiny oranges served in a sugared syrup and the light egg bread that accompanied their omelettes. She left them alone, though, as soon as she'd finished.

After she'd gone, Elspeth lifted a piece of orange to her mouth with a small silver spoon. "Nelly is right. It is a lovely breakfast, Lieutenant."

"I think you might call me by my name, Elspeth."

She fingered her ring and watched as the sunlight lit the stone. "I did not expect a ring, Val. Certainly not anything so beautiful."

"I thought you needed something to make the day special," he told her with one of his rare smiles.

"I am Mrs. Aston now," she said wonderingly.

"Yes. Does it feel like such an unwelcome change?"

"In some ways," she confessed openly.

"At least we have honesty between us, Elspeth. I can't blame you for not wanting to change your name to Aston. It is not a family name, but the name my mother adopted before she had me," he told her with a bleak smile.

"She must have been a very brave woman, your mother," Elspeth said gently. He had never spoken of his mother before.

"Yes, I suppose she was. It couldn't have been easy, pretending to be a widow and raising a child on her own."

"When did you lose her, Val?"

"She died when I was eight." There was a moment's silence and then Val got up abruptly. "Well, I must go and see to our tickets." He left Elspeth to sit there wondering what it would have been like for an eight-year-old boy to lose his mother. She suspected it would take a long time before he revealed more.

That night, Elspeth readied herself for bed carefully, slipping on a silk night rail that she had purchased the day before and brushing her hair until it shone. She settled herself against the pillows and waited.

It was not long before Val appeared at the door. "I thought I would sleep in the sitting room tonight, Elspeth," he said.

"Oh?" She should have protested or questioned him, but she was so surprised and hurt that she could find no other words.

"We will have an uncomfortable two weeks ahead of us aboard ship and you will need all the sleep you can get tonight." He hesitated. "You haven't had much time to get used to this marriage and I was not very thoughtful a few nights ago. I thought I would give you a little time to recover." He stood there for a moment, as though wanting something from her, but she didn't know what. "Well, we will need to be up early, so I bid you good night."

"Good night, Valentine," she whispered as he closed the door.

Obviously the revealing silk had no effect on him, or perhaps he had only wanted her body for comfort, she thought sadly. It was certainly not the wedding night she had hoped for. She sighed as she turned the lamp down and gave herself to sleep.

Early that day, Val had resolved to give Elspeth time before he came to her again. He had treated her thoughtlessly the first time, only using her for his needs. He decided that when they made love again it would be warm and gentle: a slow-building fire and not an instant conflagration. But it took every bit of his resolve for him not to climb into bed with her, for she looked lovely in that clinging silk and unbound hair. It took him a long time to fall asleep.

*   *   *

When they reached London, Val booked them a suite of rooms in a small hotel on the edge of Mayfair.

"I am sorry it is not Fenton's, Elspeth," he said apologetically, "but Captain Grant gave me enough only for my own lodgings." He didn't add that he had spent quite a bit of his back pay on her wedding ring.

"These rooms are very satisfactory, Val," she reassured him. "I would be happy anywhere just to be off that ship, I am ashamed to confess!"

"I have to report to Whitehall, but will make sure they send you up a good luncheon, Elspeth. You are still looking pale."

"But that is better than Nile green," she replied with a smile.

Val waited at Whitehall most of the morning until the government secretary could see him.

"I understand you have been sent by Captain Grant to further question young Devereaux?" the secretary inquired when Val was finally admitted.

"Yes. Captain Grant wants to be sure he is telling the truth before taking action against someone who would seem a most unlikely traitor," Val relied stiffly.

"I am sure that the boy is telling the truth, though I hate the thought of James Lambert being guilty as much as you."

"Where is Devereaux?"

"At his secretarial post."

"He is not under arrest?"

"You realize, Lieutenant, had we arrested him, it would have alerted the marquess," the minister said caustically.

"Of course. I hadn't thought of that."

"I understand you are Wimborne's friend?"

Val nodded.

"He is very busy shepherding his sister through the Season. As the son of the Duke of Ravenscroft, young Devereaux is also busy with the social whirl. May I make a suggestion?"

"Of course."

"I will procure you invitations for many of the same occasions they are attending. That will give you time to get acquainted with Devereaux and to lull any suspicions the marquess might have about your appearance in London."

"I doubt he would ever suspect me of spying upon him," Val said bitterly.

"Perhaps not, but we do not wish to alarm either of them. Where are you lodged?"

"We are in the Blackstone Hotel."

"We? Did you bring someone with you?"

"I escorted Major Gordon's daughter to London." Val blushed. "She, er, agreed to become my wife and we married in Lisbon."

"I see," said the minister, raising his eyebrows. "Well, I will arrange invitations for Lieutenant and Mrs. Aston, then."

"Thank you, sir."

Chapter 29

"How was your day, Elspeth?" Val asked when he returned home and found her in the small sitting room.

"I did nothing but eat and sleep all day," she confessed with a smile. "I hope that by tomorrow I will have caught up and can get out for a while."

"You should take all the time you need . . ." Val started to say and then stopped.

"But . . . ?"

"We will likely be receiving invitations tomorrow."

"I don't know how we can. Maddy doesn't know I have arrived. And no one even knows we are married," she added with a faint blush.

"The minister at Whitehall does now," Val informed her with a rueful smile. "Evidently it is necessary for the success of my assignment that I socialize, so we will be included at a number of parties. And after you send Maddie word that you are in London, we will be invited to even more, Elspeth," he added.

His voice was strained and Elspeth saw he looked worried.

"Come, sit down, Val, and tell me exactly what Captain Grant sent you to do," she said, patting the sofa.

"I suppose I can tell you," he replied as he took the chair opposite her. She gave a little sigh and wondered when he would wish to be close to her again.

"But you cannot tell *anyone*," he added.

"I am very capable of keeping a secret, Valentine, I assure you."

"Of course you are. I apologize. I told you that someone was passing information to Massena this winter?"

"Yes, and that Mrs. Tallman was one of your confederates. . . ."

"We had three suspects: George Trowbridge, Lucas Stanton, and James Lambert."

"James!"

"My own reaction," Val said sadly. "But it was indeed James who was the contact in Portugal. He was fed information from private government meetings by a minister's secretary who fancied himself a revolutionary."

"But James is no radical," Elspeth protested. "What would be his motive?"

"The late marquess ran through most of the estate. James has managed to clear himself of debt, but there would have been very little left over for his sister's Season."

"Sell secrets to the enemy to fund Maddie's come-out! I can't believe it. She would have waited a year willingly."

"He also needs to marry, Elspeth, and what father would give his daughter to someone on the edge of bankruptcy?"

"But I *know* James. . . . He is not the sort of man to do this," she said, a bewildered look on her face.

"I certainly didn't think so. But perhaps if he felt desperate enough . . . And then, even if he had wanted to get out of it, he couldn't. Lucas Stanton made sure of that."

"Lucas Stanton . . . ?"

"Was blackmailing James. He must have found out early on. So then James needed the money for himself and to keep Stanton quiet."

"And you are here to arrest James?" Elspeth said quietly, the sympathy in her voice almost palpable.

"Not immediately. I am here to question young Devereaux and make sure he is telling the truth first."

Elspeth's face brightened. "Maybe he is lying? Could Lucas be paying him to lie?"

"I would love to think so, but there is that little matter of blackmail, my dear."

"Did the letter Mrs. Tallman found name James?"

"No," Val admitted.

"I have always disliked Lucas Stanton, from the moment I met him," declared Elspeth.

"So have I, and I met him years before you, Elspeth," said Val, amused by her vehemence.

"I forgot that you were at school with him. He was the reason you left, wasn't he?" she said slowly, remembering. "Charlie said you beat him senseless. But you never said exactly why."

"He . . . er . . . degraded a young boy, Elspeth. I couldn't stand that such brutality was accepted."

"Lucas Stanton is one of those men who likes other men? He was always after some woman in the camp," replied Elspeth, a puzzled frown on her face.

"Lucas Stanton is one of those men who uses whoever is available to him, but I don't think he is of an unnatural disposition."

"He is an evil man," Elspeth said flatly. "Whatever his disposition."

"I believe so."

"Then why could *he* not be the traitor? Perhaps he was blackmailing someone else."

"I would have liked to believe that, Elspeth."

"Then *do*. Don't go into this convinced of James's guilt." Without thinking, she reached out and put her hand on his. It was the first time they had touched aside from their wedding kiss and Val could almost feel the hair on his hand and arm stir in response to her light touch. He moved his thumb caressingly along hers and wondered if she would pull away. Instead, he felt her hand relax under his touch. She was leaning toward him and, without letting go of her hand, he slipped off his chair and onto the sofa.

"Your wedding ring looks very lovely on your hand, Mrs. Aston," he whispered.

"It is a beautiful ring, sir," she answered breathlessly.

"It is a beautiful hand," Val replied as he traced its structure with one finger. "Both finely shaped and strong."

"I have always been strong," sighed Elspeth.

"Surely that is not a bad thing to be?"

"Strength is not usually the first quality men look for in a woman," she said lightly.

"And what is?" he asked gently.

"Why, you should know, being a man, sir. Beauty, of course."

"Perhaps that is true for the everyday man. But a soldier needs a strong woman."

Elspeth knew that she had no claim to beauty, but it would have been lovely had he lied, she thought wistfully. But then her heart lifted as he continued.

"This soldier is lucky to have found a woman with such beautiful hair." His hand smoothed back a few wisps that had freed themselves and were shining in the afternoon sun. "And hazel eyes flecked with green. . . ." He lifted her chin and gazed into them so intently that she lowered them in confusion.

"And freckled skin," she added, trying to dispel the tension that was building between them.

"Yes, a fine dusting," he agreed as he traced her cheek.

"So you are satisfied with your wife, sir," she teased.

"Oh, very much, madame," he replied as he lowered his face to hers and brushed her lips with his.

Her lips immediately parted, and he nibbled at her mouth with his. Elspeth gave a little moan and he pulled away. "Oh, don't stop," she whispered and pulled him down again.

This time their kiss was long and deep and when it ended, Val buried his face in her neck. "I want you, Elspeth," he whispered against her ear. "But I used you so urgently that I would not wonder if you did not want me."

"Oh, but I have, I do," she answered.

His hand caressed her breast and she shivered. "But not here on the sofa," she said with a mischievous little smile.

He slid his hand around her waist and kept it there, guiding her upstairs and into their bedchamber. When he had closed the door behind them, they stood there, looking at one another.

"It is still light out," Elspeth told him.

"Let me close the curtains, then." When Val had drawn them shut, he turned and there was Elspeth standing in the same spot.

"Have you changed your mind?"

"No," she said slowly. "I just have never undressed in front of a man before."

"Then let me help you." Val stood behind her and, as he dropped kisses on her neck, slowly unpinned her. The dress slipped to the floor and Elspeth stepped out of it and turned to face him.

"I am a little chilly, Val," she said nervously. "I'll get under the covers while you undress."

He knew it wasn't the cold but her self-consciousness. He pulled opened the buttons of his tunic as he watched her slip into the bed. He was just unfastening his trousers when she giggled. "Your boots?"

It seemed to take forever to pull the damned boots off, but he finally succeeded and stood there in his small clothes, his back to her. He debated taking them off in bed. But they were husband and wife, and she would see him sooner or later, he told himself, and he stripped right then and there.

As he was turning around, she gasped and he flushed with embarrassment. Perhaps he should have waited.

"Your back, Val," she said, her voice shaking.

He had completely forgotten about it. It had been dark the first time they had made love, so she wouldn't have seen the scars, and it had been so hurried she'd hardly had a chance to feel them.

"Yes, well, no one serves in the army for twelve years and escapes flogging," he said lightly. "That is, if you serve in the ranks," he added ironically.

"I have only seen one flogging," said Elspeth, "and that was enough. I know it may be a necessary discipline, but I could not watch another one."

Val sat on the edge of the bed and Elspeth ran her fingers over the crisscrossed weals. "How long ago was this, Val?"

"Oh, early on. I had not gotten used to not being a free man, though you'd think I would have learned after George Burton," he added ruefully.

"George Burton?"

"My aunt's husband. The blacksmith I was apprenticed to. I haven't led the life of an officer and a gentleman, Elspeth."

"Was he a hard man, this George?"

"Some would say so. Some would say no more than most."

"You told me your mother died when you were eight. Did you go directly to your aunt's?"

"Where else was there to go?" he said matter-of-factly. Her fingers were still on his back, lightly tracing the scars as if she could make them go away. He could not turn and face her, not while he could feel her pity. It wasn't pity he wanted.

"Your father's?" she whispered.

He looked down at the ring hanging around his neck and, pulling away, slipped it off. "Until I was eight, I thought my father was a soldier killed in India," he said bitterly.

Elspeth said nothing. What could she say? That she was sorry for that little boy who had lost mother and father at the same time, who'd been sent off to a harsh, perhaps cruel man? She had thought she'd understood his pride. She had even, God forgive her, thought him unduly sensitive to a situation that did not seem that important to her.

"I am sorry you were forced to marry me, Elspeth," he said.

"I am not sorry at all," she answered fiercely and sliding over to make room for him, she took his hand and pulled him down next to her.

After the first kiss, Val did not even care whether it was love or pity. He was lost in the moment, lost in the pleasure of suckling at her breast, lost in amazement when she slid her hand down and caressed him gently and rhythmically.

"Not yet," he whispered as he gently moved her hand away.

"I hope that would give you pleasure," she whispered.

"Oh, it does," he groaned. "But too much, too soon. I wish to give you pleasure this time."

When his hand found her, Elspeth realized she had been hiding all her life. From the moment she had known she was not beautiful or sweetly foolish, she had hidden her deepest self away. For why should she be there, eager and loving, when no one was there to meet her and see her for who she was? No one had ever been curious about what lay beneath the surface. No one had cared to find her until now. Until this man with his hard face and scarred soul and oh, so gentle fingers drove her up and up, seemingly away from him. But he would not let her hide. He came after her, he sought her longingly, and then she was coming down into his arms and she was free and home at last.

It was only when she clung to him, shuddering, that Val entered her. He couldn't wait, for he knew she was there, ready to meet him. And as he poured himself into her, he marveled that Elspeth could make him forget everything in the past and only be with her in the present.

They lay collapsed in each other's arms for a long time and Val dropped occasional kisses on her head. Finally they fell back against the pillows and Elspeth looked over at him and gave a soft laugh.

"What is so amusing, madame?" he asked.

She reached out her finger and traced his nose.

"You are making fun of my nose!" he said with mock indignation. "I'll have you know it is considered quite—"

"Wellingtonian," she said with a little giggle.

"Surely not so prominent as that?"

"I wonder if our children will inherit it," she said without thinking.

He sighed and she asked anxiously, "You do want children, don't you, Valentine?"

"Yes, yes, I do. It is only that I never thought to be married . . . to be a father."

He turned to her. "I suppose in my own way I am as bad as Will Tallman," he admitted. "I didn't believe a soldier should marry. Didn't imagine I would ever find a woman who would be willing to follow the drum," he said lightly.

"Well, you have found one," she replied softly.

"It seems I have," he answered, reaching for her hand and giving it a squeeze. "And you need not worry too much about the nose," he teased. "It has been broken and is not quite as prominent as my father's," he added.

"Will you go see your father soon, Val?" she asked hesitantly, hating to disturb the easiness between them.

"I promised Charlie, Elspeth. I planned to visit Faringdon House tomorrow to see if he is still in town."

"Do you wish me to come with you?"

"No, Elspeth. I thank you, but it is something I must do myself." He leaned over and kissed her. "You are a good comrade, madame wife."

Elspeth lay awake after he had fallen asleep. He had given her his body, this new husband of hers. He had helped her discover her own capacity for passion. But it seemed clear to her that for now, he came to her for pleasure and to hide himself in her. When would he let her love him? When would he let himself be found?

Chapter 30

As Val had predicted, the invitations started arriving the very next day, and after breakfast, over a second cup of tea, Elspeth began opening them.

"Here is one from the Duke and Duchess of Farron for a musicale," she exclaimed.

"I think this is the most difficult assignment Grant ever sent me on," Val complained. "I would rather face the French than attend a ton function," he confessed, only half-humorously.

"I don't look forward to it much more than you do, Val. I didn't mind coming back for Maddie, but I never expected all this," she said, waving her hand over the pile of invitations.

"I am sorry, Elspeth. I never dreamed you would be pulled into this charade."

"I will look on it as my sacrifice for God and country," she replied, her eyes twinkling. Then her face became serious. "Others have made far greater ones, after all."

"Well, I will leave you to it, then," said Val as he got up from the table. "I must make my call at Faringdon House."

"I wish you well, Val," she called after him.

*   *   *

Val didn't realize how much he was hoping that the door knocker would be missing until he got to St. James's Square and saw it hanging just where it should be. Above it hung a black bow.

"What a coward I am," he muttered as he stood there, unable to lift his hand. Finally he gave the door a few sharp raps.

"I am sorry, sir, His Lordship is not at home to anyone," said Baynes, beginning to close the door in Val's face.

"Perhaps you don't remember me, Baynes? It is Valentine Aston and I have come to offer my condolences to my father."

"Why, so it is you, sir!" said the old butler, his face reddening. "I am sorry. I will tell His Lordship you are here."

He showed Val into the library, where a fire was crackling cheerfully. Val was too restless to sit, so he scanned the shelves, skimming over titles and anxiously awaiting the earl.

When he heard the door open, he turned. Even if the earl had been his worst enemy, he would have felt sympathy for him at the loss of his son, but he was surprised at how much he felt for the man who stood before him.

"Good morning, Valentine."

"Good morning, my lord."

Val had not seen his father in years and was surprised at how much he had aged. His blond hair was silvered and he looked thinner. His cheeks were lined and his nose even more prominent. He looks like an old eagle, Val thought.

It was clear that grief had affected him as much as age, for his eyes were red-rimmed and tired-looking and his mouth drawn.

"I came to offer my sympathy, my lord," Val continued in a softer tone than he had ever used with his father.

"Please sit down, Valentine." There were two chairs facing the fire and the earl took one, gesturing Val to the other. He sat silently for a moment, as if intent on finding some meaning in the flames or the shifting of the logs. "You were with Charlie?"

"Yes, sir. We were almost seven months behind the lines."

"Ah, yes, the now-famous Lines of Tôrres Vedras. I always thought Wellington would one day display his genius. It seems he has finally done so."

"He saved Portugal, and I am convinced we will take Spain."

"Where did Charlie fall?" the earl asked bluntly.

"The French made a stand on the banks of the River Coa, sir, near a town called Sabugal. We forced them to retreat. Wellington himself said it was one of the most glorious actions his troops had ever engaged in."

"So Charlie died gloriously? I suppose that should make me feel comforted, but it does not, Valentine, it does not," said the earl, looking over at Val. "I don't suppose you know how he died? The casualty lists tell nothing and I would like to know if he suffered much," added the earl, his voice shaking.

"I was across the river on a reconnaissance mission, my lord, but I was able to find him after the battle."

"Ah, yes, Charlie wrote me that you are one of Colquhoun Grant's right-hand men. He was very proud of you. Always mentioned you in his letters. Was it quick, Valentine, or did he suffer?" The earl's voice broke and his eyes were agonized. "I don't think I could bear to know he suffered."

"It was a saber thrust through the lung, sir. I think he would have died very quickly."

"But not painlessly. . . ."

"He wouldn't have felt much," Val said, hoping it was true.

The earl buried his face in his hands.

"Perhaps I should have lied, sir, but it would not have seemed respectful to Charlie. I can assure you he died a better death than many a soldier. His face . . . it seemed more surprised than suffering."

"Thank God for that, then."

"He gave me this before the battle, sir," Val said, drawing out the Faringdon ring. "He didn't want it lost or . . . Anyway, he wanted me to give it to you personally, if anything happened to him." Val slipped the ring off the chain and held it out.

The earl took it and turned it in his hand as though he had never seen it before. "The Faringdon crest," he whispered.

"Yes, sir."

"Worn by the heir for the last three hundred years." The earl looked up and said with a great weariness, "It is yours, Valentine," and held it out to Val.

"It is . . . was Charlie's, my lord. It will now go to whoever is the rightful heir. I assume there is some cousin somewhere," he added almost harshly.

"Yes, but you are my only surviving son, Valentine." Before Val could reply, the earl got up and went over to his desk. "Unfortunately, I can't legitimize you, but here . . ." he said, lifting a paper off the desk. "Here I formally recognize you as my son. That will give you a place in Society at least."

Val was speechless. Now, now, his father would recognize him? And smile at him as though he'd given him something that Val had always wanted?

"I don't want your bloody recognition, my lord. It is years too late," he added, the steel in his voice as cutting as a sword.

"It is not the viscountcy, Valentine."

"Charlie was your son, my lord."

"As are you, and Charlie is dead. This is what he would have wished. He urged me to do it many times."

"He wanted me at school with him and so you sent me. He wanted me to have a commission and you bought it for me. But this is one thing you can't give me, my lord, for I won't accept it."

"I am not giving you a choice, Valentine. I will do this, whether you wish it or not, and not only for Charlie's sake. I would have done it years ago, had you stayed."

Val could hardly trust himself to speak. He stepped forward and put the ring on the desk. "Do whatever you like, my lord, but I cannot take this. I loved him too," Val declared, his voice breaking. He was out the door before his father could stop him.

It was a glorious May morning, but Val did not notice the cloudless blue sky or the pale green leaves on the trees, for he was still back in the library with his father. He walked at quick march pace and inside he was in a turmoil. After all these years, his father was ready to acknowledge him. Said he'd wanted to do it long ago. Then why *didn't* you, while my mother was alive? Why didn't you marry her instead of Charlie's mother? But then, of course, there would have been no Charlie. . . . Val could feel the tears rising. He would *not* cry. He'd be damned if he'd cry. He found himself at the entrance to the park and he walked in and down one of the side paths. Although it was not the fashionable hour, there were quite a few riders and carriages. Once the terrible winter had eased its grip and the ice was gone, people who had been homebound for months were out enjoying their freedom.

Val stayed off the main paths as long as he could, but eventually he came out to one of the main thoroughfares. There was not the crush there would be later in the afternoon, but there were enough riders and carriages that he had to pay more attention to what was around him. He had just stepped aside to let a curricle pass, barely taking note of the dapple grays that drew it, when the driver drew up and called down to him.

"Val! Is that you? Whatever are you doing in London?"

It was James Lambert.

Val did his best to smile, although to him it felt more like a grimace. He had his excuse ready, of course.

"Good morning, James. I was given leave to visit my father and bring him something of Charlie's."

James motioned to his tiger and, handing him the reins, stepped down to walk beside Val. He put a sympathetic arm around Val's shoulders. "It was devastating to hear the news, Val."

James's voice held a very real grief. He had known Charlie at school and university. In some ways, he knew him better than Val had. James's palpable affection and his sorrow over Charlie's death almost overset Val's control. One of the hardest things about Charlie's death had been that there was no one to mourn with. Everyone had loved Charlie, of course, but not many had known him as well as James.

"Thank you, James," he said in a strained voice. "It means a great deal to know someone else misses him as much as I do."

"I called on your father. He was devastated by the news," James replied quietly. "Have you been to see him yet?"

"This morning," Val said shortly.

"Surely you and he might grieve together?" James suggested gently.

"My father and I had very little in common besides Charlie. Now we have nothing."

"I had a few reasons to be at odds with my father, Val, but despite that, I am glad I made my peace with him before he died."

"You have always been a better-hearted man than I, James," Val declared, looking over at him with a crooked smile. "You and Charlie shared that quality."

"You are equally good-hearted, Val," James replied seriously. "In fact, I am sure that your affections, once given, run very deep indeed. You just keep your feelings well-hidden."

"He offered to . . . no, he is going to recognize me, James," Val said bitterly.

James stopped and faced him. "I think that was very well done. You are his only son now."

"He doesn't want me as his son, James. He never wanted me. Oh, Charlie wanted me," continued Val, putting his hand up to stop James's protest. "The earl only brought me to Faringdon for his sake. It should have been *me,* James, not Charlie," Val continued, his voice raw with pain. "He was sunny and gay and openhearted and all who knew him loved him."

"It was hard not to love Charlie," James admitted with a sweet smile.

"And I am a hard and hidden-hearted fellow," continued Val in a voice even he could tell was full of self-pity as well as real pain.

"If I didn't care about you, Valentine, I would wash my hands of you right now," said James, with such vehemence that Val knew there was nothing humorous in his words at all. "You are a brave and resourceful soldier, and a good friend, but you are the most blind and stubborn fool when it comes to your father. You were born out of wedlock. So were many others. Some are born even worse. We have no choice over how and where and to whom we are born, but we *can* choose how to live our lives. It is high time you came to terms with your birth, Val. It is something we all have to do," James added, his voice tight with anger and something else.

"I accepted the fact I am a bastard a long time ago, James," Val protested. "I had little choice about that."

"Until you make peace with your father, Val, you will not be at peace." Val opened his mouth to protest, but James just continued, "I have lost one dear friend, Valentine. I do not want to lose another, so let us leave the subject, shall we?"

They walked on a few moments in uncomfortable silence, which James finally broke by saying humorously, "You see, even though you are a hard-hearted bastard, I do care about you, Val." Val looked over and they both laughed.

"Thank you, James. I need you to act as a scold every now and then. And I have always been grateful you call me friend."

"Now that you are in London, you must come and meet my sister. Will you join us for dinner tomorrow night? We are going to the Duke of Farron's musicale afterward. I'll try to get you an invitation too, if you wish."

"Actually, I, er, we already have an invitation," Val stammered.

"We?"

"Yes, Captain Grant saw to it."

"Do you mean Colquhoun is in London? I would not have thought Wellington could have spared him."

"Not Captain Grant; Elspeth Gordon. No, Elspeth Aston. We are married, you see," Val finished awkwardly, his face getting red.

"I knew Elspeth would be coming to London to take part in Maddie's Season," said James, trying to make some sense of what Val had said. "But how on earth have you had time to marry her?"

"Major Gordon asked me to escort her and we were wed in Lisbon."

"It is not every young woman who marries her military escort, Val," replied James quizzically.

"It was what you might call a necessary marriage, James. In my need for comfort over Charlie's death, I, er, compromised Elspeth."

"I see."

"I had to marry her, James, after betraying her parents' trust."

"I had always suspected there was some feeling between you and Elspeth," James said blandly.

"We have always been good friends."

"Something more than that, I think?"

"I do not know that she loves me, James, if that is what you are asking."

"But do you love her?"

"Very much," Val confessed in a low voice. "And that is all the more reason I should never have put her in such a position."

"Elspeth is an uncommon woman, Val. I wish you both happy."

"Thank you, James."

"Come, let me show you how well these grays of mine move." They both mounted the carriage.

As they bowled down the path, James turned to Val and said, "You know, you are not the only one whose appearance in London surprised me, Val. Lucas Stanton arrived a few days ago. I thought I'd warn you, since he will likely be at the musicale."

"What is Stanton doing in London?" Val demanded so vehemently that James looked at him with surprise.

"Evidently his great-aunt is near death. I never took him for one with much family feeling, but then she is supposed to have mentioned him in her will," James added cynically.

Val was very quiet the rest of their ride, for the mention of Stanton's name had reminded him of why he was in London himself. Tonight he would watch Stanton and young Devereaux very carefully. Stanton's presence in London may very well mean that his faith in James was justified.

Chapter 31

Elspeth lingered over breakfast that morning feeling delightfully lethargic after the night's lovemaking. The feeling of oneness with her husband that she had experienced only made her hungrier for more. More lovemaking, she thought with a blush, but also a closer acquaintance with his heart and mind. It surprised her, this hunger, for she had so long believed herself resigned to solitude and successful in banishing the desire for intimacy with a man. She may have "married in haste," but she most definitely was not "repenting at leisure," she reflected with a smile.

She wondered how Val's visit to his father had gone. Elspeth had met the earl years ago when she and her parents had been in London to get her settled in school. They had been invited to dinner at her grandfather's house and both Charles and Charlie had been present. Elspeth wondered if the earl remembered her.

She wanted to offer her condolences to him personally and as she went through the pile of invitations next to her, she realized that she was unlikely to see him at any of these gatherings, for he was in mourning. This morning she had intended to pay a brief call on Maddie and let her know she was in town. Of course, once Maddie found out that Elspeth was now Mrs. Valentine Aston, it was unlikely to be a brief call! Perhaps on her way she might stop at Faringdon House.

As Elspeth walked up the steps of Faringdon House a few hours later, she almost turned around and left. She wasn't really sneaking around behind her husband's back, she told herself. After all, the earl was now her father-in-law. Nevertheless, she felt irrationally guilty as she lifted her hand to the knocker.

The butler repeated what he said to everyone: that the earl was unavailable.

"I think he may see *me*," she told Baynes. "Would you tell him that Mrs. Valentine Aston is here to offer her condolences?"

Baynes's eyebrows lifted in surprise, but he merely said, "Come in, madame, and I will take the news to His Lordship."

He was back quickly. "The earl will see you in the morning room, Mrs. Aston."

She was only seated for a moment when the earl walked in, his face expressionless, looking her over as though he were a blue-eyed hawk. If she hadn't already known they were father and son, she would have guessed, for the resemblance was strong.

"Baynes told me Mrs. Valentine Aston called to offer her condolences. But if I am not mistaken, you are Ian and Peggy Gordon's daughter?" he said, a puzzled look in his eyes.

"You remember me?"

"I knew your mother's family well, so I paid attention to Peggy's daughter when I met her," he told her with a smile. "But what are you doing in London, my dear?"

"I was Elspeth Gordon, my lord. I am now Mrs. Valentine Aston," she said simply. "We have been married only a short time." Elspeth hesitated. "We had come to know each other well in Portugal and Val escorted me to London. When he asked me to marry him, I was happy to say yes."

"Valentine was here this morning and said not a word about it. Not that I am surprised," the earl added ironically.

"I wasn't sure whether I should come," explained Elspeth. "But my parents and I knew and loved Charlie and I wanted to tell you how sorry we are for your loss. I realized I might not see you at all if I didn't call. I wasn't sure Val would bring me. . . ." Elspeth's voice trailed off in embarrassment.

"I suspect that you are right, my dear. He only came here to bring me this," said the earl, his eyes growing bright with tears when he drew out Charlie's ring from his waistcoat pocket. "I told Valentine it was his, and that I in-

tended to recognize him as my son. That will give you both
a place in Society."

"I am not at all the type, my lord," Elspeth said with a
smile. "I have been following the drum for years. To tell
the truth, I am dreading even these few weeks. I am only
here for Lady Madeline Lambert's sake," she added with
a confiding smile.

"It seems to me that you are just the sort of wife a
soldier needs, Mrs. Aston."

"Oh, please call me Elspeth." She was thoughtful for a
minute. "Was Val pleased that you would acknowledge
him, my lord?"

"Charles."

"Was he pleased, Charles?"

"What do you think, my dear?"

Elspeth's face grew pink. "Despite the fact that the circumstances of his birth have had a great effect on him, I am
afraid his pride would not allow him to easily accept this."

"You know him very well, indeed, my dear. Better than
I. . . . I had hoped . . . but indeed it was foolish, given our
history . . ." the earl said sadly. "I would legitimize him, if
I could."

"Then I would have been a viscountess? I am glad to
be just plain Mrs. Aston," said Elspeth with a smile. "I
only wish . . ."

"Yes, my dear?" the earl asked quietly.

"I only wish for Val's happiness, Charles. And yet I am
not sure he will ever be happy," she added sadly.

"Surely he is happy to be married to you, Elspeth?"

"Oh, yes, of course, there is that," she said brightly. "But
I think he still feels a great deal of shame over his birth.
And anger over . . . This is difficult, Charles."

"Go on."

"Anger over your treatment of his mother. He believes
you only brought him to Faringdon for Charlie's sake."

"He is right, Elspeth," the earl said quietly.

"I see," she said, feeling all the hope she had for a recon-
ciliation dying.

"I promised Sarah, Val's mother, not to recognize him.
She did not want Charlie or his mother to suffer from any
scandal. Had Charlie's mother lived, he would never have
known of Valentine's existence." The earl turned his back

on Elspeth and went to stand by one of the windows, but she had seen the pain in his eyes.

"I would have married Sarah, if she had let me," the earl said, turning back with an ironic smile.

"You wished to marry Val's mother, Charles? I'm sure he does not know this."

"He never gave me a chance to tell him. He found out about his birth very suddenly when his mother died. I must have appeared a villain to a young boy and I did nothing to change his view over the years."

"You must tell him, Charles!" Elspeth exclaimed.

"Perhaps someday. In the meantime, I beg you to keep this in confidence."

Elspeth hesitated and then agreed.

"He is as proud as his mother, you know," the earl told her with a tender smile.

"I suspect he also shares that quality with you, Charles," Elspeth told him tartly. "It is not only your nose that creates a resemblance!"

The earl laughed. "I suspect you have come to know your husband well, Elspeth."

"Would you come and dine with us one night, Charles?" Elspeth asked impulsively.

"Not yet, my dear. I do not want to force myself on Valentine."

"Then may I visit you again?"

"I would be delighted to see you at any time, my dear."

The earl watched Elspeth go down the stairs. Valentine had chosen well, he told himself. He had had a hard life, this oldest son of his. Elspeth Gordon, with her army background and common sense, was perfect for him.

She was no beauty, it was true, for she was too tall to meet Society's standards and her features, one by one, were nothing out of the ordinary. But she had a spirit, intelligence, and grace that brought everything together and made her an attractive woman, one of those women, he realized, who becomes more attractive with age.

And she loved Val. She could not hide that. Yet he could not help worrying about their marriage. Valentine had never mentioned her at all. He hoped his son loved Elspeth, not only for her sake but for his own. It was painful

to love. The earl knew that well. He had never thought to
recover from the loss of Sarah Aston. But he had kept his
heart open to Helen. And Charlie had been the apple of
his eye. He took a deep, shuddering breath as he realized
yet again that he would never again see Charlie's smiling
face, never hear his voice.

And yet despite the agony of losing Charlie, he would
never regret loving him. He would go on loving him until
he died, just the way he still loved Sarah and Helen. But
it was a hard thing, to only give your love to the dead and
not the living. He would give anything to get to know his
oldest son. He loved Val because he was Sarah's, of course.
But he wanted to love him for himself and it did not seem
that Val would ever give him the chance.

Elspeth made a visit to the Lambert town house, but
Maddie was out shopping, so she could only leave word
that she had called and hoped to see her friend at the
Farrons' musicale. By the time she returned to the hotel,
Val had been home for an hour.

"Did you have a pleasant visit with Lady Madeline?" he
asked when she joined him in the sitting room.

"Unfortunately, I missed her. She was out shopping. I
did some myself," announced Elspeth, for she had visited
Hatchards on the way home. "It is such a luxury to be able
to buy a book and not make do with whatever has survived
the latest march!"

She sat down in the chair opposite her husband and, with
her usual directness, asked how his visit with his father had
gone. "I'm sure it must have been difficult to tell him the
details of Charlie's death."

"That is one of the things I appreciate about you, Elspeth," Val told her. "You are never afraid to come right
to the point."

"I was not brought up in a household where we tiptoed
around things, Val."

He smiled, thinking of the Gordons. "No, you certainly
were not. It was a hard visit," he admitted. "It brought it
all back to me," he added, gazing into the fire so she would
not see the tears spring to his eyes.

"Yes, I imagine it would," she said gently.

Val sighed. "I must tell you what the earl intends to do,

Elspeth, for it affects both of us. He is going to officially recognize me as his son, which means you will have a more secure place in Society." When Elspeth said nothing, Val said, "Aren't you surprised? Perhaps happy that being Mrs. Aston will not be as much of a disgrace?"

Elspeth was quiet for a moment. "I am not that surprised. The earl has just lost a son. He may not be able to make you his heir, but obviously he wishes to do what he can." She hesitated. "What I wish is for you to be happy, Val. Whether that is as a soldier or someone who moves in the highest circles . . . well, that is up to you," she added with an edge to her voice. "I find myself happy to be married to you, despite the fact that you are sometimes the greatest fool in Christendom. But perhaps that makes me the greater fool," she added ironically. "I am going upstairs to change. I will see you at supper."

Why the hell couldn't she be like other women? thought Val, leaning over and angrily stirring the fire and only managing to put it out by his motions. Any other woman would have been happy to have her marriage turn out not to be such a disaster. He was happy with it for her sake. He didn't need it for his own.

Or did he? *Did* something in him want his father's recognition? Want the acceptance other men could take for granted? Want even a little of what Charlie had taken for granted all his life? It was difficult to face that thought. *Had* he been envious of his brother all these years and never even known it?

He had never wanted the title; he was sure of that. But Charlie had had more than a title; he had had his father's love.

Oh, his mother had told him his father loved him very much. But that was the make-believe father, the tin soldier who had never really existed. Had she ever been thinking of the earl when she spoke of his father?

His mother had lied to him his whole childhood, he realized. He had never admitted that before. If she hadn't died, it would never have mattered. But she had died and left him fatherless and at the mercy of George Burton and all the others who had despised him over the years.

What if his mother had lived and Charlie had found him

there? What would she had said or done, with her decep-
tion revealed? Oh, God, why was he even questioning his
mother's decisions? What choice had she had?

She could have told me the truth.

No, he would not think that. She wanted to protect me.
She did what she thought best. He closed his eyes tight and
summoned his beautiful mother, working in the rose garden, tucking him in at night, telling him a story . . . about
his hero father.

He rubbed his hand over his face. What would Elspeth
have done in a similar situation? He was surprised that the
question occurred to him, but once it was there, it wouldn't
go away. Elspeth would have told her son the truth. He
knew that in his bones. She would have told it gently and
lovingly, but she would have told it. His mother's image
faded and in its place was Elspeth's. Had he been the one
to abandon Elspeth, had she had a child, he believed she
would have prepared their son better for the world, for
surely the truth was a better foundation for one's life than
a lie? His mother had been his security and when she had
died, he had been left with none, not even the comfort of
a make-believe father.

But to admit his mother had been wrong felt like losing
her all over again, and he didn't think he could bear so
much loss. Without his mother, he would have nothing: no
mother, no father, no brother. Only his wife. And she
thought him the greatest fool in Christendom!

Chapter 32

By an unspoken agreement they avoided the topic at supper, and therefore had a very quiet meal. Elspeth's anger
was the sort that flared up and then went away soon after
she had expressed it. It was becoming clear to her that
her husband was different. She supposed he must be angry

at her outspokenness, but because he was so reserved, it was hard to tell.

Had she asked him, Val could have told her, and truthfully, that he was not angry at her. At his mother for lying to him and then leaving him, at his father who was offering to recognize him years too late, and at Charlie for dying, yes. But there was no way he could have said this to Elspeth. He could barely articulate it to himself. And so when they finished their supper, he excused himself and told her that he was going out, would likely be back late, and he hoped she would not feel obliged to wait up for him.

Elspeth stayed in the sitting room for a little while after he'd left, hoping that the new novel would succeed in absorbing her into a world where all would come right in the end. But she couldn't concentrate for long and finally gave up and went to bed.

By the time Val returned, she was fast asleep. She was lying on her side, head pillowed in her hand, and Val slipped in next to her and put his arm around her waist. He lay there for a while, feeling the soft rise and fall of her breath, wondering if it was her habit to sleep on her side. He smiled in the dark as his own breathing relaxed in the same rhythm as hers. What a paradox it was that he didn't know Elspeth well enough to know how she preferred to sleep and at the same time knew her more intimately than anyone else on earth.

They were still spooned together when Elspeth awoke and she lay there for a moment enjoying the closeness. Val's arm was around her waist and she slipped her hand in his. His hand was strong and spare and even though he was asleep, she felt protected.

After a few minutes, she shifted closer. "Are you awake, Elspeth?" he whispered, his warm breath stirring her hair. She nodded and then felt his hand move to her breast.

"So am I," he said, whispering into her ear and pulling her even closer. They were both in that early morning trance state between sleeping and waking and Elspeth kept her eyes closed as Val's fingers gently caressed her breast and his breath against her neck made her very bones soften. Soon his breath became little kisses and then his hand reached lower to lift her night rail so he could trail his fingers down her bare flesh. His touch was so leisurely that she lay there motionless, suspended between delight and fulfillment. She could have stayed there forever, but then he shifted and when she felt his hardness against her, she began to wake up, almost against her will. She gently pushed away his hand and, before he could even wonder whether she was rejecting him, turned to face him and caress him in the same easy way, pressing him against her belly as she enclosed him with her hand and moved slowly against him.

It could have gone on forever, this sleepy pleasuring, but then Elspeth moved up against his bare chest, and Val knew she was ready for him. He entered her so softly that she only felt it as a continuation of what they had been doing and when he turned her on her back, he put both his hands behind her head, almost cradling her as he moved faster.

Elspeth felt she was being rocked by a larger rhythm, like the waves of the sea. It seemed as though the waves were in her body and she in the waves. They were both of them in an underwater world and when Val poured himself into her as she came down upon him, the ebb and flow did not end but moved rhythmically through her very veins.

There was nothing separate between them because they were all liquid. They had flowed into one another and lay there until gradually their bodies returned to them and they felt bones and muscles shape around them.

When Val rolled off her, he pulled Elspeth against him so that they were spooned together again.

"So you are not sorry to be married to me, Elspeth?" he whispered.

"Not at all."

"I'm glad, for I'm not at all sorry to be married to you, my dear," he said, dropping a kiss on top of her head.

Elspeth fell asleep again, but Val lay there, watching the room become brighter as the sun rose, wondering at how everything in his hard life had come together and brought him here, holding this woman in his arms.

He missed his mother and Charlie, and always would. But it struck him that it was only because of their deaths that he was here with Elspeth. It was a disquieting thought, that their deaths had led him to her and to a life he had never dreamed of.

He sighed and eased himself out of bed so as not to disturb her. As he splashed his face at the washstand and dressed, he realized that sometime in the night, a decision had been made. He would accept his father's recognition. He wasn't sure how he had come to this, but in some strange way it felt like he was doing it for his mother and for Charlie as well as for Elspeth.

He had finished his breakfast and was reading the paper when Elspeth finally came down to join him.

"You should have stayed in bed, Elspeth. I could have brought you your tea."

" 'Tis way past the time a braw scotswoman should be up and awake," she said with a broad burr and a self-conscious smile.

Val waited until she had finished her eggs and muffin and poured them both a second cup of tea. Then he cleared his throat. "I have decided that I should accept my father's decision with better grace," he told her, a serious look in his eye.

She could only guess how difficult it was for him to take something now from a father he saw as having abandoned him. "I hope you are doing this for yourself, Val," she said quietly.

"I suppose I am, as well as for my mother and you and Charlie."

"I'm very happy to be the wife of a soldier, Val. What do you think this will mean for you?"

"I don't intend to leave the army anytime soon," he reassured her. "But this will mean that when we come back to England, it will be easier for us . . . and our children," he added awkwardly.

Elspeth reached over and put her hand on his. "I think you have made a good decision, my dear."

"What are you planning to do today, madame wife?" he asked teasingly.

"I thought I might go to the Pantheon Bazaar and look for a pair of gloves for tonight. And you?"

"I suppose it is considered unfashionable for a husband to accompany his wife shopping?" he asked with a grin.

Elspeth blushed. "It probably is, but I would very much enjoy it, Val."

When they returned from their little shopping excursion with Elspeth's gloves and a bar of lavender-scented soap and a light green ribbon that matched her dress, they were met in the hotel lobby by the proprietor, who informed them with barely concealed satisfaction that His Lordship, the Earl of Faringdon, had been waiting for them for the last half hour.

Val's face immediately clouded, but Elspeth merely nodded and, thanking the man, requested him to show the earl up. And could he please also send up a pitcher of lemonade and some biscuits?

When she had put away her purchases, Elspeth opened the curtains in their sitting room and sat down, waiting for Val to join her. When he came in, she saw that her relaxed companion of the morning was gone and the expression on his face was one of watchful reserve.

When the earl arrived, the two men greeted one another with such similar expressions and such stiffness that Elspeth had to stifle a laugh at how alike were this father and son.

"I am sorry to disturb you, Valentine. And you, Elspeth."

Val looked questioningly over at his wife, and Elspeth blushed. "I made a short visit to your father on my way to Maddie's yesterday," she admitted. "I wanted to offer my own condolences."

"Then you know we are married?" Val asked his father.

"Yes, and I was very happy at your choice of brides. I have met Elspeth before at a family dinner."

Val was both relieved and annoyed. While he was happy to see that his father clearly liked Elspeth and approved his decision, he also felt it was none of his father's business whom he married.

They all sat stiffly waiting for the footman, who had come in behind the earl, to finish serving the lemonade.

"Would you like something stronger, sir?" Val asked politely.

"No, thank you, Valentine." The earl dismissed the footman with a wave of his hand, and the air of command set Val on edge.

"I see no reason to mince words here, since we are all family," said the earl. "What have you decided to do about my recognition, Valentine?"

"Do I have a choice, then?" Val asked ironically.

"Not about what I have decided, of course. But you may choose to ignore it."

Elspeth gave Val a pleading glance and he smiled. "I have decided there is not much I can do besides accept with good grace."

The earl visibly relaxed, but all he said was, "I am glad that it is settled, then. There will be gossip, of course, but after a while something else will distract Society," he added with an ironic smile. "Do you intend to take part in the Season?"

"I am here to attend Lady Madeline Lambert's come-out, my lord. I mean, Charles," added Elspeth. "And we have already received a number of invitations."

The earl looked surprised and Val said reluctantly, "I am also here on a mission for Captain Grant that necessitates our mixing with the ton."

"Then I shall be sure to attend some of these with you," his father announced.

"But you are in mourning, Charles," said Elspeth with concern. "Surely you do not wish to be facing people yet."

"No," he confessed, giving Elspeth a grateful smile. "And it will cause some gossip. But not as much as if I recognize you as my son but do not appear with you, Valentine," he said.

"I appreciate your support, my lord, although I am not sure it is necessary," he answered politely.

"Trust me, it is," the earl told him with a wry smile. "Did you receive an invitation to the Duke of Farron's tonight?"

"We did, Charles," said Elspeth. "We will be dining at the Wimbornes' first."

"Then I will meet you at the musicale and make sure that our relationship is made clear, before too much gossip starts." The earl rose. "Until tonight, then. I look forward to hearing more about your parents, my dear. I was always very fond of your mother. Ian Gordon was a lucky man."

After his father left, Val looked over at Elspeth.

"So you visited my father yesterday?"

"I knew him through my parents, Val, and I wasn't at all sure I would have the opportunity to offer my condolences at any other time," she said apologetically.

"You might have told me."

"I would have eventually, Val. I wish no long-kept secrets between us." She nibbled on a biscuit and then said, "Your father is being very thoughtful, Valentine."

"I suppose so."

"He is making no small sacrifice to make the transition easier for you. It cannot be what he wants, to go out so soon after Charlie's death."

Val sighed. "You are right, Elspeth. I suppose if I am going to take my place in Society as his son, I should be grateful for his support. But I hope he does not expect me to express any filial affection."

"Believe me, Valentine, I do not think he does," Elspeth replied tartly.

Chapter 33

By the time they got to the Wimbornes', they were back in charity with one another and, as they walked up the steps, gave each other's hands an encouraging squeeze at the same time.

James had kept the dinner small, so that Elspeth and Maddie would have time to talk and catch up. No dessert was served after dinner and instead of the gentlemen going off to have their port, all repaired to a sitting room, where James had champagne and a small but exquisitely decorated cake from Gunther's.

"I thought we should toast the bride and groom," he announced, smiling over at Elspeth and Val.

"Oh, James, that was so sweet of you," exclaimed Elspeth.

"Well, here you are, my sister's dear friend, married to

my companion in arms, and none of us had a chance to formally wish you happy. To Elspeth and Valentine," he said, lifting his glass. "May they find their hearts' refuge in one another."

Elspeth had to brush tears from her eyes at James's words and even Val found his throat tighten.

"My father will be at the musicale tonight," he told them. "In order to lend countenance to me and my new bride."

"Why, that is wonderful," exclaimed Maddie. "I have always liked Charlie's father . . . your father, Lieutenant," she added with a flushed smile. "He has done the right thing in recognizing you."

"Indeed," echoed James.

By the time they arrived at the Farrons', the earl had been there for a half hour, and when Lieutenant and Mrs. Aston were announced, Val was disoriented for a few minutes as they went through the receiving line. Here he was, married and recognized by his father, and yet at some level he still was that lonely hardworking young boy who was George Burton's apprentice. How on earth was a blacksmith's lad going to get on at a duke's party?

His face became set in a polite smile as he was introduced to friends and acquaintances of his father. Without Elspeth at his side, he would have felt very alone and he was grateful for her arm tucked comfortingly in his. He hated to admit it, but he owed the earl a great deal for appearing tonight, for his father moved them smoothly through the crowd. Val was appreciative of his father's air of command now, for no one would have dared make an untoward comment or express surprise with the hawk-eyed Earl of Faringdon looking down at them. Not even Lucas Stanton.

When he saw Stanton, Val became ramrod stiff.

"Lord Stanton, I think you know my son, Valentine Aston?" said the earl as they reached Stanton and a group of his friends. "You and Val and Charlie were at school together, I believe?"

"Yes, my lord," said Stanton, bowing slightly. "And I know Miss Gordon from many a delightful dinner at her parents' quarters."

"Mrs. Aston now, Stanton," said the earl with a smile.

"Congratulations, Aston, you are a lucky man indeed," Stanton told Val, managing, as always, to inject a faint note of hostility into the most innocuous words.

"Thank you, my lord," Val replied with a polite smile.

"I knew that you were coming to London, Miss Gordon . . . I mean, Mrs. Aston . . . but I am surprised to see you here, Lieutenant."

"I obtained leave to visit my father and offer my condolences on Charlie's death."

"Of course. Very sad news, my lord," said Stanton, bowing to the earl. "To lose a son and heir. But how, er, lucky you are to have Valentine, then."

"I am, am I not," the earl agreed blandly and they moved on.

"*Odious* man," muttered Elspeth. "I have always despised him."

"I see my son has married himself a very perspicacious wife. I myself would call himself something worse than odious, however," said the earl. "Charlie always hated him and for good reason, wouldn't you say, Valentine?"

"Yes, sir."

"I was always thankful you were with Charlie for his first year at school, for he felt protected from such predators as Stanton. It was a shame you did not stay, but I could understand."

Val was surprised at how much the warm approval in the earl's voice meant to him.

"The same sort of thing happened when I was at school, but much as I hated them, I never did anything to stop them. Took it all too much for granted, I suppose, which is one of the dangers of privilege," he admitted. "Sometimes it takes a fresh perspective to change things."

"I don't think anything changed at Queen's Hall, my lord," Val said with an ironic smile, which the earl returned. For one moment he felt himself in complete accord with his father.

They had drawn closer to the dance floor and the orchestra, which had been tuning up, began to play a country dance.

"I see an old friend over there. Why don't you lead Elspeth out, Valentine," said the earl.

Val looked over at his wife and raised his eyebrows.

"Can you stand my lack of expertise in moving around a Society ballroom, Elspeth? I know the dance, of course, but I am used to a rowdier company," he confessed with a grin.

"So am I, Val, so am I," said Elspeth with an answering smile.

Although Val and Elspeth were conscious that the gossips were having a field day, the earl's presence protected them from any direct unpleasantness and the evening went better than any could have expected. Val's uniform and his position as one of Wellington's officers had something to do with this, for people were curious about the progress of the war and impressed by Val's "daring exploits," as Lady Madeline put it.

"I assure you, my lady, that I spent more of my time lying on icy ground watching the French for hours as they went above their very boring routines than in "daring exploits," protested Val. But he was glad for Elspeth's sake that his uniform brought him some respect to offset the reaction to his parentage.

He had had young Devereaux pointed out to him shortly after they arrived. He was a very innocuous-looking young man and if Val hadn't known, he would never have suspected him of either radical sympathies or out-and-out treason.

All the players were present—James, Stanton, and young Devereaux—but none of them spent any time with each other as far as Val could tell. He would visit the ministry tomorrow and let Devereaux know exactly who he was.

Well before the end of the evening, the earl approached Val. "You and Elspeth are welcome to stay, Valentine, but having done my part, I find I am more fatigued than I expected. I had forgotten how exhausting grief is," he added apologetically.

"We are tired too, isn't that right, Val?" said Elspeth.

"I am quite happy to leave now," Val assured his father.

"I'll have the coach drop me off first," said his father, "and then carry you and Elspeth to the hotel."

"There is no need, sir. We could find a hansom."

"Nonsense. I would not want you and your lady to be traveling in a hired conveyance."

Elspeth and the earl chatted about the evening as they drove back to St. James's Square. "Maddie is quite a success, don't you think, Charles? Although I did not notice a particular beau, there were at least three men who asked her to dance twice."

"She is a vivacious and charming young lady and no doubt will receive several offers despite the state of her family's fortune. Or lack of it, to be more accurate," he added dryly. "I was sorry to see a fine man like James saddled with his father's debts, but from what I hear, he has almost succeeded in clearing them. And Maddie has a small inheritance from her mother's side of the family, which should help."

"So you would not say that James is near bankruptcy, sir?" Val asked, suddenly interested in their conversation.

"It will take a long time to restore Wimborne Hall to what it once was, but as far as I know he has managed to extricate himself from the worst of it."

"That is very good to hear," said Val. If James was not in desperate straits, then it was clear that Devereaux was lying, just as he had thought.

"You are happy about James," said Elspeth after they had dropped the earl off.

"It removes his motive," said Val. "And I will take on that young liar tomorrow and get the truth out of him at last."

Chapter 34

Val was up and out early the next morning and arrived at the ministry only a half-hour after it opened. He found Sir Humphrey's office easily enough and there was Devereaux in the anteroom, opening correspondence. Without looking up, he announced in a dismissive voice that the minister was not in and not expected back until later in the afternoon.

"That is neither here nor there to me, Lord Devereaux, since it is you I have come to see."

The younger man looked up, surprise and annoyance clearly written on his face. "I am very busy this morning, as you can see. I can't imagine what you want with me. I don't know you, do I?"

"I am Lieutenant Valentine Aston, my lord."

"Valentine Aston? Now, why does that sound familiar?"

"Perhaps you heard it last night," Val suggested.

"Ah, yes, you are the Earl of Faringdon's . . . er . . . eldest son."

"And one of Wellington's exploring officers. I was sent from Portugal to speak with you, my lord," Val added, his voice hard.

The young man's eyes opened wide. "What do you know of me?"

"Everything," Val announced bluntly. "Is there somewhere we can speak privately? Perhaps the minister's office?"

Devereaux shuffled the papers together nervously as he stood up. "We could do that for a short while."

"So the minister will not be gone for hours," Val said sarcastically.

"It *is* my job to protect him from any riffraff that might want a favor."

Devereaux led Val into the office and closed the door. "Do you wish to sit down, Lieutenant?" he asked, gesturing to two chairs by the window.

"I don't think so." Val stood there for a few minutes, letting the silent tension build until finally Devereaux asked desperately, "What do you want?"

"I wanted to see what kind of man would give information to the enemy."

"I did it to help men like you, Lieutenant," Devereaux declared with false bravado.

"Men like me?"

"Surely, as the, er, illegitimate son of an earl, you must be stirred by the injustices in our present system of laws. You must believe in liberty and equality and—"

"Fraternité?"

"Napoleon Bonaparte is a living emblem of the Revolution."

"Napoleon Bonaparte is terrorizing Europe, you young fool," said Val, willing himself not to grab Devereaux by his cravat and choke him. "He has displaced the lawful sovereign of Spain and put his own brother on the throne. How is that equality?"

"He has been faithful to the reforms of the Revolution, sir. In the end, it will be all right itself," Devereaux said stubbornly. "And I did not reveal anything that had to do with military matters, after all. I would never have done that," he added indignantly. "I only made sure that word of the political situation reached Portugal sooner than it would have done. It seemed absolutely sure that the prince would bring in the Whigs and recall Wellington. The war would have been over and the government in the hands of men who had the people's interest at heart."

"You really believe that you have done nothing treasonous, don't you?" said Val, amazed that anyone could be no naive.

"I did what I did for my country's sake," Devereaux answered stubbornly.

"Well, let me tell you just a little of what happened because of your childish idealism, my lord." Val pushed Devereaux's chest and forced him to step back until he was against the wall, looking up into Val's eyes. "Because Massena had an accurate account of the situation here, he was encouraged to dig himself in at Santarém. Despite the fact that there was no food. Do you know what it is like to be without food, my lord?" Devereaux shook his head, his eyes wide and frightened.

"The French were starving. And when they finally moved, do you know what they did?"

"N-no, sir," Devereaux stammered.

"They revenged themselves on the people of Portugal. The peasantry. Those whom you would see as your brothers and sisters. They hung women and their babies and set fire under them to get them to reveal where food was hidden."

Devereaux closed his eyes. "My God," he whispered.

"Yes, well, your God wasn't around, my lord. The stench from the graves lingered for days."

"I didn't know. . . ."

"The easiest words in the English language . . . 'I didn't know.' Well, now you do," said Val disgustedly, releasing him. "I want to know to whom you passed information and why."

"Someone came to me months ago and requested my help. He made it sound . . . truly, he made it sound like it was all for the good, that it could possibly end the war."

"Was that whom you sent news to?"

"No. I've already told them. I sent the information on to James Lambert, Marquess of Wimborne."

"You lie!"

"Whatever you think of me, sir, I am not a liar," said young Devereaux, drawing himself up. "It was suggested to me that the marquess would be willing to do it for the money."

"How did you pay him?"

"Out of my own funds. I have an inheritance from my great-aunt as well as being my father's heir. I'm a rich man, Lieutenant, and I wished to do some good with my money," he added, his voice trailing off.

"Who suggested James to you?" Val demanded.

"I cannot tell you, Lieutenant. I gave my word as a gentleman," said Devereaux, looking into Val's eyes proudly, eager to gain back some regard.

"Bloody hell, you still think you are a gentleman?"

"I gave my word, sir."

"Well, you are going to break your word and tell me," Val informed him, the threat in his voice almost palpable.

"I can't, Lieutenant. Not even if they transport me."

Val could tell by the way the young fool was looking at him that he was stubbornly determined to cling to the one vestige of honor left him.

"You know damn well you won't be transported, or even punished, because of your family's position. So much for your *equalité* and *fraternité*! You have no problem accusing James Lambert. Why hold back the name of the other traitor?"

"I have never seen nor spoke to Lord Wimborne, except for a few polite words at ton affairs. He doesn't even know

where the information came from. I never promised him
secrecy." Devereaux was quiet for a moment and then said,
"I am sure you must despise me, but I give you my word
of honor I never realized what the consequences could be.
He made it sound so simple and easy and patriotic, really."
Devereaux added with a despairing laugh. "But if I was
even partly responsible for such depredations and because
of his prompting . . . He was very eager to involve the
marquess, you know . . ." The younger man fell silent and
Val could see the agony of indecision on his face. He
stepped back and kept still.

"I cannot break my word and *tell* you who he is, Lieutenant Aston. But I *could* make an appointment with him and
with you at the same time. It is rather jesuitical reasoning,
I know, but it is the best I can do and have any self-respect
left," Devereaux added bitterly. "I will regret this to my
dying day, sir."

"I'm at the Blackstone Hotel. Send for me there when
you contact this man."

"Yes, sir."

Young Devereaux was not the only one who believed
that England was fighting the war for fear of the revolutionary ideas that had sprung up in France. Many of the officers
in the army, like the Napier brothers, felt that the government's motive was to save rank and privilege, not to
counter tyranny.

Val hadn't given much time to political considerations
over the years. But he supposed if he sat down and thought
about it he would lean toward the Whigs himself. Look at
how rigidly the nobility held on. He didn't really want the
viscountcy, but legitimacy, well, that would have been a
different thing. Yet under the present laws, his father was
unable to legitimize him, because property and lines of inheritance were considered more important than individual
wishes.

But he couldn't understand why the radicals did not see
Bonaparte as a tyrant who was willing to fill his armies
with young boys and sacrifice them to gain more power for
himself. It wasn't *"Vive fraternité"* that French troops
chanted as they marched into battle, but *"Vive l'Emper-
eur,"* thought Val with a disgusted laugh.

So why James? he wondered, his heart sinking. How could James Lambert, a man he had so admired and, he had to admit it, so loved, act the traitor? Money was no excuse, although it might have been a reason he understood. But James, although pressed for funds, did not seem desperate. He was a Whig, but not one of the radical fringe. Yet someone had known he would be open to suggestion. Someone had told Devereaux that James was his man. Why? Had James been a spy all along, or was this the first information he had passed on? Had he seen this the way young Devereaux had, as a relatively innocuous way of helping to shorten the war?

But Val could not give his friend the same excuse, for James was an experienced soldier and knew that any action, no matter how innocent it seemed, could have far-reaching consequences.

What would they do to James? Perhaps not bring him to trial, since he was a peer of the realm. If Devereaux had gotten off so lightly, then James might. He'd lose his commission, of course. Surely they wouldn't want a trial at this time. It would be too embarrassing for the government.

How could he look James in the eye again, knowing what he knew? How could he attend Lady Madeline's ball and act as if nothing had happened, yet knowing that he had information that could condemn James to a life of exile at the very least? He was duty-bound to betray a friend and he did not know how he would live with himself afterward.

He had wanted it to be Lucas Stanton. Damn, but he had been so *sure*. But it *was* Stanton, he thought, stopping so suddenly that the man who was walking behind him ran right into him.

"Watch what you are doing, sir."

"I beg your pardon. I am a bit distracted," Val apologized, waving him on with his shako.

Lucas Stanton had to be the man he would meet at the ministry office. It fit: He would have known James's financial circumstances. But why would he have thought James would have sold information merely to buy his sister more dresses for her Season? But what if it was a cruel game that Stanton played? What if he had manipulated Devereaux, set James up, only to blackmail him later? It made

some sense, given the way Stanton gained pleasure from
exerting power and making others his pawns.

The pieces almost fit together, but there was still a hole.
What on earth would have motivated James to agree in the
first place? God, he was right back to the beginning.

Exposing Stanton as a traitor would give him the greatest
satisfaction. But he couldn't bring the bastard down without
destroying his friend.

The closer he got to the hotel, the more he felt like he
was being drawn to it, by the magnet that was Elspeth.
There were very few people with whom he'd be willing
to share his dilemma, but he knew that Elspeth, with her
combination of quiet good sense and compassionate nature,
would understand. Would help him sort things through.
Please God she was in, he prayed.

He found her in the sitting room, sewing the green ribbon on her dress.

"What is it, Val? You look blue-deviled. Was it your
meeting with Devereaux?" She slowly rolled up the green
ribbon and, putting her sewing aside, gave him her full
attention.

Val let out a deep breath and sat down opposite her. "I
have already told you that I am glad you are my wife,
Elspeth. But I am even more grateful that you are my
friend. There is no one else I can turn to with this
dilemma."

Elspeth was deeply touched, but kept her face calm and
merely waited for him to continue.

"I did speak with Devereaux. An idealistic young fool
whose stupidity cost many lives. He swears . . . and he is
very concerned that I believe in his sense of honor," Val
added sarcastically. "He gives his word that James was his
contact in Portugal."

"Oh, no," Elspeth whispered.

"James was suggested to him by a man he will not name,
having given his word as a gentleman! However, he is willing to set up a meeting with the man and inform me of the
time, so that I can be there myself."

"Who would even think to suggest James, and why?"

"I am convinced it is Lucas Stanton. Everything fits and
the letter Mags found makes perfect sense. But no matter
how I twist it and turn it, there is still an unanswerable

question: Why did Stanton suggest James in the first place?"

"Because he knew James needed money?"

"But we know he is not bankrupt, Elspeth."

"No, but perhaps with Maddie's come-out?"

"Can you see James Lambert betraying his country over a come-out ball? As a last resort, he could have married for the money."

"No, I can't," responded Elspeth immediately. "But then, I can't imagine him marrying for money either."

Or marrying at all. The thought was there before she knew it and she sat very quietly, turning her idea this way and that. It made sense, she realized. Much more sense than anything else. And it had taken her all this time to see it. "Val, what if Lucas Stanton was already blackmailing James and that is why he knew he would be open to the offer of money?"

Val thought for a moment. "It does make sense of everything," he admitted. "But what on earth could James have done?"

"You might want to ask James," Elspeth replied quietly.

"Then you think I should warn him? A confirmed traitor?"

"And a good friend."

Val groaned. "I have to warn him," he confessed, "and what does that make me?"

"Also a good friend." Elspeth could see the agony in her husband's eyes and reached out and took his hands. "Could you live with yourself if you said nothing to James and then reported him to Captain Grant? He could be hung."

"More likely transported, but even that would bring such disgrace upon him and his family." Val squeezed her hands tightly. "But if I warn him, that also makes me a traitor. I would betray my honor as an officer—and a 'gentleman,'" he added ironically.

Elspeth looked steadily into his eyes. "I am glad that I have *you* as my friend, Val. You are a most honorable gentleman to me, no matter what you decide."

Val let go of her hands and cupped her face. He leaned over and kissed her gently. "Elspeth, I . . . I am very lucky to have married you." He had almost said, "I love you." It was almost out before he thought. But what if she still only saw him with the eyes of friendship? He couldn't bear to put her into a position where she would feel she had to apologize for not loving him.

"Tomorrow is Lady Madeline's ball, thank God. I cannot confront him and ruin the evening. But I will warn him, Elspeth, and give him a chance to explain. And by God, if it's Stanton who set this thing up for his own perverted pleasure, he will pay!"

Chapter 35

The earl insisted on calling for them in his carriage and so the next evening they were all together, waiting in the long line of vehicles stopped in front of the Wimborne town house.

"You are both very quiet," observed the earl. "I hope I have not intruded upon a newlyweds' quarrel," he added humorously.

"Not at all, Charles," Elspeth replied with a reassuring smile. "It is only that we are both tired. We are unaccustomed to such social activity."

"I think it has gone well, though, Valentine, don't you?"

"The gossips fall silent with you at our sides, sir," Val admitted. "And especially for Elspeth's sake, I thank you."

"Have you given any thought at all to selling out?" his father asked. "Staying in England and taking a place in Society?"

"My place is with the army, sir, at least as long as the war goes on," Val replied bluntly.

"But what of your wife?"

"Oh, I could never be happy outside the army, Charles," she said, taking Val's hand and giving it a little squeeze.

"Look, we are finally here," announced Val, grateful that their conversation couldn't be continued. He had no desire to speak of the future with his father.

*   *   *

"It is a most satisfying crush, isn't it?" said Maddie, smiling up at Elspeth and Val as they came through the reception line. "James is the best of brothers," she added.

" 'Tis only what you deserved, Maddie," said James. "But now it is up to you to manage one of your beaus into a declaration!"

James led Maddie into the first dance and then looked on indulgently as she was swept off for every one after that.

"You do not dance, James?" Val and Elspeth had just danced a quadrille and had come over at Elspeth's prodding.

"You were right about the young men, James. They are fighting over who will lead Lady Madeline into supper. She seems to have written both their names down," Val said with a laugh.

"The little minx!"

"Do you think she has a preference, James? She has not said much to me," said Elspeth.

"I don't think so, though I would be happy to see her with either one. They are both fine . . . young men."

"You were about to say 'lads,' " Val said with a quizzical grin.

"I know I am only a few years their senior, Valentine, but I feel positively like an old man compared with either."

"I know what you mean, James," replied Elspeth with a commiserating smile. "I always felt that with my schoolmates."

"They are striking up again, Elspeth. May I have the honor? You don't mind, do you, Val, if I dance with your new bride?"

"Not at all, James."

Val was relieved, for he had seen Devereaux. He wandered over to where he stood chatting with a group of young people. "I wonder if I might have a word with you, my lord?"

"Er, of course, Lieutenant Aston. I shall be right back to claim my dance," he told one of the young ladies.

Val drew him into one of the anterooms. "Have you contacted our man yet?" he asked bluntly.

"As a matter of fact, I have. I was going to send a note 'round in the morning. He is coming to see me tomorrow at three."

"I'll be there," said Val.

"But what is going to happen?" Devereaux asked anxiously.

"We will just have to see, won't we, my lord?" Val left him standing there, imagining all the possible scenarios, regretting he had ever opened his mouth.

As Devereaux made his way back to claim his dance, he was waylaid by Lucas Stanton.

"I just saw Faringdon's bastard come out of that anteroom and then you emerged. Whatever could he have to say to you, my lord?" Stanton asked suspiciously.

"He was, uh, wondering if there were some posthumous honor that could be award his half-brother, my lord." Devereaux was amazed he had been able to think of anything resembling a reasonable explanation.

"Full of brotherly concern, is he?"

"Actually, it was quite touching, my lord," he continued, almost getting caught up in his own lie.

"I am sure," said Stanton with a derisive laugh. But he watched the viscount return to his friends with a speculative look on his face.

The evening seemed endless to Val once he had talked to Devereaux and he was very glad when Elspeth approached him and suggested they say their good-byes. "Your father is looking tired, Val," she told him. "Of course, we could have his carriage come back for us, if you wish to stay?"

"Only if you do, my dear."

"No, I have had a lovely time, but I am not one of those who must stay until the last dance has been played."

"I am sorry to leave you to your own devices today, Elspeth," Val apologized as they sat over a late breakfast the next morning.

"You will be calling on James?"

"Yes, and then I am off to Whitehall. But once this is all settled, we'll go to Portugal," he said with a reassuring smile. "And tell your parents we are married," he added, his smile fading.

"I believe they will be pleased, Val," Elspeth reassured him, "although my father may be angry at first that they did not have a chance to be there." She hesitated. "I only wish that you and your father had more time together."

"I did not realize you were such a sentimental woman, my dear," Val replied with a touch of irony.

"It is not sentimental to wish that you and he would get to know one another better now that Charlie is gone."

"I am sure I am only a reminder that the wrong son died," Val said bitterly.

Elspeth looked as though she wished to argue with him but only said quietly, "I will not discuss this with you this morning, Val. I wish you well in your visit to James and beg you to be careful later. If the instigator of all this is Lucas Stanton, he will be angry to have been exposed."

"Thank you for your care, Elspeth, but I am sure you need not worry. I will see you early this evening."

Chapter 36

Val walked around the square three times before he finally made himself knock on James's door.

"The family is not receiving yet," the butler told him.

"I know it was a late night for them, but this is a matter most urgent," Val told him. "Would you please inform the marquess that Lieutenant Aston *must* speak with him?"

"Come in, sir, and I will see," replied the butler, reluctantly admitting Val to the foyer.

When he returned, he issued him into the library. "The marquess will be down directly. He is still getting dressed," he added with a censorious look at Val before he left.

Val was too restless to sit and he was pacing the carpet when James came in a few minutes later.

"Good morning, Val. Or should I say good afternoon? The festivities went on long after you left, and none of us is fully awake yet, I fear," he said with a grin.

When Val gave him no answering smile and remained standing after his friend gestured him to a chair, James said more seriously, "I take it this is a matter of some importance? Has there been word from Wellington? Why do you look so grim, Val? And if you won't sit down, then I will," added James, perching on the edge of his desk and looking over at Val expectantly.

He didn't look at all worried, thought Val. Wouldn't he be, if it were all true?

"I have been working on something for Captain Grant these past few months, James."

"Yes?"

"It seems Massena was receiving advance information about the political situation here in London. Captain Grant asked me to investigate."

"I see," James replied calmly. Val was watching him carefully and detected no change in his expression.

"We had three suspects: Trowbridge, Stanton . . . and you."

James was disconcertingly silent as Val continued. "I was unable to discover anything myself and so I recruited Mags Casey to help us, since she had easy access to all of your tents."

"Indeed she did. Then the attack on Mags . . . ?"

"Was no robbery, James. We are sure she was seen coming out of Stanton's tent."

"Surely you don't think I am capable of brutalizing Mrs. Casey," protested James.

"I don't know what I think, James," Val said quietly. "I know what I don't want to believe: that you are the traitor. Mags found a letter in Stanton's tent which revealed that he was blackmailing a former classmate for a capital offense."

"He could have been referring to anyone, Val."

"Yes, except that at the same time I was investigating in Portugal, there was someone digging here in London. Lord Devereaux has confessed, James, and named you as the traitor."

Val watched his friend turn white and become very still.

"I see," was all he said.

"You see, James? You see? Is that all you are going to say in your defense? Tell me Devereaux is lying, even if *that* is a lie," Val asked him in an agonized voice.

"It would be a lie, Val, and I could never lie to you."

"You could never lie to me, but you could betray your country. And Devereaux could pass on information that cost the lives of hundreds of our allies but not betray his honor by telling me the name of the man who suggested the whole thing! I tell you, James, I am happy to be a bastard, if this is what being a gentleman means."

"I doubt that you will understand, Val, but I had no choice."

"Did you need money that much, James? Was Maddie's ball more important that the fate of Europe?"

James stood up and went over to stir the fire. When he turned back to face Val, his face was angry and hard.

"I assure you, money had nothing to do with it."

"Then *why*, James? You are not like Devereaux. You knew your decision would have consequences."

"I would never have passed on information regarding troop strength or strategy, believe me. Not that I am excusing myself. Of course I knew there would be consequences. I was hoping the Regency Bill would be passed sooner and that Wellington would be recalled before too many Frenchmen died of starvation."

"So you are that much a radical, James, even after seeing what Bonaparte has done to Europe," said Val unbelievingly.

James gave him a wry smile. "It is ironic, is it not, that of the two of us, it is the man with rank and privilege, not the illegitimate son, who is the Whig?"

"I am not as amused by the irony as you are, James."

"Sit down, Val."

Val just glared at him stubbornly.

"Oh, for God's sake, sit down. I am not going to escape you or the consequences. I can't," James added wearily.

The pain in his friend's voice finally reached Val and he sat down on the sofa. James gazed into the fire and then, turning to Val, gave him a smile so full of affection that it wrung Val's heart.

"You don't know, do you, Val?"

"Know what, James?"

"Oh, God, this is difficult. There are capital offenses other than treason, my friend," James pointed out dryly.

"They are innumerable, James, but somehow I can't picture you as a poacher," Val replied sarcastically.

"Why do you think I have never married, Val? Never developed an attachment to any woman?"

"Why, you were abroad . . . your father's gambling . . ." Val's voice trailed off as the unthinkable finally occurred to him.

"You are not . . . you cannot be . . ."

"A catamite? A molly? But I am."

"I can't believe it!"

"Whyever not? Charlie had no trouble believing it," James told him with a quizzical grin.

"Charlie! He knew this?"

"I do believe you have always underestimated Charlie, Val. I think many people did. But just because he was such an openhearted young man didn't mean he was naive about the ways of the world. He guessed my secret shortly after he got to Oxford."

"But Lucas Stanton is the one who . . . ?"

"Buggered young boys?" James said sarcastically. "I told you then, Val, that Stanton would have rogered anything available."

"You protected them from him. . . ."

"Whenever I could. Of course. I don't bugger young boys, Valentine." He paused and said more gently, "It is not all about buggery. For me it is about whom I love."

"Then you have . . . loved men?" Val asked, trying unsuccessfully to hide the distaste in his voice.

"Oh, God, Val," groaned James. "What are you asking? Have I made love to men? Yes, I have. Not often, because of the risk involved. Have I been in love with a man? Yes, I have. I met him in Oxford. He was a year ahead of me and quite . . . wonderful. Not really handsome, but quick and brilliant. And betrothed since childhood to his next-door neighbor's daughter," James added, the pain in his voice almost palpable.

"So he was not, er, like you?"

"Oh, he was exactly like me," James replied with a wry smile. "We fell madly in love. I tried to convince him to give it all up, to come to the Continent with me. But he couldn't do it. Said he couldn't disgrace his family, his future wife. . . ." James looked bleakly at Val.

"So he married her?"

"Yes. I was at their wedding. She is a lovely girl. If he had to marry anyone, I would have wished someone like her . . . but . . ."

"But?"

"He is living a lie with every good-morning kiss; with every breath, Val, he denies himself. I couldn't do it then. I can't do it now."

"So Lucas Stanton knew?"

"I think he probably suspected it at the Hall, though God knows why, for I never let myself get close to anyone there. Except for you, Val," he added. "You were an outcast too, just like me, though of course you could never see it. We were both born something we had no control over: you a bastard, and I a man who happened to love men rather than women. . . . Anyway, Stanton saw me with a man in Lisbon almost a year ago. It was no one important, but enough for him to gain a hold over me."

"And so he threatened you?"

"I would have resisted him, I think, if the information seemed more crucial. But the more he threatened me, the more I realized what would have happened to Maddie should the truth come out. My father's behavior was hard on her, but this would have destroyed her and any chance of a good marriage."

"I can see that," Val admitted quietly. "So you took money to pay Lucas Stanton off."

"Yes. I had enough, just barely, after selling off one of our small estates and settling my father's debts, to bring Maddie out. But certainly not enough to pay Lucas's blackmail."

"But he doesn't need money."

"Of course not. He gets pleasure from causing people pain, Val. You saw that at school. The money was only incidental." They were both quiet for a moment and then James continued, "I don't want to make myself out such an innocent in this, Val. The truth is that, while I do not support Bonaparte, at least he did keep the reforms established by the Revolution. In Europe, under Napoleon, I would be able to live my life without fear. I suppose the contrast between their laws and ours had some sort of influence on me also," he added bitterly.

"I can even understand that, James," Val confessed. "I never thought much about the laws against, er, men like you."

"Two of us were hanged last year, you know."

"I feel a fool compared to Charlie," Val said. "I never guessed."

"Charlie and I had a longer acquaintance, Val, so in some ways it is understandable."

"You were my first real friend, James," said Val, working hard to keep his voice from betraying his emotion. "You saw me for myself, not just as the bastard son of Faringdon. You always acknowledged me as your equal."

"Because you are any man's equal. I can see I'll have to start supplying you with Whig pamphlets, Val," he added with forced humor. He fell silent and then asked, "What are you going to do? I don't ask so much for myself, but so I can prepare Maddie for whatever comes."

"They are not going to prosecute Devereaux because of his father's influence. The least that could happen to you, James, is that you lose your commission. I don't think they want a scandal just as Wellington is pushing the war into Spain, but you are guilty of treason and . . . sodomy," Val added uncomfortably. "I suppose they could transport you. . . ."

"What if I resigned my commission and exiled myself to Italy or Greece? It would save Whitehall and the army the scandal and would also spare my sister and the rest of my family."

"I will do my best to persuade them, James. Of course, that means Stanton may escape punishment also," he added bitterly.

James's hands, which were still holding the poker, tightened and he lifted the piece of iron as though it were a weapon and then got up and replaced it carefully by the hearth.

"There is nothing you or I can do about that, Val," James declared, keeping his voice calm.

"I know," said Val with suppressed fury. "But it galls me to think that someone so despicable might get off scot-free. It is one thing to have Devereaux learn his lesson. But Stanton . . . damn his rotten soul to hell!"

"He will be returning to Spain, won't he? He may well be in hell sooner than we think, Val," replied James with a wry smile.

"But *he* will know what it is to live with fear, James, I swear. I will make sure of that," Val said vehemently. "For now *I* have information that could hang *him.*"

"Be careful. Lucas Stanton is not a man to play games with."

"Believe me, James, I am not playing," Val told him. He stood up. "I can delay sending my news to Captain Grant, James. And then it will take several weeks for my dispatch to arrive. You have some time to do what you need to do. . . ." Val's voice trailed off unhappily.

"Thank you, my friend. I can still call you that?" asked James with a smile that could not hide his vulnerability.

"Of course, James," Val replied, offering his hand stiffly. He cursed himself for his formality when he saw the look in James's eyes as their hands touched only briefly. But he felt so awkward. He loved James, almost as much as he had loved Charlie, but however could he express it, now that he knew what James was?

Val had almost an hour to waste before his appointment at Whitehall and as he walked down the street, he realized he was only a block away from Faringdon House. It was utterly irrational, he told himself as he found himself walking in that direction. He had nothing to say to his father. But he had nowhere else to go and there he was, lifting the knocker.

"Is the earl at home, Baynes?"

"Yes, sir, in the library."

The earl was behind his desk again and looked up with a hesitant smile when Val was admitted.

"It is good to see you, Valentine," he said, coming around the desk. "Bring us some sherry, will you, Baynes?"

"Yes, my lord."

"Sit down, Val." The earl looked expectantly at his son.

"I was in the neighborhood and thought I would call and see if you had recovered from last night," Val explained stiffly.

"You don't ever need a reason to call on me, Valentine,"

the earl told him quietly. "You are always welcome here. Indeed, I wish you would consider it your home also." As the butler came in with the sherry, the earl thanked him. "Just put the glasses down here. Will you have a glass, Val?"

"Thank you, sir, I will."

They sipped their sherry, each keenly aware of the tension between them. Finally Val said, "I don't know *why* I am here. Perhaps it is because of Charlie. . . ."

The earl looked up from his glass. "Even though he had been in the army for a while, I still think he will bound down the stairs for breakfast," he confessed with a sad smile. The earl cleared his throat. "Well, whatever brought you, I am glad you came, Valentine, for I have something to discuss with you. I know you intend to return to Spain."

Val nodded.

"I am proud of you, of course, but I feel as though I have already given enough," the earl said softly.

"It is my job, sir. And now I have a wife to support."

"Yes, that is what I wish to talk about. When you first came to Faringdon and we discussed your future, one thing I mentioned to you was managing one of my estates. Do you remember?"

Val nodded, his eyes on his glass as he swirled the amber liquid. He tried to keep his emotions under control.

"I have made a new will, Val. If it were allowed to me under the law, I would make you my heir and you would inherit Faringdon. But since I can't, I have made sure that you inherit everything I have that is not entailed. Faringdon will go to my second cousin, but you will still be a wealthy man."

"I don't want your money," Val replied stiffly.

"Then you can always give it away, can't you?" said the earl with wry humor. "And I am a healthy man, Valentine, so no use getting angry about it yet! In the meantime," he continued, "I am putting you in charge of my Yorkshire estate. You may apply the income from the estate to upkeep and any improvements you deem fit as you raise your family. And since it is not part of the entailment, it will be yours after I die."

Val was moved despite himself. Damn it, he didn't want to be moved. He didn't want his father's money. He wanted . . . he didn't know what he wanted or why he was here. He stood up suddenly, jarring the small table between them with his knee so the glasses rang as they shattered, sending bright shards all over the carpet.

"Damn. I am sorry, sir," he said, leaning down and starting to pick up the pieces.

"Just leave it, Valentine. Baynes will be in shortly."

Val straightened up and looked down at his father. He wanted to despise him as he always had, but he couldn't.

"It would have been better if I had never known about you at all." The words were out of his mouth before he knew it. "I always dreamed that maybe the army had made a mistake, that maybe Sergeant Aston would come marching home. And then my mother died and I had nothing. I had a lead soldier I made believe was my father," he said bitterly. "I melted him down in George Burton's forge. . . ."

"I am very sorry, Valentine. It doesn't make up for anything, but—"

"Don't. I am ashamed to have said anything. I don't know why I came, but I must leave or I'll be late," he said, ignoring his father's hand on his arm and his plea to stay.

After Val left, Charles Faringdon sat there, trying to imagine the boy Val had been. It wasn't too difficult, for he had been given a glimpse of him just now.

"You were wrong, Sarah," he whispered. "You let your pride get in the way. I don't blame you, my dear, for God knows what I would have done in your situation. But perhaps there is a chance for our son and me. He came here for something, even if he doesn't know what it is."

Chapter 37

Val felt his cheeks burning as he strode toward Whitehall. No one knew about that soldier. No one. And after all these years, he told the story to his father! It was all James's fault, damn it. He'd thought he had known James and it

turned out he hadn't known him at all. Shouldn't he have
guessed? Shouldn't there have been something about James
that would have alerted him? Although, to be honest, there
wasn't anything about the two men he remembered from
years ago. If he hadn't known about them from the village
gossip, he probably wouldn't have guessed. Not that he
understood the vagaries of human desire then, he thought
with a smile. It wasn't until school that he had confronted
the . . . variations. And in the army, of course, one saw
everything: men who were drawn to men, men who were
only satisfied when they hurt women, even one man whom
they had found hanging in a barn unconscious; Evidently
that was yet another way to heighten pleasure. I am the
simpleton, the fool in all this, he thought. For all my experience in the world, Charlie knew more than I.

He had reached Whitehall just five minutes before Stanton was expected and he hurried up the stairs. Devereaux
was sitting at his desk and when Val entered he looked up
fearfully, his face white. "Lord . . . uh, the man you have
come to see will be here any moment. Do you want to wait
in the minister's office?"

Val nodded. He had been so upset by James's confession
that he hadn't given much thought to anything beyond getting here in time.

"You can leave the door open a bit and hear everything.
In fact, perhaps that is all you really need to do," Devereaux suggested nervously. "Just find out who he is. There
is no need for a confrontation, is there?"

Val only slipped into the office. Devereaux was right, he
supposed. He merely needed to confirm that Lucas Stanton
was the traitor and then inform Captain Grant. The army
would decide what to do with him. Then he heard the outer
door open and he stood quietly, holding his breath.

"You wanted to see me, Devereaux?"

Val let his breath out softly. It was Stanton's voice.

"Er, yes, Lord Stanton," the younger man replied, barely
able to keep his voice from shaking.

"Well, are you going to tell me why?"

"Of course. It wasn't really that important, Lucas. I just
wanted to reassure you that Wimborne's is the only name
I've given."

"But we had already agreed that you would keep my identity a secret. You gave me your word."

"I gave you my word that I would never reveal your name."

"And what of your conversation with Aston?"

"Only social, I assure you."

"That had better be so, or I would have to do something I would rather not."

There was a moment of silence and then Devereaux protested, his voice high with fear, "There is no need to threaten me like that, Stanton. I give you my word of honor as a gentleman that your name never arose in my conversation with Lieutenant Aston." His chair scraped against the floor as though he were trying to get as far away from Stanton as he could and Val heard the sound of a pistol being cocked and the pleasure in Stanton's voice as he said, "You *do* understand me, my lord?"

It was really time someone made Stanton suffer, thought Val, as he opened the door and stepped out.

"He's telling the truth, Stanton, so take your gun from his head." Val stood there, his own pistol drawn and cocked. "I couldn't get your name from Devereaux, could I? So I forced him to invite you here. But you have no more power here, Lucas, so you may as well leave. Devereaux will not be prosecuted."

"Ah, but what of the Marquess of Wimborne, Devereaux? You *did* tell the lieutenant his name, so now everyone will know, won't they?" Stanton said with a smile.

"Know what, Stanton? That James passed information to the French? Or that you were blackmailing him?"

"That he is a damned catamite, of course."

"I don't think that needs to come out," Val replied thoughtfully. "On the other hand, the fact that you were behind the whole scheme—that might be made public," he added.

"Oh, I don't think so, Aston," Lucas said silkily. "The government does not want a political scandal or they would be prosecuting young Devereaux here. But they wouldn't mind charging James with being a molly. And they will take my word over Faringdon's bastard any day."

"James has agreed to resign his commission and settle indefinitely on the Continent. So you have no more power over him, Stanton. I, on the other hand, have a little over you and I will see that you are cashiered. I am sure that Captain Grant and I can come up with some reason between us," he added with a smile.

Stanton turned his pistol on Devereaux again. "You little whoremonger! 'Word of a gentleman'! If I kill him, Aston, then there is no evidence against me."

"But if you kill him, then I will have to kill you," Val replied calmly, trying to reassure Devereaux with his eyes, praying the young fool wouldn't move.

Lucas's shot was only a second ahead of Val's, but it was enough. Val felt the pain in his side just as his finger pulled the trigger. His own aim was better, he thought from far away as he watched Stanton fall. After all, he was still standing, he thought ironically as he reached out to support himself on the desk.

"My God, you got him right through the heart," Devereaux gasped.

"Oh, I am sure not," whispered Val as he sank to his knees. "The man had no heart."

"He meant to kill me."

"Yes, I do believe so." Val was slumped against the side of the desk, his hand holding his side. "He's succeeded with me, I fear," he whispered as he slumped to the floor.

They brought him to Faringdon House. The earl was still in the library and when Baynes opened the door without knocking, he looked up, a faintly annoyed expression on his face. "What is it?"

"Your son, my lord, the lieutenant. He's been shot."

The earl was disoriented, frozen in his seat. "I know that Charles is dead, Baynes," he said quietly.

"No, no, I mean Valentine, my lord."

The earl moved so quickly that his chair fell behind him. "Get him upstairs to the guest room," he ordered the two Home Guard officers who were carrying Val. "Has anyone sent for a doctor?"

"I did, my lord," said Devereaux. "He saved my life," he added brokenly.

"I will be upstairs in a minute. Now tell me what happened, sir."

"The lieutenant was in London on mission for Wellington and Captain Grant. I had been forwarding information to the enemy, you see, and was found out. The lieutenant was here to confirm that Wimborne was my confederate."

The earl's head was spinning. "Never mind that. Who shot him?"

"Lucas Stanton, my lord. He was the other party involved. Stanton had a pistol to my head. Then he turned so suddenly . . . I could not stop him in time."

"All right, lad," said the earl.

"Is there anything I can do to help?"

"You did the right thing by calling the doctor right away. And bringing him here."

"I didn't know where else to go, my lord."

"Mrs. Aston needs to be told. Are you up to calling on her and bringing her here? I will have my chaise sent 'round. William," the earl called to one of his footmen, "get His Lordship a glass of brandy and settle him in the library."

By the time the earl reached the guest room, Val had been laid on the bed and the two soldiers were standing by helplessly.

"William, get me some washing cloths," barked the earl to the footman who had followed him up. "Here, you two, pull his boots off. Gently, mind you."

Val's uniform was soaked through with blood and the earl's fingers were shaking as he unbuttoned his tunic. "Damnable buttons," he muttered as another one seemed to fight being pushed through the buttonhole. When the tunic was open, the earl gestured to one of the guards. "Hold him up while I slip this off."

Now he could see the wound and his heart sank. It seemed to be low and left of the heart, thank God, but it was so close to the lung and it was bleeding so damn much.

"Here, my lord," said William, handing the earl some linen cloths.

"Good man, William." Faringdon ripped open Val's shirt and, placing the cloth over the wound, pressed down with his hand. Val groaned and tried to move away from the pressure, but his father held him. "There, there, I know it must hurt like the very devil, but I must stop the bleeding."

The doctor arrived only fifteen minutes later, though it

seemed like hours to the earl. "You can relax for a moment while I examine him, my lord," the doctor said kindly. "You did well, for I can see that the worst of the bleeding is over."

The earl moved away and watched as the doctor probed the wound. "Here, help me lift him," he told the footman.

"No, let me," said the earl. "I've got blood on me already."

"Ah, good, a clean exit, so I shall not have to poke and probe him. The bullet went right through, you see. That's why he's bleeding like a stuck pig." They lowered Val back down. "He is a lucky man, my lord. The bullet missed both his heart and lung."

"So he will live?" the earl whispered.

"There is always the danger of infection," the doctor warned.

"He will get the best care."

"I have no doubt about that, my lord. You know him well?"

"No," said the earl with a sad smile. "But he is my son."

"The first forty-eight hours are critical. If no infection develops, he'll heal quickly after that."

Elspeth arrived just as the doctor was leaving.

"This is Mrs. Aston, Doctor," the earl told him.

"How is he?" asked Elspeth, barely able to control her voice.

"Now, don't you worry, Mrs. Aston. I was just telling His Lordship that your husband should heal quickly."

"Where is he, Charles?"

"Come, my dear, I will take you up." The earl nodded a good-bye to the doctor and, taking Elspeth's hand, led her up the stairs.

She stood very still for a long time, just looking down at Val, and then the earl pulled a chair over.

"Sit down, my dear." Elspeth sat and, reaching out to where Val's hand lay on the coverlet, covered it with her own. "My dearest," she whispered, with such love and pain in her voice that the earl's eyes filled with tears.

"What happened?" she asked, without turning her head from her husband.

"Well, that is what I don't know. Devereaux told me that Lucas Stanton was responsible for this."

"I'll kill him," Elspeth whispered passionately.

"From what the young man told me, he is already dead."

"Good."

A quick smile flitted across the earl's face at her vehemence. "Devereaux also mentioned James. Do you know anything about this, Elspeth?"

"It is a long story, Charles, and I don't know all of it. But from what Val discovered, Lucas Stanton was blackmailing James and forcing him to pass information on to the French. Val has had a hard time believing that James would do anything like that. He tends to see things as black and white. Perhaps if his mother hadn't died when he was so young . . . He has always seen her as perfect and you the villain, from what I gather."

"And what of you? How does he see you, my dear?" the earl asked gently.

"We were friends first, Charles. But he felt he *had* to marry me. I have hoped that love would develop over time . . . but now we may not have the time," she said with a little sob.

"Nonsense, my dear. The doctor seemed very optimistic."

The fever developed the next day, and when the doctor was called, he only shook his head. "He may yet pull through this, Mrs. Aston. He is a healthy young man."

"He was worn out when we left Portugal, Charles," said Elspeth, wringing her hands after the doctor left. "With the strain of Charlie's death and James . . . what resistance will he have?"

"*You* will have none at all if you don't get some sleep, my dear," the earl told her. "I will sit with him for a while."

But although she tried, Elspeth could not sleep and returned to join the earl in his vigil.

It was so hard to watch Val toss and turn. So hard to feel his forehead get hotter and hotter, to hold his hand in hers, dry and lifeless. If he died . . . no, she would not let him. But if he did, she would never have had the chance to tell him she loved him.

It was even harder when after a day of tossing and muttering incomprehensible phrases in English and Spanish and

Portuguese, he then lay still, his breathing forced and so shallow his chest barely lifted the covers.

"The fever *must* break soon, Charles," said Elspeth, looking up and seeing the agony in the earl's eyes, which she was sure mirrored her own. Dear God, surely to lose two sons in a few months of each other was too much.

"You look utterly exhausted, Charles. Why don't you rest."

The earl ran his hand over his eyes and nodded. "You will call me if anything changes?"

"Immediately," Elspeth assured him.

Charles Faringdon entered his bedroom, looked at his bed, and gave a short laugh. He could not lie down, much less sleep, not with Val so close to death. He opened the curtains and gazed out over the garden. It was an hour before dawn, that time of early morning when it seems that daylight will never return, the time when death holds sway over life.

"Oh, Sarah," he whispered brokenly. "If you are anywhere you can hear me, help our son."

It was ridiculous, of course, to be talking to her as if she could hear him, though he'd been doing it for years. He bowed his head in despair. They had loved each other, but so had many others. She had died and their love had died with her. And in the morning, the only living proof of their love, their son, would be gone, he was sure of it.

Chapter 38

Val was being drawn down into the dark. He was alone, although once in a while he thought he could hear someone calling him. Elspeth. But Elspeth was not here with him. He kept moving forward; he had no choice, for he was being pulled, inexorably, through dark and mist.

Then, suddenly, as though someone had lifted a veil in

front of him, he could see. Charlie was walking toward him, tall and healthy, smiling a welcome. Val wanted to stop, to clasp Charlie in his arms, but in this borderline country he had to keep moving.

Then he saw her. There was a blinding light behind her, and at first he thought he might be mistaken. But as she walked toward him, he saw that it was his mother. She was dressed simply, in the old dress she used for gardening. She looked so familiar and so dear. And small. Val smiled as he realized she was looking up at him.

"Mama?" he whispered.

She did not speak. It seemed that wherever they were, words were not necessary. She gazed at him with both pride and love. The tears ran down Val's cheeks as he took in what she conveyed wordlessly. He knew, in that moment, that his whole life he had been wanting her to see him and bless him for who he had become.

"Where are we?" he wondered, looking around and half-expecting to see an angel winging by.

She smiled, as if to say, "No angels and no golden choirs; there is only the Light."

"It is blinding," he told her, trying but unable to look directly at the Light from which she had emerged, of which she seemed a part.

"Only for those who are not ready."

"But I can't lose you again," he protested.

"No one is ever lost when there is love, Val."

She spoke without words, directly to his heart, telling him all he needed to know: that she had done what she thought best for both of them, out of love. That she had let his father go, out of love. That she had made mistakes out of love, for human love was flawed and partial.

" 'When I was a child . . .' "

He could almost hear her voice, reading to him when he was a boy. He had enjoyed the adventurous stories from the Bible, but although he had heard these words both from her and from the pulpit many times, he had never understood them.

" 'When I was a child,' " he repeated, " 'I thought as a child.' He hesitated and then continued. "I saw you as the victim and my father as the villain. 'But now I am a man. . . .' "

It all unfolded in an instant. He saw his whole life and how all was connected. Had his mother not refused his father, then Charlie would never have been born. What kind of life would he have had without Charlie? One thing depended upon another: Charlie led him to school, which brought him to the army, and all, all of his whole life had brought him to Elspeth. To love.

" 'And now we see face to face,' " he whispered. He understood, then, how pride and shame had always distorted the image in his mirror. He had seen a man unworthy of love, unable to inspire love. And afraid to receive love, lest he lose it again.

His mother's image was shifting, changing from second to second from her beloved form to all the colors of the spectrum and back to herself again. Whatever had pulled him to her and toward the Light was letting go and as he watched, she shimmered rainbowlike one more time and then all was clear Light and she only a small spark of it. And then he fell back into darkness.

The crisis came just before dawn. Elspeth watched each labored breath and wondered that Val's skin did not catch fire, for it was so dry and hot. She held his hand and murmured over and over, "I love you, Val, I love you," as though her litany might reach him, wherever he was, and bring him back.

Suddenly she realized that the hand she held had become moist and she lifted her eyes to her husband's face. "Charles!"

The earl raised his head.

"I think the fever may have finally broken." Elspeth reached out a shaking hand to feel Val's forehead. It was still hot, but it was also moist with sweat.

"Pull up another blanket, Elspeth," said her father-in-law, and they piled the covers on and watched as what seemed like a miracle occurred. Val's breathing became less ragged and his pulse, which had been faint, began to beat more steadily.

Elspeth and the earl looked at each other and smiled. Charles could not trust himself and, standing up and muttering, "I'll send for the doctor," left Elspeth alone with her husband. Leaning down, she pressed her lips to his forehead. "Welcome back, my dearest."

The first few days of his recovery, Val slept most of the time, opening his eyes only for a few moments. He would see either Elspeth or his father watching over him. He wanted to speak with them, but didn't even have the strength to smile.

Then he began to be awake for longer periods of time. He couldn't feed himself, but at least he was aware when he was being spoon-fed water or gruel. At first he whispered a thank-you to either Elspeth or his father, but by the end of the week he actually had the strength to push the spoon away and whisper a request for "something with more taste, please."

Elspeth's eyes stung with tears of joy when he made his first complaint. "The doctor wants you to continue with this for another day or so. When you gain some strength, you can have some beef tea," she explained.

"I don't see how I can gain any strength on this pap," he complained, trying to pull himself up into a half-sitting position.

"Lie still, Val, and I'll see if I can get the doctor to change his mind," Elspeth promised.

After a week during which he felt like a weak kitten, Val felt his physical energy begin to return. By the end of a fortnight, he was able to sit up in a chair and take a few steps about the room, leaning on a footman's arm. His wound healed rapidly and whenever the doctor came to check on him, he would smile and shake his head and say, "It is amazing the powers of recuperation a young man has, Lieutenant. Of course, you have gotten the best of care."

Val knew that. He would have had to be blind not to see the concern and affection on Elspeth's and his father's faces. But although his body was gaining strength, he felt in some sort of emotional limbo. He had not fully returned from where he had been.

One morning, almost three weeks after he had been shot, he was sitting in the small garden on the side of the house. It was a sunny day made delightful by a gentle breeze that carried the scent of roses. One side of the yard had been given over to rosebushes, Val realized, and he got up and walked slowly over to appreciate the perfume and the profusion of crimson flowers.

"They were your mother's favorite," said his father's voice behind him. Val started, having been so absorbed in the sight and scent that he hadn't heard anyone come out.

"Yes, I remember. I still have one pressed in the old Bible she gave me," he confessed.

"I was so angry she had sent me away that I ripped the one she gave me to shreds," admitted his father with a rueful smile.

Val walked back to the garden bench and sat down. His father sat next to him and, looking down at the worn path and pushing the green velvet moss that grew between the bricks with the toe of his boot, said quietly, "I did ask her to marry me, you know."

"Why didn't you ever tell me?"

"I don't believe you ever gave me the chance, Valentine," his father said dryly as he looked up and smiled at his son.

"I suppose not," Val admitted.

"Perhaps I should have *made* her marry me," continued the earl. "But she was a strong, stubborn woman. You remind me of her, Valentine," he said with another smile.

"Did you never want to see her . . . or me . . . ?"

"Always. But she made me promise to stay away. She did not want to take anything away from Helen or any children we might have." The earl was silent for a moment. "When she died . . . well, by that time Charlie had been born and his mother and I had a good marriage. I thought that Sarah's sister would take good care of you, so it seemed better just to continue sending money. Had I known about George Burton, Val, I assure you—"

"It is all right, sir." And it was, Val realized. Whether his mother or father had been right or wrong in their decisions, what was done was done. He had had a hard life, it was true, but he had known many men who had had much harder.

The earl reached into his waistcoat pocket and drew out Charlie's ring. He turned and faced Val and said, his voice trembling, "I want you to have this, Valentine. Charlie would have wanted you to have it. I may not be able to give my son Faringdon or the title, but I can give him this. Please take it."

Val hesitated and then, taking the ring, slipped it onto his right hand. "Thank you . . . Father," he said awkwardly.

The two men sat there quietly, watching the summer breeze toss the roses and lift the fallen petals into tiny crimson maelstroms. There would be another time to say more of what was in their hearts, but for now it was enough to sit and take in the sun, the roses, and the silent presence of the woman they had both loved.

That night after a quiet supper, Val followed Elspeth up the stairs, and as she started to open the door to her room he placed his hand on hers.

"I had my things moved to your room, Elspeth," he said quietly. "I will join you there in a few minutes?" Elspeth heard the question in her husband's voice and, blushing slightly, nodded her head yes.

She was sitting on the edge of the bed in her night rail when Val came in.

"I have missed being with my wife," he said as he closed the door behind him. "I can't promise that we will do anything but sleep, though," he added with a smile. He sat down on the bed beside her and gently undid her hair.

"But I just got finished braiding it, Val," she said in halfhearted protest.

"I love your hair down, Elspeth," he told her, combing it out with his fingers. He lifted the covers with one hand and pulled her under. They lay there, spooned together, and although Val felt himself becoming aroused, he had no strong need to act on it. They lay still until both fell asleep.

They slept late and when Val opened his eyes, the sun was pouring through a gap in the drapes. He buried his face between Elspeth's neck and shoulders and nuzzled her awake.

"Oh, Val," she whispered as she turned to face him, "I was so worried I was going to lose you."

Val kissed her gently on the forehead.

"I don't think I could have left you behind, Elspeth. I love you too much."

"And I, you, Val."

"I know that, Elspeth, at long last." He was quiet for a

moment and then said hesitantly, "When I was so ill . . . I thought I had died. . . ."

"You almost did, Val."

"I saw my mother. It was as if she had been waiting for me. She didn't really speak, but somehow I understood what she wanted to tell me. I can't explain it," he said helplessly. "But I realized love is always there, connecting all of us. We only have to let it in." He closed his eyes for a moment and when he opened them again, Elspeth could see the sheen of tears. "I always thought love was about loving, Elspeth, but now I know it is also about being loved. You helped me learn that, my dearest love."

Elspeth reached out and traced his cheek with her finger. As she began to press gentle and then harder kisses on his mouth, he buried his hands in her hair and pulled her against him.

"Perhaps we shouldn't be doing this yet," worried Elspeth. "You are still weak."

"Not that weak," Val reassured her, guiding her hand down to feel his arousal. He started to roll over, but she pressed him back. "No, Val, truly, you shouldn't," she sighed.

"Perhaps if you help," he suggested with a shy smile.

Elspeth sat up and drew her gown over her head while Val lay there, watching. She placed her hand on his chest and gently fingered the newly healed wound. "Are you sure, Val?"

When he nodded and clasped her waist with his hands, she relaxed and, smiling mischievously as she straddled him, said, "You will just have to lie there and let me see what I can do."

At first she only kissed him gently on the mouth, but then, with a soft moan, she slid down and nuzzled under his arms. "I love the way you smell," she whispered as she moved a little and then lazily circled his nipples with her tongue. At the same time she was moving rhythmically against him and he groaned.

"Am I hurting you?" she asked, beginning to lift her weight off him.

"Not in the way you think," he muttered as he pulled her back. He could feel her moist against him and thought he might die of the pleasure. Letting go of her waist, he found her with his fingers and she gave a little gasp.

"I don't know how long I can wait, Elspeth," he whispered.

She lifted herself off him and, cupping him in her hand, guided him into her. She held still for a moment, enjoying his fullness, and then started moving again, slowly at first and then faster and faster as he lifted his hips to meet her. Just as he felt himself about to explode, he sought her out again and she threw her head back as he drew her up and up and then brought her down to him. She collapsed with little sobs and cries as they reached their climax together.

Val lay there, stroking her hair and murmuring little nothings into her ear. She was such a strong woman, his Elspeth, and yet she had let him into that secret place where she was most vulnerable and most herself. And he had let himself lie there and lose the hard-won control he had exercised all his life. She had made love to him the way he would a woman and he had felt ecstasy in letting himself receive her love as well as give to her. Her passion had opened every door he had ever closed behind him, until she reached his very soul.

"Oh, God, I do love you," he whispered.

Elspeth lifted her head. He was looking straight into her eyes and there was nothing hidden, nothing held back. "I never dreamed I would ever have this, my love," she murmured. Then Elspeth slipped off him and fit herself against his back and put her arm around his waist. He clasped her hand in front of him as they fell asleep.

Chapter 39

Val had put all thought of Stanton and James out of his head as he recovered, but a few mornings later, he looked up from his breakfast and addressed his father.

"Has there been anything in the paper about Stanton? Or James?"

"Evidently Whitehall thought it best to put it about that

Stanton had been shot in some dispute over cards," the earl told him with an ironic smile. "If they had revealed what happened, it would have caused a monumental scandal, which is exactly what they have been trying to avoid."

"And James?"

"His name has never been connected with it at all."

"Thank God," said Elspeth.

"I have heard, however, that now that Lady Madeline has received a proposal, he has decided to resign his commission and make an extended visit to Italy. His decision has raised some eyebrows, but people only think of it as vaguely unpatriotic of him, while there is a war on. On the other hand, he *is* the head of his family, so it is better he not risk his life. . . ." The earl's tone so accurately mimicked the gossips that Val had to smile.

"Do you think I did the right thing, Charles?" Despite the moment in the garden, Val did not feel comfortable addressing the earl as his father. They were grown men, and for now, his father's name came to his lips more readily. The earl did not mind, for Val referred to him in conversation as his father and their friendship was growing stronger by the day.

"I do not think ruining James or his family would have served any good purpose, Val."

"He called many times when you were ill, Val, and Maddie tells me he leaves in two days' time," Elspeth told him. She would never judge him, but he could tell from the look in her eyes that she wished he could see his way to saying farewell to one of his oldest friends. He knew she was right, but he wasn't sure he could do it.

James's revelation had become all mixed up with the events at Whitehall, and the pain of discovering his friend's treachery had become almost indistinguishable from the pain caused by Lucas's pistol shot. He had had no time to take in what James had told him, and when he tried to remember their conversation, he only remembered how foolish and embarrassed and, yes, somewhat disgusted he had felt.

His father and Elspeth had taken themselves off for a walk in the park, something that had become a daily ritual, and Val sat at the breakfast table over a cold cup of tea.

If he didn't call on James today, he would most likely not see him again for years.

Their talk a month ago had been stiff and cold. But he had felt so damned uncomfortable. How could he have given James any gesture of affection, now that he knew what James was?

And who is that, Val? he asked himself. What exactly has changed about James? He is still intelligent and charming and warm. A man who takes responsibility seriously. Look at how hard he has worked to bring his family back from ruin.

Only to place his family in far greater jeopardy, Val reminded himself. James had been an excellent soldier and a trusted officer, damn it, and he had betrayed a great trust. Yet he had been placed on the horns of an unresolvable dilemma, Val had to admit. Pay off Lucas Stanton or see the family he had rescued disgraced in a far more lasting way. The damage done to Lady Madeline, had her brother been revealed as a catamite, would have been irreparable.

Maybe what was holding him back was that he himself felt betrayed. Why hadn't James trusted him enough to tell him? Even Charlie knew. For God's sake, James, what did you think I would do, turn my back on you?

He hadn't turned his back, had he? He had been surprised, that was all. And scared, he had to admit that. For if James was what he was, then what *did* he feel for Val? Or Val for him?

Val sat there agonizing, and then the answer came to him: James felt the same affection that Val felt for any of his friends, of course. James loved Val, just as James had loved Charlie. Just as Val loved James. Why should that be any different now?

He remembered their walks over the moors at school, and how James had helped him with Latin. There had never been a hint of desire in any of their interactions, then or now. If any had existed, well, James had hidden it well, thought Val with an ironic grin.

He pushed his chair back from the table and called for his shako. He was going to say good-bye to his friend.

When Val arrived at the Lambert town house he was told James was out but expected back shortly. The butler showed Val into the morning room, where he paced nervously until he heard the door open and turned to see James standing in the doorway.

"Val," James said quietly and, closing the door behind him, started over with his hand outstretched. He stopped midway and gestured instead toward the sofa. "Sit down, Val. You look thin, but aside from that, completely recovered, I hope?"

"I am finally feeling myself again, although I am not quite ready for one of Colquhoun Grant's assignments. It will take another few weeks for that."

"So you will be returning to Spain? I thought you might consider selling out, after your father's recognition."

"Elspeth and I are agreed: We have been in the army too long to give it up now. After the war is over . . . well, then it may be different. My father has an estate in Yorkshire that he has turned over to me and that would give us something to return for. I haven't had a home except the army for many years," Val said quietly.

Both men sat uncomfortably silent for a few minutes and then Val finally spoke. "Elspeth and my father tell me that you visited almost every day when I was ill, James. I am very grateful, but I wonder why you have not come by since my recovery."

"I did not think you would want to receive me," James said simply.

"I may not have been able to, James, although I am sorry to admit it."

James gave Val one quick painful glance and then looked down as he said, "I don't blame you, Val. If I hadn't given in to Stanton's blackmail, you wouldn't have been at the point of death. You were very lucky, my friend, from what I've heard," he added, his voice tight with emotion.

"I *am* very lucky. Being that close to death . . . I can't really describe what it was like, but it made me realize just how much I have: a loving wife, a father after all these years . . ."

"So at last you have come to an understanding with Charles," said James, looking up at Val with a bittersweet smile. "I am glad that something good has come of all this."

"I hadn't finished counting my blessings, James," Val

said humorously. "I was about to say that I am also lucky to have had your friendship all these years."

James sat very still, and unable to tolerate the tension between them, Val stood up and walked over to the window. The day had started out sunny and warm, but now gray clouds were scudding across the sky and the first fat drops of rain were hitting the glass and running down the pane. Val turned. "You were wrong to do what you did. It was treasonous, but I understand why you were driven to it. I am not sure what I would have done under the same, er, circumstances," he stammered.

"And the 'circumstances,' Val—what do you think of them?"

"I can't pretend it is easy for me to understand. In fact, I am not sure I do. But I have thought about it a lot and I would choose you as my friend all over again, James. I find that who you are is far more important to me than whom you love. You offered me the same acceptance, James, despite my birth. How can I do less?"

James was silent, and Val turned abruptly and said, "Well, I must go."

James stood up and they walked to the door together. "I am glad you came, Val," James said quietly. "I leave tomorrow."

Val turned to face him. "Damn it, James, I hate to lose someone else I love," he choked out.

"I will only be in Italy and I *will* write. After a few years, when the war is over, perhaps I will be able to come home for a visit. I'll come to Yorkshire and see you and Elspeth and your children and we will tramp the moors together the way we did in Devon," he added with a sweet smile and an extended hand.

This time, Val pulled James into a warm embrace. "I must go," he mumbled, after they separated.

"Take care of yourself in Spain, Val," James told him, resting his hand on his friend's arm for one moment before opening the door. Val was gone quickly and James walked over to the window, where he stood for a long while, watching the English rain beating down until he could see nothing because of the rain and his tears.

Two weeks after James left, Val and Elspeth returned to Portugal. Their sail took longer this time, for the wind was

not with them. But the weather was warn and their return
journey seemed an idyllic interlude, taking them away from
the difficulties of the past two months and toward the un-
known challenges facing them in Spain. Every evening they
walked the deck, hand in hand, and watched the stars. Then
they returned to their cabin, some nights to make love,
others just to fall asleep in each other's arms.

Their journey through Portugal to Spain was uncomfortable but uneventful, yet Val felt himself getting more and
more anxious the closer they got to Wellington's army.

"What will I tell your parents, Elspeth?" he asked her
one night as they sat in front of their campfire.

"The truth, my dear. That we discovered we loved each
other and decided we could not wait to be married."

"That is not quite the truth, madame wife, and you know
it. We discovered we loved each other only after our
marriage."

"But you did love me, Val, and I, you, long before."

"Oh, yes, my dearest," he answered, giving her a kiss.

"When *did* you know you loved me, Val?"

"I think I loved you almost from the beginning, Elspeth,
but I knew it when I heard you say Mrs. Casey's vows.
You looked so lovely, just like that red rose in the Burns
song that your father loves to sing. As I listened to you, I
realized how much I wished you were saying those words
to me."

"You needn't worry about my parents, Val. All they
have ever wanted was for me to have what they have with
each other. I never thought I would," she whispered
wonderingly.

Val pulled her into his arms and started to hum the
Burns tune that had haunted him since the first time he'd
heard it. "It is a beautiful song, Elspeth."

"But even more beautiful with the lyrics, Val."

"I don't ever want to leave you, Elspeth," he said,
"though I will often have to, until this bloody war is over.
But I will always 'come again, my love, though it were ten
thousand mile.' I will come back if it is ten times ten thousand miles, to be with my rose. My bonnie *wee* lass," he
added, pulling her closer. Elspeth laughed softly, and when
the fire died down, they warmed each other with the love
that would burn for the rest of their lives together.

□LAIRD OF THE WIND   0-451-40768-7/$5.99

In medieval Scotland, the warrior known as Border Hawk seizes the castle belonging to the father of the beautiful Isabel Scott, famous throughout the Lowlands for her gift of prophecy. During the battle, Isabel is injured while fighting alongside her men and placed under Border Hawk's protection. As the border wars rage on, the warrior and prophetess engage in a more intimate conflict, discovering their love for the Scottish borderlands is surpassed only by their love for each other.

Also available:
□THE ANGEL KNIGHT   0-451-40662-1/$5.50
□LADY MIRACLE   0-451-40766-0/$5.99
□THE RAVEN'S MOON   0-451-18868-3/$5.99
□THE RAVEN'S WISH   0-451-40545-5/$4.99

Coming in April 1999 HEATHER MOON
□0-451-40774-1/$6.99

Prices slightly higher in Canada

Payable in U.S. funds only. No cash/COD accepted. Postage & handling: U.S./CAN. $2.75 for one book, $1.00 for each additional, not to exceed $6.75; Int'l $5.00 for one book, $1.00 each additional. We accept Visa, Amex, MC ($10.00 min.), checks ($15.00 fee for returned checks) and money orders. Call 800-788-6262 or 201-933-9292, fax 201-896-8569; refer to ad #TOPHR1

Penguin Putnam Inc.	Bill my: □Visa □MasterCard □Amex_____(expires)
P.O. Box 12289, Dept. B	Card#_____
Newark, NJ 07101-5289	Signature_____
Please allow 4-6 weeks for delivery.	
Foreign and Canadian delivery 6-8 weeks.	

Bill to:
Name_____
Address_____City_____
State/ZIP_____
Daytime Phone #_____

Ship to:
Name_____ Book Total $_____
Address_____ Applicable Sales Tax $_____
City_____ Postage & Handling $_____
State/ZIP_____ Total Amount Due $_____

This offer subject to change without notice.